BTL

$\rightarrow$ Sou
6/19

25 MAR 2021

This book should be returned/renewed by the latest date shown above. Overdue items incur charges which prevent self-service renewals. Please contact the library.

Wandsworth Libraries
24 hour Renewal Hotline
01527 852385
www.wandsworth.gov.uk

Wandsworth

Workhouse Nightingale

HOLLY GREEN

Workhouse Nightingale

EBURY
PRESS

1 3 5 7 9 10 8 6 4 2

Ebury Press, an imprint of Ebury Publishing
20 Vauxhall Bridge Road,
London SW1V 2SA

Ebury Press is part of the Penguin Random House group of companies
whose addresses can be found at global.penguinrandomhouse.com

First published in the UK in 2018 by Ebury Press

www.penguin.co.uk

A CIP catalogue record for this book is available from the British Library

ISBN 9781785035661

Typeset in 12.25/15.5 pt Times LT Std
by Integra Software Services Pvt. Ltd, Pondicherry

Printed   p.A.

Pengui   for
our   e

Prologue

'Whore!' The venomous hiss carried all the violence of pent-up hatred. 'Get out of this house. I knew from the moment my husband forced me to take you in that I would live to regret it. Your mother was a whore and you have turned out to be the same. Bad blood will out!'

'My mother was not a whore, and neither am I.' Dora's voice shook, but it was as much with rage as with fear. 'She loved my father and he loved her.'

'She bewitched your father. There is only one name for a woman who seduces a married man away from his family and lives with him in sin, and that is whore. And now you have proved yourself as bad as her. How else do you explain your condition?'

'I am not the one at fault here,' Dora cried out.

'Then who is? I suppose you are going to tell me this is some kind of immaculate conception, that the seed growing in your womb was planted there without your knowledge. That would be to add sacrilege to your sin.'

'No.' Dora lowered her voice. 'I am not such a fool. But the fault is not mine. He forced me.'

'Forced you? Then why did you not report it? Who is responsible? Do you even know his name?'

'Very well. It was Hector.'

'*Hector!* You dare to suggest that my son did this to you?'

'It is the truth.'

'You expect me to believe that!' Mrs Latimer lifted a bell from the table at her side and rang it violently. 'How dare you make such an allegation? You were brought into this house when your mother died, against my will. But you have had bed and board here, and benefited from the same education as my own daughters, and this is how you repay me?'

A parlourmaid appeared at the door, her expression apprehensive. 'You rang for me, madam?'

'Is Mr Hector in the house?'

'I believe he is in the billiard room, madam.'

'Ask him to step in here for a moment, please.'

'Very good, madam.' The girl's eyes slid from her mistress's face to Dora's and Dora thought she detected a smirk. She had never been popular with the servants, existing as she did in a kind of limbo between their position and membership of the family.

She turned back to Mrs Latimer. 'I have always done my best to please you. I know you do not want me here, but I have tried to be of service.'

'Huh! You have always had ideas above your station. But if you have tried to seduce my son ...'

'Seduce him! He is my half-brother!'

'So we have been led to believe. I have always had my doubts about your true parentage.'

'My parentage? You know ...'

Her protest was cut short as the door opened to admit Hector Latimer. At nineteen years old, he was a pale, languid young man with limp fair hair and very pale blue eyes.

'You wanted me, Mama?'

'My dear boy! A most monstrous accusation has been made against you by this ... this ungrateful girl. I need to hear you deny it to her face.'

Hector's eyes did not flicker. 'What accusation, Mama?'

'That you are the father of the child she is carrying.'

'Child!' Hector's gaze switched from his mother to Dora and for a second she saw an expression of shock cross his face. It vanished as soon as it appeared and he turned his eyes back to his mother. 'Dora is with child?'

'Yes.'

'And she claims that it is mine?'

'More than that. She accuses you of taking advantage of her.'

The blue eyes widened in an expression of injured innocence. 'Taking advantage? My dear Mama! Can you seriously believe me capable of such a vile act? And with ... with her, of all people?'

Mrs Latimer smiled indulgently. 'Of course not. I just needed to hear you deny it in front of her.' She turned her attention to Dora. 'You have heard what Hector says? He denies it.'

'Of course he does!' Dora said bitterly. 'And you believe him.'

'Of course. My son is a gentleman. He would never stoop to such a vile act.'

'And yet, it is the truth, and I have the proof of it here, in my belly.'

'Disgusting creature! Get out of this house. You have no place here anymore.'

'But ... but where shall I go? I have no other home, no money, no friends who will take me in.'

'What do I care? You have forfeited any right to my consideration. You have told wicked lies and impugned the honour of my son. You have shown yourself no better than that whore, your mother. Get out, before I call John and William to throw you out.'

Chapter 1

''Ere! Where do you think you're going? You can't just walk in.'

'Please! I need somewhere to stay, a shelter until ... until ...'

'What do you think this is, a hotel? It ain't the effing Adelphi, you know.' The porter's voice changed as Dora buckled over with a spasm of pain. 'What's up? What's the matter with you?'

A woman's voice interposed. 'What's going on here? Let me see her.' A hand gripped her shoulder and Dora struggled to stand upright. 'Dear God, Sam! I think she's in labour. Quick, fetch some of the women. They will know what to do.'

For a few moments Dora's whole consciousness was focussed on another wave of pain. When it passed she became aware that she was being supported by two women and half-carried over a roughly cobbled surface. She had an impression of high brick walls surrounding soot-blackened buildings, which rose on either side of a narrow roadway. She was hustled through a door and lowered onto a bed. Faces loomed over her, then her skirts were lifted and a hand probed her private parts.

'Dinna worry, pet! I've birthed many a bairn in my time. I'll see you all right. You hold her, Betsy. Lie back, pet. It'll be over soon.'

From then on Dora ceased to be aware of anything except what was happening within her own body. Her muscles had taken on a separate life, over which she had no control. The pain ebbed and flowed, grew stronger and then eased. Time lost all meaning and resolved into an eternity of struggle.

Dimly she heard voices. 'It's taking too long. She doesn't have the strength, poor girl. Is there nothing we can do?'

'Give me some oil. I'll have to drag the child out of her.'

She screamed as a hand was inserted into her vagina. 'Push, now! Push!' came the command and there was a sensation as if her body was being ripped apart.

Voices above her cried out in relief and celebration. 'It's a boy! A fine, strong child. See? See? You have a son.'

A bundle was thrust into her arms, but she did not have the strength to hold it. Finally she could allow herself to sink into oblivion.

When consciousness returned she knew she was in a different place. It was the smell that penetrated her mind first; a sharp, acrid odour of urine and excrement and decay. She opened her eyes. She was in a large, dimly lit space and she was not alone. There were rustles and groans and the low mutter of voices. She turned her head. She was lying on a low pallet and stretching away on either side were other, similar beds, each occupied by a hunched figure. On the floor there was a layer of straw. From the quality of the light she guessed it was night, or very early morning. She became aware of a raging thirst. She wanted to get up, to go in search of something to drink, but when she raised her head a wave of dizziness swept over her and she sank back again.

Time passed, she did not know how much, and then there was a stir in the room. The light was stronger. People were moving about. Footsteps approached and a woman leaned over her.

'You're awake at last! I was afraid we were going to lose you. Here, drink.' A hand raised her head and a cup was held to her lips. Her mouth was so parched that it was difficult to open it. Water trickled in and dribbled down her chin. The cup was removed and she whispered desperately, 'Please! More!'

'In a moment. Not too much all at once. Here, take another sip.'

The water revived her and she was able to speak. 'Where am I?'

'In the workhouse infirmary. Do you remember what happened?'

'I came ... I came because ... The baby! I had a baby!'

'Yes, you did.'

'Where is it?'

'In the nursery. One of the women is nursing him. She had a child of her own a week or two ago and she has milk enough for two. No need to worry.'

'Is it a boy or a girl?'

'You don't remember? You had a boy.'

'Can I see him?'

'Later. You're too weak to go down there and it wouldn't be wise to bring him up here.'

'Why am I here?'

'You had a very long labour and you lost a good deal of blood. You have been very ill for several days.'

'Several days? How long?'

'Three ... nearly four. Now, lie back and rest. I'll bring you some broth in a little while.'

For the first time Dora looked properly at her companion. She was a woman in middle age. Greying hair was drawn back from a face criss-crossed with lines. Her cheeks were sunken as if she had suffered a long period of privation, but her eyes were clear and kind.

'What is your name?'

'Edith – Edith Barnes. What's yours?'

'Dora. Dorinda Latimer.'

'That's a pretty name. Now, you must rest. I'll be back soon.'

Dora closed her eyes and let her mind drift. She had a son. A faint tremor of pleasure rose from somewhere deep inside her and then dissipated. A son, yes – the child of a man she hated. How could she ever love him, remembering the manner of his conception? And how could she ever provide for him, homeless as she was? It would have been better if he had died, better if they both had.

Somewhere nearby she could hear voices. 'Who is she?'

'No idea. Turned up out of the blue and almost gave birth in the street, I was told.'

'That dress. Forget the dirt and the ragged edges, that didn't come cheap.'

'Hand-me-down from some charitable lady, maybe?'

'Or earned lying on her back!'

'Heard her talking in the night – rambling, like. She don't speak like us. Quite genteel sounding.'

'You think?'

'Yeah. Fallen on hard times, if you ask me.'

'Fallen's the word, all right.'

Once again, time ceased to have meaning. Dora was by turns shivering with cold and burning with heat. At times she thought she was back in the Latimer household, being chivvied by the two legitimate daughters. 'I'm sorry, Georgiana! I can't! I can't do it any faster ...' Then she was back in the little house by the docks where she had grown up. 'When is Papa coming home? Will he bring me a present? Can I go on his ship?'

Sometimes she was aware of Edith bending over her, holding a cup to her lips, spooning a trickle of broth into her mouth, bathing her face. Then she would slip back into the darkness.

Someone was saying, 'Leave her, Edith. You're wasting your time. She'll never make it.'

'No! There's still a chance. Come on, Dora love. Stay with us. Remember your little boy. He needs you.'

A day came at last when she opened her eyes and knew where she was, and why. She was almost too weak to move and the rough blanket she lay on was soaked with sweat, but her mind was clear. Edith, bringing more broth, smiled at the sight of her face.

'There! You look better. We'll have you back on your feet in no time. Can you sit up if I help you?'

She struggled into a sitting position, her back propped against the wall, and Edith began to feed her, dipping pieces of bread into the thin broth to soften them.

'How long have I been here?'

'Days – eight, no nine days. You nearly died.'

9

'I think I would have done if it wasn't for you.'

'Oh well. I've seen too many women in your condition slip away. I wasn't going to let you do the same.'

'Can I see my son?'

'All in good time. You're not strong enough to move yet. Rest. I'll be back soon.'

Dora lay back and looked around her. The long room was lined with low beds, so closely packed that there was scarcely room to walk between them. Each one was occupied. Some of the women lay still, staring at the ceiling; others tossed and turned, groaning with pain or muttering in fever. A few beds away one lay curled like a foetus, muttering to herself in a constant monotone. The straw which covered the floor was dark and moist, and it stank. From time to time she heard rustling, and realised with horror that it was the sound of rats moving through it.

A few of the women were well enough to talk, and even to move around. One of them came to stand by her, looking down with curiosity.

'Where you from then?'

'What do you mean?'

'Where were you born?'

'Here. I mean, near here, down by the docks.'

'You're not from here, though, are you? Don't see many with skin your colour round here.'

'My mother came from Jamaica.'

'Slave, was she?'

'No! My father was a sea captain, trading to the West Indies. He met my mother there and fell in love with her. He brought her back to Liverpool.'

'Sea captain, was he? So how come you're in here?'

'He ... he went away. His ship sank in a storm.'

'Ah, right! Left you to fend for yourself, eh? That why you had to go on the game?'

'Do what?'

'Aw, come on! There's no need to be ashamed. Many's the girl who's had to take to the streets to keep body and soul together.'

'I didn't! I wasn't!' A wave of exhaustion swept over Dora and she sank back on the bed and turned her face away.

Sometime later Edith brought a bowl of water and helped her to wash. She realised for the first time that she was wearing nothing but her shift, which was stiff with blood.

'What happened to my clothes?'

'I've got your dress safe, but I'm afraid it will never be wearable again. It's badly stained. Don't worry, I'll find you something else to wear when you are ready to get up.' She squeezed out the sponge she had been using and sat back on her heels. 'How old are you, my dear?'

'Seventeen.'

You speak like a woman with some education. How did you come to be in this state?'

Dora bent her head. 'I was forced.'

'I thought that might be the answer. You don't strike me like a street girl. Who did it?'

'My own brother! Well, my half-brother.'

Edith gave a small gasp. 'Merciful God! How could that happen?'

Dora kept her eyes down, twisting in her hands the piece of rough cloth she had been given to dry herself with. 'My mother died of the typhus, three years ago now. She was never married to my father because he already had a wife and family – two daughters and a son. When she died, my father insisted that I go to live with them. He said I was to be treated like one of them, but his wife always hated me. I suppose it's not surprising. When he went away to sea she made it clear that I was only there on sufferance. Then, a bit more than a year ago, his ship went down in a hurricane and after that she didn't have to worry about his reaction when he got home. She started to treat me like a servant, made me act as maid to her daughters. I never liked the son – Hector. He was a spoilt boy, his mother's darling. One night he came to my room ...' her voice faltered. 'He'd been drinking. He tried to kiss me. When I pushed him away he got angry, said that I owed it to the family to do everything I was asked to do. That really I was just a slave, like my ancestors had been, and he had a right to do what he liked to me. Then he threw me onto the bed and forced me.'

'You poor girl! Didn't you tell anyone what he had done?'

'Who could I tell? When I started to show, his mother, Mrs Latimer, demanded to know who the father was. When I told her, she refused to believe me. She threw me out of the house.'

'How long ago was that?'

'About six months.'

'Where have you been since then?'

'I found work, helping a woman who took in washing. It was hard, but she gave me a bed and my food. Then, when my pains started, she kicked me out, told me to come here.'

'How can anyone be so heartless!' Edith put out a hand and smoothed Dora's hair back from her face. 'But you've survived. And you are among friends here. We have all fallen on hard times, but we care for each other as best we can. Take heart!'

Dora reached for the hand that caressed her hair and squeezed it. 'Thank you! If everyone could be as kind as you, what a wonderful place the world would be!'

For the first time she saw a hint of bitterness in the other woman's expression. 'If kindness was all that was needed ...' She stood up and picked up the bowl of water. 'I must get on. There's plenty of poor souls that need a bit of kindness in this place.'

Over the following days, as she slowly grew stronger, Dora learned something of Edith's history. Her father had been a Methodist preacher and her upbringing had been happy, though discipline was strict. At the age of eighteen she had been found a place as governess to a respectable family who were also Methodists. She smiled wryly as she spoke of that time.

'A governess's position is not a happy one. She is neither a servant nor a member of the family. There were three children, two boys and a girl, and their father was very strict with them. As a result, when they found themselves in the charge of an inexperienced young woman, they took the opportunity to – well, to kick over the traces, as the saying goes. I was not allowed to discipline them myself, but if I complained of their behaviour to their father he preferred to believe that it was my incompetence rather than their wickedness that was to blame.' She sighed. 'Eventually, it was decided that I was not "suitable" and was sent back to my family. I tried to earn my keep by giving private lessons in French to local children, but it never brought in much money. The parents were poor and often the lessons were never paid for. My father grew sick, became forgetful and was unable to carry out his duties. I knew I had to find a way to make a living and I went back to being a governess in a different family. This time it was easier and for a while I lived quite happily, but the children grew up, as children do, and I was no longer needed. My parents were both dead by this time. I found another position, looking after an elderly gentlewoman who was very sick. When she died I discovered that she had passed on the same contagion to me. My savings were soon used up. I was ill and penniless. I had no option but to come here.'

'But you recovered from your illness?' Dora said.

'Yes, by the mercy of God – and through the care of some of the women here. That is why I now devote my time to looking after others, like you.'

'You are a saint!' Dora said.

Edith shook her head. 'Very far from it. I do what I can, that is all.'

Slowly Dora's strength came back. The workhouse diet was monotonous, consisting mainly of gruel and broth and dry bread, but once a week there was lobscouse – a stew of meat and vegetables – and on Sundays there was beef. It was as good as the fare she had lived on while she worked for the washerwoman. When she was able to stand, Edith brought her a clean shift and a plain blue dress. She did not conceal the fact that it had belonged to a woman who had died in the infirmary, but assured her that it had been thoroughly washed. Dora experienced a shiver of distaste as she put it on, but she forced herself not to think about its former owner and soon it came to feel like her own.

She began to move around the ward and even to help out with the care of the other patients. Once a day a woman in a black dress and white gloves walked through the ward, casting a rapid glance at each inmate and asking a few curt questions. She was, Edith explained, one of the three superintendents who were in charge of the infirmary. Her name was Mrs Carter.

'Is she a nurse?' Dora asked.

Edith shook her head. 'Women like that wouldn't sully their hands with nursing the sick. They might catch something! Any nursing that's to be done is down to us, the ones who volunteer for the job. And most of them are not here out of a Christian desire to heal the sick. They do it because it gets them out of other work, like picking oakum, and they get to eat better. I've caught more than one taking food that was meant for a patient.' She sighed. 'Well, that's human nature for you. We have to take the good with the bad and do the best we can.'

One day Edith said, 'I think you're strong enough to leave now.'

'Leave? You mean leave the workhouse?'

'Oh no. Once you're in here it's not so easy to get out. I mean leave the infirmary. Go down to the nursery. Don't you want to see your son?'

Dora stood still. It felt as if she had suddenly walked into an invisible wall. For several days now, she realised, she had not thought about the child she had given birth to.

'No,' she heard herself say. 'I don't want him.'

15

'What! He's your baby, your own child. Of course you want him.'

Dora looked at her. 'Why? What can he ever be to me but a reminder of my shame?'

Edith took her by the shoulders and looked into her face. 'The shame is not yours. It belongs to the man who abused you.'

'Then perhaps the child should belong to him too.'

'You don't mean that.'

'I do. What can I give a child, stuck in here? There's no future for him here.'

'There's no future for him anywhere, if you abandon him. You gave birth to him, whatever the circumstances, so he's your responsibility. You have a duty to care for him.' Edith shook her gently. 'Go and find him. As soon as you have him in your arms you'll feel differently. Go on!'

With leaden feet Dora made her way through the narrow lanes towards the nursery. Twice she had to ask her way. The workhouse was like a small town, with alleys and courtyards and staircases. A glance through a grimy window showed her rows of women working at looms or sitting stitching. In another room, men sat at the monotonous task of picking oakum. As she passed the chapel, a bell rang and she stood aside as a file of boys, the oldest about twelve, the youngest perhaps four years old, filed up from the basement and went into a room which she could see was set out as a dining hall. They walked in silence, their faces pinched and pale, followed by a sallow-faced man who carried a cane. Was this, Dora asked herself, what her son could expect, if he had to grow up here?

Finally she found her way to the complex of buildings that housed the nursery, the lying in rooms and the associated offices like the laundry and the bath house. Entering, she was met by the sound of babies crying and the smell of wet nappies. Dora gazed around. There were women suckling babies, others rocking slightly older children. There were babes lying in cribs, some asleep, other squalling; a couple of sour-faced older women in the uniform of paupers were occupied changing the nappies of two others. There was a general atmosphere of squalor and a sense of bitter resignation on the majority of faces. There was one exception. In one corner, a young girl was bouncing a golden haired child on her knees and singing to it. Dora watched, puzzled. Surely this could not be the girl's own child? No, she was far too young.

She withdrew her gaze as a woman with a grizzling child on her hip came over to her.

'Yes?'

'I ... I've come to see my son.'

'What do you mean, come to see him? Is one of these brats yours?'

'Yes, I suppose so.'

'What do you mean, you suppose so?'

'I ... gave birth here, but I've been ill. I've never seen him.'

'Oh!' Understanding and surprise crossed the woman's face in quick succession. 'You're the one who ... we all thought you was dead. Now I know who you mean. Nancy! Come 'ere. This is the woman whose kid you've been suckling.'

A large woman hoisted herself out of a chair and came towards them, a child on each arm. Dora caught her breath. There was no doubt about which of the two was her son. His skin was the colour of golden syrup and there was already a network of black curls stuck to his scalp.

'You made it, then?' the woman said. 'I wouldn't have given much for your chances when they took you away. Here.' She thrust the baby into Dora's arms. 'He's yours, all right. No question about that. And a right greedy little monster he is, too. Would have sucked me dry if I let him and left nothing for me own bairn.'

Dora looked down at the swaddled bundle in her arms. The incubus that had grown in her belly for nine months was now a separate, living being. Her child. She waited for the flame of maternal love to kindle, but felt nothing. The small head twisted from side to side, the red mouth searching. Then he opened his eyes and Dora felt suddenly sick, as if she had been punched in the stomach. The eyes were pale blue, the same forget-me-not shade exactly as his father's.

She tried to thrust the bundle back into Nancy's arms. 'I can't! I can't. I don't have any milk for him.'

It was true. In her weakened state her milk had dried up. Her breasts were sore, the nipples so tender that she could hardly bear her clothes touching them. The thought of even attempting to suckle the child filled her with revulsion.

Nancy pushed her away. 'No you don't! I've done my bit. Find someone else to feed the brat.'

She turned away and stomped off to her chair, where she put her own child to her breast as if to demonstrate her determination. Dora looked at the woman who had first spoken to her.

'Is there someone else ...?'

She shook her head. 'There's no one. We've only got three nursing mothers now and they all have their work cut out to feed their own babes. Most of the women who end up here have had a rough time, hard work, not enough to eat – it's a miracle they haven't lost the child, let alone have the milk to feed them.'

'What can I do?' Dora asked.

'You sure you can't do it yourself? Let him try. The milk may come. Here, take a seat. I'll help if I can.'

Unwillingly Dora let herself be led to a chair. She undid the front of her dress and held the child, who was now yowling and thrashing in her grasp, to her chest. After a brief struggle he located her breast and Dora suppressed a cry of pain as the small mouth fastened on her nipple. A moment later he twisted his head away, screaming in frustration. She tried again, offered the other breast, with the same result. It was with a sense of relief that she held him away from her and pulled her dress closed.

'It's no good. I told you. Nancy will have to take him back.'

'There's no "have to" about it,' the other woman said with some asperity. Dora could see that she was unimpressed with her efforts.

'But he'll die if he doesn't get food.'

'You can try getting cow's milk into him, but in my experience children don't thrive on that.' She paused and looked around the room. 'I'll have another word with Nance. Maybe I can persuade her.'

In the end, after much begging, Nancy agreed take him back, but only for a limited time.

'You need to find someone else,' she said. 'There's women on the outside would take him.'

'But they would want to be paid,' Dora pointed out.

'Well, where's the father? He should take some responsibility.'

The first woman gave a cackle of laughter. 'And pigs should know how to fly! How many of us are in here because men never want to take on any responsibility for anything they've done to us?'

But the words had set a train of thought in motion in Dora's mind. She remembered what she had said to Edith. Hector should take his share of the shame, and his share of the consequences.

'Are we allowed out of here?' she asked.

'Only on the last Thursday of the month, for a few hours in the afternoon,' she was told. 'If you're thinking you might go and talk to the father, you're in luck. It's the last Thursday this week.'

'What day is it today?' Dora asked. 'I've lost track.'

'Tuesday.'

'The day after tomorrow, then.' She looked at Nancy. 'If you can put up with him until then, I promise I'll find another solution on Thursday.'

Dora made her preparations carefully. She found an osier basket which was used to carry laundry and took one of the rags that were used as napkins off the washing line in the little courtyard outside the laundry room. When the midday meal was over she took the baby from Nancy. She had just fed him and he was quiet for once.

Nancy looked at her suspiciously. 'You're not going to do anything stupid, are you?'

'Of course not,' Dora replied.

She laid the child in the basket and covered him with the cloth. Then she made her way to the main gate. A crowd of men and women were pushing their way out, eager to make the most of their few hours of freedom. No one took any notice of Dora. It was further than she remembered from Brownlow Hill to Canning Street, where the Latimers resided, and in her still weakened state her burden seemed to grow heavier by the minute. She plodded on, along the length of Hope Street, and found herself at last outside the familiar door. She rang the bell and waited. It was opened, as she expected, by Clara, the parlourmaid

The girl stepped back with a gasp. 'You! What are you doing here? You'd better shove off before the mistress knows you're here.'

Dora thrust the basket, the still mercifully sleeping child hidden beneath the cloth, into her hands.

'A gift for Mr Hector.'

She turned away and walked as fast as she could back in the direction from which she had come.

Chapter 2

'Dora!' Edith's worn face melted into a smile. 'How are you? And how is your little baby?'

Dora shrugged. 'He didn't survive.' She had gambled that there was little communication between the nursery and the infirmary.

Edith gasped. 'Oh, no! My dear, I am so sorry.'

'It was probably better like this,' Dora said. 'After all, what kind of life could he have had, growing up here?'

Edith frowned at her. 'Just the same, it is a terrible blow. You must be grieving.'

'I never really knew him. He was forced upon me against my will and I nearly died giving birth to him. I can't grieve for what I never had and never wanted.'

Edith shook her head, baffled and saddened. Dora understood why. She could hardly understand her own feelings. What she had just said was true, and yet underneath the cold rationality of the statement was an aching sense of loss and emptiness. She had not wanted the child, the very sight of him repelled her, yet she still felt as if a part of herself had been ripped away.

She took a breath and straightened her shoulders. 'What I need is an occupation. Can I help you here in the infirmary?'

'You really want to work here? You've seen from the other side how dire the circumstances are and how little we can do.'

'All the better to keep my mind away from my own loss. And I may be able to help more than you think. My mother told me that back in Jamaica, where she grew up, her family were known as healers and sick people often came to her mother for help. While she lived here she tried to carry on the tradition by caring for people in our neighbourhood. I learned a lot from her.'

'Then you will be doubly welcome,' Edith said. 'Lord knows, there are few enough of us and an extra pair of hands will be a great help. So—' her tone became practical '—let me take you round and show you what is needed. There are two wards, one for men and one for women, plus two fever wards, the lying-in ward, where you were taken when you first came here, and another for those who have contracted what people call "the itch".'

'The itch?' Dora queried.

Edith cleared her throat. 'There are ... diseases ... which are passed from men to women when they have ... relations of an intimate nature.'

'Oh,' Dora nodded. 'You don't have to be so delicate with me. My mother treated women with those afflictions.'

Edith looked at her. 'I can see you are going to be a great asset here. So, let us start here, in the women's ward.'

Dora already knew at first-hand what it was like to be a patient, but her perceptions had been clouded by pain and weakness. Now, as she and Edith walked the length of the long room, she saw that her companion's description of the conditions as 'dire' was fully justified. Little light penetrated the grimy windows, cobwebs hung from the rafters and in the airless atmosphere the stench was nauseating. She soon realised that while some of the women were able to get up and hobble to the privy at the far end, many could not, which explained why the straw beneath their beds was matted with urine and excrement. As they passed many of them called out, begging for water.

'Are there not two other women who are supposed to help?' she asked. 'Where are they?'

'Gossiping by the tap in the yard, I expect,' Edith said, pursing her lips. 'That is where I usually find them.'

Dora looked along the line of beds. 'What is wrong with them all? Why are they here?'

'All sorts of reasons. The two at the end of the ward, there, have consumption. There are two cases of acute diarrhoea and seven of scurvy. Old Ma Garvey is so crippled with arthritis she can hardly get out of bed, and Dot Parsons has a broken arm. She came back from a Thursday outing drunk and fell down the stairs. Jessie cut herself when she was working in the kitchen and the wound has festered. She is in a great deal of pain, I'm afraid. The surgeon says the arm may have to come off. Poor little Fanny over there – well, no one seems to know what is wrong with her. She simply refuses to eat. And Peggy Watts is mad. She sees things and hears voices. She should be in an asylum. And in the fever ward we have five cases of scarlet fever.'

'The scurvy cases,' Dora said, 'surely they could be cured with fruit? Oranges for example.'

'Hah!' Edith laughed bitterly. 'Who is going to buy oranges for the likes of us?'

Dora said no more, but her mind was working to recall the remedies she had seen her mother use for sick neighbours. She could think of several, but the means to come by the ingredients was a different problem.

'Set me to work,' she said. 'What shall I do first?'

For the rest of the day she fetched water from the tap in the yard and held cups to the lips of those unable to drink alone. She bathed fevered faces and changed dressings. She and Edith lifted woman out of soiled beds and changed the linen, and helped those who could stand to get to the privy. The other women who were supposed to be helping saw what was happening and were shamed into following suit, though it was clear that they resented having to make the effort.

By bedtime Dora's back was aching and her hands were raw from being continually in cold water, but that, she reminded herself wryly, was no change from the months she had spent working for the washerwoman. At least here she had the comfort of a friendly fellow worker in the shape of Edith.

As they withdrew to the small dormitory they shared with the other helpers, she was horrified to see Mrs Carter, the superintendent, who had paid little attention to what was going on during the day, take a bunch of keys from her belt and lock the door of the ward.

'That can't be right!' she exclaimed. 'What about those who need help and care during the night?'

'They have to wait until morning, I'm afraid,' was the reply. 'We can't have patients wandering around in the middle of the night.'

'I could sit with them, make sure no one wandered out.'

'And go without sleep yourself? You would soon nod off and then anything could happen.'

Dora began to protest again, but the woman walked away without a backward look.

That day set the pattern for the days that followed, days in which Dora became increasingly frustrated by how little she was able to do to ease the suffering of the women in the ward.

'Is there no doctor to care for these people?' she asked Edith.

'The medical officer comes round every two or three days, but he has the whole workhouse to look after. And the truth is there is very little he can do that we cannot. Most of these diseases have no cure, as you well know.'

'But they could be alleviated, if only the right medicines were available,' Dora said.

'In my experience, these patent medicines that promise such miracle cures do very little good,' Edith said. 'I prefer to put my faith in God. I pray every night for him to have mercy on these poor women.'

'And does he answer?' Dora said, angrily. Then she saw that she had offended her friend and apologised.

One afternoon, seeking some fresh air after the foetid atmosphere in the ward, Dora wandered out into what was ironically termed the 'garden', an open space behind the infirmary. It was true that at some time in the past some-one had attempted to cultivate a few flowers there, but now the beds were choked with weeds and more had thrust their way up between the paving stones around the edge.

Minutes later, she hurried back to where Edith was sitting by Fanny's bedside, trying to persuade her to eat.

'Look! See what I have found?' She held out a handful of green shoots of various kinds.

'Weeds?' Edith said, puzzled. 'What is so exciting about them?'

'Not weeds! Herbs! They are growing out there in the garden and I can't understand why no one has noticed them before. See, this is yarrow. A poultice of this helps wounds to heal cleanly. This here is St John's wort. That is good for burns and eases pain. And here is horehound, a sovereign remedy for coughs, and feverfew which does as its name suggests and reduces fever.'

'And all these are growing out there, in our garden?'

'And more besides, probably. I haven't searched thoroughly.'

'Do you know how they should be used?'

'I've watched my mother. I remember what she did.'

Edith stood up. 'Dora, are you quite sure you have identified them correctly? It would be so easy to make a mistake and perhaps do more harm than good.'

'I know them as well as I know my own hands! I used to go out with my mother to collect them. They are not hard to find. They will grow on any bit of waste land, or along the sides of roads. Let me show you how they can be used. I promise you, we can do so much to ease the suffering around us.'

'I'm not sure …' Edith looked down the ward uneasily. 'We should probably ask the superintendent …'

'She knows nothing about these things. She would probably forbid it out of ignorance. Let me try. I promise you it will do no harm, and it may do much good.'

'Very well.' Edith made up her mind. 'What do you need?'

'A basin or something like that to pound the leaves in. Some boiling water to make a tincture. Linen for poultices. I'll begin with this.' She held up a bunch of slightly woolly leaves. 'A tincture of horehound will help those two poor women who cough so painfully.'

There was a small kitchen attached to the infirmary. Most of the food was sent in bulk from the main kitchens, but this had been designed with the idea that special dishes could be prepared for those who required it. Unfortunately, the ingredients for such delicacies were in short supply and even what was there was tended to vanish, spirited away by the carers to sell or give to their families outside. It did, however, provide Dora with the implements she required. It took only a few minutes to pound the hairy leaves into a pulp and pour boiling water over them. Dora drained off the resulting liquor and sipped it.

She wrinkled her nose. 'It is better if it can be sweetened. Do we have any sugar?'

Edith searched the cupboards and shook her head. 'There should be some, but it has gone, like most of the good things.'

'Well, we shall just have to persuade our patients to drink it as it is,' Dora said.

'Is it very bitter?'

'Not unbearably. Taste.'

Edith took a cautious sip. 'Well, I've tasted worse medicine. Let us try it on our two consumptives.'

The two women lay side by side at the far end of the ward. Both were very pale, exhausted by the constant racking coughs that shook their fragile bodies. Dora knelt beside the first one.

'I have a medicine here which will ease your cough. Will you try it?'

'What is it?' the woman asked, her voice a husky whisper.

'Tincture of horehound. It is an old remedy, but a good one. Take a little, please.'

The woman sighed. 'I can't feel any worse. Give it to me.' She sipped and made a face, but then finished the draft and lay back on her pillows. The second woman was weaker, but she swallowed the medicine without question.

Dora straightened up. 'It may need several drafts to show any improvement. We must be patient. Now, I am going to make a poultice of yarrow to put on Peggy's arm. It should help to take away the inflammation.'

As the hours passed, she went back several times to check on the two consumptives. Towards evening she persuaded them both to take a second dose and as they made the rounds to dish out the milk soup that comprised the evening meal Edith said, 'Listen!'

'Listen? To what?'

'No coughing.'

It was true. Both women lay asleep, resting more peacefully than they had done for many nights.

'Will it cure them?' Edith asked.

Dora shook her head sadly. 'I fear there is no cure for consumption. All we can do is make their last days more comfortable. But it's something, at least.'

In the following days Dora worked at her herbal remedies. Drafts of feverfew reduced the hectic flush on the faces of the sufferers from scarlet fever and quieted their restless muttering. She compounded dandelion leaves and mallow flowers to make a drink for the scurvy sufferers. And her yarrow poultice was so effective on Peggy's arm that the wound began to heal. She was soon hailed as a healer with almost magical powers.

Not everyone was pleased with her efforts, however. The two other women who had volunteered to care for the patients regarded her with great suspicion. One day she heard them muttering together. 'If you ask me, it's some kind of black magic she learned from the people back where she came from,' one said.

'You're right,' the other agreed. 'Time was, she'd have been burned as a witch.'

One night Dora woke to the sound of distant shouts and the frantic ringing of the workhouse bell.

'What's going on?' Edith was on her feet already. 'There's some kind of emergency.'

The other women were awake now, protesting drowsily at being disturbed. Dora pulled a shawl over her nightgown and went to open the window. The noise grew louder and she smelled smoke.

'There's a fire somewhere!'

Edith peered over her shoulder. 'It looks like one of the dormitories.'

Dora followed her pointing finger and saw a plume of black smoke rising above the rooftops. 'Should we evacuate the patients?'

'No, I don't think there's any danger. It's not close. But they may be worried. We had better do what we can to reassure them.'

As soon as they stepped out into the corridor they could hear shouts and screams coming from the locked wards and someone was pounding on the door of the men's ward. Mrs Carter appeared in her dressing gown, followed by her male counterpart.

'Be quiet in there! There is no need for panic,' she shouted.

'Quiet! Go back to bed!' the man boomed.

'Please,' Dora begged, 'unlock the doors. The poor creatures are terrified.'

'And have them all come rushing out and going heaven knows where?'

'They won't rush out. Most of them can hardly walk! Let me go in and talk to them. I can calm them down.'

Mrs Carter exchanged glances with her fellow officer. The noise from the wards had not abated. He shrugged and turned back towards the main entrance.

'I'll see what is going on out there.'

Seeing that he had abrogated all responsibility, Mrs Carter took the keys from her dressing gown pocket and unlocked the women's ward.

'Very well. Just make sure no one slips out. I hold you responsible.'

Inside the ward most of the women who were able to stand had congregated by the door; one or two others were standing on stools in an attempt to see out of the grimy windows set high up in the walls. Others cowered under their bedclothes, whimpering. It was some time before Dora and Edith could make themselves heard.

'There's no danger,' Dora repeated again and again. 'The fire is nowhere near here. You are quite safe.'

Eventually calm was restored and they managed to get all the patients back into bed. Back in the corridor they discovered that the two volunteers who worked in the men's ward had arrived, somewhat belatedly, and been let in. They could hear them ordering the men back to bed, with threats of punishment. Mrs Carter was nowhere to be seen.

'Gone back to bed, I suppose,' Edith said.

'So how are we supposed to lock up?'

'We can't.'

'We can't risk one of them deciding to wander off,' Dora said. 'I'll sit up with them.'

'We both will. It's not fair for you to do it all on your own.'

So they both spent what remained of the night in the ward, soothing the terrified and bathing the faces of the feverish, until at last quiet descended.

'I was thinking,' Dora whispered as they settled on a pair of stools near the door, 'suppose the fire had started here? These poor souls might be burnt alive before we could get the door unlocked.'

'The same thing occurred to me,' Edith agreed. 'But there's nothing we can do about it.'

Next morning Mrs Carter called them into her office.

'I'll wager it's not to thank us for what we did last night,' Dora murmured as they reached the door.

'More likely to moan at us for disobedience,' Edith said.

In the event it was neither. Mrs Carter was a small, dried up twig of a woman, with a waist so small that Dora had the impression she might snap in half if put under stress. Her sharp features were normally almost devoid of expression, but that morning it was clear that she was agitated.

'I do not know if you have heard the cause of last night's panic?'

'No, ma'am.'

'The girls' dormitory caught fire. No one seems to know how it happened, but the results have been tragic. Twenty-two children and two nurses dead.'

'Twenty-two!' Edith gasped.

'Dear God!' Dora murmured.

'Did anyone survive?'

'A few, yes, and that is why I have sent for you. There are two girls in particular who have survived but have suffered burns. They have been sent here, naturally, but the governor wishes them to be kept separate from the other patients.'

'Why is that?'

'It is ... sensitive. I do not want what I am going to tell you to go any further. You understand me?'

'Yes, ma'am.'

'I believe you are both women of discretion, not given to idle gossip. That is why I have chosen to take you into my confidence. The reason why one of the two girls sustained serious burns is that she had been tied to her bed by one of the nurses.'

'Tied! Why?' Dora exclaimed.

'It seems she was apt to walk in her sleep and this disturbed the other girls. We shall never know the full story, because the nurse responsible was one of those who died in the blaze. What matters is this. When the fire broke out, all those who were able to escaped by the staircase, but of course the one who was tied down was unable to do that. One of the others saw her predicament and returned, at risk of her own life, to untie her.'

33

'Are they both badly burned?' Edith asked.

'The girl who was tied down has quite severe burns to her face. I'm told a roof beam splintered in the heat and part of it fell on her. The other, the rescuer, was more fortunate, but her hands are burned from struggling to untie the smouldering ropes that held the other girl down. I want you two to make them your special care.'

'Of course,' Edith said. 'Where are they?'

'In the small room where we put new arrivals until we find out what is wrong with them. You had better go to them straight away.'

'What are their names?' Dora asked.

'The girl who was tied is called Jeannie. The other one is May. Oh, there's one other thing. For some unknown reason she had a small child in bed with her. Strictly against the rules.'

'What happened to it?'

'She managed to hand it on to one of the others before she went back to help Jeannie. I'm told it has been safely returned to the nursery. Just as well! It should never have been removed in the first place.'

'I don't understand why the governor wants them kept separate from the others,' Dora said, as they headed for the room.

'I do,' Edith said grimly. 'There is bound to be an enquiry into the cause of the fire and he doesn't want the inspectors finding out that that poor girl was tied to the bed. It would reflect badly on his management. But never mind that now. Dora, do you have any herbal remedies for burns?'

Dora's mind was already busy with that question. 'St John's wort would be the best thing. I will prepare it straight away.'

In the little kitchen that had become her laboratory she pounded the yellow flowers of the St John's wort into an oily paste and then spread it onto strips of clean linen to form a bandage. In the small room off the main ward she found the doctor who served as the medical officer for the workhouse stooping over the beds. His name was Wentworth and Dora estimated that he was in his early twenties, recently qualified and obliged to take on this thankless job until he was able to set up in practice for himself.

'This poor child is going to be badly disfigured, I'm afraid,' he said grimly.

'Are they both still unconscious?' Dora asked.

'I have given them both a dose of laudanum. It will keep them asleep for an hour or two, until the worst of the pain has eased.'

'Then we must do what we can before they come round,' Dora said.

'Do?' he queried. 'What do you mean?'

'I have an unguent here, a herbal remedy. I think it will help.'

He looked sharply at her and for a moment she was afraid that he was going to forbid her to apply the bandages. Then he shrugged, 'These folk remedies sometimes work. You might as well try it.' He straightened up. 'I have done all I can for the moment. I will come back later to see how they are progressing.'

When the doctor had gone, Dora moved to Jeannie's side. 'Can you support the child's head for me?'

With Edith's help she wound a bandage impregnated with the herbal paste around the girl's face, which was marked with a long, scarlet scar. Then she turned her attention to the other bed, and realised with surprise that she recognised the girl lying there. It was the one she had seen nursing the little girl with golden hair on her first visit to the nursery.

'What a little heroine!' she murmured, as she carefully anointed May's hands.'Will her hands heal,' Edith asked, 'so she can use them, do you think?'

'If this works as it should, I hope so,' Dora said. 'The burns are not as deep as on the other girl's face.'

She sat by the two girls until the one called May opened her eyes and tried to sit up. She put a hand gently on her shoulder and pressed her back onto the pillows.

'Lie quiet, sweetheart. Everything's all right. Just you rest.'

For the next few minutes she devoted herself to soothing the girl's anxiety about her injured friend and the small child who had been with her when the fire started. By the time Edith came to relieve her she had drifted off to sleep again.

'She keeps asking after Angel,' she murmured to the other woman. 'I thought at first she was delirious, but it seems that is what she calls the little girl. She appears to be devoted to the child.'

Later that day one of the other girls, who had survived the fire, came knocking at the door of the infirmary. She was holding a slightly singed rag doll.

'One of the workmen found this when they were clearing up. It's May's, I think. It was in her bed. I thought she might want it back.'

Dora took the doll and regarded it with a degree of surprise. Surely, she thought, May was too old to need the comfort of a toy like this. But she took it with her when she went to give the two girls their supper.

'This was found in your bed when they were clearing up after the fire. Is it something you were given as a little child?'

'Oh, no! It's not mine,' May said. 'It's Angel's. She'll be missing it. Can you take it to the nursery for her, please?'

'It's all grubby and it smells of smoke. She won't want it now.'

'Oh, yes she will. She adores that doll. Please take it to her.'

Dora put the doll on May's bed. She had no intention of going anywhere near the nursery. 'Best you give it to her yourself when you see her. I've got enough to do without trekking down there.'

In a few days May was well enough to get up. The doctor examined her hands and was plainly surprised at how well they had healed. He told her she could go back to the rest of the girls and resume her normal routine. For the first time Dora considered what sort of life children like her – orphans whose only family was the workhouse – might have.

'What do they do all day?' she asked Edith.

'Oh, they have a programme of education, such as it is,' Edith said. 'They learn to read and write and do basic arithmetic, but most of what they are taught is designed to fit them to go into service when they are old enough to leave here. They learn housework, how to clean silver, mend clothes, some simple cooking, that sort of thing. Most of them will find jobs as maids-of-all-work. With luck the brightest among them might work their way up to being parlour maids.'

Dora shook her head sadly. She had spent long enough in the Latimer household to know the kind of life a servant might expect, particularly in the lower ranks, for the hier- archy of service was as rigid as that among the gentry who employed them. 'It's not an inviting prospect, is it? That May seems to be a girl with a lot of character. She could grow up to be quite pretty. And she's brave. Quite a little heroine. I'd like to think she had something better in store for her.'

'We might have hoped there was something better in store for us,' Edith responded wryly. 'But fortune is fickle, as we are often told.' She sighed. 'It's little Jeannie I feel sorriest for. There's no getting away from the fact that she is going to be badly disfigured. No one is going to want to employ a servant looking like that where other people might see her. All I can see for her is a life of drudgery below stairs, if that. And that's not all. The pretty ones have some hope of marriage one day. I can't see that happening to Jeannie.'

After a day or two Dora decided that it was time to remove the bandages from Jeannie's face. The girl put up her hand and touched her cheek with anxious fingertips.

'It feels strange. What's wrong with it?'

Dora looked at her. A jagged red cicatrix ran from her left temple to the corner of her mouth and the skin on either side was stretched and shiny. The scar had drawn the corner of her eye downwards and the corner of her lips upwards, giving her face a lopsided leer.

'Now, you keep your hands away from it, you hear me?' Dora said. 'If you pick at it I shall have to put the bandages back on. It will heal better in the open air, as long as you don't touch it.'

'When can I go back to the others?' Jeannie asked.

'Soon. In a day or two, when you're a bit stronger.'

Dora reflected sadly that the longer she could keep her in the seclusion of the infirmary the better. She knew that there were no mirrors in the workhouse, the official view being that such vanity would be misplaced among women who had fallen so low, but she suspected that even so there were a few treasured shards kept concealed in pockets or under pillows. It would not be long before some misguided individual decided that Jeannie had a right to know how she looked. But even without that, she would soon realise from the reactions of the other girls that her appearance shocked them.

'Have you got a lot of friends?' she asked.

Jeannie shrugged. 'Not many. They think I'm weird because I walk in my sleep.'

Dora turned away to hide the fact that tears had sprung to her eyes. That night, when she said her prayers, as she always did, she prayed that some of the girls would have the charity to befriend Jeannie when she returned to them.

Mrs Carter sent for her next morning.

'Dora, it has come to my notice that you are using some medications of your own devising on the patients. Who gave you authority to do that?'

'No one, ma'am,' Dora admitted. 'But they're not of my own devising. They are herbal remedies which have been used for hundreds of years.'

'Among your own people, perhaps. But you must understand that you now live in a civilised country. We have our own doctors who are far better qualified in these matters.'

Dora felt her cheeks burning. 'I don't know what you mean by "my own people". I was born and brought up here in Liverpool. These herbs grow here and have been used by the people who live here for centuries. Most of them cannot afford to call in your "civilised" doctors. And when they do, all the doctors can prescribe are quack medicines or laudanum. My herbs have helped the women here. Ask them.'

'It is well known that people can convince themselves that they feel better, just because someone tells them that they are being cured. You may not have done any harm, so far, but I cannot allow you to continue. Many of the plants you use may have curative properties, but there are many which are very dangerous. I cannot risk the possibility of mistakes.'

'You think I don't know the difference between herbs that cure and those that kill?' Dora exclaimed. 'I was taught by my mother and she never in all her life harmed any one with her medicines.'

'That may be, but what you are doing is upsetting some of the other women who work here. It is causing anxiety and division. I must insist that you stop at once.'

Dora forced back tears of anger and frustration. She knew that her potions had helped people and to be forced to abandon them, out of ignorance and prejudice, was infuriating. Then she had an inspiration.

'Perhaps we should refer the matter to Dr Wentworth. I think he may see things differently.'

'Dr Wentworth is a qualified physician. I am quite sure he will have no truck with your folk remedies.'

'We could ask him, couldn't we?'

'No, we could not! I forbid you to bother him with such trivial matters.'

Dora had no intention of obeying that order and when the doctor came the following morning she was determined to make her point. Wentworth examined Jeannie's face and said that the burns were healing up nicely and she could re-join the other girls.

As she followed him out of the room Dora said, 'Excuse me, sir. Would you say that the St John's wort dressings I used were helpful in the healing process?'

She expected him to put the enquiry aside with a casual comment, but instead he stopped and looked at her seriously.

'I believe they did. They certainly seemed to ease the pain and there was no infection. Where did you learn to do that?'

'From my mother, sir. She was regarded as a healer by a great many people.'

'Do you know any other similar remedies?'

'A good many, sir.'

'Such as?'

'Horehound for coughs, yarrow to heal open wounds, feverfew for fevers. If I could only come by white willow bark, that is better still for fever, but I have to make do with what I can find in the garden here.'

'And have you tried these remedies on the patients here?'

'Yes. I have.

'I should like to speak to them.'

Dora felt a thrill of triumph. 'This way, sir. I'm sure they will tell you they have found them helpful.'

As they headed for the main ward Mrs Carter came out of her office.

'Ah, Mrs Carter,' Wentworth said, 'I am going to inquire into the results of Dora's herbal remedies.'

Carter looked furious. 'There is really no need for that, doctor. I have already forbidden her to continue with them. I knew you, as a man trained in the sciences, would have no truck with what is, at best, mere superstitio.'

'I don't know about that,' Wentworth said. 'There are more things in heaven and earth, Horatio ...'

It was clear from Carter's expression that the quotation was completely lost on her, but Dora smiled. He looked at her quizzically.

'You can complete the quotation?'

'Than are dreamt of in your philosophy,' she supplied.

His eyes met hers as if he was seeing her for the first time. 'You know your Hamlet?'

Dora looked down. 'I had the ... the good fortune to share in the education of two young ladies of quality for a few years. Our tutor believed that any well educated person, male or female, should have some acquaintance with the works of Shakespeare.'

'What an enlightened man!' Wentworth said. 'You were fortunate.'

Dora thought back to the lessons with the two Latimer daughters and remembered how they had yawned and giggled their way through them and then demanded that she write the essays set for them by the tutor. 'Yes,' she murmured, 'I was fortunate.'

Mrs Carter was looking from one of them to the other with barely suppressed irritation. Wentworth turned his attention to her. 'Well, shall we see what the patients have to say on the question?'

Dora followed him and Mrs Carter down the ward. He asked her which patients she had treated and then enquired from each of them what the effect had been. Without exception, they insisted that her medicines had relieved their symptoms and eased their suffering. When he had finished his inspection Wentworth turned to the superintendent with a smile.

'Well, Mrs Carter, there may be little scientific knowledge behind Dora's remedies, but the fact is they do seem to help. I see no reason why she should not continue.'

Dora expected Mrs Carter to be furious, but she saw instead that she looked embarrassed, as if she had been caught behaving in an unprofessional manner. 'Of course, doctor. It is for you to say.'

Dora ducked her head to conceal her grin of triumph.

Chapter 3

From that day on, Dora's life settled into a steady routine. She helped Edith and the other women in the day-to-day care of the patients, the back-breaking work of fetching water and changing linen and carrying those unable to walk to the privy. The rest of her time was spent in hunting for suitable herbs and concocting her various remedies, and then in administering drafts and applying poultices. And all too often hours were spent sitting beside the beds of the dying and then in laying them out. There were brighter moments, too, when one of the patients recovered enough to leave the infirmary. The scarlet fever epidemic subsided and most of the patients recovered, but in its wake came measles, which mainly affected the children. One of the helpers went down with it as well, leaving them more short-handed than ever, but Dora and Edith seemed to lead charmed lives and neither of them caught any of the diseases they were treating.

After her triumph with Dr Wentworth she expected Mrs Carter's antagonism to increase but instead she found herself treated with greater respect. One of the fruits of that was to persuade the superintendent that it was inhuman to lock the wards at night, particularly in view of what might have happened had the fire broken out closer to hand. It meant that one of them, usually either herself or Edith, had to stay in the ward overnight, sleeping fitfully on a camp bed near the door and waking frequently to carry chamber pots or help a patient to the privy, but they reaped the reward of having fewer wet beds to change in the morning.

It was during these uneasy nights that Dora found herself thinking about the child she had given away. Initially she had closed her mind to it, immersing herself in work and so tired every night that she fell asleep at once, allowing no time for introspection. Now she was no longer able to banish the memory. She had little recollection of the actual birth, except as a time of agony and fear, and the few short hours she had spent in the nursery, with a baby who refused to feed and whose blue eyes were a constant reminder of the man who had fathered him, had been filled with such a confusion of emotions that she had wanted only to be free of them, and of him. Now that she had time to think she had to admit a sense of guilt. Violent as his conception had been, she had carried him and given him life. It was her duty to make that life as enjoyable and trouble free as possible. But that, she reasoned, was exactly what she had tried to do. She knew what happened to children brought up in the workhouse, given only a basic education and destined for menial work when they were old enough to leave. Was that what she wanted for her son? It occurred to her that she had never even given him a name. By returning him to his father, she told herself, she had given him the chance of growing up in a wealthy household, with all the advantages that could bring. She told herself this over and over again, but as time passed she could no longer suppress the cold realisation that the outcome might be very different. Why should she imagine that Hector would wish to be burdened with an illegitimate son? And even if he did have some feeling for him, his mother would never allow her family to be shamed in such a way. Almost certainly they would have looked for someone to adopt the child, perhaps paid some poor family to take him or ... and on this thought a chill ran through Dora's veins ... they might have sent him back to the workhouse as a homeless orphan left on the doorstep. He might even now be in the nursery, which she refused to visit. If he had been returned, she reasoned, he would have been recognised. His skin colour alone made him distinctive. And in that case surely she would have been summoned to look after him. But then, who in the nursery knew that she had come back to work here? The last they knew of her was when she set out that Thursday afternoon, carrying her child, and, as they thought, had never returned.

The dilemma of what she should have done and what the consequences of her actions might have been went round and round in her mind, disturbing her much-needed rest at night and distracting her during the day. Seeing the change in her, Edith one evening sat down with her and asked what was troubling her.

'It's nothing – nothing important. It's just that sometimes ... sometimes I wish my little boy had lived. I know I said at first it didn't matter to me, that I didn't want him. But now I think it was wicked of me to feel like that.'

Edith took her hand. 'You couldn't help the way you felt, my dear. You had been so terribly abused and then the birth was so difficult. If you had been able to hold him when he first arrived it might have been different, but as things were it is not surprising that you didn't care for him. You must tell yourself that it was God's will to take him and perhaps in His wisdom He knew it would be for the best. We must trust in Him.'

Dora bowed her head. If she had sinned, she had increased her culpability by spinning such a falsehood to cover it, but it was too late to go back now. She resolved to put the whole matter to the back of her mind and con-centrate on her work. Surely she could find redemption in alleviating the suffering of others.

Dr Wentworth continued to take an interest in her rem-edies. One day he asked if he could see how she prepared them and she took him into the little kitchen and demon-strated how she boiled some herbs and pounded others into a paste or made a kind of tea with them.

He said, 'You told me once that there was one herb that you could not find here in the workhouse.'

'Oh, there are many I wish I had,' she said. 'But the one I mentioned was not a herb exactly. It is the bark of the white willow, which has great power in the relief of pain.'

'What are the others?'

'I would like lavender. Oil made from that is excellent for healing wounds and treating burns. Valerian is a sed-ative and promotes healing through allowing the patient to rest. A syrup made from rose hips is good for treating scurvy – though of course oranges and lemons are better still. But it is too early in the year for rose hips.'

'I think I know gardens where lavender grows. I am sure I could bring you some of the flowers. And I think I know valerian. It grows on dry, heathland areas, does it not? I like to walk in such places and I have long been interested in the plants that grow there.'

'It can grow in any waste place. I remember finding it with my mother growing on a wall down near the docks.'

'Is it the flowers that you need?'

'No, the root.'

'And white willow. Is that the weeping willow?'

'No, but all willows have a kind of watery sap under the bark, which is what I need.'

'Well, I know where to find willows, down by the river. I shall bring you some.'

He was as good as his word and after that he quite frequently sought her out with offerings of plants or flowers he had culled on his walks. Some of them she was able to plant in the little garden and others she dried. Soon her little pharmacy was stocked with most of the things she needed. He told her that he had begun a study of the scientific literature concerning herbal remedies and was thinking of preparing a paper on the subject for the interest of colleagues.

One thing that distressed Dora particularly was the fact that she was forbidden to go into the men's ward. The patients there were cared for exclusively by male attendants and she suspected that the care they received was pretty rough and ready. One day she mentioned her concern to Dr Wentworth.

'I am sure that many of the men could benefit from my remedies, but since I cannot visit them I do not know what might be of use.'

'I could speak to the superintendent about the matter,' he suggested.

The male superintendent, a Mr Bellow, was, however, adamant; the men's ward was no place for a woman, particularly an unmarried woman.

'Some of these men have wounds or conditions on areas of their bodies which no innocent female should have to look upon,' he announced ponderously. 'And the language some of them use should not afflict feminine ears.'

Wentworth persisted and at length won the concession that men whose conditions might respond to Dora's medicines could be brought out to the small room where new arrivals were accommodated, so that she could prescribe the appropriate treatment, with the proviso that she could only apply any local remedy to areas above the shoulder or below the knee. Treatment to any other part of the anatomy would be administered by a male attendant after she had left the room. A few men presented themselves with open wounds or fevers, but not many. When Dora expressed surprise Wentworth looked embarrassed.

'There is some resistance, I must admit. Some of them object to being treated by a woman, and one or two because of the colour of your skin – but there is a foolish story going round that your cures are the product of black magic. I have pointed out that that is nothing but ridiculous superstition but it's hard to dislodge the idea from their minds.'

'Well, I can guess where that story came from,' Dora said bitterly.

'Don't be too downhearted. When the others see how effective your potions are I'm sure they will come round.'

One day, when he had made his rounds, the doctor said, 'I have a compatriot of yours in need of your help.'

Dora gave him a sideways look. 'You mean a fellow Englishman?'

He had the grace to blush. 'I'm sorry. I should have said someone of your colour. I know you were born here.'

'What is wrong with him?' she asked.

'His breathing is restricted. I'm not sure at the moment whether it is asthma or a bronchitis. He's in the small ward. Shall we go and see him? His name is Jem, by the way.'

Dora realised at once that Jem, like herself, was of mixed blood. She was surprised to see that, in contrast to most of the people she treated, he was obviously strong and well-nourished. His shirt was open to the waist and the rolled up sleeves showed muscular arms, but his shoulders were raised and his face was beaded with sweat from the effort of breathing.

Wentworth said, 'I'm going to listen to your chest, Jem. Just try to breathe as normally as possible.'

He produced from his bag a device Dora had never seen before. It was a short trumpet-shaped tube of polished wood with an ivory disc at one end. He placed the disc against Jem's chest and put the other end in his ear. When he had repeated the process in several locations, both on Jem's chest and back, he straightened up.

'There is considerable congestion. Dora, is there anything you can do to help this poor man breathe more easily?'

She had been thinking hard. 'An infusion of horehound should work. But there is another plant, which I do not have. It is called butterbur and it grows in moist places, like along the banks of streams. That would be better, if we can find some. Also liquorice can be beneficial. Can you obtain some for me?'

'Certainly. And I can look for the butterbur. What does it look like?'

'It has spikes of purple flowers, quite densely packed.'

'Well, I'll see what I can do. Meanwhile?'

'A steam inhalation with aromatic herbs will help. I'll prepare that straight away, and the horehound infusion.' She smiled at Jem. 'I'm sure we can make things better for you.'

He managed a smile in return. 'Feeling better already, ma'am,' he wheezed.

'No need to call me ma'am,' she responded. 'My name is Dorinda – Dora if you prefer. Wait here. I will be back as soon as I can.'

As he closed the door behind him Wentworth cocked an eyebrow. 'Dorinda, eh? Why have you never told me that?'

She shrugged. 'It's not important. Too much of a mouthful for most people. Please, what is that instrument you used in there?'

'It is called a stethoscope. It was invented by a French doctor about fifty years ago, but the design has been refined somewhat since then. With it I can hear what is going on inside a patient's chest much better than just by putting my ear against it. One day I'll let you try it, if you like.'

She hesitated. There was something in the doctor's manner which disturbed her, though she could not say why.

'I'd best get on. That poor man needs help as quickly as possible.'

In the kitchen she boiled water and placed a selection of herbs in a basin, choosing sage and rosemary and thyme and a few sprigs of lavender. She crushed the horehound leaves and added boiling water to make an infusion, then carried the resulting liquor, together with the kettle, the basin of herbs and a towel back to the small ward where Jem waited.

'Now—' she set a low table in front of him and placed the basin on it '—put this towel over your head and breathe in the steam.'

She poured the hot water onto the herbs and stood back as Jem bent his head over the table. After a while, he raised it again, his face dewed with droplets of water.

'Has it helped?'

He drew in an experimental breath. 'I believe it has!'

'Good. Now drink this.' She handed him the cup with the horehound infusion and watched him drain it.

'I'll bring you another inhalation in an hour or two. You had better stay here, instead of going back to the men's ward. Just try to rest now.'

She placed a pillow at the end of the bed, so he could lean his back against the wall and he settled back. She paused.

'Your name is Jem, yes? Short for Jeremy?'

'No, ma'am – Dorinda. Short for Jeremiah. My da was keen on biblical names, but I guess he didn't study the story of Jeremiah too closely.' His voice was husky and his breathing was still laboured but she saw a glint of humour in his eyes and responded with a smile.

'Never mind. Jem does very well. Can you tell me how you came to be in this condition? You look a strong man, not like most of those who end up here.'

'Working in the stokehold of one of these new steam ships,' he said. 'Breathing coal dust all day. Guess my lungs are as choked up as a chimney flue.'

'Well, I hope we can improve on that,' she said. She was tempted to linger, but reminded herself of all the work waiting to be done. 'You shouldn't talk too much yet. I'll be back later.'

She kept her word, bringing him fresh inhalations every couple of hours, and was gratified to see that his struggle to breathe eased after each one. Next morning Wentworth arrived triumphant, carrying a basket of plants with purple flowers.

'Is this what you want? I found them growing along the side of the canal.'

'Yes, that is butterbur,' she responded. 'How clever of you! And how good of you to give up your leisure time to hunting for it.'

He smiled at her. 'I take pleasure in doing it – and I am learning new things all the time.'

She met his eyes and experienced the same uneasy sense of intimacy that she had felt the day before. He came to the kitchen with her and watched her as she prepared a new draft and once or twice as she reached for more of the flowers his hand brushed hers.

'I hope the concentration is right,' she murmured, to deflect his attention as much as to voice her own doubts. 'I have never used this herb before.'

She carried the new concoction to the small ward, where Jem had remained, and he drank it without querying its efficacy. For the rest of the day she watched him for signs of any adverse side effects, but saw none. Next morning she heard him coughing and he began to bring up gouts of dark yellow phlegm, flecked with soot. By evening, it was clear that his condition was much improved.

'You are a true angel of mercy,' he told her. 'I thought my number was up for a while, back in that big ward. I'll never forget what you've done for me.'

'I hope that doesn't mean you are thinking of leaving,' she said. 'You are far from well yet.'

'Where would I go?' he asked. 'I have no home, no job now. It's the workhouse or nothing.'

'There must be something you could do, once you are fully recovered,' she said. 'As long as you don't go back to stoking.'

'No chance of that!' he replied.

She lingered, searching for a way to prolong the conversation. 'What did you do before that? Those steam ships are new. Did you come over on one?'

'Come over?'

'From ... wherever it was. Where were you born?'

'Not far from here, on a big estate in Cheshire. How about you?'

'Here in Liverpool.'

He gave a wheezy laugh. 'So we're both English. So how did that come about, for you?'

'My father was a sea captain. He brought my mother back with him from Jamaica.' Then, before he could ask for more details of her upbringing she added, 'And you? What's your story?'

'Oh, I'm more of a native here than you,' he said with a grin. 'My grand pappy was brought here as a slave, when he was only ten years old, to be a page and companion to the son of a wealthy family, the Deveraux. They treated him well and he grew up alongside their son and was given the same education, but when the son

went away to university he had no need of my granddad.
But still, the family were good to him. They gave him a
job as a groom, which he was very happy with because
he loved horses. He married one of the kitchen maids, a
black girl who came over on the same boat as him, and
they lived in a tied cottage on the estate, and had four
children. My father was the eldest. There was a smithy
on the estate, producing shoes for the family's horses and
tools for the farm, and when my da was old enough he
was apprenticed to the smith. Of course, by that time the
government had passed the abolition of slavery act, so
technically my dad was a free man. He did well, so well
that he married the smith's daughter – a white girl. I was
born the following year, 1837, but my ma contracted a
fever and died.'

'So you never knew her?'

'No.'

'That's very sad.'

'Is it? They say what you've never had you don't miss,
don't they?'

'Do they?' Dora looked away. This was too close to her
own abiding conflict with her conscience for comfort.

'Anyway,' Jem went on, 'I grew up on the estate, helping out in the smithy and in the stables. I liked that best,
because I loved horses, like my granddad. I was happy
there, thought that was going to be my life, but when I was
sixteen, a horse my da was shoeing kicked out and caught
him on the head, killed him instantly.'

'Oh no!'

'Oh yes. I never understood how it happened. He was a
man who could gentle the worst-tempered beasts. Horses

who played up with anyone else would stand like lambs for him. But something went wrong that day.'

'What happened to you?'

'Well, I had my job as a stable boy by then and I'd have been there yet, I daresay, but the family fell on hard times. Old Sir George, who brought my grandfather over from Jamaica, was a good man. But his son, Percy, who inherited the estate, was a gambler. He gambled away the family fortune and the estate had to be sold. The man who bought it had made his money in the cotton mills. The family weren't interested in keeping horses. So that was me, out of a job.'

'What did you do?'

'There wasn't any work for me in the neighbourhood, so I came to the city. I did some odd jobs on the docks, nothing regular but enough to keep body and soul together. Then someone told me there was work to be had stoking the engines in these new steam ships, work that paid good money. He was right about that. The money was better than anything I could make on the docks. But I knew by the end of the first day I'd made a mistake. I reckon the stokehold of a steamer's about the closest thing to hell you'd find anywhere. Hot, filthy, air full of fumes and coal dust. I stuck it out for two round trips, promising myself that if we ever called at Jamaica I'd jump ship. Reckoned with what I'd earned I could live for quite a while there, until I could find something else. But it wasn't to be. On the last voyage home I started to cough and it got so bad I couldn't do my work, so as soon as we made port I was paid off. "Thanks very much, here's your wages. Go and die somewhere else!" I went to the seamen's hostel, but they couldn't look after me. They told me to come here.'

'It's a cruel world,' Dora said, 'if you are without money and friends.'

'Never a truer word ...' he agreed. 'So what brought you here?'

Dora picked up his empty cup. 'What am I thinking about, standing here chattering? Dr Wentworth will be here on his rounds soon and I have several more patients waiting for medicine. I must get on.'

'Dr Wentworth, eh?' Something in his voice made her turn back to him. 'You want to watch out for him.'

'I don't know what you mean.'

'Don't tell me you haven't noticed the way he looks at you. It's none of my business, of course, but just ... watch out.'

'I don't know what you are talking about,' she said stiffly. 'His interest is purely professional. He is studying my remedies for a paper he's writing.'

'Professional, is it?' Jem said. 'That's not how it looked to me. He's taken a shine to you.'

'Rubbish!' she responded tersely and left the room.

Once outside, however, she could not get his words out of her head. 'The way he looks at you ...' There had been looks, looks that disturbed her. Was it possible? But what good could come of it? She shook herself mentally and got on with her work. Whatever the doctor might or might not see in her there could never be any relationship between them, other than the mutual interest in herbs and their uses. But occasionally, in the brief intervals between one task and the next, she found her mind drifting, seeing herself as the wife of a respectable doctor, with a home and servants ... and children. At that point she pulled herself up short. She had a child, somewhere; a child she had abandoned. And what respectable doctor could afford to marry someone that society would regard, however unjustly, as a fallen woman?

Dora always avoided any contact with the inhabitants of the rest of the workhouse. She never went to eat in the communal dining room, preferring to share the food that was sent in for the patients in the infirmary. Her abiding fear was that one of the women who had attended her at the birth of her son, or who had nursed him during her illness afterwards, would recognise her and demand to know where he was. As the months passed her anxiety lessened, but the guilt that gnawed away at her in quiet moments never went away. Over a year had gone by, and she felt dimly that she ought to remember the child's birthday, but she realised that she had only the haziest idea of the actual date on which she had given birth to him. Sometimes she tried to imagine what he would be like now, but she had never had much to do with small children and she found it hard. He would be learning to speak, and to walk perhaps. Would his first word be to call some other woman 'mama'?

About a week after Jem's arrival, while he was still confined to the small ward – an expedient that she justified by saying that his coughing would disturb the other men if he was returned to the big one – she came out of the kitchen carrying a tray of medicines and found herself face to face with Nancy, the woman who had suckled her child.

'You!' Nancy exclaimed. 'What are you doing here?'

'Same as you,' Dora managed to say. 'Earning my daily bread and keeping a roof over my head.'

'Where's the child?'

'He died.'

'Died? How? He was a fine thriving boy when you took him from me.'

'Yes, I know. But soon after that he took sick and died.'

'Took sick where? Where did you go with him? Last time I saw you, you was heading out of this place, and taking the child with you.'

'I went ...' Dora was improvising desperately, 'I went to a place where I thought he would be taken care of, where we both would. But it was not to be.'

Nancy took a step forward and thrust her face close to Dora's. 'You killed that babe. You knew you couldn't feed him. I've never seen a child fight against being put to the breast like that, as if he knew your milk was poison. You took him away, knowing it would be the death of him. Why?'

Mrs Carter came out of her office.

'What is going on here? I can hear you through the walls of my room. Please be quiet.'

'She's a murderer! A child killer!' Nancy insisted, without lowering her voice.

'Nonsense! You are deranged. What are you doing here?'

'Sent here, wasn't I? To get something done about this.' She pulled up her sleeve and exhibited a jagged, festering wound on her forearm.

'How did that happen?' Carter asked.

'Got into a bit of a fight, didn't I? The other whore slashed me with a broken glass.'

'Well, if you want to be treated you will have to modify your behaviour and not launch baseless accusations at the women who look after you. Dora, can you do anything for this?'

'I'm sure a poultice of yarrow would help,' Dora said uneasily. The prospect of being in close contact with her accuser was disturbing, to say the least.

'I'm not letting her anywhere near me!' Nancy exclaimed. 'She'll poison me, like as not.'

'Don't be ridiculous!' Carter turned her attention to Dora. 'If you prepare the poultice, could someone else apply it?'

'Oh yes, easily. Edith knows what to do.'

'Very well then. Now, you—' she turned back to Nancy '—come with me and we'll find you a bed.'

'I ain't staying here!' Nancy protested. 'I know what happens here. You goes in and you comes out in a coffin.'

Carter began to expostulate but Dora cut in quickly. 'Ma'am, if Edith poultices the wound she ... this woman ... could go back to ... to her usual place. I think she works in the nursery. She can come every day to have to wound dressed. There is no need for her to take up a bed.'

'*This woman ... I think she works in the nursery*,' Nancy hissed. 'You know damn well who I am and where I work.'

'That is quite enough of that,' Carter said. 'I want no foul language here. You had better keep quiet if you know what is good for you. Dora, go and prepare the poultice and tell Edith what is required. You—' she turned to Nancy '—can go and wait in the main ward. Someone will see to you shortly.' She opened the door and ordered Nancy through with an imperious gesture. Then she turned back and spoke in an undertone to Dora.

'Whatever has got into the woman? Is she deranged, do you think?'

'I think,' Dora said carefully, 'that perhaps the evil humours from the wound have got into her brain and created a fever there. I will prepare a soothing draft, as well as the poultice.'

Later Edith said, 'That unpleasant woman with the festering wound kept accusing you of killing your baby. Whatever can have put that into her head?'

Dora had had time to think. 'She looked after him for a few days, while I was too ill. I suppose she blames me for his death because I wasn't there to care for him myself.'

Edith nodded. 'Perhaps she feels guilty because she was unable to keep him alive, and she wants to tell herself it was your fault, not hers.'

'Yes, perhaps that's it,' Dora agreed. She tried to tell herself that the problem was dealt with but she slept little that night. She had devised an explanation for Nancy's behaviour that seemed to satisfy Edith and Mrs Carter, but there was no knowing what she might be saying to others, back in the nursery.

Her fears were realised the following morning, in a way far more terrifying than she had ever imagined. She was in the kitchen, preparing the medicines for the morning round, when Dr Wentworth looked in.

'Anything new today?'

'No, just the usual routine.' She looked at him and felt her pulse give an unaccustomed leap.

'Right,' he said. 'If you're ready ...'

He was interrupted by a violent banging on the outer door and a chorus of angry voices. Hurrying out into the main corridor, they found Mrs Carter and Mr Bellow converging in the doorway. Bellow flung open the door and demanded furiously, 'What in the name of God is going on here? Have you all taken leave of your senses?'

Outside the door a group of a dozen of more women, including Nancy and Bet and Judy, the volunteers who worked in the infirmary, who were pushing each other to get inside. Their voices rose in a shrill chant.

'We want the witch! Bring out the witch! The witch! The witch!'

Chapter 4

'The witch! The witch!' The chant went on.

'Be quiet, all of you!' Bellow thundered, then, when the voices had subsided to a grumbling murmur, he went on, 'Now, what is all this about? Who are you accusing?'

'Her!' Nancy pushed herself forward, pointing at Dora. 'She's in league with the devil. She brews up spells and potions. It's black magic.'

'That is nonsense.' Dr Wentworth stepped forward. 'Dora produces herbal remedies, using ingredients that have been known for their healing powers for generations. What you are saying is pure ignorance. This is not the Middle Ages; it is the nineteenth century and we trust in science, not superstition.'

'If she's so innocent, ask her what happened to the child she bore last year. She took him from my arms and he was never seen again.'

Wentworth turned and stared at Dora. 'You had a child?'

'The devil's spawn if ever I saw one,' Nancy went on inexorably. 'I saw the struggle she had birthing him, and then he wouldn't feed – not from her. He knew she meant him harm. She took him, and sacrificed him to her master, in exchange for the power to cast spells.'

Wentworth continued to stare at Dora in silence. It was Bellow who spoke.

'Let us get to the bottom of this.' He looked at Dora. 'Is it true you had a child?'

Unable to speak, she nodded.

'And who is the father?'

'I told you!' Nancy said. 'Satan himself.'

'Dora?' Bellow said. 'Answer the question.'

The tears she had been struggling to hold back broke out in spite of her. 'I was forced!' she cried out, her voice harsh in her own ears. The tray she was holding clattered to the ground, spilling the various drafts and poultices. 'Taken advantage of by my own half-brother! I didn't want the child, but I never harmed him.'

'What did you do with him?'

'I gave him back to the man who fathered him.'

'What do you mean?'

'I took him to the house, the house where I grew up, and I gave him to the girl who opened the door. I said it was a gift for the young master.' She was sobbing helplessly now.

'Can you prove that?'

'I don't know.' She drew in a breath and forced herself to think. 'You could ask the girl, I suppose – Clara, the parlourmaid.'

'And what has happened to the child now?'

'How should I know? I haven't set eyes on him from that day to this.'

Bellow studied her closely for a moment, then he turned his attention to Nancy and the other women.

'Go back to your proper quarters. You have made wicked accusations, based, as Dr Wentworth says, on ignorance and superstition.'

'You going to take her word for it then?' Nancy demanded. 'How do you know she's not lying? She could have murdered the child and made up that story.'

'Rest assured, the matter will be fully investigated,' Bellow said. 'But it is not your place to involve yourselves. I want to hear no more foolish talk about the devil and black magic, and if it comes to my ears that you have been perpetuating this story I shall be forced to take steps to put an end to it. You can expect to be severely punished. A spell in the oakum picking shed will teach you to keep your tongues from wagging. Now go!'

Unwillingly the women turned round and shuffled out of the door. Bellow closed it behind them and turned to Dora.

'I shall personally visit the house where you say you left the child, to see if your story can be substantiated. What is the address?'

Dora gave it.

'And the family name?'

'Latimer.'

'Is that not also your name?'

'Captain Latimer was my father.'

'But Mrs Latimer is not your mother. Is that right?'

'Yes, sir.'

'Dr Wentworth, can you guarantee that the potions Dora has been making are beneficial? There are no ill effects?'

Wentworth glanced in Dora's direction and then looked away again. He gave a small shrug, as if absolving himself from responsibility. 'I have seen none.'

'Just the same, I cannot allow you to continue to treat the patients here until I can verify your story. I shall make enquiries, but I warn you, if the results are not satisfactory I may have to refer the case to the police. Until then, you can spend your time picking oakum.'

'But ...' Dora began but the superintendent cut her short.

'Mrs Carter, a word if you please, in my office.'

When the two superintendents had closed to door behind them Dora looked around her, first at Edith and then at Wentworth. Edith was white faced, but she immediately stretched out a hand to Dora. Wentworth ducked his head and turned aside.

'I have patients to see,' he said gruffly. He vanished into the men's ward, where Dora could not follow.

She stooped to pick up the tray and collect the scattered cups and pots of ointment. As she straightened up, she caught sight of Jem standing in the doorway of his room. Their eyes met, but she could not tell if the expression in his was one of shock or sympathy.

In the ward Edith turned to face her. 'Why did you not tell me the truth? Why did you say the boy died?'

Dora lowered her eyes. 'I was afraid that you would think what I had done was wicked.'

'That man attacked you brutally. And yet you sent your son back to be brought up by him?' Edith's eyes were compassionate, but puzzled.

'I know. I did wrong, but I could see no other way out. I couldn't bear to bring the child up. His eyes were just like his father's, blue. I couldn't bear to have that reminder of what happened constantly with me.'

'What did you expect to happen to him?'

'I dreamed of him being brought up in the family, with all the privileges that means. But I see now that was foolish.' She cast a look of appeal at her friend. 'I cannot believe they would harm him. He, the father, is spoilt and wicked but not a monster. They will have sent him away somewhere, I hope to some poor but honest family who will give him a decent upbringing.' She shook her head, beginning to weep again. 'But I don't know ... and I never shall know. That will be my punishment.'

Edith put her arm round her shoulders. 'There, don't cry. You did what seemed best to you at the time. That's all any of us can do.'

Mrs Carter came out of the office. 'Dora! What are you doing here still? You were told to go to the oakum picking hall. Get along there at once.'

'Please, ma'am,' Edith said, 'I really need Dora here. And I can supervise her. I promise she will not be any danger to anyone.'

'That is not the point. Mr Bellow has given his orders and they must be obeyed. Dora, go!'

In the oakum picking hall women sat in rows at long tables, their heads bowed over their work. The air was thick with dust and the grimy windows let in little light. A woman she did not recognise came over to her.

'Yes? What do you want?'

'Please, I've been told to come here.'

'Ah!' The woman smiled grimly. 'So what have you done to annoy the governor? Disobedient, drunk and disorderly ...?'

'No!'

'Well, you're here now so you'd better make the best of it. Ever done this work before?'

'No, never.'

'Right. Here's an apron. You'll need this. Sit over there, next to Florrie. She'll show you what to do.'

The woman named Florrie looked up as Dora took a seat beside her but made no attempt to greet her or ask her name.'

'Like this,' she said gruffly, and took from the basket in front of her a piece of tarred rope about three inches long. 'You pull it apart, like so. Then you rub it on your knee until it breaks up into little threads, like this.' She reached into a second basket and pulled out a shapeless clump of material.

'What use is that?' Dora asked.

'Caulking the seams on ships, to stop the water getting in.'

'Where does this stuff come from?'

'Junk? That's what they call it. Comes from ships – ropes that are no good, too weak, too short, I dunno.'

The supervisor dumped a basket of rope ends in front of Dora. 'Less chatter and more work. You won't complete your quota else.'

Dora picked up a piece of rope and began to prise apart the tightly woven strands. It was hard, and very soon the tips of her fingers were sore. Glancing at Florrie's hands she saw that her fingers were calloused and in places there were open sores. How long would it be, she wondered, before hers were the same, if she had to stay here. She forced the thought out of her mind. She was not going to be here long. Mr Bellow's enquiries would exonerate her and she would be able to return to her work in the infirmary. She would see Edith again, and Jem – and Dr Wentworth. That thought brought another painful memory, of the look on his face when he'd said, 'you have had a child?' What she had always feared had come about. From now on he would see her as a 'fallen woman'.

These thoughts occupied her mind while her hands struggled with the unyielding rope. She looked at Florrie. 'I can't get the hang of this.'

'You will,' was the terse reply. 'We all feel like that to begin with.' Florrie glanced down at Dora's hands. 'Mind, not many of us have lady's hands, like yours.'

'Lady's hands!' Dora looked down. Months of working as a washerwoman had coarsened her skin but over the last year, while she had spent most of her time preparing her remedies, they had healed. She had rubbed them with an ointment made from St John's wort and lavender oil to keep them soft. Now she was beginning to regret it.

'How much of this do I have to do?' she asked.

Florrie nodded towards her basket. 'That's your quota. You have to pick a pound and a half every day.'

'All this!' Dora stared at the basket. 'I'll never do it.'

'Oh, you will,' Florrie said. 'You won't get out of here or get any supper until you do.'

For Dora the next two days were a kind of hell. Her fingers bled from the effort of pulling the rope apart, the dust that filled the air made it hard to breathe and there was not even the solace of conversation to relieve the tedium of the work. The women worked with their heads down, scarcely speaking, and if Dora tried to talk the supervisor was quick to reprimand her with her mantra of 'less chat, more work!'

It was on the third morning that someone came to the door and spoke to the supervisor.

'Latimer?' she called.

'Yes?'

'Governor wants to speak to you.'

Dora put down her work and went quickly to the door. Her knees were shaking. She knew that the summons must mean that some conclusion had been reached about her guilt or innocence and she told herself that the news must be good, or she would simply have been left to the endless toil of the oakum hall. Nevertheless, by the time she knocked on the governor's door her nerves were so stretched that she could hardly breathe.

Inside the room she found not only the governor but Mr Bellow and Dr Wentworth. She tried to catch the doctor's eye, to get some notion of the outcome of the investigations, but he gazed past her without acknowledging her appearance in the room.

'Latimer?' The governor was a small man whose face was almost obscured by a thick mat of ginger beard and whiskers.

'Yes, sir.'

'Some very serious accusations have been made against you.'

'Yes, sir, I know. But they are false.'

'Mr Bellow, I believe you have made some enquiries into the matter.'

'I have, sir. Latimer maintains that she took the illegitimate child to which she had given birth to the home of the man she says is the father and left it there. I am of the opinion that the easiest way to determine the truth of the matter is to bring her face to face with the gentleman in question. Accordingly, I have arranged for us to visit the Latimer residence this morning.'

'This morning!' Dora gasped.

'Are you afraid to confront the man you accuse?' the governor asked.

'No! But he will deny everything, as he always has.'

'If the child was left with him, or with someone in his household, he can scarcely deny it,' Mr Bellow said. 'Come, we are wasting time. Your bonnet and cloak are here. Put them on. Mrs Carter will accompany us.'

They drove to the house in Canning Street, which Dora had at one time called home. A nervous-looking Clara admitted them.

'Mrs Latimer said to tell you that Mr Hector is not at home, but she will see you, sir.'

Dora drew a deep breath. It was a relief to find that she did not have to confront Hector, but she knew that she was unlikely to receive any help from his mother. They were ushered into the drawing room, where Mrs Latimer, tightly corseted and swathed from neck to ankle in the purple tones of half-mourning, which she had adopted on her husband's death, was awaiting them. She cast one look at Dora, her nostrils flaring in disgust, and turned to Mr Bellow.

'Well? How can I help you?'

'I understand this young woman was resident in your household for some years.'

'She was, until I sent her packing after she tried to blame her … her condition on my son.'

'We are not here to determine the truth or otherwise of that accusation. She gave birth to a son in the workhouse and the child has since disappeared. She maintains that she brought it here and left it for the man she believes to be the father to bring up. We need to know if that is true.'

Mrs Latimer glared at him. 'How dare you come here with such a suggestion? The girl is lying, as usual. She has disposed of the child somewhere and now wishes to hide her guilt by inventing this tale.'

'Let me be quite clear. Dora did not bring her son to this house?'

'No! She did not.'

'It's a lie!' Dora broke out. 'I brought him here. He was alive and well when I left him.'

'Silence!' Mr Bellow bowed slightly to Mrs Latimer. 'Thank you for seeing us, ma'am. I apologise for troubling you. We will not detain you further.'

'But she's not telling you the truth!' Dora cried desperately. She broke free of Mrs Carter's restraining hand and advanced on Mrs Latimer. 'What have you done with him? Where is he?'

'Take her away,' was the response. 'The girl is deranged. She should be locked up.'

'Don't worry about that, ma'am,' Bellow responded. 'I shall see she is dealt with in a fitting manner.'

Dora was hustled out of the room, weeping tears of fury and frustration. In the hall the maid, Clara, instead of opening the front door, stepped closer to Mr Bellow and whispered, 'Begging your pardon, sir. I couldn't help hearing what was being said and I can't stand by and let Miss Latimer here suffer for a lie. She did bring the child here. She handed him to me and ran away before I could stop her.'

'Oh, Clara! Thank you! Thank you!' Dora felt her legs go weak with relief.

'You are quite sure about this?' Mr Bellow asked.

'Quite sure, sir.'

'So what did you do with the child?'

'I took him in to the missus, sir. She ... she wasn't pleased. She told me to take him to the kitchen and tell Cook to feed him – he was crying, see. Course, he was too young to take anything we could give him, but Cook had a married sister who'd had a babe not long before. She came round and let the little chap suckle. Then Mrs Latimer came in and said she had found someone who would take him and she went off with him in the carriage. We never liked to ask what had happened to him after that.'

'You don't know where he was taken?' Dora asked.

Clara looked at her and her face said plainly that she felt she had done her duty and that was more than Dora had any right to expect. 'No, I don't,' she said shortly.

Mr Bellow said, 'You have behaved very properly in difficult circumstances. We are all grateful to you. You have prevented what might well have been a miscarriage of justice. Thank you.'

He reached out and coins passed from his hand to Clara's. The girl curtsied and thanked him, then she opened the front door and Dora was hustled out and into the carriage.

Back in the governor's office Bellow reported what had taken place. The governor peered at Dora. 'It seems that she has been telling the truth after all. However, there is a secondary accusation, that Latimer has been indulging in the black arts, that her remedies are the result of witchcraft. We are not so backward as to believe such nonsense, but I am concerned that she has been allowed to contrive medicines that are not part of the regular pharmaceutical repertoire. Dr Wentworth, I believe you have been party to this activity. Can you assure me that the remedies are effective?'

Dora looked at Wentworth, appealing to him with her eyes, but he refused to meet her gaze.

He shrugged. 'I believe they may have had what is termed a placebo effect, that is to say the patient feels better because he, or she, believes in the efficacy of the drug.'

'But you have seen no ill effects?'

'No, of course not. Had I done so I would have put a stop to the experiments.'

Dora stared at him, wondering how he could deny his former interest and enthusiasm for her work. Could the fact that she had born a child out of wedlock discount all the good effects they had both seen?

'What do you think should be done with this young woman, Mr Bellow?' the governor asked. 'I am told she has done useful work in the infirmary. Should she be returned there?'

'I leave that decision to Dr Wentworth,' Bellow said. 'He is best able to determine whether she can be trusted.'

Once again Dora fixed her eyes on the doctor. For a moment it seemed that he was undecided. Then he said, negligently, 'I see no reason why she should not return. An extra pair of hands is always useful.'

Edith welcomed her with a warm hug when she reached the infirmary.

'I'm so glad to see you! The governor accepted your story, then?'

'Eventually.' Dora searched her friend's face for any hint that the revelations had changed her attitude but found none.

'I've missed you badly,' Edith told her. 'Apart from anything else, it has been hard managing things here on my own.'

Dora looked around the ward with some apprehension. 'Where are Bet and Judy?'

'I made it clear to them that they were not welcome, after they chose to join in with that gang who accused you.'

'So they have gone? Where to?'

'Back to the workhouse, and good riddance. They were always more trouble than they were worth.'

'Well,' Dora said, 'I can't say I'm sorry to see the back of them. But I don't know how you have coped on your own.'

'I've managed somehow, but I'm afraid some things have been neglected,' Edith said. 'The patients will be glad to see you back. Old Ma Johnson has been asking for another dose of your sleeping draft every night and little Gracie has been crying because her stomach hurts and she needs your special medicine. Oh, and Jem keeps asking when you are coming back. He's much better than he was but he says he still needs your inhalation. So you'd better get into the kitchen and start brewing your magic potions.'

'Oh, please don't call them that!' Dora exclaimed.

'Sorry!' Edith responded. 'That was thoughtless of me. But they do seem to work like magic on some of the poor souls here.'

'Dr Wentworth doesn't think so. He told the governor it was just a ... what did he call it ... something that makes people feel better just because they think it will.'

'Hmm,' Edith said. 'I'm beginning to think less of that man. After all the encouragement he has given you, the least he could do is stand by you.'

'Yes, well, we both know why he's changed his tune, don't we,' Dora commented. 'I'm not sure if I'm supposed to go on with the herbal remedies. He didn't make it at all clear.'

'There will be a lot of disappointed people in this place if you don't,' Edith said. 'Ignore him and get on with what you do so well.'

Dora took her advice and her doubts were swept away by the welcome she received from the patients. Most of them had not heard anything of the accusations that had been levelled against her so she felt at ease with them, but she approached the room still occupied by Jem with some hesitation, knowing that he had witnessed the humiliating confession that she had been forced to make.

He got up from the bed with a warm smile as she entered. 'Thank heaven, my ministering angel is back!'

'I'm no angel,' she responded, 'as you very well know.'

'You are as far as I'm concerned,' he said. 'Those wicked women should be punished for what they said about you.'

'That isn't what I meant,' she said.

He put out a hand and touched her arm. 'There's someone else who deserves worse punishment, from what I heard, but I don't suppose there's much chance of that.'

She smiled at him, relieved and touched by his sympathy. 'I don't really care what happens to him, as long as ... as long as my friends understand.'

'If I can be counted as one of those,' he said, 'then I think myself very lucky.'

Their eyes met and something in his look unleashed the tears she had been holding back. She sank down on the edge of the bed and wept helplessly. She felt him sit down beside her and then his arm went tentatively around her shoulders.

'I hope you are not crying because I said I would like to be one of your friends.' There was a gentle, reassuring humour in his tone.

'Of course I'm not,' she managed to say. 'It's just … just … oh, I'm tired, that's all. It was horrible in the oakum picking room and … and I kept thinking about my little boy.' She looked up at him through eyes blurred with tears. 'They wouldn't tell me what they had done with him, or where they had sent him. I shall never be able to find him, to try to make up for what I did.' She took a deep breath and rubbed the back of her hand across her eyes. 'Where do you think he might have been sent, Jem?'

He sat back, rubbing his chin thoughtfully. 'A baby farm somewhere, at a guess.'

'A baby farm!' she repeated. 'That sounds terrible, like children were just animals.'

'Not as bad as that,' he said. 'It just means some woman who will look after unwanted children for money. There was one in the village near where I grew up. We had a boy as an apprentice in the stables who came from there. He … he was all right. Needed feeding up, but …' He trailed off.

Dora looked at him. 'You mean the children didn't get properly fed?'

'Well, I expect some of them did. It would depend on whether the money was paid over regularly. As long as that came in on time, she … the woman … would make sure the child was in good health, in case the parent, or someone employed by them, came to check up.'

'And if they didn't?'

'As soon as the child was old enough to be some use she'd send them off to a farm to work, or if it was a girl she'd send them into service, if there was a house nearby that would have them.'

'Did they ... the children you knew about ... did they get any education?'

'Not as far as I could tell, from the lad who came to work for us.'

Dora shook her head, miserably. 'What have I done? I gave him away because I thought he would have a chance of a better life. Now it seems he would have been better off here.'

He patted her hand. 'Don't be too hard on yourself. I'm only telling you what I saw. Chances are, your man will have found a better way. He won't want a child of his to grow up to be a disgrace to the family, will he?'

She sniffed. 'I don't know. He won't accept that it is his child. Nor does his mother..'

'He must know, surely.' He got up. 'I've said too much, let my tongue run away with me. There must be plenty of better places than the one in our village. Now, what about that inhalation? My chest always feels better after I've had that.'

She stood up as well. 'It's gone cold. I'll have to boil another kettle.'

As she waited for the kettle to boil, Dora found herself remembering the touch of Jem's hand, the arm round her shoulders, the way he smiled at her. The thought was comforting. Dr Wentworth might despise her now, but Jem had not judged her by the standard of society's morals.

Next morning, as she and Edith prepared for the morning round, Dora said, 'Should we not wait for Dr Wentworth?'

Edith gave a small snort of contempt. 'Oh, we haven't seen much of that gentleman in the last day or two, and when he does show his face he's in and out before anyone has a chance to talk to him.'

Dora shook her head sadly. 'Can he really care so little? I know he despises me, but that should not prevent him from doing his job.'

'If you ask me,' Edith said, 'he's embarrassed by his own conduct, as well he might be. But he's young, and he has his way to make in the world. I think he's frightened that it may harm his reputation among his fellow doctors if it gets out that he has been dabbling in herbal remedies.'

'I hadn't thought of it like that,' Dora said. 'I suppose we must make some excuse for him.'

'Hmm! I don't see it as excusable,' Edith replied. 'I see it as lily-livered cowardice. But there it is. We must get on without him.'

When the doctor did appear some time later he did his rounds as rapidly as possible and made no attempt to address Dora. Some of the patients began telling him how much they had been helped by one or other of Dora's remedies, but he cut them short with a few brusque words. When he had finished in the main wards he went into Jem's room, closing the door so that Dora could not follow him. He came out a few minutes later, tucking his stethoscope into his pocket.

'That man is perfectly well now. There is no reason for him to take up a bed here, I have told him to go to the men's dormitory in the main workhouse and report to the supervisor.'

'He mustn't be sent to pick oakum,' Dora blurted out. 'His lungs will not stand the dust there.'

Wentworth shrugged. 'That is not up to me. It is up to the supervisor.'

Dora went into the room and found Jem packing his few personal possessions into a canvas bag. He looked up with a smile.

'I've been told to sling my hook – and the doctor's right. I'm fit enough now, thanks to your medicines.'

'I ... I'm concerned that you might be sent to pick oakum, and I know that would be very bad for your lungs.'

'Can't be worse than the stokehold,' he said.

'Maybe not, but it won't be good for you.'

'Well—' he grinned at her '—if that's the case I might find myself back here, being ministered to by my guardian angel.'

'Don't joke about it!' she said. 'I don't want you to be ill again.'

He came closer to her and he had stopped grinning. 'You're the first person since my da was killed who has really cared about my well-being. I shall miss being here with you.'

'I shall miss you, too,' she said.

He held her eyes for a moment, then turned aside. 'I've been kicking myself for my damn stupidity, talking to you about baby farms and putting those terrible pictures into your head. What do I know, really? Will you forgive me?'

'There's nothing to forgive,' she said. 'I'm glad you said what you did. When I get out of here, I shall search for places like that, and maybe in one of them I shall find my son.' She paused and added, 'If I ever do get out of here.'

'You will,' he said. 'You're not like most of these wasters. You've got something about you.'

She sighed. 'I don't know. Where could I go? Who would employ me? I shall carry the taint of the workhouse wherever I am.'

He came back to her and took her hand. 'Don't think like that. You are a fine woman, with a good head on your shoulders. You will find a way out, one day soon. And so shall I. As soon as I can I'm going to look for a job – and I won't give up until I find one.'

'Of course you will,' she said. 'I shall miss you, but I wish you the best of luck.'

He looked into her face. 'How about when I get myself settled I come back for you.'

'You mean ...' she felt colour rushing to her face. 'I don't understand.'

'Yes, you do. We make a good pair, you and me. There's a future for us out there. Just you wait.'

He bent his head and kissed her on the lips. It was the first time a man had ever kissed her and her first instinct was to draw back, but then every nerve in her body quickened with desire and she let herself sink against him, so that their two bodies seemed to become one. His tongue touched her lips and probed inside and something like liquid fire began to run though her senses. For a long moment she clung in his embrace, oblivious of everything except his mouth on hers and his arms pressing her close. Then the real world reasserted itself and she drew back.

'I ... I don't ... we shouldn't be doing this.'

He let her go with a regretful sigh. 'Not now, not here, perhaps. But one day ... One day I shall come to you and say, I have a job and there is a home waiting for you, if you want it.' She made to speak but he put a finger on her lips. 'Don't say any more now. When the time comes you may have better things to do, better prospects. And if that's the way of things ... well, that's it. I expect I'll survive.'

He turned away and picked up his bag. 'I shan't be far off for the time being, at least. Can I come and talk to you sometime?'

'Yes, oh yes, please. That is, if they'll let you.'

'Just let them try to stop me!' He moved towards the door, then stopped and caught hold of her hand. 'Take care of yourself. Even angels can get ill, I suppose.'

'I'll be all right,' she said.

He kissed her briefly and went out and she heard him saying goodbye to Edith and then the sound of the outer door closing. For a few minutes she stood without moving, trying to get clear in her mind what had just happened. The word had not been spoken, but she understood that she had received a proposal of marriage, and that something in her had responded in an urgent, visceral manner she had never experienced before. Did she want to be married to Jem? She simply did not know.

Chapter 5

'Something is going on.' Edith peered from the door of the ward along the corridor towards the main entrance. Dora joined her and saw that Mrs Carter and Mr Bellow were waiting by it, dressed in their smartest clothes. Mrs Carter was smoothing her hair and Bellow was fiddling with his cravat, both obviously in a state of nervous expectation.

'Looks as if we are going to have a visit from an inspector,' Edith said.

'Do you think so? There hasn't been one in all the time I've been here.'

'No, it doesn't happen as often as it should,' Edith agreed.

Before she could say any more the door opened to admit Mr Fitzgibbon, the senior supervisor, and a well-dressed, middle-aged gentleman with a high forehead and bushy side whiskers. They were followed by Dr Wentworth. The gentleman was introduced to Carter and Bellow and as they were shaking hands Edith murmured, 'That doesn't look like an inspector to me. Come on, we'd better look busy,' and led the way back into the women's ward.

It was not long before the visitor was brought into the ward by Mrs Carter, whose hands, in their white gloves, were fluttering nervously.

'This is where the female patients are cared for, sir,' she simpered. 'There are a good many, as you can see, and we do not have the best conditions for them, but we do our utmost to make them as comfortable as possible.'

'You mean, some of us do,' Edith muttered. 'I've never seen you lift a finger.'

The gentleman advanced down the ward, looking from side to side with a sharp curiosity, but also, Dora thought, with an expression of compassion. She had been about to administer some of her medicines when Edith had called her attention and now she set down her tray beside a woman who had been admitted the day before with acute stomach pains and diarrhoea.

'Has the draft I gave you this morning helped at all, Margaret?'

'Yes, bless you, it has. The pain is much less now,' the woman replied. 'Can I have more?'

Dora was aware that the visitor was close by and that he was accompanied not just by Mrs Carter but by Dr Wentworth. She wondered if he would intervene and forbid her to administer the medicine, but she took up the cup and supported Margaret's head as she held it to her lips.

'And who is this?' she heard the gentleman say. He spoke quietly, without the harsh authoritarian tones she heard so often.

Dora laid Margaret back and stood up.

'This is Dora, sir,' Mrs Carter said. 'She is one of the inmates who has volunteered to help. Dora, this is Mr

Rathbone, who is interested to see how things are run here.'

'A noble action, to volunteer for such a task,' Rathbone said. 'Tell me, do you have any training in this work?'

'Training, sir?' Dora said. 'I'm not sure what you mean.'

'Have you been taught how to care for the sick?'

'I only know what I learned from my mother.'

'Ah, I thought that was probably the case. What is in the cup?'

'In this, sir?' Dora hesitated. 'It is a herbal remedy of my own making.' As she spoke she looked past the visitor at Dr Wentworth.

He stepped forward. 'Dora has some knowledge of folk remedies, Mr Rathbone. I have observed closely and, though they may have little medical value, I am confident they do no harm.'

'And what is in this remedy, if I may ask?' Rathbone enquired.

'It is a decoction of chamomile and borage, sir,' Dora told him. 'This patient is suffering from acute stomach cramps.'

'I see.' Rathbone turned his attention to Margaret. 'And has it helped?'

'Oh, it has, sir!' the woman said. 'It works like a charm!'

Dora winced inwardly at the term but Rathbone smiled and nodded. 'Well, I am very glad to hear it.' He turned back to Dora. 'Do you have other remedies in your repertoire?'

'I do, sir,' Dora replied, and found herself conducting him along the row of beds, describing as they went the particular medicines which she had given to each patient. He stopped often by the bedsides of various patients, asking questions about their illness and how they were being treated, enquiring not just into Dora's remedies but about the conditions in the ward and the problems she encountered.

At one point she informed him that three of the patients were suffering from scurvy and he turned to Wentworth and exclaimed, 'But that is easily treatable, is it not?'

'It is, sir, if we had the means to provide the fresh fruit and vegetables required.'

'And you do not?'

'Such things are expensive, and the Vestry only allows us a limited budget for each patient.'

Rathbone rubbed his chin. 'I see, I see.'

'I do what I can with a tea made from dandelion leaves,' Dora said, 'and when the right season comes, rosehips are very beneficial, if I can obtain some.'

'But failing that ...?'

'Oranges would be the ideal answer, sir.'

Rathbone continued round the ward and was then led away to inspect the men's ward.

'Well,' Edith said when he had gone, 'what was that all about, I wonder. Does the gentleman intend to do anything or was it just idle curiosity? I hope it is not going to become a regular event. We have enough to do, without being a public entertainment as well.'

Next morning, a crate of oranges was delivered to the infirmary.

'Well, I never expected that!' Edith said. 'At least something good came out of that visit.'

A few days later Mrs Carter called Dora and Edith into her office.

'There are going to be some changes here, some quite big changes,' she said, and Dora thought she sounded rather put out. 'The gentleman who came round the other day, Mr Rathbone, is a wealthy man and a philanthropist. He is also a member of the Vestry, which as you know is responsible for the running of the workhouse and the infirmary. It seems about four years ago his wife died, but during her last illness she was cared for by a trained nurse, who was a great help to her and to him. Her work so impressed him, in fact, that he feels that such care should be available to everyone, and not just to those who can afford to pay for it. Have you heard of Miss Florence Nightingale?'

'Of course we have,' Edith said, rather irritably. 'We may be paupers, ma'am, but that does not mean we're totally without wit or education.'

'Well,' Carter went on, 'it seems Mr Rathbone has been in touch with Miss Nightingale and has arranged, at his own expense, for her to send a team of her trained nurses to take over the running of the infirmary.'

'To take over?' Edith repeated.

Mrs Carter shifted in her seat. 'Do not misunderstand me. Mr Fitzgibbon, Mr Bellow and I will still be in charge. But Miss Nightingale's nurses will manage the everyday running of the wards.'

'Does that mean we shall no longer be needed?' Dora asked. Her memory of oakum picking was still vivid and she had a sickening presentiment that she and Edith would be returned there if their presence in the infirmary was no longer required.

'I know no more than you do about that,' Mrs Carter said. 'We shall have to wait and see when the new nurses arrive.'

'When will that be?' Edith asked. 'Do we know yet?'

'That I cannot tell you, but I imagine such things cannot be arranged at a moment's notice.'

Dora and Edith adjourned to the kitchen to talk over what they had heard.

'Do you think we will be sent away?' Dora asked.

'I hope not. There is always so much to do. I don't know how many of these nurses are coming, but I can't believe there will be so many that they will not be glad of some extra help. We must make sure that they see how useful we can be.'

'Florence Nightingale,' Dora murmured. 'Of course, I have heard of her, but I'm not sure why she is such an authority on caring for the sick.'

Edith looked surprised. 'You must have read how she looked after our soldiers in the Crimea, during the war there.' She stopped and shook her head. 'Of course not. It was over eight years ago and you cannot have been more than a girl. You were what ten, eleven in 1856?'

'I must have been about eleven,' Dora said. 'It was before my mother died and I still lived with her. She did not take a great deal of interest in such things, I'm afraid. But it was a long time ago. Why is she so important now?'

'From what I have read, she has made great changes in the way hospitals are run in this country, and has set up schools to train nurses in her methods.'

'What are her methods?'

'That we shall just have to wait and see, I suppose,' Edith said.

Their wait was shorter than they had expected. A week later Mrs Carter appeared in the ward with a soberly dressed young woman whose eyes swept her surroundings with a sharply assessing gaze. Mrs Carter beckoned to Edith and Dora.

'This is Miss Agnes Jones. She has been sent by Miss Nightingale to find out what is required here before the rest of her team arrive. Miss Jones, these are two of my most valued helpers. This is Edith and this is Dora.'

Miss Jones bent her head in greeting to each of them. 'I am very glad to make your acquaintance. I am sure we shall work together very happily.' Her voice was quiet, but there was something about its tone and her whole air of self-possession that gave it authority. Dora's heart lifted. If they were going to work together, that meant she was not going to lose her job here.

'Do you look after this ward alone, or are there more of you?' Miss Jones enquired.

'There were two other women, but they decided to withdraw,' Edith said. 'There was ... a difference of opinion. But we could ask for more volunteers from the women in the workhouse.'

'There will not be any need for that,' was the reply. 'I shall bring my own team of nurses up from London, as soon as I have assessed what needs to be done. Now, I should like to have a good look round.'

'Of course,' Mrs Carter said.

They moved on down the ward and Dora and Edith followed. Dora noticed that Miss Jones had a small notebook attached to her belt by a fine chain, in which she made occasional notes. She looked up at the grimy windows and the cobwebbed rafters.

'Who is responsible for cleaning here?'

'We do our best,' Edith said, 'but we do not have time to do more than change the beds and try to keep the patients clean.'

Miss Jones turned to Mrs Carter. 'I shall need a group of women whose sole job is to scour this place until there is not a cobweb or a stain anywhere. Miss Nightingale is adamant about the need for cleanliness, but it will not be my nurses' duty to clean. Can that be organised?'

'I am sure we can find women who will volunteer for that work,' Mrs Carter said. 'Or, if not, the governor can direct some of the inmates to do it.'

'When were those windows last cleaned?' Miss Jones continued.

Miss Carter was visibly embarrassed. 'I ... do not exactly recall.'

'They have never been cleaned while I have worked here,' Edith said firmly. 'And I have been here for three years, almost.'

'Can they be opened?'

'Opened?' Mrs Carter looked as if she had asked for something unheard of. 'Oh, we would not risk our patients' health by exposing them to drafts.'

'Fresh air is an absolute requisite for recovery,' Miss Jones said. 'Miss Nightingale insists that each patient should be near a window, so that they have natural light and clean air. The miasma in this room is enough to make anyone ill, even if they were not so already. I shall speak to the governor and make sure that the windows are cleaned and opened.' She turned and gazed around her. 'I can see that there is a great deal to be done here. Now, show me the other wards, if you please.'

Later Dora was busy in the kitchen preparing some more medicines when Miss Jones came in.

'May I ask what you are doing?'

'Yes, miss. I'm preparing a poultice of yarrow and lavender for one of the men who has a septic wound on his leg.'

'Ah, of course! Mr Rathbone mentioned you when he asked me to come here. Dora, isn't it?'

'That's right, miss.'

'Dora what? It does not seem right for me to call you by your first name on such a short acquaintance.'

'It's Latimer, miss. But the only time anyone uses that is if I'm in some sort of trouble. I prefer Dora.'

'As you wish. My name is Agnes, but I'm afraid we Nightingale nurses prefer a more formal mode of address. You should call me Nurse Jones.'

'Very well, miss,' Dora agreed.

'Mr Rathbone told me that you seem to have a real talent for producing remedies from very humble ingredients. He thought you really cared for the people you were nursing, unlike so many of the men and women who work here.'

Dora nodded. 'Yes, I do, and so does Edith.'

'But you didn't come here of your own free will, as I understand it. Circumstances forced you to it.'

'Into the workhouse, you mean? Yes, that's true, like everyone else here. None of us would be in here if we could make our own way outside. But I volunteered to help in the infirmary.'

'Why? Forgive me for asking, but I am interested.'

Dora thought for a moment. 'I was looked after here, when I first arrived, and I came to know Edith. Then, later, I wanted ... I needed something to occupy my mind; some kind of work that had a purpose to it. Then I started to remember how sick people used to come to my mother for help and I thought I could use what she taught me to help the patients here.'

Agnes nodded, studying her face. For a moment it looked as if she was about to ask another question but then she said, 'I mustn't pry any further. I hope you don't feel that I have been too intrusive.'

'I don't mind,' Dora said, and realised that it was true. There was something about the new nurse's quiet manner that made it easy to confide in her.

The door opened to admit four men carrying between them huge steaming containers. They were followed by a woman carrying a basket of dry bread.

'What is this?' Agnes asked.

'The patients' dinner,' Dora told her, moving her poultices out of the way so that the men could put the containers down.

Agnes lifted the lid of one and sniffed. 'What is it?'

'Today is Thursday, so it will be lobscouse.'

'Whatever is that?'

'Small pieces of beef boiled with potatoes.'

Agnes took a spoon and lifted a small portion to her lips. She chewed for a moment, then turned to Dora. 'Is this given to all the patients?'

'Yes.'

'Even to those who have a fever, or stomach troubles?'

'Yes, they all get the same.'

'And do they eat it?'

'Not all of them. It's too tough for those with bad teeth, for one thing. Some of them manage the broth and the potatoes, but a lot gets left.'

'And what happens to that?'

'I think it goes to feed pigs somewhere.'

Agnes made a sound of exasperated disapproval and made a note in her little book. 'Such waste!'

Edith came in. 'Is that the dinner?'

'Yes.' Dora reached for a stack of tin plates. 'If you will excuse us, Nurse Jones. We should take this round while it's still hot. Some of the patients, at least, will be glad of it.'

That evening, after Miss Jones had left and while Dora and Edith were eating their meagre supper of bread soaked in warm milk, there was a tap on the door. Jem stood outside.

'Jem!' Edith exclaimed. 'Come in a minute. How are you?'

'I'm well enough, thank you.' He smiled at Edith, but immediately his gaze turned to Dora.

She felt the hot blood rising in her face and was glad that the colour of her skin made her blushes less obvious. Her heart had begun to beat faster and she found she could not meet Jem's eyes.

'What are you doing now?' Edith asked. 'I hope they haven't put you to oakum picking.'

'No, no.' Jem gave a low chuckle. 'I've escaped that, thanks be. I've had a stroke of luck. When I told the governor I grew up on a farm he decided to put me to work in his own garden. He's raising a couple of piglets and some chickens, and of course he has a horse for his carriage, so there's plenty to do.'

Dora remembered Agnes Jones's disapproval of the waste of food. So that was where it ended up! She made herself look at Jem.

'You look well, Jem. I'm so glad.'

'Well, it's thanks to you and your magic potions,' he said, with a cheeky grin.

A silence fell. Dora knew that Jem was hoping Edith would leave them alone, and she was not sure whether she wanted that or not. Either way, Edith had no inkling of what had passed between them and so saw no reason for a tactful withdrawal. She made conversation for a few minutes, enquiring further about Jem's work and asking after one or two patients who had been in the ward with him and had now been discharged.

Then, to Dora's relief, Jem said, 'Well, I mustn't interrupt your supper any longer. I'd better get back, before Mrs Carter or Mr Bellow know I'm here. I don't suppose they approve of you ladies receiving gentleman visitors.' He winked at Dora, nodded to Edith and went to the door. 'I'll wish you both good evening.'

Dora roused herself at the last minute. 'Thank you so much for coming, Jem. I have been thinking about you and wondering how you were getting on.'

He smiled at her. 'No need to worry about me. I'll call again, shall I?'

'Yes, do that. I ... we will always be glad to see you.'

Over the next weeks and months the infirmary underwent a great change. Agnes Jones's team of twelve nurses arrived very quickly, business-like in their uniforms of high-necked brown dresses with starched white aprons and caps. To Dora and Edith's amusement, they were known, collectively, as Nightingales. They took over the running of the wards with a smooth efficiency that some of the established volunteers found offensive. When they made to enter the men's ward they were met by a scandalised Mr Bellow.

'This is not a fit place for young women!' he expostulated.

Agnes Jones swept him aside with a brusque, 'Nonsense, sir. My nurses are used to dealing with male patients in any state of dress or undress. Nothing here will shock them – unless it is the lack of basic hygiene which seems to prevail under your jurisdiction.'

A squad of 'scourers' ordered by the governor appeared, armed with buckets and brooms. The floors were swept and scrubbed, the cobwebs dislodged and the windows cleaned inside and out. They were also opened, producing a chorus of protests from the patients at the chill, in spite of the fact that it was now high summer. Dora ignored the objections. It was a delight to be able to walk the wards without the prevailing stench of sweat and stale urine. New bedding arrived to replace the old, stained sheets and blankets and there were clean nightshirts for the patients.

One day, a team of workmen arrived and began to install water closets, something most of the inmates had never seen before, and which they viewed at first with considerable suspicion. Dora and Edith were only too glad to see the back of the smelly privies that had been in use before.

Some of the men who had worked in the wards as volunteers resented the intrusion of the nurses and took themselves off, and it was soon made clear to the others that they were no longer needed. Instead, word was spread among the female paupers that there was an opportunity for them to become probationers, helping out while learning the basics of nursing. Edith and Dora were enrolled at once and Dora was still permitted to prepare and administer her herbal remedies. Dr Wentworth continued to be in overall charge of treatment and Agnes Jones and the other nurses were punctilious in their respect, but somehow managed to convey that his former, rather cavalier attitude would no longer be acceptable. From then on he made his visits with greater regularity than before. To Dora he behaved as if there had never been anything more between them than between him and any of the other volunteers. He never asked her directly about any of her preparations, but she noticed that he often enquired of the patients if they had been given one of them and what effect it had had. She also overheard him once or twice discussing the efficacy of a particular medicine with Nurse Jones. For her own part, she avoided any contact with him as far as possible.

In all the bustle and confusion of the changes she found little opportunity to think about Jem and what he had said to her. He called in, from time to time, and they snatched a few moments conversation. He was fit again now and the outdoor life in the garden suited him, but he declared that he was restless and longed to leave the confines of the workhouse. Once or twice they managed to be alone for a short time and then he took her in his arms and kissed her, and she felt herself melt against him as before. She loved the way he looked at her, loved the feel of his arms round her, but when he had gone and she had time to think she found herself wondering what future there could ever be for the two of them.

Christmas was approaching. In the New Year four years would have passed since Dora entered the workhouse for the first time. Sometimes, at night, she still lay awake, thinking about the child she had abandoned and wondering what had become of him. On the verge of sleep she dreamed of a vague future, in which she was able to leave the workhouse and live an independent life. She imagined herself searching for women who took in unwanted babies and finding one who was caring for a child with her dark skin and his father's blue eyes. But in her waking moments she knew that this was just a fantasy. She could see no prospect of being able to make her own living, other than a return to the drudgery she had experienced working for the washerwoman. She knew no respectable family would take in a woman from the workhouse as a cook or a chambermaid, and even if they did, her spirit rebelled against submitting to such servitude. There had been a time in her life when servants had tended to her needs, albeit somewhat grudgingly. While her father lived, he had insisted that she be treated as a member of the family. She had no wish to return to such an invidious position, caught between the resentment of her stepmother and sisters and the barely concealed contempt of the upper servants. At least here she had work, which, in spite of its hardships, she enjoyed and felt was worthwhile. She was treated with respect by grateful patients and even Agnes Jones spoke to her with courtesy, not perhaps as an equal but not, either, like an underling to be ordered about. Above all, she had the companionship of Edith. They had developed a close friendship that allowed them to share jokes and irritations in equal measure, and which was a constant source of support and encouragement. Whatever happened, she told herself, she could never go anywhere and leave Edith behind.

One evening, Jem appeared in the corridor as she was, heading towards the kitchen with a tray of used cups.

'Can we talk for a minute – in private?'

Dora glanced round. 'Come in here.' She led him into the kitchen. It had become her particular refuge, almost her own domain, except when there were meals to be served. Inside, she put down the tray and turned to him.

'What is it?'

'I'm leaving. I've found a job.'

Dora's heart gave a jolt. She knew he had often spoken of going, but somehow she had never believed it would happen.

'What sort of job?'

'At a livery stables. Today was the last Thursday in the month, you know, when we're allowed out. You never bother to go out, but I do. Every time I've gone looking for work, and today I happened to spot some gents riding by and I heard one say to the other, "we'd better get the horses back, or they'll be charging us extra". So I knew they must have hired the beasts from a livery stable some-where. I managed to follow them and when they'd paid their dues and left I found the boss and asked if he could use an extra hand, someone who was used to dealing with horses. As it happened, he'd just lost one of his men. He'd decided to try his luck in America, apparently. So he said he'd take me on.'

'Did you tell him where you were living now?' Dora asked.

Jem wriggled his shoulders. 'I didn't see much point in that. I told him where I was brought up and about my da being a smith and how he'd been killed. He didn't seem to want to know more than that. Anyway, what difference does it make? I know horses and I'll do a good job. That's all that will matter to him.'

'Where will you live?' Dora was still struggling to come to terms with his news.

'He says I can sleep in the loft and eat with him and his family. It's not perfect, but it's a start.'

Dora swallowed hard. 'I'm really glad for you, Jem. Congratulations.'

He took hold of her hands. 'You remember what I said, all those months ago? I said one day I would find a job and then I'd come back for you. I'm not in a position to ask you to come with me yet. But one day soon, when I've put a bit of money behind me, I'll find a place where we could live. When that day comes, will you come to me – as my wife?'

Dora felt her head swimming. 'Oh Jem! I don't know ... I like you, I'm very fond of you. But I don't really know you. We've had so little time together.'

His face clouded but he nodded. 'I understand what you're saying. I think I know you. I've watched you with the people you look after. And I've seen how gentle you are, how kind. That's good enough for me. But I can see you've never seen me as I really am. So what's to do?'

'I don't know,' she whispered.

'Here's an idea. When I'm a bit more settled, I'll come for you one of those Thursdays, when the gates are opened, and we'll walk out together, like courting couples should. Then, when you've had a chance to get to know me better, I'll ask you again. What do you say?'

Dora's heart lifted. 'Oh, yes! Yes, I think I should like that very much.'

'That's settled then,' he said. 'Will you kiss me to seal the bargain?'

She held up her face and he put his arms round her and kissed her, a long, deep kiss that set her blood racing.

At length he stepped back. 'I must stop there, before I go too far and make you angry with me. Take care of yourself, my angel, till we meet again.'

'Are you going now … straight away?'

'No time like the present. I must be off before the gates are locked. But I'll be back next month. You can depend upon it.'

He kissed her briefly on the forehead and was gone before she could think of anything more to say.

Chapter 6

One of the nurses put her head round the kitchen door. 'Dora, Mrs Carter wants to see you in her office.'

'What for?'

'Don't ask me.'

Dora dried her hands and smoothed her hair. A summons to the office usually meant that Mrs Carter had a complaint of some kind. At the door she paused, took a deep breath and knocked.

'Come in.'

Mrs Carter was not alone. To Dora's surprise Mr Rathbone was with her. A variety of possible reasons for his presence passed through her mind in rapid review. Had there been a complaint about one of her remedies? Had someone told him that she had had a child and abandoned him? Or had Agnes Jones found out and decided she was no longer fit to work in the wards?

'Dora, come in.' To her surprise he rose to greet her, as he would have done to any lady. 'Come and sit down. I want to talk to you.'

She took the chair he indicated and he seated himself again opposite her.

'I have a suggestion, a proposition, I should like to put to you. I have been interested, as you know, in the various herbal remedies you produce, but beyond that, I have the impression that you have more education than is usually found amongst women ... women in your position. For example, Dr Wentworth mentioned once that you know your Shakespeare.'

Dora regarded him with puzzlement, wondering what this could be leading up to. 'I was ... fortunate enough to live for some years in a household where ... where education was valued rather more than is perhaps usual for young ladies. I was able to share in some of their lessons.' She broke off, afraid that he would want to know more details about why she had been there and why she had left. To her relief he merely nodded as if this confirmed what he already knew.

'What else did you study?'

'Mathematics, geography, history, a little Latin. But the other girls were never really interested, so we did not pursue any of it very far. They preferred drawing and singing.'

Mr Rathbone nodded and said dryly, 'As young ladies do whose only interest is in finding themselves a husband. But you, I fancy, had different ideas.'

'I like learning, sir, if that is what you mean.'

'It is. Nurse Jones speaks highly of your dedication to the welfare of the patients and your willingness to learn. She and I have discussed matters and we have come to the conclusion that with the proper training you would make an excellent nurse.'

Dora let out a breath of relief. 'Oh, I am always glad to learn anything Nurse Jones can teach me, sir.'

'Yes, yes, I know that. But what I have in mind is something rather more ... radical. I think, and Nurse Jones agrees with me, that you should go to London, to train in the school for nurses set up by Miss Nightingale herself.'

'London!' Dora stared at him. 'But how could I do that? I've no money, no way of supporting myself.'

'You need have no worries on that count. You would live in the nurses' home and have all your meals provided for you.'

'But ... would they have me? I mean, a girl like me ... black, well, half-caste.'

Rathbone smiled reassuringly. 'Have you ever heard of Mary Seacole?'

Dora hesitated, searching her memory. 'I think so, somewhere.'

'She was of mixed race, like you. She grew up in Jamaica but she always had a desire to care for the suffering. When the war broke out in the Crimea she went there and set up a sort of hotel, where the wounded were cared for and weary soldiers could find some respite from the fighting. She is still held in high esteem by the military. I see no reason why you should not follow her example.'

'Oh!' Dora exclaimed suddenly. 'I've just remembered where I heard the name. My mother knew her, when she was a girl, before she came to England. Mary's mother was known as a healer and so was mine. Everything I know about medicinal herbs comes from them.'

'Well, there you are,' Rathbone said. 'Everything falls into place. You will follow in their footsteps.'

'And I am really to go to London in spite of ... in spite of everything?'

'I have already arranged it. Miss Nightingale will accept you on my recommendation.'

Dora's thoughts were in turmoil. 'But London ...? How would I get there?'

'I will pay your train fare – and I will make you a small allowance during your training, enough to provide you with any small necessities and perhaps a little over to allow you to sample some of the delights of the metropolis. So, what do you say?'

Dora's mouth had gone dry. She tried to swallow. 'How ... how long would I be away?'

'The training takes a year.'

'And ... and after that I would come back here?'

'If you wished to. But not as an inmate. As a qualified nurse, as part of the team working here.'

Mrs Carter spoke for the first time, an edge of impatience to her voice. 'Dora, do you not realise what you are being offered? Mr Rathbone is giving you the chance to make a respectable life for yourself, a chance to earn your own living, away from this place. How can you be so ungrateful?'

'Oh, I'm not! I'm not, really. It's just ...'

Rathbone smiled at her gently. 'It is a great deal to take in and I have sprung it on you quite suddenly. I understand that you may need time to think.'

Dora shook her head. 'Oh no! No, I want to do it. Mrs Carter is right. It is a wonderful chance and I am grateful, very grateful. It's just that this has been my home now for four years, more than that. I ... I have friends here, a friend. Please, could Edith come with me? She is already a better nurse than I am. I know she would do very well.'

Rathbone's expression was regretful. 'I fear that for Edith this comes too late. She is not a young woman. I fancy the upheaval of moving to London would be too much for her, and also I have to consider the fact that after her training she might not be able to give so many years of service to the community as ... as a younger woman like you. I'm sorry.'

Dora looked down at her hands. She had once thought that she could never leave Edith alone, but now that the prospect of a new life, a life of independence, was opening up she knew she would be a fool to turn it down.

'It would only be for a year?' she said.

'Yes.'

'And then I could come back?'

'Only if you wished to. You might want to take up a position in one of the great London hospitals.'

'No, no ... I should wish to come back here ...' Suddenly a new thought came to her – a thought that might put an end to all her hopes. 'Sir, there is something you should know about me. It may make you change your mind.' *Why am I saying this?* she asked herself. But some half understood impulse of honour made her go on. 'I ... I have had a child. It was not ... not of my own wish ... and I ... I let him go. I should not wish you to think that I had accepted your kind offer without telling you the full facts.'

To her surprise and relief Rathbone's expression did not change. 'I am aware of all this. Mrs Carter has told me the full story. As I understand it, the pregnancy was forced on you. There is no justice in making you suffer more for it than you already have. My offer stands.'

'Then—' Dora got up '—then I should like to accept – and I shall always be grateful for your benevolence.'

'It is not a question of benevolence entirely,' he said, rising in his turn. 'I have made it my life's work to see that poor people can have proper care from a qualified nurse when they fall ill. You will be one more nurse able to offer that care. That is enough for me.'

A new thought struck her. 'When do I have to leave?'

'Soon after Christmas. The new course starts in the New Year. But we will speak again before then. We shall have to make sure that you are supplied with everything you need for your new life.' He held out his hand. 'Until then, I will wish you good day ... Miss Latimer.'

She had the presence of mind to curtsy. 'Good day, sir. And thank you again.'

In the kitchen she found Edith setting out plates for the patients' dinner.

'Oh, there you are. What did Carter want?' She turned and caught sight of Dora's face. 'Oh, goodness, what has happened? Is something wrong?'

'No, not wrong.' Dora was battling with contrary emotions of euphoria and disbelief. 'Mr Rathbone was there. He ... he wants me to ... he is sending me to London to be trained as a proper nurse.'

Edith dropped a pile of tin plates with a clatter. 'Sending you to London! When?'

'Next week. I'm to live in the nurses' home and be taught with the others – like Nurse Jones and the rest of them.'

Edith came across and took hold of her hands. 'Oh, my dear, I am so pleased for you. It is just what you deserve. You will do well, I know you will.'

'I don't want to leave you behind.' Tears started to Dora's eyes. 'I asked if you could come too but ...'

'But I should not want to,' Edith said. 'I am too old to start learning a new profession, and I should feel out of place among the other young women. You mustn't worry about that.'

'I shall come back!' Dora promised. 'It's only for a year, and then I can come back and be like one of the other nurses.'

'If that is what you want to do. But you mustn't feel bound by that. There will be so many opportunities opening up for you. When do you leave?'

'After Christmas, Mr Rathbone said. I'm not sure when.' Her tears flowed more freely and Edith pulled her into an embrace.

'There, there, don't cry. It's good news.'

'Yes, I know.' She drew back, sniffing. 'It's just ... so unexpected. I never dreamed ...'

'Yes, I know. It will take time to get used to the idea, but it is something to look forward to.'

'I shall miss you.'

'And I shall miss you. You must promise to write to me and tell me everything.'

'Oh, yes. I will, of course.'

The clatter of the food containers being carried along the corridor recalled her to the present. She rubbed a hand across her eyes.

'That's the dinner. We'd better get on.'

Dora was in the middle of helping one of the weaker patients, an old woman called Millie Sykes, to feed herself when another complication came to the surface of her mind.

Jem! Jem would arrive on the last Thursday of the month to take her out. He had promised and she had no doubt that he would keep his word. That would be December 28th and by then she might be gone. She imagined his disappointment when he found she was not there – would not be there for at least a year. She had no idea where he was working, so there was no possibility of writing to him to explain. The best she could do would be to leave a note for him with Edith. She felt a tremor of regret. She had been looking forward to their next meeting, to 'walking out' with the man who might one day be her husband. That line of thought brought her up short. Was she throwing away the chance of marriage? Would Jem wait for her to come back? And if he did, would she be able to abandon the career she had been trained for to marry him?

As she contemplated that prospect Agnes Jones came into the ward and paused to look around her, her gaze alert and confident. Dora found herself thinking, 'That could be me!' Two contrasting images presented themselves to her imagination – herself in the uniform of a nurse, taking charge of a ward, and herself with a baby in her arms, maybe two small children at her feet, Jem coming home from work. The two pictures were in such perfect equilibrium that she stood temporarily paralysed.

'Are you all right, ducky?' Millie was looking up at her with concern. 'You look like you've seen a ghost.'

'No, no. I'm quite well.' Dora pulled herself together. 'Oh, you've eaten all your dinner! Well done, Millie. I'm glad to see you are getting your appetite back.'

She took the empty plate and began to make her way back towards the kitchen. As she passed Agnes an impulse brought her to a standstill.

'Nurse Jones, can I ask you something?'

Agnes turned from a contemplation of the ordered scene in the ward. 'Oh, Dora. Has Mr Rathbone spoken to you?'

'Yes, he has. I want to thank you for speaking up for me, for recommending me to him.'

'I was happy to do it. I am sure you will make an excellent nurse.'

'It's very kind of you to say so.'

'What was it you wanted to ask me?'

'It ... it's rather personal. I hope you won't be offended.'

'Well, if I can help in any way, I'll try to answer you. What is it?'

'You have never married, have you.'

'No. I have always felt that I had a calling that outweighed any ... personal desires.'

'A calling? You mean, from God? Like a nun?'

'Very much like that, yes.'

'You believe that God wants us to do the work you do.'

'Some of us, yes. I believe that those of us who have the ability and the opportunity to relieve suffering have a duty to pursue that object, to the exclusion of other distractions.'

'I see.' Dora thought for a moment. 'Thank you. That was – very helpful.'

That night, when she and Edith were settling to sleep, she said, 'Can I talk to you about something?'

'Of course you can. You know that.'

'You know Jem – well, of course you do. Did you know that ... that ...'

'That he's sweet on you. Of course, it was obvious. And you like him, don't you?'

'Yes, I do. He's got a job now, and we agreed that next time we are allowed out he will call for me and we'll, well, walk out together. He's asked me to marry him, once he's settled and got some money behind him.'

'I see.' Edith's tone was thoughtful. 'And now you are faced with a choice. That had not occurred to me. How do you feel about it?'

'Confused,' Dora confessed. 'I want to go to London. I like the idea of being properly qualified. But I like the thought of being married to Jem, too.'

'Is it not possible to have both? Surely Jem would wait for you. It would give him a chance to get himself in a position to be able to provide for you.'

'Maybe. But I was talking to Nurse Jones. She says nursing is a vocation, a calling from God, and we have to put everything else aside.'

'Hmm,' Edith said. 'Perhaps that is how she sees it, but I can't imagine all the young women who are being trained feel the same way. There must be room for compromise.'

'I don't see how,' Dora said. 'I couldn't work here, or in an ordinary hospital, if I had children to look after.'

'No, that's true,' Edith responded, 'but there are other kinds of nursing. Remember, the thing that made Mr Rathbone decide to use some of his fortune to train nurses was the way one looked after his wife in their own home. There must be plenty of families who would be glad to employ a trained nurse when one of them is ill. You might be able to do that, as a part-time job.'

'But not if I had children of my own to look after.' Dora sighed. 'Oh, I don't know. It would be wrong to let Mr Rathbone pay for me to be trained and then not use what

I'd learned – but I should like to have a home of my own – and children. Though perhaps I don't deserve them, after what I did with my baby.'

Edith turned on her side in bed and propped herself up on her elbow. 'Dora, listen to me. You must not miss this opportunity. You have the chance to be independent, to be able to support yourself without needing a man to look after you. I know you want everything marriage can bring, but sometimes things do not work out the way they are supposed to. Jem is a good man, I'm sure, but he does not have a trade that would give him a secure position. He has a job now, but there is no guarantee it will last, or lead to anything better. And he could fall ill again or be injured in some way. Then how would you fare?'

'That's something to consider, I suppose,' Dora said.

Edith lay back on her pillow. 'When I told you how I came to be here, there was one thing I omitted. Before I took up my first position as a governess, I was going to be married. He was a young man studying to become a minister, like my father, and I loved him very dearly. One day, he went swimming in the sea when it was far too cold. He took a chill, which became pneumonia, and he died. After that, I had no option but to earn my own living, but I was always dependent on the goodwill of the families I worked for, and there were times when I would have given a great deal to have some means of supporting myself, doing work that gave me some pleasure, instead of the drudgery of a governess's lot. And in the end, when I could no longer do even that, I had no option but to come here. If you go to London and qualify as a professional nurse you will never be in that position.'

'Oh, Edith, I am so sorry!' Dora said. 'Why didn't you tell me before?'

'It didn't seem important, and it is not something I like to think of too much. But now you see why I am urging you not to miss this wonderful chance. Jem will wait, if he really cares for you, and when you come back you can make up your mind what you want to do. But at least you will have a choice. That is not something that many women are allowed.'

'Yes, you are right,' Dora said. 'Thank you, Edith. I can see I should be a fool to say no. I shall go to London.'

Next day she was summoned again to Mrs Carter's office, where she found a dressmaker waiting to take her measurements and a boot-maker with a selection of shoes for her to try on for size. On the third day after that she was sent for again.

'The clothes have come for you to try on,' the superintendent said. 'You had better come into my bedroom where you can have a bit of privacy.'

Dora followed her through a communicating door into a simply furnished room with a narrow single bed and a chest of drawers. Laid out on the counterpane was a dress and a skirt and jacket and a hooped petticoat.

'Which one do you want to try first?'

Dora looked at her. There was something in her voice and in her face that suggested excitement. It occurred to her that this sudden break in the routine of what was, after all, a fairly cheerless existence had brightened her life. She looked at the two garments.

'I'll try that one first.'

She undid the simple blue dress that was the uniform garment provided for women in the workhouse and slid it off. Then she stepped into the petticoat and tied it at the waist. The skirt was made of fine wool in dark green, trimmed with silk ribbons in a lighter shade and decorated with a deep row of pleats at the hem. The jacket had a high neck and was worn over a white lawn blouse, the sleeves of which showed below those of the jacket.

'That is very suitable,' Mrs Carter declared. 'A nice, sensible garment for travelling in, and with plenty of wear in it. Have a look in the mirror.'

She opened a wardrobe door and showed a mirror fixed to the inside. Dora looked at herself and for a moment almost failed to recognise the image in front of her. The last time she had seen herself in a mirror was at the Latimer's house. She had been wearing a dress much finer than this, made of pale blue silk with a low neck. She had never liked it much because, like most of her clothes, it had been passed on to her from Fenella, Mrs Latimer's elder daughter. She had been studying herself in the mirror, wondering how much longer she could fasten the buttons over the swelling of her belly. But it was not the difference in the clothes that caused her to stare at her reflection in shock. The girl she remembered had looked very different. There had been a softness, an almost childish plumpness to her face. Now the face that looked back at her was a woman's, its curves lost, its structure defined in planes and hollows.

'Well, what do you think?' Mrs Carter said.

'It's ... very smart.'

'Try the other on.'

The second dress was made in a lighter material, a silk poplin in stripes of amber and bronze, with a lower neckline trimmed with a fichu of cream lace.

Mrs Carter caught her breath. 'Oh, that really suits you. You look ... quite pretty.'

Dora studied her reflection and allowed herself a moment of vanity. Yes, she did look pretty. At the Latimer's house she had been constantly reminded that with her dark skin and curly hair she could never be regarded as meeting the standard of beauty set by the creamy complexions and silky locks of the two legitimate daughters. Now, for the first time, she recognised that she had her own beauty.

Mrs Carter was bustling over to a large case set on the bed. 'Now, see what else we have here.' She opened the lid and took out a cape of greenish tweed with a small fur collar. 'You will need that in this cold weather. And look what else there is.'

Dora moved across to the bed and looked. The case contained another white lawn blouse, a corset, two chemises and four pairs of stockings, and a nightgown.

'Mr Rathbone seems to have thought of everything,' she said wonderingly.

'Oh, I suspect he took some advice from the dressmaker, or another lady,' Mrs Carter said. 'And that is not all.'

From under the bed she produced a hat box. 'Open it!'

Dora did so and found a bonnet trimmed with the same green ribbons as on the suit, the underside of the brim lined with ruffles of cream lace.

'All this must have cost Mr Rathbone a great deal of money,' she said. 'How am I ever going to repay him?'

'I shouldn't worry your head about that,' Mrs Carter said. 'He is a wealthy man and I am sure the only recompense he requires is that you make the most of the opportunity he is giving you and turn your training to good account. Now, we had better pack all this away. I will keep it safe for you until you are ready to leave.'

'Please, ma'am,' Dora said, 'may I take the two dresses to show Edith? I should like her to see them.'

Mrs Carter hesitated a moment, then gave in. 'Very well. But you must take the greatest care of them, and bring them back before you go to bed. They are not to be worn in the wards, remember.'

'Of course not,' Dora said and gathered the two garments in her arms.

She had to wait until the patients had been given their supper and settled for the night before she had a chance to put them on for Edith's inspection.

'Well,' Edith said, when Dora had displayed them both, 'Mr Rathbone – or someone he knows – has excellent taste.'

'I didn't expect anything like this,' Dora said. 'Just something respectable enough to travel to London in. I'm not sure when I am expected to wear the other dress.'

'I suppose you are not going to be shut up in the nurses' home all the time. You may want to go out to a concert, or the theatre. Or perhaps you might be invited to take tea at the home of one of the other girls.'

'I hadn't thought of that,' Dora murmured. 'Somehow, I can't quite believe in it.'

Edith gave her a hug. 'You will, in time. I'm so happy for you, my dear.'

'I just wish you could be with me.'

'No, no. I'm well enough here. I'm too old for all that sort of thing.'

'Oh, nonsense,' Dora said, but Edith changed the subject.

'We should do something with your hair, don't you think?'

'Do what with it? It will not lie flat, like it does for other ladies. I used to try all sorts of ways, but nothing really worked.'

'No, but perhaps there is another way. Sit down and let me try.'

'My mother used to plait it tightly and tie it with ribbons but the Latimer girls laughed at that.'

Since entering the workhouse Dora had scarcely thought about her appearance. She had washed her hair when she had her weekly bath, but for the rest of the time she had hidden it under a mob cap, like all the other women. Edith produced a comb and patiently worked out the tangles. After a little she said, 'There, I think this will do.'

She took a metal plate from the kitchen shelf and polished it with a tea towel, then held it up so that Dora could see a rather blurred image of herself.

'See, I've formed the front into little ringlets, and the rest can be plaited and coiled up at the back of your head. You need some hairpins to hold it. Perhaps Mrs Carter might oblige.'

'You are clever, Edith,' Dora exclaimed. 'Thank you!'

'Oh, it's nothing. When I was a girl I used to love doing my friends' hair. But we had to keep it secret. My papa would not have approved of such vanity!' She stood back. 'Well, you're ready, as far as possible. When do you leave?'

'I still don't know. I suppose Mr Rathbone will send a message.'

In the event, on the day after Boxing Day Mr Rathbone came in person to deliver the news. Once again Dora was summoned to Mrs Carter's office.

'So, Dora,' he said with a smile, 'are you happy with your new wardrobe?'

'Very happy, sir, and I thank you for your generosity. I shall do my best to deserve it.'

'I'm sure you will. I have every confidence in you. Are you ready to leave?'

Dora felt a tug of apprehension somewhere in the region of her heart but she responded firmly, 'I am, sir.'

'Good. You will catch the ten a.m. train from Lime Street Station the day after tomorrow.'

Dora took a quick inward breath. The day after tomorrow was Thursday, when Jem was supposed to call for her, but she knew that to quibble about the date would raise questions about her commitment to the new life she was being offered. She said nothing and Rathbone continued, 'You will be met at King's Cross Station by a young lady named—' he referred to a slip of paper that he drew from his pocket '—named Elizabeth Warrender. She is one of the new intake of probationers and she will take you to the nurses' home and introduce you to the matron. You will recognise her, because she will be wearing the same uniform as the nurses who are working here.' He opened a small case and took out a purse. 'In here is your railway ticket and a small amount of money to cover any immediate needs you may have. I am going to make you an allowance of four pounds a month, which you will receive in the form of a cheque, which you can cash at any bank. It will allow you to participate in some of the social activities which may be on offer. But be warned: London is an expensive city. You will have to husband your resources carefully.'

'I will, sir,' Dora promised.

'There is one matter you need to be aware of. There are two classes of probationer. Some of them come from relatively humble backgrounds. They are termed students, and are paid a small sum per month while they are studying. The others are ladies, educated young women of independent means. I have enrolled you in the latter group.'

'But ...' Dora stumbled over her words, 'but I am not a lady. I never could be.'

A vivid recollection came to her. She was in the schoolroom with her two half-sisters and their governess. They were practising walking with a book balanced on their heads and Fenella had lost her temper and thrown the book across the room. The governess had told her she should take a leaf out of Dora's book, because her behaviour was much more ladylike. Fenella had looked at Dora, her lips curling in a cruel smile. 'Oh, she may be lady*like* but after all, she can never be a lady.'

Rathbone smiled at her. 'That is a term that has a variety of definitions, in my opinion. You are definitely not one of the common sort. You have received an education and you have the deportment and manners fitting for a lady. You would not, I think, be comfortable in the society of uneducated women, however well intentioned. Some of the young women you will be studying with will be drawn from the higher reaches of society, with wealthy parents, but I do not believe they will be given to extravagant displays. They have all chosen to dedicate themselves to the care of the sick and I know that Miss Nightingale has no time for these who wish to play the society lady. You will be in good company.'

'May I ask you something, please?' Dora said hesitantly.

'Of course.'

'Will they ... will the people I am going to work with know where I have come from?'

'Ah, yes. That is a point I intended to raise with you. Mrs Wardroper, the matron in charge of the probationers, has already been told your story. I felt it was my duty to ensure that she had a clear understanding of your circumstances. But I see no reason why your fellow probationers should be told. I suggest that you tell them that you are an orphan; that you were taken in to his family by Captain Latimer and brought up with his daughters, but when you were of an age to make a decision about your future you felt impelled to follow your mother's example in caring for the sick, so you volunteered to work in the infirmary. There is no need to mention the fact that you were compelled to enter the workhouse.'

'But would I not be, well, less than honest, if I tell them that?'

'What elements of the story I have outlined are untrue?' he asked.

Dora thought about it. 'I suppose there is nothing that did not actually happen.'

'Well, then. It is for you decide, of course, but that would be my solution to the problem.'

'Thank you, sir. That does lift a weight from my shoulders.'

'I'm glad. I should not like you to have to start your new life under a cloud. Regard this as a new beginning and put the past behind you. Now, is there anything else you need to know?'

'No, I don't think so. Except ... I have never been to Lime Street Station. I have passed it, of course, when I ... before I came here. But I am not sure how ... how to conduct myself.'

'I understand. Mrs Carter, is there not somebody here who could accompany Dora to the station and see her safely on the train?'

'I shall do that myself, Mr Rathbone. You may rely on me.'

'Very well. So I shall wish you goodbye and *bon voyage,* Dora.'

He held out his hand. Dora took it and felt tears pricking her eyelids. 'Goodbye, sir. And thank you again.'

'I hope we shall meet again, when you return to take up your vocation here, as a fully qualified nurse.'

'I shall look forward to that,' Dora said.

That evening Dora begged paper and an envelope from Mrs Carter and sat down to write what she thought would probably be the most difficult letter she would ever pen.

Dear Jem,

I know that when you receive this letter it will be a disappointment to you, because you will be expecting to find me waiting for you. I hope you will understand why I am not. I have been given a chance to escape the workhouse, just as you did, and I know you will not blame me for taking it.

I have been offered the opportunity by Mr Rathbone, the gentleman who is paying for the Nightingale nurses, to take over the running of the infirmary, to go to London to learn to be a proper nurse at the school Miss Nightingale has set up. I shall be gone for a year, but at the end of that time I shall have a qualification that will allow me to lead an independent life. Perhaps it seems strange to you that I should want that. It is not what most women expect, but after my experience of trying to make my way in the world without the help of a family or a protector it seems to me a most desirable thing.

It would be wrong of me to ask you to wait for me. A year is a long time and you will probably meet someone else who will be only too glad to join her fate with yours. Since we last spoke I have cherished the idea of marriage to you, and of having children – children in whom I can take real joy, instead of reminding me of my shame. It is still something I dream of. But when I return, even if you were to wait for me, I shall be honour bound to repay my debt to Mr Rathbone by taking up a position as a nurse here. I have every intention of so doing and I cannot see how that could be combined with the responsibilities of marriage and bringing up children.

Dear Jem, I shall always remember your kindness and warmth. I believe I could very easily fall in love with you, if circumstances were other then they are. But I cannot turn my back on the chance of a new life. I hope you can forgive me.

With my warmest good wishes,
Dorinda.

She sealed the letter and gave it to Edith for safe keeping.

Waking the next morning, her stomach felt hollow with apprehension and regret. In another twenty-four hours she would have to say goodbye to the one real friend she had ever known and to the place that had been her home for nearly four years. To most people it was a place of shame and deprivation and yet she had found here a purpose and a security that she had not known in her earlier life. She was going out into the unknown, as surely as an explorer heading for a new continent.

She spent the day making up as many of the herbal remedies she had concocted as possible, and saying goodbye to the patients and the nurses. The nurses had tended on their first arrival to either ignore her or condescend to her, but over the months both she and Edith had been accepted as valuable partners in their work and she was on friendly terms with most of them. They had been told where she was going and she was offered good wishes, and sometimes small pieces of advice.

'Watch out for Sister Samson. She's a real tartar if you get on the wrong side of her.'

'Make sure your apron is always spotless. I was made to display mine in front of all the patients because it had a stain on it.'

Her last farewell was to Agnes Jones.

'Well,' she asked, 'are you looking forward to starting your training?'

'Yes, I am, of course, but ...'

'But not without some trepidation. Of course, that is natural. But you need have no worries. If you show yourself as willing and dedicated as you have here, you will do very well. Now—' she reached into the pocket of her apron

'—we have all clubbed together to buy you a little parting gift.' She held out a small package. 'It was hard to decide what might be most suitable, but I think you will find this useful.'

Dora opened the parcel. It contained a small, sturdily made watch, with a ribbon attached that could be pinned to a dress. She caught her breath. 'Oh! What a wonderful gift! Of course, it will be most useful – and it will be a lasting reminder of all of you. Thank you so much!'

'I am glad you like it. We shall all miss you. Just make sure you come back to us when the year is over.'

Dora was up early the next morning. She collected her travelling clothes from Mrs Carter's room and put them on and Edith pinned up her hair with borrowed hairpins.

'There! You look really smart. A real lady.'

'I don't feel like one. I feel like an imposter.'

'Nonsense. You are an intelligent, educated young woman and you have more about you than these vapid girls whose only thought is of flirting with every good-looking man who comes along. Now, come along. You don't want to miss your train.'

Mrs Carter was waiting outside her office, with Dora's portmanteau beside her. A young man was standing awkwardly nearby.

'I've asked Wilfred, one of the porters, to accompany us to the station. You cannot manage this all on your own. At the other end of the journey you will be able to get a station porter to carry it for you. Say goodbye. It's time we were going.'

Edith hugged her tightly and whispered. 'Goodbye, my dear. And the very best of luck.'

Dora swallowed back tears. 'See you in a year's time.'

'Yes, yes. Go now. Take care of yourself.'

Lime Street Station frightened Dora so much that, had she not had Mrs Carter at her side, she would have turned and fled. Under the huge vault of the roof the noise of gates clanging, the hiss of steam and the shouts of the porters rose to a cacophony that to Dora's ears, used only to the subdued noises of the infirmary, was almost unbearable. The locomotive standing at the platform spat sparks and smoke and just as they passed it gave out a great snort of steam that made her nearly jump out of her skin. Mrs Carter took her by the elbow and guided her firmly along the platform until they reached a carriage that carried the sign 'Ladies Only'.

'This will do nicely,' she said. 'Climb in. Now, your case is in the luggage van. It will be got out when you reach King's Cross Station and you can get a porter to carry it to where your guide will be waiting. The train will call at several other stations on the way, so do not be tempted to get out. You cannot go beyond King's Cross, as the train terminates there.'

Dora mounted the steps and seated herself in a corner of the carriage. She was glad to see that two middle-aged ladies already occupied the two places on the opposite side. They nodded amiably to her, but did not interrupt their conversation.

'Oh, I almost forgot!' Mrs Carter leaned in through the window with a small package in her hand. 'I put up a few sandwiches for you, in case you get hungry.'

Dora took the package and felt a sudden rush of guilt. She and Edith had always regarded the superintendent as, if not exactly an enemy, certainly someone whose purpose was opposed to their own. She was aware that over the years a subtle change had happened in their relationship and that now Mrs Carter had assumed an almost motherly attitude to her. She leaned over and kissed her on the cheek.

'Thank you so much, for everything you have done for me. I hope I haven't caused you too much trouble.'

'Trouble? Goodness, I don't know what you mean.'

Her words were cut short by a shrill whistle from the engine and the sound of doors being slammed all along the train. She stepped back onto the platform and the train jerked into motion.

'Goodbye! Take care of yourself.'

'Goodbye. See you next year.'

The train glided forward and a gust of steam enveloped Mrs Carter, hiding her from view. Dora waved once and sat back. For better or worse, she was on her way.

Chapter 7

If Lime Street had been daunting, King's Cross Station was doubly so. Dora climbed down from the train, stiff from prolonged sitting, and was almost swept away by the flood of people hurrying along the platform towards the barrier at the end. She followed them and was greatly relieved when she reached the guard's van to see her suitcase waiting for her. As she hesitated, a man wearing a peaked cap and pushing a trolley came up to her.

'Need a porter, miss?'

'Oh, yes, please.'

He lifted her case onto the trolley and headed through the crowd towards the barrier. Dora hurried in his wake, afraid of losing sight of him. At the gate, she had to fumble in the bag Mr Rathbone had given her for her ticket. Then she was through and looking around her, wondering how she would ever find the young woman who was supposed to escort her to the hospital. The air in the station was cloudy, she supposed from the smoke and steam generated by the engines, and it was hard to see any distance.

'Miss Latimer?' A figure seemed to materialise from the mist, a slender girl wrapped in a fur cape under which showed the brown uniform of a Nightingale nurse. 'I am right, am I not? My name is Elizabeth Warrender.'

'Oh, yes. Yes, I'm Dora Latimer.' Dora was prepared for a look of surprise, even of shock, but the stranger's smile did not falter. Of course, she thought, she must have been forewarned. How else could she recognise her so easily?

'I thought you must be.' A gloved hand was extended towards her. 'Hah d'you do?'

It took a second for Dora to translate the words. She had been surrounded all her life by people who spoke scouse, the rough accent of Liverpool, and even her stepmother and half-sisters, who would have regarded their manner of speaking as faultlessly upper class, had still retained a northern accent. She was uncomfortably aware that hers would sound uncouth to this southerner's ears.

She touched the offered hand briefly. 'How do you do?'

'I'm so pleased to meet you.' The warmth in the voice sounded genuine. 'Now, I'm sure you are worn out after such a long journey, but we still have a bit further to go. Come along. We must find a hansom cab.' She turned to the porter. 'Take us to the cab rank, please.'

She tucked a hand under Dora's arm and urged her forward. 'Is this the first time you have been to London?'

'Yes, it is.'

'I expect it seems rather overwhelming, if you are not used to crowds. But you will get used to it.'

'You know the city well, do you?' Dora hazarded.

'Oh yes. I was brought up here. That's why Mrs Wardroper chose me to come and meet you. She knows my mother through some of the charity work she is involved with.'

They threaded their way through the crowd until they came out to an open space, or so it seemed to Dora. It was hard to be sure, because the mist here was thicker than ever. She could just make out a variety of vehicles, which loomed up and disappeared through the murk. There were smart horse-drawn carriages and pony traps, and large drays pulled by great cart horses and others full of people, which she recognised as omnibuses. She sniffed the air. It smelt of smoke.

'It seems rather foggy.'

'Yes, we've got a real pea-souper, I'm afraid. Not the ideal conditions to introduce you to London.'

'A what? Pea-souper? Why do you call it that?'

'Because it's thick and yellow, like pea soup.'

'Does it happen often?'

'Quite often, during the winter.'

A line of hansom cabs was drawn up by the kerb. The porter loaded Dora's case onto the one at the front and Elizabeth pressed a coin into his hand. Dora felt embarrassed. She should have been ready to do that.

They climbed into the cab and Elizabeth said, 'Surrey Gardens, please, driver.'

'Surrey Gardens?' he queried. 'You sure you want to go there? It's all closed down now, you know. The zoo's gone and the music hall.'

'Yes, we know that,' Elizabeth said. 'We are going to the hospital.'

'Hospital? What hospital?'

'St Thomas's. It's been moved there while we wait for the new building to be completed.'

'Well, that's news to me! Right you are, then.' The driver clicked to his horse and the cab moved off.

Elizabeth turned to Dora. 'I don't know if anyone told you that we are not in the original hospital any longer?'

'No, no one mentioned that.' Dora had had no idea where the hospital might be and she had never thought to enquire.

'They are going to extend the railway line to a new station at Charing Cross, and it will go right through the middle of the old building, so everyone had to move out. There is going to be a new hospital, right by the end of Westminster Bridge, but until it is finished we are making do out at Newington.' Elizabeth laughed. 'It's quite comical, really. There used to be pleasure gardens there, with a zoo and a huge music hall. They had concerts and firework displays and all sorts of things, but it stopped being popular – I'm not sure why – and closed down. So St Thomas's has taken it over. The main wards are in the old music hall, there is a laboratory in a pavilion in the grounds and the dissecting room is in what used to be the elephant house. Can you imagine!'

'It does seem strange,' Dora agreed. 'Have you been there long?'

'Listen to me! Chatting on as if I'm an old hand! No, I only started yesterday, but as I told you my mama is a friend of the matron's. She told me what to expect.'

'It doesn't sound very ... convenient,' Dora said.

'No, I suppose it isn't. But it might be quite pleasant when the weather improves. The grounds are still beautiful. They were planted up with all sorts of exotic trees and shrubs, with little hidden pavilions and summer houses. I had a stroll round yesterday and I think it will be nice to be able to walk out there when we are free. Nice to get some fresh air.'

'Fresh air?' Dora queried, looking out of the cab at the tendrils of fog curling round them.

'Don't you have fogs in Liverpool? That is where you are from, isn't it?'

'Yes. We get sea mists, but they smell of salt and seaweed and usually the wind off the sea blows them away quite quickly.'

Elizabeth sighed. 'I wish we had sea winds to blow away the foul air here. It can be worse in the summer.'

'Worse?'

'My father says there are too many people living here now and they all produce – well, you know, waste products. A lot of it ends up in the River Thames and when the tide goes out it is left on the mud to bake in the sun. You never heard about the Great Stink?'

'What?'

'A few years ago the smell was so bad that the government was afraid some of the members of Parliament would get ill from it. The old Palace of Westminster was right by the river before it burnt down, so they got the full force of it. Now they are supposed to be building new sewers to take the waste away, but I haven't noticed much difference yet.'

'Oh dear,' Dora said. She was beginning to wonder if her bright new future was going to be quite as bright as she had imagined.

'Oh, there I go again!' Elizabeth said. 'I do tend to rattle on, sometimes. My papa often speaks to me about it. You mustn't think it's all doom and gloom. London can be a wonderful city in good weather. It's such a pity the fog is so thick. I can't point out any of the famous landmarks to you. But I'll show you another day, when the fog clears.'

'Will we be allowed to go out?'

'Yes, on Sundays, unless we are on duty. There will be a rota. Well, that's what my mother told me.'

The cab crept forward at a walking pace and other vehicles appeared out of the mist and passed by. Dora had a vague impression of buildings on either side of the road and from time to time there was a glow from what she thought must be shop windows, but that was all. They passed people muffled up in cloaks and coats, their heads hunched forwards as they strove to see what was ahead of them. After a long time she felt the cab climbing an incline and Elizabeth peered out of the window.

'We're crossing the river. It may be a little clearer on the other side.'

She was proved right. Slowly the fog gave way and they could see that the road was lined with small terraced houses, behind which the occasional glimpse of the top of a tree hinted at gardens. Then the road widened and the cab turned into a wide sweep of drive and drew up in front of an imposing building.

'This is the old Manor House,' Elizabeth said. 'This is where our quarters are. Come on. Let's get inside. I expect you are chilled to the marrow and dying for a cup of tea.'

She led the way through the open front door and the driver followed with Dora's case, which he dumped on the floor. Dora felt in her bag. She had no idea how much the journey had cost. She could only hope Mr Rathbone had given her enough to cover it. Before she had a chance to get her money out Elizabeth said, 'No, let me. Mrs Wardroper gave me the money for the fare.'

When the driver had gone back to his cab she said, 'You had better leave your case there for the moment. I'll take you up and introduce you to Mrs W.'

Dora followed her up a wide staircase. It was clear that this had once been a grand house, but signs of neglect were everywhere, in the chipped banisters and the dirty marks on the wallpaper. Elizabeth tapped on a door and a voice called, 'Come in.'

Dora drew herself up and braced her shoulders. She was very tired, but she was determined to make a good impression.

Mrs Wardroper was sitting behind a desk covered in papers. She wore a dress of black bombazine and a white cap with streamers that hung over her shoulders. Dora's first impression was of a face full of purpose, a wide forehead, straight nose and brown eyes which fixed on her with a sharp assessing gaze.

'Excuse me, Matron,' Elizabeth said. 'This is Dora Latimer.'

'Come in.' Mrs Wardroper beckoned her closer. 'Welcome to St Thomas's. Warrender, ask Jackson to take Miss Latimer's case up to room 4, please. Then you can come back here to collect her.'

Elizabeth made a small curtsy. 'Very good, matron.'

When she had left, Mrs Wardroper said, 'I have heard a good deal about you from Mr Rathbone. He obviously thinks very highly of you.'

'It's very kind of him to send me here,' Dora said. 'I shall try to live up to his expectations.'

Mrs Wardroper nodded approvingly. 'That is the right attitude.' She regarded Dora with her head slightly on one side. 'You have not had quite the sort of upbringing that would normally suit you for this situation. I understand from Mr Rathbone that you have suffered considerable hardships in your life.'

Dora swallowed. 'It is true that there have been ... difficult times. But I have also been very fortunate. I have found friends and a ... a way of life that has enabled me to atone for past mistakes, at least to some extent.'

'I am glad to find that you have such a positive view. Some young women would regard themselves as the victim of circumstances and expect the world to make allowances in compensation.'

'No, I do not ask for that,' Dora said. 'I only wish to make a new life, in which I can be of service to others.'

'Splendid!' Mrs Wardroper exclaimed. 'That is exactly the sort of attitude I expect from all the probationers. Now, I want you to know that none of what Mr Rathbone has told me will be passed on to the other members of staff who will be teaching you, or to any of your fellow probationers. What you tell them about your background will be entirely up to you. But bear this in mind: Miss Nightingale requires her nurses to have unblemished characters. To her, character is more important than nursing skill. I think you have the potential to live up to her high standard. It will be up to you to prove me right.'

'I shall do my best,' Dora said. She understood the unspoken context of the remark. Her past history meant that there was a question mark over her future conduct, and she would have to be extra vigilant to eradicate it.

There was a tap on the door and Elizabeth returned. Mrs Wardroper dismissed them both and Elizabeth said, 'I'll show you where your room is, and then we'll go down to the common room. It will be tea time soon.'

The bedrooms in the old house had been roughly subdivided with partitions of plywood to give a series of small private cubicles. Elizabeth pushed aside a curtain, which served as a door, and revealed a bed, a chest of drawers with a mirror and a wash basin and ewer, and a rail for hanging items.

'It's a bit basic, I'm afraid,' she said. 'But the beds are comfortable and that's the main thing.'

Dora thought of the little room she had shared with Edith, with its rough blankets and uncarpeted floor. *You don't know what basic is,* she thought. The gulf between her own experiences and those of the girls she was about to meet suddenly seemed unbridgeable.

'Your case is here,' Elizabeth said. 'Do you want to freshen up after the journey?'

'Yes, please. I should like that.'

'I'll show you the bathroom. There are eight of us on this floor and we all have to share it, so I'm afraid there can be a bit of queue sometimes.'

Dora opened her case and took out her few items of toiletries – a toothbrush, a small piece of soap and a ragged facecloth. Holding them close, so that Elizabeth could not see how poor they were, she followed her to the end of the passage.

'Here you are,' Elizabeth said, opening a door. 'I'll wait outside.'

It was the nicest bathroom Dora had ever seen, for all that some of the enamel on the bath and the basin was chipped. To her relief, there was a water closet, which she quickly made use of. There were taps over the hand basin and the roll-top bath. She tried them, and discovered that there was both hot and cold water. She remembered that there had been talk of installing a system in the Latimer's house, before her expulsion, and the workhouse had a bath house where the inmates were given their weekly bath, but it was the first time she had had access to running water in a private bathroom, albeit one she would have to share with eight others. She washed her hands and face and re-joined Elizabeth in the passage.

On the ground floor what had once been a grand dining room now contained two long trestle tables with benches on either side. In the drawing room there were rows of desks and a blackboard, but at the rear of the house the library had been given over to the probationers as a common room. There were a dozen or so young women present when Dora was shown in by Elizabeth, and she was immediately aware that there were two distinct groups. Although they were all dressed in the brown uniform of a Nightingale nurse, the posture and the hum of well-bred conversation of those seated nearest to the fire identified them at once as girls whose upbringing had accustomed them to society. On the periphery of the room small huddles of other girls looked on, exchanging muted murmurs as if afraid of giving offence.

Elizabeth led Dora into the circle by the fire. 'Ladies, this is Dora Latimer. She has just arrived all the way from Liverpool.' She looked round at the others. 'I think I had better let you introduce yourselves, since we only met this morning and I'm not sure I remember everyone's names.'

Now she did see the reaction she had expected, surprise on some faces, something stronger on others. In the workhouse she had been a familiar sight, and not the only black face to be seen. Before that, her father had constantly told her that she was beautiful and should feel at no disadvantage to her white half-sisters. But after his death they had been at pains to point out the difference between them. Now, being introduced into a new circle, she knew she might encounter prejudice. How hard it might be to overcome remained to be seen.

A girl with chestnut-brown hair, worn in ringlets that fell to her shoulders, stood up with a smile. 'I'm Hope Standish,' she said 'Welcome to London, Dora.'

Dora bent her head in recognition. 'How do you do?'

After a fractional pause a tall, dark-haired girl stood up and extended her hand. 'Good afternoon. My name is Julia Fellowes. How do you do?'

'How do you do?' The hand she touched was quickly withdrawn.

After that the others in the group introduced themselves but there were too many names and faces to fix themselves in her memory all at once. Then someone said, 'Hey, come along, Phyllis. Say how do you do to our new arrival.'

Dora looked round. In a window embrasure a young woman was lounging on a chaise longue with a book in her hands. She put it aside and stood up. She was as tall as Julia, but where Julia's figure was elegantly slender hers was broader and the hand she extended was strong and capable. Her expression showed curiosity but not surprise.

'Please call me Phil. I abhor Phyllis.'

Dora found herself smiling as she responded, 'As you please, Phil.'

There was a pause in the conversation and Dora was uncomfortably aware that she was the focus of several pairs of eyes.

'So!' Julia broke the silence. 'Perhaps we should tell each other a bit about ourselves – where we come from, who our families are ... that sort of thing. Shall I begin?'

'Oh yes, please do,' Hope said.

'My father is a colonel in the Hussars. My uncle, his elder brother, has an estate in Lanarkshire.' It was clear to Dora that in Julia's mind this established her in a secure position in the social hierarchy. 'How about you, Hope?'

'Oh, nothing as grand as that. My father is the vicar of Chalfont St Peter in Buckinghamshire.'

'Oh, the church and the military have always been closely related,' Julia said generously. 'Elizabeth, what does your father do?'

Elizabeth hesitated for an instant and Dora saw her colour slightly. When she spoke there was a hint of defiance in her tone. 'He's an industrialist. He owns a factory.'

'A factory?' Something in Julia's tone made the word sound faintly improper. 'What does he make?'

'Tools of all sorts. Machines. I don't know much about it.' Elizabeth's blush had deepened.

'And you, Dora.' Julia turned her eyes in her direction. 'What do your people do?'

Dora took a deep breath. This was the inquisition she had been dreading. 'I have no ... people, as you put it. I am an orphan.'

'Oh, that's very sad for you!' Elizabeth's voice was full of sympathy.

'Yes, it is sad. But it is not unusual. I have been luckier than some.'

'How so?' Julia asked.

137

'I was taken into the home of a sea captain and brought up with his children.'

'Latimer,' Julia mused. 'That's a very English sounding name.'

'It was the name of the captain who adopted me.'

'Oh? So what was your original name?'

'I ...' Dora floundered.

'Oh, come on, Julia,' Phil interrupted. 'How do you expect Dora to remember that? I imagine she was just a baby when she was adopted.'

Julia shrugged. 'I just wondered.'

'You haven't asked me about my background,' Phil said, 'since you seem to be keen to establish our social credentials.'

'I don't ... that is, I just thought it would be nice to know something about each other. So, tell us about your family.'

'Oh, we farm. We have some land in Hertfordshire.'

'Ah, my father always says that the yeoman farmer is the backbone of England.'

Julia smiled warmly, happy in having established her own superior position.

'I'm sure he is correct,' Phil said mildly. 'But it doesn't really apply to us. My father is Lord Delamere. It's an old title, dating back to the Conquest.'

Julia's face was a study. Across the group Dora caught Elizabeth's eyes and they exchanged grins.

The rattle of tea cups interrupted the conversation and a maid appeared pushing a trolley.

'Praise the Lord!' Phil exclaimed. 'Tea at last. I am famished!'

There was a general movement towards the table in the centre of the room. The maid was setting out plates and dishes loaded with buttered crumpets and sandwiches of white bread with the crusts cut off. There was a Dundee cake, the top glistening with glacé cherries, and a dish of gingerbread and a sponge cake filled with jam. Dora felt the saliva rise in her mouth. It was years since she had seen a spread like this, and having had no dinner, apart from the sandwiches Mrs Carter had given her, she was hungry. The girls she had been introduced to were casually filling their plates and accepting cups of tea from the maid, but the others, the quiet ones, hung back as if unsure whether the food was intended for them. Dora guessed that these were the students, the girls from poorer backgrounds. She experienced a flush of indignation. These privileged young women had no conception of what it was to go hungry. What gave them this sense of entitlement, so that they accepted the good things of life so unquestioningly?

She looked round. Some of the other girls had drawn closer and reached hesitantly for plates. She picked up a dish and offered it to the nearest one.

'Have a crumpet.'

'Oh, thanks.'

The girl reached out with a hand that showed the signs of regular exposure to cold water.

You've scrubbed a few pots and holystoned a few doorsteps in your life, Dora thought.

Aloud she said, 'My name's Dora. What's yours?'

'Lily, miss. Lily Baker.'

'You don't have to call me miss – or any of the others. We're all here for the same thing, aren't we?'

'Well said!' A voice spoke at her elbow. 'I'm Phil. Pleased to meet you, Lily. And who's your friend?'

A small girl with blonde hair and wide blue eyes stood next to Lily.

'Pearl,' Lily said. 'Her name is Pearl.'

'Hah! A pearl beyond price!' said Phil, reaching for a plate. 'Have a sandwich, Pearl.'

Dora became aware that Elizabeth had followed her example and was offering round plates of cake and ginger-bread and little by little the conversation became general as the two groups exchanged names and information about where they came from and what had brought them there. She noticed that Julia remained aloof, unwilling, or per-haps unable, to find the right words. Impelled by curiosity, she took her plate and teacup and found a seat near her.

'What made you want to take up nursing, Julia – if I may ask?'

Julia gave a small shrug. 'It's my father's idea, really. He fought in the Crimea. He saw what Miss Nightingale did for the wounded there, and he was so impressed he decided that I ought to learn to do the same.'

'And do you think you will enjoy it?' Dora asked.

'I don't expect to, but I have to keep my side of the bar-gain. Papa agreed that if I undertook a year's training here he would let me come out next year and do the Season – you know, balls and parties and so on. If I haven't managed to find myself a husband by the end of it, I suppose I can always fall back on nursing.'

'Oh, Julia!' Hope had joined them in time to hear that last remark. 'I don't mean to be rude, but do you think that is the right way to look at things?'

'It's how I look at it,' Julia responded curtly.

'What about you, Hope?' Dora asked.

'Oh, I think it is a duty. My papa is a man of God, and he says it is our bounden duty to succour the afflicted.' Hope's delicate face was suffused with a glow of conviction.

'Oh dear, you make me feel a bit of a fraud,' Elizabeth said. 'I'm doing this as a way of escape.'

'Escape from what?' Hope asked, sounding slightly shocked.

'From a future of arranging flowers and organising dinner parties,' Elizabeth said with a laugh. 'That's the sort of life my mama would like to see me leading.'

'Personally, I can't see anything to object to in that,' Julia said. 'But what about you, Dora? What brings you here?'

'I ... have already had some experience,' Dora said, choosing her words carefully. 'A gentleman by the name of Mr Rathbone, who is a great local benefactor, suggested I should come here. He is a friend of Miss Nightingale.'

'Oh well,' Julia said with a shrug, 'you will be able to show us all what to do.' Her off-hand manner signalled quite clearly that Dora's explanation had confirmed her first impression – that Dora did not belong to the same class as she did. Dora looked at her for a moment and then turned away. So Julia did not like her. Well, the feeling was mutual.

A laugh from the other side of the room drew every-one's attention. Phil was still chatting to Lily and Pearl. Something Lily had said had apparently struck her as funny and her laugh was loud and uninhibited. Dora had been drawn to her from the start and this confirmed her attraction. She moved across to join the three of them. Lily and Pearl were giggling helplessly.

'What's so funny?' Dora asked.

'Ssh!' Phil cast a glance over her shoulder at the girls by the fire. 'Lily here is a first-class mimic. You should have heard her impression of Julia doing the Season.'

Lily gave a hiccup of laughter, 'Oh, I shouldn't, really. It's wicked of me. I don't know what it means even, but it's the way she said it.'

'Well, it's like this,' Phil said. 'Have you ever been to a cattle market?'

'There's one at Smithfield every week. Why?'

'Well, the Season is a kind of upper-class cattle market, only instead of cows it's for girls.'

'Ooh, that's awful!' Lily clasped a hand over her mouth. She and Pearl looked again at the others and dissolved once more into giggles.

Dora stifled a desire to join them and said instead, 'So what brings you here, Phil?'

Phil smiled wryly. 'I suppose I failed to reach a good enough price at market. No, the fact is, I turned down three good offers, so my papa decided that if I was going to be an old maid I had better learn to do something useful.'

By the time the tea things were cleared away the two groups had begun to mix and the atmosphere was more relaxed. By then Dora was finding it very hard to stay awake. It was a relief when a bell sounded and Elizabeth said, 'That's the signal for bedtime. It will be "lights out" in twenty minutes.'

'Anybody would think,' Julia complained, 'that we were at boarding school.'

'Well, I suppose we are, in a way,' Hope responded.

In spite of her tiredness, it was some time before Dora was able to get to sleep. After the enforced seclusion of the workhouse, her brain seemed unable to process all the new faces and new impressions that crowded in on her. The social divisions disturbed her. She felt that she did not fit into either group. She was sufficiently educated to pass muster among the 'ladies', but the gulf between her background and theirs seemed impassable. Yet she was seen by the others as not one of them, though she felt far better fitted by her experience of life to belong there. Scraps of conversation and images of faces flitted through her mind, dragging her back from the brink of sleep, until at last she reminded herself that these challenges were just part of the new life that was opening up for her and somehow or other they would be overcome. At that point she slept.

The sound of the bell woke her and for a confused moment she thought she was back in the workhouse and there must be some kind of emergency. Then she opened her eyes to the unfamiliar surroundings of her little room and heard the yawns and groans of the other women as they dragged themselves out of bed. She looked at the little watch she had been given. 6.30am. By now Edith and the Nightingale nurses would be up and dressed and beginning the day's work. She poured water from the ewer into the basin and washed quickly, then dressed for the first time in the brown uniform dress and put on the freshly starched apron and cap. She knew she must look like the nurses she had come to admire in the infirmary and wished she had a full-length mirror to see the effect.

At breakfast the distinction between the two classes was apparent. While the 'ladies' yawned and complained about the early hour, the others were tucking in to an ample meal with every sign of pleasure. Early rising was no novelty to them.

When the meal was over they were summoned into the room which had been set up as a classroom. A woman wearing the same uniform as the rest of them but with a more elaborate cap came in. She was, Dora guessed, around forty, with strong, rather horsey features and a high colour. Impelled by the same instinctive respect for authority, they all rose.

'Good morning, ladies,' she began, and Dora thought she heard a suppressed giggle from Pearl who was standing behind her. 'My name is Sister Andrews and I am the sister tutor in charge of your education. Now, before we go any further, I want to emphasise one important point. One of the cardinal virtues, inculcated by Miss Nightingale herself, is cleanliness. It is her belief that dirt is the greatest enemy to health and therefore everything connected with the nursing of the sick must be kept immaculate. And that starts with the personal cleanliness of all those involved. So I am going to inspect all of you, to make sure that you understand the high standards we require. Please stand by your desks and hold out your hands so I can see them.'

Dora glanced sideways. Julia was standing next to her and her face was a study in offended sensibility. Phil looked as if she might burst out laughing at any minute; further away, Lily was trying to shove an unruly strand of hair under her cap. One by one, Sister Andrews made her way along the lines.

'What is your name?'

'Peggy West, miss ... ma'am ... sister.'

'Your finger nails are dirty. Before we go to the wards you must scrub them.'

'Yes, sister.'

'And your name is ...?'

'Mary Jones, sister.'

'You need to wash your hair. Make sure you do it before you go to bed tonight.'

She reached Hope. 'What is your name?'

'Hope Standish, sister.'

'Those ringlets need to be tied back and tucked away under your cap. There is no place for vanity here.'

'Oh yes, sorry, sister.'

Dora saw a deep blush rising up Hope's neck. She hoped that the sister would find something to criticise in Julia but she passed her with a nod and came on to Dora. In front of her she paused, took her hands and turned them over, and Dora guessed she was trying to determine whether their colour might conceal a lack of cleanliness. Then she stood back and looked her up and down.

'Very neat! You are the only one who seems to understand how the cap should be worn. Your name is ...'

'Dora Latimer, sister.'

'The rest of you could do well to study how Latimer has tucked all her hair out of the way under her cap. This is the way it should be.'

It was Dora's turn to blush.

'These uniforms are not designed to make you look attractive,' Sister Andrews announced. 'In fact, their purpose is quite the opposite. You will be dealing with men as well as women, and you do not want to be the object of unwanted propositions. Patients should see the uniform, and not the woman inside it.'

'Can't see that being a problem for her,' a voice murmured in Dora's ear.

Sister Andrews completed her inspection and said, 'Very well, you may sit down and I will explain to you what form your training will take. You will receive lectures on anatomy, chemistry, physiology, sanitation and food hygiene. You will also be given instruction in ethics and the correct professional approach to your work. But the largest and most important part of your work will take place on the wards, where you will assist the trained nurses in caring for the patients and observe the work of the doctors. Now, you will have realised that we are operating under distinct disadvantages while we wait for the new hospital to be built, but nevertheless we are determined to provide the same standard of care that was the norm in the old St Thomas's. So this morning I am going to take you on a tour of the wards, so you can get some idea of what is expected of you.'

They trooped out of the manor house and followed the path that led them to what had once been a music hall. The cavernous interior had been divided up with temporary partitions. There were two main wards in what had once been the stalls, one for men and one for women, and the galleries above housed two surgical wards, a lying ward and a fever ward. Sister Andrews led them first into the women's ward and Dora caught in a quick breath at the sight of it. Windows had been pierced in the outer walls so that daylight flooded in. The fog of the previous day had dissipated and pale winter sunshine cast long beams across the space. The beds were well separated and there were clean sheets on them. The floor had been polished to a high shine and there were flowers, even at this dead time of year, on the bedside tables. It was their perfume that struck her more forcibly than anything. After the crowded beds and the pervading smell of human excretions that she associated with the infirmary it was hard to believe that this place was full of sick people. No wonder Agnes Jones had been horrified by her first inspection.

'You will notice,' Sister Andrews said, 'that the ward is light and well ventilated. It is one of Miss Nightingale's prime requirements. She is of the opinion that it is the miasma arising from dirt and foul smells that is the primary cause of disease. In her notes on nursing she says that only Nature can heal, but it is our job to provide an environment in which that healing can progress without hindrance.'

The tour of the hospital occupied most of the morning and after dinner there was a lecture in which Sister Andrews outlined what their duties would be. They were divided into three groups, Red Watch, Blue Watch and Green Watch. Dora was pleased to find that Elizabeth and Phil were both in Red Watch with her, though she was less delighted by the inclusion of Julia.

'You will work in shifts,' Sister Andrews said. 'Commencing tomorrow, and for the rest of the week, Red Watch will be on duty from six in the morning until two in the afternoon, Blue Watch will take the shift from two o'clock until ten and Green Watch will take the period from ten pm until six am.'

There was a collective gasp from the members of Green Watch. 'When are we supposed to sleep?' asked a querulous voice.

'You can sleep when you come off duty,' Sister Andrews replied crisply. 'Shifts will rotate each week, so you will all get your turn on night duty. The exception to this pattern will be on Thursdays, when you will all attend lectures. When each shift reports for duty you will be allocated to work in the various wards, depending on the particular needs of the day. You will work at all times under the direction on a qualified nurse, who will expect unquestioning obedience. Is that understood?'

That evening they all had tea together for the last time until Thursday came around and afterwards they sat around the fire in the library. As before, Phil settled herself on the window seat and became absorbed in a book. Dora remembered with a surge of nostalgia that when she lived with the Latimers there had been occasions, few and far between but all the more precious for that, when she had been able to lose herself in a novel. It struck her that she had not opened a book for four years. She looked at Phil and wondered what it was that held her attention so completely. She felt it would be impolite to interrupt, but after a while her curiosity overcame her.

She crossed the room and took a chair near the window. Phil glanced up and gave her a smile.

'Forgive me for intruding,' Dora said. 'I was wondering what it is that you are reading.'

'This,' Phil said, holding out the book. 'It is by a woman called Charlotte Brontë and it is quite brilliant.'

'By a woman?' Dora said. 'The only woman writer I ever heard of was Miss Austen. Is it a novel?'

'Yes. It is the story of a girl called Jane Eyre. I believe Miss Brontë had to pretend to be a man to get it published. But she says so much that strikes a chord with me, things I have vaguely felt but never put into words. Listen to this, for example.' She flicked through the pages to find the passage and read, '"It is in vain to say human beings ought to be satisfied with tranquillity: they must have action; and they will make it if they cannot find it. Women are supposed to be very calm generally: but women feel just as men feel; they need exercise for their faculties, and a field for their efforts, as much as their brothers do; they suffer from too rigid a restraint, too absolute a stagnation, precisely as men would suffer; and it is narrow-minded in their more privileged fellow-creatures to say that they ought to confine themselves to making puddings and knitting stockings, to playing on the piano and embroidering bags. It is thoughtless to condemn them, or laugh at them, if they seek to do more or learn more than custom has pronounced necessary for their sex." There! Do you see? Isn't that exactly why we are all here?'

Dora frowned. 'It's too much to take in all at once. Can I read it for myself?'

'Of course.' Phil handed her the book and she studied the text in silence. After a while she said, 'You are right. It does put into words what has only been dimly felt – or perhaps it is more accurate to say, from my point of view, it makes me think in a way I have never thought before.'

'But you must have felt it,' Phil said, 'or why are you here?'

Dora gave a rueful smile. 'Do not credit me with too much initiative. I am not here because of any decision I made, but because of a chain of circumstances over which I had little control.' She looked round the room. 'I wonder how many of us here could honestly say we are here because we have a real desire to escape from the sort of life most women expect. Julia is here because her father insisted on it, and Hope is here because her father told her it was her duty to God. And I suspect girls like Lily and Pearl are here to escape from a life of poverty.'

'And you?' Phil asked.

Dora dropped her eyes. How could she explain without giving away all the shameful facts of her life? She was saved from her dilemma by Julia.

'What are you two so engrossed in? Just a silly novel?'

'It is not silly!' Phil said hotly. 'It is extremely profound.'

Julia laughed. 'In that case, I don't think I shall try it. It may suit you, Phil, but I have no desire to be a blue stocking.'

'A what?' Dora asked.

'Oh, you know. A woman who wants to be as educated as a man.'

'And why not?' Phil asked.

'Because it is a very unfeminine thing to wish for. No man wants to marry a woman who is as clever as he is.'

'I think that is rubbish!' Phil began. 'Why ...'

The argument was cut short by the bell for bedtime and Dora said, with some relief, 'We should all get some sleep. We have an early start in the morning.'

Chapter 8

Red Watch reported for duty, yawning and shivering in the chill morning air. They were greeted by Sister Andrews who divided them up between the various wards. Dora found herself working on the main women's ward with Julia and Lily, under the direction of a small, plump, fresh-faced young woman with a brisk manner, who introduced herself as Sister Waters. Dora soon found herself falling back into the morning routine she had learned under Agnes Jones, handing out cups of tea, helping patients who could walk to get to the newly installed water-closets, carrying bowls of water to wash the bed-bound.

'You have done this before,' Waters commented after watching her for a while.

'Yes, I have ... had some experience,' Dora agreed.

Before she could be asked to explain further Waters turned sharply away. 'You!' indicating Julia who was standing in the middle of the ward gazing about her. 'Help Mrs Phillips back to bed. Can't you see she is feeling unwell?'

A gaunt, shrivelled woman was making her way back from the WC, bent almost double and swaying as she walked. Julia went to her and tried awkwardly to take her arm. Dora left the patient she was dealing with and moved to her other side, but as she reached her the woman clutched at her stomach and vomited copiously over Julia's feet.

Julia jumped back. 'Ugh! Ohh! Oh, how horrible! What shall I do?' She began shaking her skirt and trying to brush off the vomit.

'Do?' said Waters. 'Clear it up, of course. Latimer, get Mrs Phillips back to bed.'

'I can't! I can't! I'm going to be sick myself,' Julia wailed.

'No, you are not! You are going to fetch a mop and a bucket and clear up this mess,' Waters said.

Dora helped the old woman back into bed. Julia was standing helplessly in the same spot, whimpering. She went over to her.

'Don't worry. I'll see to it. You go and clean yourself up.'

At the same moment Lily appeared at her side with a mop and bucket and the two of them set to work. Lily glanced over her shoulder at the retreating Julia.

'That's the trouble with fine ladies! Never had to clean up after themselves.'

'It doesn't bother you?' Dora said.

Lily grinned. 'Got three little brothers and two sisters, haven't I? I've mopped up a fair bit of puke in my time – and worse.'

Julia returned after a few minutes, looking pale but composed. She had succeeded in removing most of the vomit from her shoes and her skirt was wet where she had scrubbed it.

'Ah, you've decided to re-join us, have you?' Waters said tartly. 'See Mrs Beck over there? She's been sitting on that bedpan for the last ten minutes. Go and get her off it and empty it.'

Dora and Lily exchanged grins. For the rest of the shift, if a bedpan had to emptied, it was always Julia's job to see to it.'

Over the next days, as they were allocated to different wards, a number of images impressed themselves on Dora's mind: Elizabeth's scarlet face as she helped to give a bed bath to a large, tattooed sailor; Phil tenderly lifting a young boy, so crippled by rickets that he could not stand, and carrying him to the window so he could see the first snowdrops blooming under the trees outside; an old lady cackling with laughter at a sly comment from Lily.

The shifts were long and the work was hard, and a good deal of it involved cleaning up mess of one sort or another, scrubbing and polishing. It was clear that this was not quite how the more delicately reared 'ladies' had pictured it and there was initially a tendency to relegate that kind of work to the students, who accepted it as part of the natural order of things. Dora objected to this and tried to set an example by never refusing to do her share of the menial tasks. Phil's attitude was more robust.

'Don't let Julia give you all the nasty jobs!' she adjured Lily. 'Let her do her own dirty work!'

One morning they were informed that they were to have the privilege of attending Dr McIntyre on his rounds. McIntyre was, as his name suggested, a Scot and it was clear from the start that he regarded young women who wished to involve themselves in medical matters as, at best, a source of amusement and at worst an impertinence. As they progressed from bed to bed he singled out all the most unsavoury cases and made a point of asking questions which would cause embarrassment to his listeners. He was fond of exhibiting or describing the symptoms of a patient and then asking if anyone among the trainee nurses could diagnose the cause. It was often one of the students who answered. Most of them were familiar with the symptoms of scarlet fever or measles and rickets. Dora recognised most of the maladies, but she kept in the background, still unwilling to reveal to her colleagues how she had acquired her knowledge.

They came to the bed of a man whose face was covered in sores. McIntyre threw back the covers with a dramatic gesture and pulled the man's nightshirt up to his waist, revealing his genitals, which were swollen and ulcerated.

'There, ladies!' Macintyre exclaimed with the panache of a conjuror producing a particularly large rabbit. 'I do not suppose any of you can tell me what is wrong with this man.'

Dora glanced at her colleagues. Many had their hands to their mouths; some had turned away, others stared with horrible fascination. She looked at the patient and saw his face distorted with humiliation. Instinctively she stepped forward and drew up the sheets.

'It is syphilis,' she said coolly.

McIntyre fixed her with eyes like gimlets. 'And how would you know that, madam?'

'I have seen cases before. I have worked in an infirmary in Liverpool. Such cases were not infrequent among sailors returning from abroad.'

'Indeed! Indeed! So we have an expert amongst us.' McIntyre's sarcastic tone bore witness to his irritation at having his *coup de theatre* spoiled. 'Would you care to explain to your lady companions how such a condition is acquired?'

Dora kept her voice level. 'Through sexual congress with an infected person.'

'Quite so, quite so.' McIntyre nodded, but his expression was anything but approving. 'And is there any treatment?'

'I believe the application of an ointment containing mercury is regarded as being effective; but I have seen no evidence of it.'

'No evidence, eh? So you question established medical practice, do you?'

'I can only speak from my own experience,' Dora replied.

Behind her, Dora could hear little gasps and whispers as her colleagues reacted to what they had heard.

At the bedside of another patient McIntyre said, 'This man is suffering from acute diarrhoea and stomach pains. Now—' he turned to Dora '—what would our medical expert prescribe in this case?'

Dora knew that she had made an enemy, but she refused to be intimidated.

'If he were my patient, I would give him a decoction of chamomile, liquorice and ginger.'

'Chamomile, liquorice and ginger!' the doctor repeated. Then he gave a grim chuckle. 'I should have known! These nostrums may be seen as effective where you come from, madam. But this is a civilised country. Here we put our faith in science, not witchcraft.' Before Dora could respond he turned to the ward sister who was accompanying them. 'There is only one treatment which will be efficacious here. He must be bled and purged. I will see to the bleeding now and give you the purgative to administer later. Bring me a bowl.'

A nurse scurried away and McIntyre turned back to the trainees, a gleam of pure devilry in his eyes. 'Now, how many of you have seen a man bled before?' One or two of the students murmured assent but he ignored them. 'I shall require an assistant. Now, let me see ...' His gaze raked the faces of the young women and fixed on Elizabeth. 'You! Come here.'

Elizabeth advanced to the bedside. Watching her face, Dora could see the struggle between fear and determination in her widened eyes and tightly compressed lips. The nurse came back with an enamel bowl and a roll of bandages. McIntyre delved into a pocket and produced a lancet.

'Hold out your arm, my man,' he demanded. The patient complied, turning his face away with a grimace. 'Now, young lady, hold the bowl under his arm – there, like that. Good. Now, I trust that you are not one of those who faint at the sight of blood?'

'I ... I don't know,' Elizabeth whispered.

'Well, you will never make a nurse if you do,' the doctor told her. 'Now, hold the basin steady.'

Behind her, Dora heard a collective intake of breath as the scalpel punctured a vein. Blood spurted and then flowed in a steady stream into the basin. She saw that Elizabeth had gone very pale and her hands shook.

'Hold it steady, I said!' McIntyre barked.

Elizabeth's jaw muscles stood out as she gritted her teeth. The bowl was filling up and Dora shook her head involuntarily. She had seen this procedure many times before and it had never produced the desired results. At last McIntyre declared that the amount was sufficient, the wound was bandaged and Elizabeth rose shakily to her feet, still holding the basin.

'What ... what shall I ...' she asked tremulously.

'Give it to me,' the nurse who had brought it said and quickly removed it. Dora took hold of Elizabeth's arm.

'Well done!' she whispered. 'That's one test you've passed with flying colours.'

'I thought I was going to faint,' her friend murmured.

'But you didn't. That's what matters.'

McIntyre was preparing to move on. He was looking faintly dissatisfied and Dora guessed that he would have preferred it if Elizabeth had passed out, thus confirming his view that women were unsuited to anything connected with medicine.

They entered the women's fever ward, where there were two cases of typhus.

'This disease is the product of unwholesome air, the miasma arising from human detritus,' McIntyre pronounced.

Phil has said little up to that point. Now she said, 'Excuse me, doctor. I was wondering what you thought of the theories propounded by Dr Pasteur in France.'

McIntyre's eyebrows shot up and he gave a bark of laughter. 'You refer to germ theory? My good woman, you surely cannot give any credence to the notion that there are tiny creatures, too small to be seen by the human eye, which float about in the air we breathe and cause disease! We might as well believe in the old stories of elves and goblins who attacked men and women while they slept and inflicted boils and pustules. We are not living in the

Middle Ages now. This is the age of science, of scientific thinking, not the age of superstition.'

'I thought from what I read . . .' Phil began.

'You have read too much, by the sound of it!' McIntyre exclaimed. 'This is not the sort of literature which is suitable for the female sex. Stick to novels and magazines like *Household Words*. That is suitable reading for young women.'

'You do not approve of women studying medicine, then?' Phil asked. 'What is your opinion of Elizabeth Garret Anderson?'

'A disgrace to her sex, and to the medical profession!' McIntyre's face was dark with fury. It crossed Dora's mind that he was one case that might benefit from bloodletting. 'That is enough for one day,' he continued. 'I shall complete my rounds tomorrow – without the attendance of these presumptuous females.'

As soon as their watch was over Phil and Dora were summoned to the office of Mrs Wardroper.

'I am given to understand that you both had the temerity to question Dr McIntyre's conduct of his cases this morning.'

'I merely asked for his opinion of germ theory,' Phil protested.

'You are not required to study far-fetched theories, still less to question their validity with a qualified medical professional. And you, Latimer. You actually suggested he should prescribe some herbal concoction which, I assume, you learned from your negro ancestors.'

'I learned it from my mother, certainly,' Dora said, 'but experience has shown me that it is effective.'

Mrs Wardroper drew herself up. 'Listen to me, both of you. You may not question the doctors or advance your own theories. Miss Nightingale has made it quite clear that we nurses must always defer to the superior wisdom of our male colleagues. She believes that men are in every respect superior to women and we must act accordingly. Now, if you wish to continue your training here, you must learn respect. If I hear any further complaints I shall have to ask you both to leave. Is that understood?'

Dora caught Phil's eye and gave her a warning shake of her head. She knew already that the other girl found it hard to back down in an argument. Then she lowered her eyes and murmured, 'I'm sorry, ma'am. I didn't mean to cause offence. It won't happen again.'

'And you?' Mrs Wardroper fixed her gaze on Phil.

After a second's hesitation Phil also dropped her eyes. 'Sorry, Mrs Wardroper. I'll be more careful in future.'

Back in the manor house they joined their colleagues for dinner. Immediately Dora was assailed by a barrage of questions.

'How do you know so much?'

'How did you know what that horrible disease was?'

'Have you really worked in an infirmary?'

Dora saw that it was time to fall back on the second part of the story Mr Rathbone had suggested to her.

'Yes,' she responded to the last questioner. 'I have. I told you I was brought up in the family of a sea captain. I did not feel it would be right for me to pursue a life of idleness at their expense. So I volunteered to help in the infirmary attached to the workhouse. I learned a great deal there, but conditions were very bad until Miss Nightingale sent one of her nurses to take charge. It was her idea that I should come here to learn how things should be done.'

'You volunteered?' Hope said. 'That was noble of you.'

'It is only what all of you have done, after all.'

'What you said about that herbal mixture ...' Phil said. 'Would it have helped?'

'More than bleeding and purging,' Dora responded grimly. 'I feel sorry for that poor man.' Then, realising that she was on dangerous ground, she added, 'but please don't tell anyone I said that! Mrs Wardroper is already threatening to dismiss me.'

'Don't worry,' Phil said. 'You can trust us – can't she, ladies?'

There was a murmur of agreement and the conversation turned to other matters.

As the weeks passed and the shifts rotated the prospect of a Sunday when Dora and her friends would be free until the beginning of the night shift came round. On the previous Friday Elizabeth fell into step beside her as they walked back to the manor house.

'I was thinking ... should you care to come to tea with my family on Sunday? We could take a little time to look at some of the London sights first. What do you think?'

'I should like that very much. Thank you.'

It was expected that all the trainees would attend the morning service in the local church, unless they were on duty, so as soon as dinner was over Dora dressed herself in the clothes she had worn to travel to London and joined Elizabeth in the hallway of the manor house. It was March, a day of blustering wind and brilliant sunshine, and the grass under the trees in the park was bright with daffodils. The smoky air of London seemed to have been blown away. Dora took a deep breath. Not since her expulsion from the Latimer household had she been at liberty to stroll in the open air. The high walls of the workhouse had given only glimpses of the sky and the tiny garden where she cultivated her herbs could be crossed in a few paces. Since she arrived at the hospital, her life had been largely confined indoors, except on the brief walk from the manor house to the wards and back. This new freedom was exhilarating, but at the same time she could not escape the feeling that she was in some way transgressing, that some higher authority would soon summon her back within the walls.

Elizabeth seemed to partake in this sense of liberation.

'Come on! Let's not waste a minute. We can take an omnibus from outside the gates.'

The omnibus took them to Trafalgar Square. Dora had seen much to amaze her on the journey but she was unprepared for the huge scale of the square.

'Well, what do you think?' Elizabeth was eager to impress her new friend.

'It is wonderful. There is so much space. I thought London was all crowded streets and small houses.'

'Well, I suppose there are plenty of those, but thank heavens we have room for somewhere like this.'

Dora craned her neck. 'Who is it at the top of that column?'

'It's Admiral Nelson, of course, the victor of the battle of Trafalgar.'

'Of course. I should have guessed. What is that building on the far side?'

'That is the National Gallery. Are you interested in pictures?'

'I have very little experience in that respect, I'm afraid.'

'Well, maybe we will go there one day, but there isn't time now. It is an impressive facade, isn't it?'

Dora thought privately that in her recollection the facade of St George's Hall in Liverpool was more impressive, but she forbore to say so.

They strolled down the Mall until they stood in front of Buckingham Palace. There, Dora had to admit disappointment.

'It doesn't look like my idea of a palace. I expected – I don't know – towers and pinnacles – like the pictures in story books.'

'I know exactly what you mean,' Elizabeth said with a laugh. 'I felt the same the first time I saw it.' She reached into her reticule and took out a watch. 'There is so much more I should like to show you, but there isn't time. My family will be expecting us. Come on, we can walk through the park.'

Dora would have been happy to linger in the park. The wide open expanse of grass, the trees and the flowerbeds full of spring flowers impressed her more than the grand buildings they had seen. But Elizabeth urged her forwards until they came to a terrace of tall stucco-fronted houses in a wide street just off Berkeley Square. She rang the door-bell of one of them and the door was opened not, as Dora expected, by a parlour maid but by a butler, who greeted Elizabeth with a respect that seemed to Dora tinged with a certain reserve.

'Morton, this is my friend Miss Latimer,' Elizabeth announced.

The butler inclined his head. 'Good afternoon, miss.'

As he preceded them to the door of the drawing room Elizabeth whispered, 'Morton doesn't really approve of me. He thinks I should sit at home a sew a fine seam.'

'Miss Elizabeth, madam, and Miss Latimer.'

A tall, slender woman rose to greet them. Dora saw at once that it was from her that Elizabeth derived her English rose fairness, but she recognised at the same time that her friend had a robust solidity that her mother appeared to lack. Mrs Warrender's delicate features and willowy form made her look almost fragile in comparison.

Elizabeth advanced and kissed her on the cheek. 'How are you, Mama?'

'I'm very well, and very pleased to see you.' The voice was surprisingly deep. 'How do you do, Miss Latimer?'

Dora took the proffered hand. 'How do you do, ma'am.'

'I'm so glad to meet you. Elizabeth has mentioned you often in her letters. Please, take a seat.'

As they settled into their chairs Dora had a chance to look round the room. She remembered her stepmother's drawing room, which had been adorned with every kind of ornament. The same impetus has been at work here, unrestrained by any consideration of expense. The walls were papered with an elaborate design of fruits and flowers in pinks and green against a gold background. Swags of gold brocade hung at either side of the windows. There was a deep-piled green carpet, over which were laid several Persian rugs. In the centre of the room there was a round table covered in lace cloth, on which was a collection of ornaments, many of which she recognised as having originated in the far east. Captain Latimer had often brought similar objects back from his voyages and his wife had set great store by them.

'So, Miss Latimer ...' her hostess's voice recalled her to the present. 'Are you of the opinion that what you are learning at the Nightingale school is going to prove worth the effort?'

'Most certainly,' Dora responded.

'And how do you intend to apply your knowledge when the course is over?'

'I shall return to Liverpool and offer my services at the infirmary.'

'Indeed? Do you intend to dedicate your life to such employment?'

For a brief moment the image of Jem's face flashed across Dora's memory, but she banished it. 'Yes, probably.'

'Really, Mama,' Elizabeth protested. 'Dora came here for tea, not to face the inquisition.'

'Forgive me,' Mrs Warrender said. 'Elizabeth has probably told you that I was against her taking up this training. I am unable to understand what possible advantage it can be to a young woman in her position. Of course, I realise that for some people it may have a more direct relevance.'

'I think,' Dora said slowly, 'that it can never be a waste of time to learn how to alleviate the suffering of others – whatever the future may hold for us.'

'There you are, Mama!' Elizabeth exclaimed. 'Dora has put it in a nutshell.'

The door opened to admit the butler. 'Mr Edward, madam.'

A young man entered. Dora had heard Elizabeth speak of her brother but even without that it would not have been hard to identify him. He had the same blond hair and blue eyes and that which in his sister appeared as sturdiness expressed itself in him in the form of broad shoulders and an athletic build. With his fair beard and moustache he reminded her of pictures she had seen of Viking warriors.

Mrs Warrender said, 'Good afternoon, Edward. This is an unexpected pleasure. Will you stay for tea?'

He hesitated in the doorway, looking around the room. His gaze passed over Dora and then returned. She saw the familiar reaction of surprise but also something more subtle, harder to define.

'Forgive me, Mama,' he said. 'I did not know you were entertaining visitors.'

Elizabeth jumped up. 'Goodness, Ned, you don't regard me as a visitor, do you? Don't be so stuffy! I want you to meet my friend, Dora Latimer.'

He inclined his head to her. 'Delighted to make your acquaintance, Miss Latimer. Tell me, have you come from some far distant clime to brighten our dull London scene?'

'Not so very far,' Dora replied.

'I hope you are not finding our climate too uncongenial.'

'It differs very little from Liverpool,' Dora said dryly.

'Liverpool?' If she had thought this might take the wind out of his sails she was wrong. 'I knew it must be somewhere exotic.' His eyes met hers but the expression in them puzzled her. Was he laughing at her? She sensed a challenge of some kind. 'Of course,' he went on, 'that city has long had close connections with Africa and the West Indies.'

She knew very well what the implication of that remark was. He was assuming that her parents, or at least her grandparents, must have come to the city as slaves. She decided that Edward Warrender had far too good an opinion of himself.

'That is true,' she responded. 'My father, who was a sea captain, frequently voyaged to those parts.'

The appearance of the tea trolley interrupted the exchange. It was accompanied by another member of the family whom she realised at once must be Mr Warrender, and it was apparent that it was from him that his children derived their sturdy build. He was a large man, wide shouldered and barrel chested, with large hands that enveloped Dora's when they were introduced.

'So!' he said, kissing Elizabeth, 'is this a temporary escape, or have you decided to give up and come home?'

'I have no intention of giving up,' Elizabeth responded.

'Good for you!'

'Mama,' Edward said as he took his teacup, 'I came to ask you something. I should like you to invite someone to dine with us. His name is Will Barnaby. He's just joined our Chambers and he's an absolutely capital fellow.'

'Then of course I will invite him, if you wish it. Would Wednesday be convenient?'

'Wednesday would be perfect.' He turned to his sister. 'I particularly want you to meet him, Lizzie. He's just the sort of chap to appeal to you.'

'I'm afraid I shall not be there,' Elizabeth replied. 'I shall be working on Wednesday evening.'

'Working! Just what does this "work" consist of?'

'Mostly it involves a great deal of cleaning. Miss Nightingale believes that healing cannot take place if the surroundings are not hygienic.'

'But surely,' Edward said, 'there are others better used to that kind of thing.' His eyes flickered towards Dora. 'You were not brought up to that.'

'There are others, certainly, but I would not ask them to take on my duties as well as their own.'

'Really, Lizzie!' Her brother's voice had taken on an edge of exasperation. 'Are you determined to bury all your prospects in that place?'

'I do not know what you mean by prospects. The prospect that most interests me at the moment is that of becoming a fully qualified nurse.'

Edward threw up his hands in exasperation and turned away.

Mr Warrender turned to Dora. 'Do you share Elizabeth's ambition?'

'Absolutely,' Dora confirmed.

'And are your parents as puzzled by your decision as we are by Elizabeth's?'

'I have no parents. I am an orphan.'

She was aware of a frisson of shock around the room. Mr Warrender recovered first.

'You have other family, perhaps? Where do you live?'

'I live in Liverpool, but I have no family there.'

'And none here in London?'

'No.'

'Then you must regard us as substitutes and call on us whenever you wish,' he said. There was a warmth in his tone that made her feel that the invitation was genuine.

'That is very kind of you,' Dora responded, feeling a catch in her throat. 'But I am occupied most of the time at the hospital.'

'Surely,' Mr Warrender said, 'you must get some time off. They can't keep you cooped up all the time.'

'Well, we have a holiday at Easter, just over the weekend,' Elizabeth said.

'Well, then,' her father responded jovially, 'why don't you and Miss Latimer come down to our country place for the holiday? I expect you could both benefit from some country air.'

Elizabeth glanced at Dora. 'Should you like that?'

Dora hesitated. 'I should not wish to intrude on a family gathering.'

'Nonsense,' said Mr Warrender. 'We enjoy having guests. You will be most welcome.'

'Anyway,' Elizabeth said, 'if you don't go, I shan't go either.'

That settled the matter and soon after that, Elizabeth declared that they must be heading back to Surrey Gardens. Edward insisted on accompanying them to the omnibus. As they were about to climb aboard he took Dora's hand.

'I hope I have not offended you. If I did I apologise.'

'I accept your apology,' she replied. 'Let us say no more about it.'

On the bus she turned to Elizabeth. 'I'm sure Sister Andrews would let you go for once if you want to have dinner with your family.'

'But that's just it! I don't,' Elizabeth responded. 'I know exactly what Edward is after. He wants to see me married off and he thinks this Barnaby fellow might be a possible suitor. I've had quite enough of his matchmaking, thank you.'

'Why is he so keen for that?'

'Because he thinks I might be bad for his career. He's studying for the Bar, as you know, and he's afraid that an unmarried sister who is ... well, behaving unconventionally ... might be bad for his reputation.'

'That is ridiculous!' Dora said.

'I know, but it's the way the world works. Women are supposed to stay at home and knit. Mother is on his side, of course. She's afraid that I might spoil my value on the marriage market and end up an old maid.'

'Well, any man who's frightened off marriage to a beautiful girl like you, just because she's had the strength of character to learn something useful, isn't worthy of you anyway,' Dora said. After a pause she went on, 'I must admit, the more I hear about your brother, the less I like him.'

'I was afraid of that,' Elizabeth said with a sigh. 'Please don't make up your mind yet. He likes to tease but he doesn't always think how it affects other people.'

'That doesn't sound like the ideal qualification for a barrister,' Dora commented.

'I know. It was father's idea he should go in for the law. He wanted him to have a profession, but I'm not sure he is really suited to it. Don't judge him too harshly. He's very warm-hearted, when you get to know him, and he can be great fun, too.'

'I'll try to give him the benefit of the doubt, for your sake,' Dora said. After a moment she went on, 'What is this "place in the country" your father mentioned?'

Elizabeth laughed briefly. 'Oh, it's a crumbling old pile down in Surrey that he's bought and had refurbished so he can play the country squire.' Her expression became more serious. 'Because our money comes from industry, people with inherited wealth look down on us. We're "new money" so we are not supposed to have the same standards as they do. I don't care, personally, but Mama does. She really is the squire's daughter and grew up on the family estate in Hertfordshire. I'm afraid she sometimes feels she has married beneath her and Papa is desperate to make up for it.'

'How did they come to marry, in the first place?'

'My grandfather wanted to bring some of the farm machinery up to date. He asked my father to advise him. Father went to see what was needed, met mother and swept her off her feet, as the saying goes. I think he was a very good-looking man in those days.'

'He still is,' Dora said.

Elizabeth reached out and squeezed her hand. 'I'm really looking forward to Easter now. We'll have a good time. Just you wait and see.'

Chapter 9

One of the most distressing aspects of the work, for Dora and for her fellow trainees, was the number of children who were brought to the hospital. Dirty and ill-fed, many needed treatment for injuries that might have been avoided if a little more care had been taken. There were burns from unguarded fires, scalds from overturned kettles, cuts from knives left carelessly within reach. It seemed for all Dr McIntyre's vaunted 'scientific age' there was little that could be done, particularly for the burns and scalds.

One evening, after she had been sitting by the bedside of a small girl with a badly scalded arm, she exclaimed to Lily who was working alongside her, 'I don't understand it. How can people allow these things to happen?'

'If you saw the way most folks live, you wouldn't need to ask,' Lily replied.

'How do you mean?'

'Well, if you've got six little 'uns all under your feet in one small room, it's hard to keep an eye on all of them. ''Specially if you've got some out-work to do, sewing and the like, to keep them all fed – and a man coming in and wanting his dinner.'

'Is that how a great many people live in London?' Dora asked.

'Don't you have poor people where you come from?'

'Yes, of course. I've met plenty of them in the work-house infirmary. But I haven't seen what their homes are like.'

Lily put her head on one side and considered her. 'I can't make you out sometimes. You talk like a lady, and you act like a lady, but you work like you was one of us. Have you ever known what it's like to be poor?'

Dora had a vivid memory of the months she had spent between leaving the Latimer's house and being taken in to the workhouse, but that was part of her history that she had no intention of sharing with anyone.

She side-stepped the question. 'I've seen what it does to people.'

'You want to see how folks live round where I come from? Come with me, next time our shift ends at two o'clock. I'll show you.'

Dora realised that she might have given offense. 'But you, Lily ... you don't live like that, do you?'

Lily shook her head. 'We're some of the lucky ones. My pa has a trade. He's a butcher, works down Smithfield market, brings home a decent wage. Not but what it doesn't go far with so many mouths to feed, but he brings back bones for soup, offal sometimes. We've never gone hungry. But there's plenty of folk round about who struggle to make ends meet and live in pretty poor conditions. Will you come?'

'I should like to, very much, if you are sure I will not be ... well, intruding.'

'No need to worry about that. My ma will be glad to meet you. And you ought to see that side of life. Genteel folk like Julia have no idea how the rest of us live and don't want to know. But you ... you're different.'

A few days later Dora boarded the omnibus with Lily and took a ticket for Shoreditch. As they travelled she realised that she knew very little about Lily's family, apart from what she had told her on that first day on the ward.

'You said you had younger brothers and sisters, Lily. How old are they?'

'Well, there's Dan, the eldest. He's sixteen. He works with our dad, learning the butchery trade. Then there's Meg. She's fourteen, but you won't meet her today. She's gone into service with a dentist's family. Biddy's twelve. She works in the grocer's up the road from us. That leaves the two boys. Johnny's still at the board school – he's seven, and then there's Micky. He's four.'

'So Johnny is the only one at school.'

'Biddy was until last summer. We all went to school until we turned twelve. Like I said, we were some of the lucky ones.'

'What did you do, then, between your twelfth birthday and starting the nurse's training?'

'I was at home, helping to take care of the little ones. But now they're mostly off my mother's hands I have a chance to do something to improve myself.'

'You certainly deserve it,' Dora said.

'Here we are,' Lily said. 'We get off here.'

The street here was lined with small, respectable-looking houses. Lily led her to the door of one of them and knocked. It was opened by a small boy, who threw his arms around her yelling, 'Ma, Lily's here! Come quick!'

The front door led straight into a living room, shabbily furnished but giving an immediate impression of homely comfort. A door on the far side opened to give a glimpse of a kitchen, where clothes were hanging to dry on a folding clothes horse, and a woman came through it. Her hair was grey and her figure was broad but spare and bony, except where the swell of her belly proclaimed that she was expecting yet another child. She hurried forward and embraced Lily.

'Oh, it's good to see you, luv. You look well! They must be feeding you all right at that nurse's home.'

'Yes, they feed us very well,' Lily said with a smile. 'See, Ma, I've brought a friend with me. This is Dora Latimer.'

Mrs Baker turned her attention to Dora. 'Pleased to meet you, I'm sure.'

Her tone expressed a certain reserve and Dora guessed that she was trying place her in the hierarchy of students.

Lily said, 'Dora's one of the ladies, but she works alongside the rest of us. We get on well, don't we, Dora?'

'Yes, we do. Lily's worth two of most of the others. She's got more sense than the rest of them put together.'

'Well, I'm glad to hear it,' Mrs Baker's face warmed in a welcoming smile. 'I'm always glad to meet a friend of Lily's. You'll stay and have a cup of tea with us?'

Dora hesitated, unwilling to place an extra burden on what she guessed was an over-stretched budget but not wanting to give offence by refusing.

Lily stepped in. 'I'm going to show Dora the Old Nicol. I want her to see how some folks have to live. We'll be back for tea later.'

'Well, you mind how you go,' Mrs Baker said. 'It's a rough place, full of bad people. I'd leave your bag here, if I was you, miss. Otherwise you might get it snatched.'

Dora took her advice and followed Lily outside. A short way beyond the house a narrow alley pierced through the red-brick terrace and at the far end of it she found herself in a very different world. The alley opened out into a muddy courtyard. On three sides there were houses, three or four stories tall, their facades twisted and sagging as if they were leaning against each other for support. On the fourth side a row of doorless privies gave forth a powerful stench of excrement. In the centre stood a pump. A thin-faced girl was working the handle and Dora saw that the water was a sickly greenish brown.

'Why is the water that colour?' she asked her companion.

Lily grimaced. 'I've heard people say that the cesspit under the privies leaks and that gets into the well.'

They passed through another alleyway on the far side of the court and came out into a street. Here the houses showed signs that they had once been respectable dwellings, but at ground level more alleyways had been pierced through to reach others behind them. Many of the ground floor rooms lacked doors and windows and displayed a conglomeration of broken chairs, stained rugs, tin baths and sacks of rubbish. Few of the upper windows had glass in them. Some had been boarded up, others had pieces of sacking stuffed into the gaps, the roofs sagged and in several places the tiles were missing. Down the centre of each alley there was an open drain, which emptied its effluvia into the gutters on either side of the street.

Lines of washing stretched from one side of the street to the other, so that Dora had to duck her head to pass under them. Women leaning in their doorways shouted to each other across the space. On a corner a group of men stood smoking and regarding Lily and Dora with suspicion. A little band of ragged children abandoned their game of hopscotch and clustered round, holding out their hands for money.

'I've nothing to give them,' Dora whispered, ashamed.

'Just as well,' Lily responded. 'Let anyone see you have money on you and you won't keep it long. Come this way. I know the people who live here.'

She went to an open doorway that gave on to a rickety flight of stairs and called, 'Peggy, are you there? It's me, Lily.'

After a brief pause a young girl appeared at the top of the stairs, with a baby at her breast. 'Who's that with you?' she asked.

'It's a friend, someone who's learning to be a nurse, like me. Can we come up?'

The girl stood back and Lily led the way up the stairs. 'Mind where you step,' she warned over her shoulder. 'Some of the treads are rotten.'

A door led off the stairway into a room where Peggy was waiting for them. It was furnished with an iron bedstead on which was a stained mattress and a thin blanket. There was a small table bearing a chipped china basin and a small collection of unwashed plates and cups and beside it two chairs with sagging bottoms. In one corner a second mattress was laid directly on the floor. Rough planks had been nailed across the space where a window had once been, except for a corner where a dirty pane of glass let in a little light.

Lily made the introductions and explained, 'Peg and I were at school together, but she got married soon after we left. How's Sid, Peggy?'

The girl shrugged. 'Drinks too much, like all of them.'

'So how many babes have you got now?'

'Four, including this one.'

'Where are they now?'

'Jack'll be at work. He's gone for a climbing boy, working for a chimney sweep. Pol sells matches, down Covent Garden way. The little un's out there somewhere.'

'And what is this little one called?' Lily reached out her arms and took the child.

'He's Billy.'

The baby began to yell and Lily rocked him. 'Ah, bless him. We've interrupted his dinner. Here, Dora, do you want to hold him for a minute?'

Dora looked at the child, at the contorted face, the tiny open mouth, the face turning this way and that, blindly searching for the breast, and a tidal wave of memory rose inside her. She almost pushed away the child Lily was holding out to her. 'No, no!' Then recovering herself, 'I think we should go, Lily. We are stopping Peggy feeding him.'

'Oh, don't worry about that,' the girl said. 'He won't mind.'

She opened her blouse and put the baby to her breast. Against her stick-thin arms and bony shoulders the swollen breast struck Dora as almost obscene.

To distract herself she asked, 'How many people live in this house – if you don't mind me asking?'

Peggy screwed up her eyes. 'Let me think. There's the Coulters on the next floor, her and him and their five children; then there's old Ma Robinson and her son below us. And the top floor's let out by the night to anyone who can pay tuppance for a mattress and a blanket. But they'd have to be pretty desperate. There's a hole in the roof you could drive a horse and cart through.'

'That's terrible,' Dora murmured. 'Terrible.' But all she could think of was an urgent desire to get away. She had known poverty, when she worked for the washerwoman and slept on the floor in the back kitchen, but she had been too stunned by the change in her own fortunes to pay much attention to what was going on around her. In the workhouse she had seen the results of deprivation and bad living conditions, but even at its worst the infirmary had never produced the sense of hopelessness she was experiencing now.

To her great relief Lily stood up. 'We should go, Peg. My ma is expecting us to have tea with her.' She bent and kissed the other girl quickly on the cheek. 'Take care of yourself – and the little fellow.'

Outside, as they made their way back along the foul smelling alleyway, Lily said, 'I think this has given you a bit of a shock. I'm sorry if it has upset you.'

'I should have to be made of stone not to be upset to see people living like that,' Dora said. 'But what help is there for it? Someone should do something.'

'Aye, so they should,' Lily agreed grimly. 'The question is, who.'

'The government, I suppose.'

'Parliament is full of rich men who have no idea what life is like for the poor.'

'So, what's the answer?'

'You should talk to my dad. He's joined something called the Reform League. They think every man in the country should be able to vote.'

'Every man?' Dora repeated. 'Even men like that?' She nodded towards the little knot of men smoking on the corner.

'Why not? It's their lives that are affected when the government make new laws.'

Dora looked at her. 'I didn't realise you were interested in politics.'

Lily gave a half ironic shrug. 'It's hard not to be, when you live with a man like my dad.'

When they reached Lily's house they found that her father had returned, bringing her eldest brother with him. Soon they were joined by Biddy and the family sat down to tea. The fare was not as varied or as copious as it was in the nurses' home, but Dora was relieved to see that there was enough to go round, even with an extra mouth to feed. The talk centred to begin with on their experiences in the hospital and Biddy announced that when she was old enough she intended to follow in her sister's footsteps. Then, in a break in the conversation, Lily said, 'Pa, I've been showing Dora how some people live in Old Nicol and she agrees with us that something should be done. I started telling her about the Reform League and I think she'd like to hear more.'

'Now then, Lily,' her mother admonished her. 'I've told you before, politics is men's business. It's not something for you to get mixed up in.'

'But surely,' Dora said, 'it is something that should concern us all. I'd like to hear more, Mr Baker, if you don't mind.'

'It's very straightforward,' he said. 'We believe that all adult men should be able to vote, whether they own property or not. The old reform act went some way in the right direction, but it still only allows men who have land or a steady income to vote. It's time it was extended to all of us. We have been holding meetings for best part of a year now, and the membership is growing every day.'

'But what can you actually do?'

'We can bring pressure to bear on the government, and it looks like it's working. Mr Gladstone is on our side and he's promised to bring forward a Bill at the earliest opportunity.'

'Mr Gladstone!' Lily exclaimed. 'If he's on our side we are bound to win.'

'Let us hope so,' her father agreed. 'But he'll have his work cut out to convince his own party, let alone the Tories.'

The discussion went on until Lily exclaimed, 'Look at the time! We need to get on the next omnibus or we shall be late for lights out.'

As she prepared for bed that night Dora turned over in her mind what she had seen and heard that day. It was becoming apparent that her life in the workhouse had given her a very limited view of society and she knew nothing about politics. She scarcely knew the difference between Liberals and Tories and had always assumed that the government of the country was something so remote that it was no concern of hers. She saw now that she had a great deal to learn.

These thoughts, however, were not the ones that kept her awake that night. For the first time in many months, as she drifted on the edge of sleep, she allowed the memory of her son to come to the surface of her mind. The sight of Peggy's baby had triggered a stab of guilt and later, while she was having tea with the Bakers, little Micky had climbed onto Lily's lap and snuggled down with his head on her shoulder. Her own boy would be just about the same age. Where was he now, this child to whom she had never even given a name? Was there someone who would take him on her lap and cuddle him? Or was he like one of the children she had seen playing in the street, dirty and half-starved? Had he been forced to become a climbing boy, scrambling up chimneys to dislodge the soot? Was he begging, or selling matches? Who would give him his next meal? Dora rolled over in bed and pressed her face into the pillow to stifle the sound of her sobs.

Waking the next morning, the scramble to get ready in time for her early shift left no time for introspection and she plunged into her work as a welcome refuge. Later, walking back to the manor house, Phil fell in beside her.

'I saw you and Lily heading for the omnibus,' she said. 'Where were you off to?'

It struck Dora that Phil was probably, of all her friends, the most likely to be interested in what she had seen and learned yesterday. She gave her a brief description of conditions in the Old Nicol.

'It's not just in the cities,' Phil said. 'I've seen terrible poverty in the countryside as well. Townsfolk think that because poor farm labourers live in the middle of nature's bounty they need never go hungry, but you can still be given six months' hard labour for poaching a rabbit. I've seen women in the winter grubbing in the soil for turnips that might have been missed during the harvest; young boys who should be in school sent out to scare the birds off the crops, or watch over the herds; old men almost crippled by rheumatism staggering out to work in the fields because they can't afford to lose a day's wages.'

'Surely something should be done – but isn't it up to the government to put it right?'

'Why should they want to? Most of them are landowners and they don't want Parliament interfering with the way they farm their land. The mill owners and the mine owners don't want to lose the cheap labour children provide. The MPs don't want to risk losing the support of the men who vote them in.'

'Lily's father thinks the answer is to allow all adult men to vote. He belongs to something called the Reform League. He says Mr Gladstone is going to put a Bill before Parliament to permit it.'

Phil shrugged ironically. 'I wish him luck, but I cannot see it getting through.'.

Dora's thoughts had been so taken up with what Lily had shown her that she had almost forgotten her meeting with the Warrenders, until the next day Elizabeth caught up with her as they headed for the wards.

'I've got a letter from Edward. He wants to take us both to the theatre.'

'Both of us? Are you sure?'

'Yes.'

Dora shook her head. 'I don't believe he really wants me to come. Why don't you go on your own?'

'No, he's very insistent. He says he thinks he made a bad impression on you and he wants to put it right.'

'Well, he's certainly right about the bad impression.' Dora agreed.

'Oh, do come!' Elizabeth said. 'Ned's really quite a good sort when you get to know him. And if you are coming to stay over Easter it will be much better if you've broken the ice first.'

Dora hesitated. 'When does he want us to go?'

'Next week. On Thursday, when we don't have our regular shifts.'

'I ... I don't know. What would we see?'

'He suggests we might go to a music hall. Would you like that?'

'I've never been to a music hall.'

'No, nor have I. Do let's say yes!'

'Oh, very well, if you are really keen to go. I suppose it would be uncivil of me to refuse his offer.'

'Excellent!' Elizabeth said. 'I'll write back by return of post.'

Dora had many misgivings about the projected outing. She disliked the idea of putting herself under any sort of obligation to Elizabeth's brother, but she did not want to offend her friend. Besides that, she had never been to any sort of theatre. The Latimers had not been in the habit of attending performances and while she was in the workhouse such a thing was out of the question. She had the impression that there were rules regarding etiquette and dress that she did not know. Above all, she was not sure what to expect from Edward. She just knew that it was very important not to embarrass herself in front of him.

When the day came, she put on the striped silk poplin that had been made for her in Liverpool and wrapped her cloak over it. They took the omnibus to Leicester Square and found Edward waiting for them outside the Alhambra Theatre. He kissed Elizabeth and offered his hand to Dora.

'I'm delighted that you accepted my invitation. I was afraid that I had blotted my copy book once and for all in your estimation.'

'You apologised and I accepted,' Dora said stiffly. 'So perhaps we can make a fresh start.'

'Yes, please! That is all I ask for,' he agreed.

When they entered the theatre Dora found it was not at all as she had expected. Instead of rows of seats men and women were sitting around tables and most of them had glasses of wine or beer in front of them. The air was thick with the smoke of cigars and cigarettes and loud with conversation.

'I hope you approve of my choice,' Edward said. 'I could have suggested a play at one of the legitimate theatres, but that can be rather dry fare. Here we should get a pretty varied programme and it is pleasant to be able to chat over a drink.'

He led them to a table and when a waiter approached he asked, 'Now what can I get you ladies to drink?'

Dora felt a moment of panic. She had no idea what to ask for. Elizabeth came to the rescue.

'I should like a glass of ginger beer, please. I don't want anything alcoholic.'

'I'll have the same,' Dora said.

Edward ordered a beer and while they waited for it to arrive he turned to Dora. 'How do you find London compares with Liverpool?'

'I have seen so little of it that it's hard to judge,' she answered.

'But do you miss your own city? Are you homesick?'

Dora shook her head slowly. How could she be homesick, when she had no home?

Elizabeth filled the pause. 'We're far too busy to think about home. You have no idea how hard we work, Edward.'

Edward raised his eyebrows. 'Well, it beats me why you want put yourselves to so much trouble. After all, when you have families of your own all you will be required to do is soothe the fevered brow and let the doctors do whatever else is necessary.'

'You don't understand ...' Elizabeth began, but she was cut short by the sound of a gavel beating on a table. The hubbub in the auditorium subsided and faces turned to the stage, where a florid man with a huge moustache was seated on a high stool beside a table.

'My lords, ladies and gentlemen, welcome to the Alhambra ...'

From that moment Dora forgot about Edward. She even forgot about the hospital and the workhouse. She was carried away on a tide of music and lights and brilliant costumes. There were dancers and singers and a conjuror and a man who recited comic monologues, and another man who told jokes that she did not understand but which had the rest of the audience roaring with laughter.

In the interval they strolled around the foyer to stretch their legs. Elizabeth left them to go to the ladies' room and Edward paused and looked at Dora.

'Would you be offended by a personal compliment?'

'I don't know what you mean.'

'I just want to say how much I admire that gown. It suits you to perfection.'

Dora felt herself blush and could only murmur, 'That's very kind of you.'

To her relief the bell sounded to indicate that the interval was over and they returned to their seats.

When the show was over Edward said, 'I hope you enjoyed that.'

Dora was able to answer quite sincerely, 'Oh, yes! I did, very much. Thank you inviting me.'

He flatly refused to allow them to travel back to the hospital on the omnibus and insisted on escorting them in a hansom cab. On the journey they discussed the various acts they had seen, and he showed a lively sense of humour but also a critical appreciation of the more serious items, particularly the musical ones.

Apropos of one of these latter items he said, 'Are you fond of music, Dora?'

'I enjoy listening,' she replied, 'but I'm afraid I am quite uneducated in that respect.'

'Perhaps you would care to accompany me to a concert one day,' he suggested.

Without stopping to think she replied, 'Yes, I should like that very much.' Then she glanced at Elizabeth, who responded with an encouraging smile.

At the door of the manor house he handed them both down from the cab, kissed Elizabeth and then took Dora's hand. 'It has been a great pleasure to get to know you a little better, Dora. I hope we can meet again soon.'

There was something about the expression in his blue eyes that made her heart beat a little faster. 'I see no reason why we shouldn't,' she responded.

Before she could withdraw her hand he bent his head and kissed it. Then he swung himself back into the cab and it pulled away. Elizabeth squeezed her arm. 'I'm so glad you've seen a different side of my brother. He's quite nice, really, isn't he?'

Dora smiled back at her. 'Yes, I suppose he is.'

On 22nd March, while Dora was eating breakfast prior to starting the 10am shift, Phil placed a folded copy of the *Morning Advertiser* in front of her.

'Well, Gladstone has kept his word. The Bill has been published, but that is just the start. I very much doubt it will ever be passed into law.'

'But it is a start, isn't it? 'Dora said. 'Where's Lily? She must see this!'

Lily was triumphant. 'It's really happening, at last. All the work my dad and his friends have put in is paying off.'

But the excitement was short-lived as further newspaper reports told them that the Bill was bogged down with dozens of amendments. Dora gave up trying to follow its progress and turned her mind to a more immediate prospect. Easter was only a week away.

As the time grew closer, Dora's anxious apprehension grew stronger. She had no idea what might be expected of her or how she should conduct herself. More urgently, she was worried about what to wear. Apart from her nurse's uniform she still had only the travelling dress she had arrived in and the striped silk poplin. She hesitated to ask Elizabeth for fear of embarrassing her so in the end she turned to Phil for advice.

'Fashion has never been my strong suit,' Phil responded, 'but I suppose I have endured enough country house weekends to have some idea of the basic requirements. Let's see. I expect there will be country walks during the day, and parlour games or cards in the evening. You can arrive in the green wool, but it would be a shame to risk getting it muddy on a walk, so I suggest a sensible tweed skirt with a nice blouse for daytime. The silk poplin is very attractive but perhaps you need something a bit more sophisticated for evening.'

'But I've left it too late!' Dora mourned. 'I don't even know a dress maker who could produce what I need in time.'

'You are probably right there, but there is a solution. There are places where you can buy ready-made clothes. There is a shop in Pall Mall called the Grand Fashionable Magazine. I'm sure they would be able to fit you out. Tell you what, we are on the early shift next week. I'll come with you if you like.'

'Would you? I should be so grateful.'

In a drawer in her little cubicle Dora had three envelopes containing the monthly cheques that Mr Rathbone had sent, as he promised. She had never cashed them, partly because she had not needed any extra money but also because she had never been inside a bank. On the omnibus heading for Trafalgar Square she confessed as much to Phil.

'I'm afraid I have lived a very sheltered life. I know so little of how the world works, outside of a hospital.'

Phil sighed. 'You are not alone. So many women are brought up to know nothing of money or financial matters, so that they have to depend on husbands and fathers for even the most basic necessities. Luckily, I have always insisted on my independence. You can trust me. I'll show you what to do.'

With £12 in her reticule, Dora followed her guide into the Fashionable Magazine and found herself in a new world, a world of colour and scent and movement, as vivid as a kaleidoscope. There were hats and scarves and gloves in profusion and women in elegant gowns strolled among them. Dora would have wandered aimlessly, but Phil's business-like approach whisked her up to the department that dealt with ladies' fashions, where she buttonholed an assistant.

'This young lady requires an ensemble suitable for country walking and an evening dress.'

Half an hour later, Dora was in possession of a tweed skirt in a blend of muted lilacs and mauves, a high-collared blouse in a deeper purple, and a low-necked evening dress in red silk, with a flounced skirt drawn back into a train and supported by a bustle.

'There,' said Phil, 'you are equipped for any eventuality. Go and enjoy yourself.'

Chapter 10

Lillden Hall was set on the south-facing slope of the North Downs, not far from Guildford. Elizabeth explained, as they approached it in the open carriage which had brought them from the station, that it had been originally a rather plain Georgian house, which her father had brought up to date with a number of additions. These included at one end of the building an octagonal tower surmounted by a pointed turret, mullioned windows, a gabled roof and a series of twisted chimneys. The drive leading to it ran through park land and was shaded by an avenue of limes and in front of the house the ground was laid out in a series of formal beds, bright with spring flowers.

The carriage came to a standstill at the foot of a double flight of steps leading up to the main door.

'Here we are!' Elizabeth said. 'Come along in.'

Dora followed her up the steps with a chill feeling of anxiety in the pit of her stomach. This was far grander than any house she had ever been in, even in the days when her father was alive and the Latimers were entertained by local gentry in Liverpool. She did not know what to expect and she was afraid of making some *faux pas*, which would betray her ignorance. When the door was opened by Morton, the butler, with his habitual expression of disapproval, her fears were confirmed. The spacious entrance hall lived up to her first impression. The floor was marble and the walls were panelled in dark wood. To one side, a grand staircase with elaborately carved banisters swept up to a galleried landing and hanging on the wall beside it were a number of oil paintings, their colours and outlines dim with age. She hesitated, uncertain what to do next, but moments later reassurance arrived in the shape of Mr Warrender, who came running down the stairs and swept Elizabeth into his arms.

'I thought I heard the carriage. It's good to see you. Are you well?'

'Very well, thank you, Papa.'

'And Miss Latimer. I'm so glad you decided to accept my invitation. Welcome to Lillden Hall.'

Dora took his proffered hand. 'Thank you for inviting me.'

He made an expansive gesture that took in their surroundings. 'Well, what do you think? Does the old place make a good first impression?'

'It's very ... grand,' Dora said.

'It is, isn't it?' he agreed earnestly. 'Grand! That's exactly it. Now, you are not to stand on ceremony. Make yourself at home, and if there is anything you require, don't hesitate to ask.'

'Thank you.'

'You'll be needing some refreshment after the journey, but perhaps you would like to see your room first, eh, Elizabeth? Is that the best way?'

'Yes, that would be best,' his daughter agreed. 'At least give us time to take off our bonnets.'

'Of course, of course. I believe we've put Miss Latimer in the blue room, next to yours.'

'Good. Come along, Dora. I'll show you where.'

Dora was slightly disconcerted when Elizabeth opened the door of the room to find that her luggage had already been brought up and a young girl in housemaid's uniform was busy unpacking it. She stopped as Dora entered and bobbed curtsy.

'Good morning, miss. My name is Freda. I'll be looking after you while you are here.'

Dora tried to look as if she took such attentions for granted and thanked her.

'You'll be wanting to wash your hands and face, I expect,' the girl said. 'There's warm water here, and the bathroom and the WC are just at the end of the passage. Mr Warrender's had all the modern conveniences installed. I hope you will be comfortable.'

'I'm sure I shall,' Dora responded.

A short time later she followed Elizabeth down to the dining room, where a selection of sandwiches and a pitcher of fresh lemonade awaited them. While they were eating, the door opened to admit Edward.

'Ah, you're here! I was down in the stables so I didn't hear you arrive.' He kissed his sister and turned to Dora. 'I'm so glad you decided to join us. We shall have a capital time. The weather seems to be set fair and I have planned for all sorts of jaunts.'

'What have you got in mind?' Elizabeth asked.

'Well, it depends on what Dora wants to do. Do you ride?'

'Ride?' Dora repeated. 'No.'

'Pity! Never mind, there are plenty of places to go to on foot, or we can take the dog cart. Now, has Lizzie shown you round?'

'I haven't had a chance,' Elizabeth said. 'We only arrived a few minutes ago.'

'Good! Then I can do the honours. Are you ready?'

He insisted on giving Dora a comprehensive tour of the house. It was certainly impressive but as they went from one room to another Dora found herself overwhelmed. There was so much opulence, so much marble and velvet and gilded cornices, so many paintings and ornaments, that she began to long for simplicity and space. She remembered Mr Warrender's eager response when she said the house was grand, and Elizabeth's remark about him wanting to play the country squire. All this was intended to put him on an equal footing with the local gentry.

So far she had not seen her hostess. Mrs Warrender arrived in time for dinner and explained that she had been to call on some families in the nearby village.

'Poor old Mrs Stevens is losing her sight,' she reported. 'I sat and read to her for a while. And I took Ada Jackson some calves foot jelly. She's still quite weak after the birth of the baby.'

Clearly, Dora thought, she was in her element playing the squire's wife. In contrast to her husband's bonhomie, her attitude to Dora was somewhat distant. Dora could not decide whether this was because of her colour, or because she could not lay claim to any well-born relatives – or perhaps simply because she disapproved of Elizabeth's decision to study nursing and saw Dora as encouraging her.

'Now then,' Mr Warrender said as they finished the meal, 'I don't know what you young people have got planned but I have a couple of suggestions. I should like to have arranged a ball, but I'm told that it would not be appropriate in view of the religious nature of the holiday. But I have invited a few guests to join us tomorrow evening – just local people – and I dare say we shall manage a bit of dancing. And on Sunday afternoon I thought we might all go for a picnic on Leith Hill, if the weather stays fine. What do you think?'

There seemed to be no objections so the plan was approved.

The afternoon was spent exploring the extensive grounds attached to the Hall. It was a glorious spring day, with a lively breeze that sent small white clouds bowling across the sky and set the daffodils under the trees dancing. The impression of space and air made Dora feel almost dizzy. Elizabeth led her through the formal garden, which fell away in a series of terraces, and into the woods beyond. Dora came to a standstill, breathless with wonder. On all sides the silvery columns of beech trees rose towards the sky and at her feet the ground was carpeted with bluebells.

'Oh, this is wonderful, wonderful!' she murmured.

Elizabeth took her arm. 'Yes, it is, isn't it!'

Edward had declined to join them, citing pressure of work, but at tea time he took a seat beside Dora.

'Tell me a little more about what you are learning at the hospital. There must be more to it than scrubbing and cleaning.'

Dora told him about the lectures in anatomy and physiology and the experience of following doctors on their rounds.

'And what is your impression of the treatment they prescribe?' he asked.

'They talk about this being the age of science, but their methods have not changed, as far as I can see, since the Middle Ages.'

'You would do things differently?'

'Perhaps. But who am I to criticise qualified doctors?'

'I have been reading reports in the newspapers about this new theory put forward by Dr Pasteur.'

'Germ theory? Dr McIntyre laughed it out of court when someone asked him about it.'

He sighed and shook his head. 'Why is it so hard to get people to accept new ideas? The law is the same. Because things have always been done in a certain way, they must continue to follow the same pattern.' He looked at her. 'There is more to all this than I realised. I begin to see that nursing can be regarded as a profession – something I have always denied before.'

She raised an eyebrow. 'I am sure Elizabeth will be very grateful for your revised opinion.'

'You are mocking me!'

'Not I.'

'You think I am being condescending.'

'There is a saying – something about caps and fitting.'

'I see. But I assure you, my interest is genuine. I hope I shall be able to make you believe that.'

She met his eyes and saw that he was serious. It occurred to her that perhaps she needed to revise her first opinion of him.

Later, when the tea things had been cleared away, Elizabeth suggested that it was time to change their clothes for the evening. Dora put on the striped silk poplin, keeping the red evening dress for the more formal occasion on the next day. Her anxiety had returned, remembering what Phil had said about party games and cards. In the event, music was the chosen entertainment. Mr Warrender had a fine baritone voice and sang a selection of popular songs, accompanied by his wife on the piano. Then, after some protests, Elizabeth was persuaded to join him in a duet. Then came the moment Dora had been dreading.

'Perhaps Miss Latimer would give us a song,' Mrs Warrender said. 'Or do you play the piano?'

'I'm afraid not,' Dora said. 'And I have no singing voice either.'

'Oh, come now,' her hostess persisted. 'Surely you must have studied some form of music when you were growing up.'

Edward came to her rescue. 'Leave Dora alone, Mama. Not everyone likes to perform. Anyway, it's my turn now.'

'Very well.' Mrs Warrender left the piano and Edward took her place.

At once Dora was transfixed. She recalled that he had told her he was fond of music and had spoken of taking her to a concert, but she had never suspected that he might be a talented musician himself. The Latimer girls had had music lessons, in which Dora had joined, but neither of them had shown any aptitude for the piano. Dora would have liked to play, but she was never allowed sufficient time at the piano to practise. The best part of the lessons had been when the teacher could be persuaded to play for them, which was not difficult, since he obviously found this more satisfying than listening to their inept attempts.

Listening to Edward recalled some of the happier times of her girlhood. He played a Chopin *étude* and then one of Mendelssohn's 'Songs without Words', and for that space of time Dora forgot her worries and allowed herself to become completely absorbed in the music.

She would have been happy to listen all evening, but Mr Warrender had other ideas and she found herself persuaded to join the others in singing a series of well-known popular songs. When they had run out of suggestions and everyone settled again in their seats Edward paused beside her.

'You said you had no singing voice. It's not true. You are hiding your light under the proverbial bushel.'

'It's kind of you to say so,' she responded. 'But I should much rather listen to you playing. You play so very well.'

He gave a sigh. 'Not as well as I should like, but I have no time for the piano in London. But I am glad you enjoyed it.'

Settling to sleep that night, she decided that she had been too quick to take a dislike to Elizabeth's brother.

The next morning Edward suggested that they take the dog cart to visit some of the local beauty spots. It was another beautiful spring day and Dora gazed around her with delight as the trap rolled down narrow lanes which had carved themselves deep into the slopes of the Downs, so that the branches of the beech trees almost met overhead and their delicate new leaves formed a fluttering canopy.

'I asked one of the local people why these lanes are so deep,' Edward commented. 'He told me that it is because for centuries people have walked or driven along them and the constant passing has worn them down to their present level.

It gives me pleasure to think that we are following in their footsteps.'

They came out into a broad valley and the road wound along beside a small river, whose waters ran crystal clear over its pebbled bed. When they came to a place where a narrow wooden bridge spanned the stream there was a small clearing. Edward drew the pony to a standstill and suggested that they might stretch their legs. He looped the reins over a post and, leaving the pony to graze, they walked out to the middle of the bridge and stood looking down.

'Oh! Look, there's a fish!' Elizabeth said. 'I wonder what sort it is.'

'It could be a trout,' Edward said, 'but I don't know for sure.' He looked at Dora. 'The truth is, we two were born and bred in the city and we know nothing about the countryside. Father only bought Lillden two years ago and we are still trying to learn how to fit in.'

Dora was studying the banks of the river. 'I don't know about fish, but I recognise some of the herbs growing here.' She made her way to the far side and stooped to gather some sprigs of greenery. 'This is butterbur, an infusion of this is an excellent remedy for coughs and diseases of the lungs. Oh, and here is yarrow. A poultice of this heals wounds.' She looked around her, suddenly reminded of her childhood days when she went collecting herbs with her mother. 'Oh, look! Elderflower. That is good to treat fever.'

She turned back to the others to find them gazing at her in surprise.

'How do you know all this?' Elizabeth asked.

Dora realised that she had revealed more of her own story than she had intended, but there was no going back now. 'My mother was known as a healer. She taught me the uses of herbs and other plants.'

'Oh, I remember now!' Elizabeth said. 'You suggested something like that to Dr McIntyre and he called it medieval superstition.'

'And do these remedies really work?' Edward asked.

'In my experience, they do more good than bleeding and purging, which is all doctors seem to know.'

'How fascinating!' Elizabeth said. 'Could you teach me?'

Dora shook her head. 'It would take a long time, and you would never be allowed to use the knowledge. As nurses, we are obliged to follow the instructions of the doctors.'

Edward looked at her, his head tilted slightly to one side. 'I have a feeling that once you have qualified, it will take a very determined doctor to stop you using your knowledge.'

Dora met his eyes and they exchanged a smile. 'You may be right. But that is my battle to fight. Not one for Elizabeth to get involved with.'

They remounted in the trap and drove on until they came to a small village, where an inn offered rustic tables and benches outside in the sun. Edward bought ginger beer for the two women and ale for himself and the inn-keeper's wife provided them with fresh bread and slabs of crumbly white cheese. Dora leaned back and raised her face to the sun, glad for once that she could do so without worrying about acquiring an unbecoming tan. The atmosphere was relaxed and companionable and they talked or fell silent as the mood took them. She sensed that Edward no longer felt the need to challenge her.

They drove back by a different route and as they entered the stable yard Edward said, 'It seems we have visitors.' A carriage stood there, a stable boy holding the bridles of a pair of smart bay horses.

'Oh no!' Elizabeth groaned. 'It's the Peverills. Do you think we can sneak up the back stairs and hide till they go away?'

'No chance,' her brother said. 'Morton is bound to give the game away.'

'What is wrong with the Peverills?' Dora asked as they entered the house.

'Sir Lancelot is a real bore. His land borders ours, but his family have owned it for generations so he sees us as parvenus. He likes to think of himself as the leading figure in local society. He's the MFH and a JP and all the other initials you can think of.'

'MFH?' Dora queried.

'Master of Fox Hounds,' Edward supplied. 'Hunting is frightfully important to people round here, so Father is determined we should join in. We have ridden out with them a few times, but I can't say I enjoy it, and don't like the way he treats his horses. He's far too ready with the spurs and the whip.'

'I wonder why he has called this afternoon,' Elizabeth said. 'I'm sure Papa will have invited them this evening.'

'At a guess, he's after borrowing money,' her brother said. 'He may be top dog socially but he is also an inveterate gambler and he's always short of cash. I know Father has helped him out more than once.'

They had reached their bedrooms. Elizabeth said, 'I expect you want to wash and tidy yourself. I know I do.

Take your time. The less we have to spend making conversation with the Peverills the better.'

Dora took off her bonnet and rinsed her hands and face and combed her hair. She wondered if she should change her clothes. She was wearing the serviceable tweed skirt, which had been ideal for their morning's expedition, but she was not sure it was right for chatting to guests in the drawing room. On the other hand, there was the evening's festivities to come and it seemed too early to put on the red silk; so she decided to stay as she was. She waited a while, hoping that Elizabeth would call her when she was ready to go down, but there was no knock on her door. After a while, she looked out and saw that Elizabeth's door was open and the room was empty, so there was nothing for it but to sally down on her own.

She was almost as the bottom of the stairs when the door of the library opened and a thickset man with a very red face stumped out. He stopped and looked around him and his gaze focussed on Dora.

'Ha! You'll do! Go and tell my man to bring the carriage round. I'm ready to leave.'

Dora's first instinct was to obey, but then her pride overrode it. She descended the last stairs and drew herself up. 'I beg your pardon, sir. To whom do you think you are speaking?'

'To you, you impudent chit! Don't stand there gaping. Go!'

The drawing room door opened and Edward came out. It was clear from his expression that he had heard the last remark. He walked over to Dora and took her by the hand.

'Sir Lancelot, I do not think you have been intro-
duced to our guest. Dora, this is Sir Lancelot Peverill.
Sir Lancelot, I have the honour to present Miss Dora
Latimer.'

The expression on Sir Lancelot's face was almost sufficient compensation for her embarrassment.

Morton entered the hall. 'You rang, sir?'

'Sir Lancelot is ready to leave. Please send someone
to tell his coachman to bring the carriage round.' Morton
acknowledged the order with a bow and Edward waved an
arm in the direction of the drawing room. 'Sir Lancelot?
Shall we join the ladies?' Then he offered his arm ceremo-
niously to Dora and conducted her into the room.

It was clear that there was a certain constraint in the
atmosphere. Mrs Warrender, presiding over the tea table,
wore an expression of lofty unconcern. Her companion, a
dumpy, faded woman in an over-elaborate dress, looked
uneasy, almost, Dora thought, frightened – an expression
that was intensified by the sight of her husband's face as
he entered the room. The baronet was clearly in a fury and
Mr Warrender, following him from the library, also looked
grim.

When the visitors had left Edward said, 'What was
wrong with Sir Lancelot?'

'I told him that I was not going to cover his gambling
debts until he repaid the last loan,' Mr Warrender said. 'I
do not think we shall be seeing him here again – for a while
at least.'

'Good!' Edward exclaimed. 'The man is a boor. He was
unforgivably rude to Dora.'

'How so?'

'He obviously mistook her for one of the servants and started ordering her about.'

'Good heavens!' Mr Warrender turned to Dora. 'My dear lady, I am so sorry you have been embarrassed.'

'It doesn't matter, sir,' she replied. 'Please think no more about it.'

Nevertheless, the incident had shaken her confidence. She was more than ever aware that she did not fit into this society and never could.

When the tea things had been cleared away everyone retired to dress for the evening. Dora found that Freda had laid out her crimson silk dress. There was a contraption of whale bone and linen to be tied around her waist first, to support the extra fullness at the back of the skirt and then Freda slipped the dress over her head and did up the buttons.

'If you'll take a seat, miss,' the girl said, 'I'll arrange your hair for you.'

Dora sat in front of the dressing table mirror. It was a strange experience to have this comparative stranger combing and pinning her hair. The only person who had ever done that for her had been Edith. Freda gathered her hair into a chignon and fastened it expertly with a small circlet of red silk roses and white ribbons, which Dora had purchased to complete her toilette.

The process complete, Dora stood up and turned to face her. To her surprise and confusion the girl clasped her hands together and exclaimed, 'Oh, miss! Oh, miss!'

'What is it?' Dora enquired. 'What's wrong?'

'Oh miss, nothing's wrong. You just look so beautiful! That dress, it's perfect on you. You'll have all the gentlemen at your feet, you wait and see!'

'I don't think that is very likely,' Dora said, 'but thank you. I could never have managed without your skilled help.'

She turned back to the mirror. Since that first shock at her changed appearance, when she looked at herself in Mrs Carter's mirror, she had become accustomed to seeing herself as she hastily thrust her hair under her nurse's cap every morning, but she had not noticed how several months of good food had softened the outline of her face and given her skin the glow of health. The red dress was a perfect foil and looking at herself now she had to admit that the effect was not unpleasing.

Freda took up an object lying on the table by the bed and offered it to her. 'Miss Warrender said to give you this, because she thought you might not have brought one with you.'

It was a fan of white silk, bordered with a delicate design of fruit and flowers. Dora took it with a momentary constriction in her throat. Elizabeth had understood how restricted her wardrobe was and had chosen this tactful way of supplementing it.

'There, you're ready, miss,' Freda said. 'I hope you have a lovely evening.'

The bedrooms were on the second floor and the ball-room was at the back of the house on the first floor. As Dora began to descend she heard the first guests arriving at the front door. She took a deep breath and lifted her chin. The double doors leading into the ballroom were open and she saw Mr and Mrs Warrender waiting there to receive their guests, with Edward and Elizabeth just behind them.

As she reached them, Mr Warrender spread his hands in a gesture of delighted surprise. 'By George! I believe we have been entertaining a goddess in disguise! My dear lady, you will be the chief ornament of our little soirée.'

Dora felt herself blush. She made a small curtsy and murmured, 'You flatter me, sir.'

'Not at all. Not at all!' he responded.

Guests were coming up the stairs and he turned from her to welcome them. She looked at Mrs Warrender, who was ethereal in dove grey and lilac, and saw her lips compressed in disapproval, but whether of her or her husband's outburst Dora could not be sure.

Edward stepped forward and offered his hand. 'Dora, you look stunning. You quite take my breath away. Doesn't she look magnificent, Lizzie?'

Elizabeth was in cornflower blue with yellow and white flowers in her hair. 'Yes, she does,' she agreed.

'Thank you for the fan,' Dora said. 'It was very thoughtful of you.'

She turned away, seeing visitors waiting to greet their host's children, and made to withdraw further into the room, but Edward caught her arm.

'No, you must stay here with us and be introduced,' he declared.

Mr Warrender's idea of a few friends for an informal evening where there might be a 'bit of dancing' differed very little, as far as Dora could see, from a full-scale ball. She was presented to so many ladies and gentlemen that she quickly gave up trying to remember their names and very soon the room was filled with an animated crowd. It was a spacious room, with long windows on one side looking onto the garden, that were now covered with crimson velvet curtains, and matching mirrors on the opposite wall, reflecting the candle light from a row of elaborate chandeliers hanging down the centre. At one end was a platform, on which was assembled a small orchestra.

Mr Warrender stepped up onto the platform and raised his voice above the general hubbub.

'Ladies and gentlemen, welcome to this little celebration. It is intended to be quite informal, so there is no fuss with dance cards and that sort of thing, but we shall have music and if you feel inclined to dance then I, for one, shall be delighted. So, shall we make up sets for the quadrille?'

The orchestra struck up and Dora found Edward at her side, offering his hand to lead her onto the floor. For the first time, she felt grateful to the Latimers for what she had been taught in their household. They had ensured that their daughters were instructed in all the accomplishments required by society and whereas the two girls had monopolised much of the time given to the piano there had been less chance for them to do so during dancing lessons and Dora had discovered a natural sense of rhythm and delight in movement. She stepped out at Edward's side with a confidence she had not felt for some time.

When the intricate figures of the quadrille had been completed someone in the gathering called out, 'Let's have something a bit more up to date!'

The leader of the orchestra acknowledged the request with a flourish of his bow and struck up a waltz. A dark-haired young man in a fancy waistcoat approached and offered his hand with a bow, but Edward interposed.

'Oh no you don't, Ralph! Dora is my guest and I claim the first waltz. You can wait your turn.'

As they stepped out onto the dance floor Dora had a vivid recollection of the anxious conclave between Mrs Latimer and the dancing master as to the propriety of allowing young ladies to dance in such close contact with a man. At the time, faced with the prospect of being held in the embrace of one of the callow youths who attended the class, she had felt the same misgivings, though for different reasons. Now, as she felt Edward's arm go around her waist, she had no such qualms. With his Viking fairness and his athletic build he was by far the best-looking man in the room, and the laughter in his blue eyes as they met hers was a challenge, not to her, but to the possible disapproval of the older members of the gathering. She relaxed in his grasp and gave herself up to the heady delight of whirling round the room on the current of the music.

For the rest of the evening she never lacked for a partner and danced till her feet ached. She noticed that Edward found no shortage of partners too. There were a number of young ladies among the guests and she saw that he was welcomed into family groups, where the parents smiled benignly and their daughters chattered flirtatiously or lowered their eyes and blushed in maidenly modesty according to their dispositions. It was evident that, whatever the local people's reservations about the source of Mr Warrender's wealth, Edward was regarded as a catch. She could not detect, however, any sign that he preferred any of his partners above the others.

When supper was announced Edward claimed her again and she went into the dining room on his arm. The 'simple cold collation', as Mr Warrender termed it, lived up to his usual extravagant standards. There was cold turkey, jugged hare, chicken fricassee, oysters and crayfish, elaborate jellies and puddings decorated with gold lace and candied fruits. As Edward heaped her plate, Dora was momentarily transported back to the workhouse, to the diet of hasty pudding and milk soup and lobscouse. She laid a restraining hand on Edward's arm.

'Please, that's enough. I really cannot eat any more.'

For a few minutes the shadow of the workhouse dimmed her enjoyment. She thought of Lily, and the poverty she had seen in her company.

'Do you sometimes think, Edward,' she said, 'that it is wrong for people like you – your family, all these other people here – to have so much, while others have so little?'

He looked at her with his head on one side. 'I notice you except yourself from the group.'

She met his eyes. 'It is true. I am more fortunate than many, in that I have a generous patron who has made it possible for me to study at the Nightingale school with ladies like your sister. But for myself, I have nothing and when my training is finished I shall depend for my living on what I can earn as a nurse.'

He took her arm and drew her a little apart from the crowd round the buffet table. His eyes were serious. 'I understood something of that from Elizabeth, and I admire you for your courage. As to what you say about the uneven distribution of wealth, I can only answer that my father raised himself from comparative poverty as a boy by his own efforts and his talent for mechanics. Elizabeth and I are the fortunate inheritors of his success, but I am aware of the great gulf that separates us from the mass of common people. If – when – I qualify for the Bar, it is my intention to use my talents, such as they are, to defend the less fortunate against the powerful who might seek to oppress them. Meanwhile—' he cast a glance round the room and smiled '—the food is here to be eaten and it would be wicked to let it go to waste. Do you not agree?'

She hesitated for a moment and then allowed herself to return his smile. 'Yes, you are right. It would not benefit the poor to have it thrown away – and it is delicious!'

When the supper had been eaten and the music started up again it banished the sobering thoughts from her mind and she gave herself up to the enjoyment of the moment, but she stored what he had said in her memory, for proper consideration when she had leisure.

When the last guests had departed and she had wished Mr Warrender and his wife goodnight, she was about to make her way to her room when Edward came bounding up the stairs from the hall, where he had been seeing the last visitors on their way. He took hold of both her hands and looked into her eyes.

'I have enjoyed this evening more than I can say. Thank you.'

She felt a tremor pass through her body, as if for an instant she stood on the brink of a precipice. Then she drew a breath and calmed herself.

'I have enjoyed it too. Thanks to you. And now I must go to bed. Goodnight.'

He held her hands a few seconds longer, then lifted one to his lips and released her. 'Goodnight. Sleep well.'

Chapter 11

Dora woke next morning with a guilty sense of having overslept, but before she could drag herself out of bed there was a tap on the door and Freda came in with morning tea on a tray.

'I'm afraid I am terribly late,' Dora said, as the maid set the tray on her lap.

'Oh, don't worry about that, miss,' came the response. 'No one's up yet. I've just taken Miss Elizabeth's tray in and she said to tell you there's no hurry.'

Dora took her at her word, and when she finally entered the dining room she found Elizabeth about to begin a leisurely breakfast. They had just finished when Edward came in, brisk and energetic, as if he had been awake for hours.

'Ah, you two slug-a-beds are finally up!' he said. 'Good morning, sis.' He kissed Elizabeth on the top of her head and smiled over her at Dora. 'And good morning to you. I hope you slept well.'

'Extremely well,' she told him.

'I was wondering,' he went on. 'Would you think us terribly rude if we went out for an hour's ride this morning? It is something we both enjoy and we get so few opportunities.'

'Not at all,' Dora said quickly. The prospect came as a relief. She felt unsure how to behave towards Edward after the previous evening and the thought of an hour's solitude to gather her thoughts was welcome.

When her two friends had changed into riding clothes she walked with them to the stable yard, where a large black horse and a smaller chestnut carrying a side-saddle were waiting. Elizabeth went up to the chestnut and stroked its nose fondly.

'Come and meet Star, Dora,' she said, adding as Dora hung back, 'she is the gentlest creature. I promise she will not hurt you.'

Dora advanced cautiously and laid her hand on the warm, glossy neck. The horse lowered her head and nudged Elizabeth's arm.

'She's looking for a titbit,' Elizabeth said and reached into her pocket, producing a piece of apple. Dora watched as she held it out and the horse nuzzled her hand and took it.

'Aren't you afraid she'll bite you?'

'No, of course not. I told you, she's as gentle as a lamb.'

Edward joined them. 'Are you sure you wouldn't like to try a short ride? I could teach you the rudiments.'

Dora shook her head. 'There's no point. I shall never have the opportunity to progress any further.'

'Well, at least let me put you up on Star for a minute, just to get the feel of it. With the side saddle you'll be perfectly safe.'

'Oh, very well,' she yielded.

He took her by the waist and lifted her into the saddle. 'There you are. Now hook your right leg round the saddle horn and put your left foot in the stirrup. See? Safe as houses.'

He took the reins from Elizabeth and clicked his tongue and Dora gave a small shriek as the horse walked forward, but she soon realised that there was, as he said, no danger and she was surprised by how her body accommodated itself to the movement. He led her once round the yard and came back to where Elizabeth waited.

'Did you enjoy that?'

'Yes, as a matter of fact I did.'

'Well, next time you come down I'll give you a proper lesson. Now, unhook your leg and let yourself slide down.' He held out his arms and lowered her gently to the ground. For a moment they were face to face, inches apart, and she experienced the same vertiginous sensation as on the previous evening. It was so strong that she stepped back sharply, collided with the horse and stumbled, so that he had to catch hold of her again.

'I'm sorry!' she said breathlessly.

'Are you all right?' he enquired simultaneously.

Dora felt herself flush and saw, to her surprise, that under the fair beard the colour had risen in his cheeks as well. Elizabeth had moved the horse away and she recovered her balance and stepped back again.

'Thank you. I can see what fun it must be to ride properly, but as I said, I shall never have the opportunity.'

'Don't be so sure,' he responded.

'Shall we go?' Elizabeth asked, and he turned away to lift her into the saddle. Then he swung himself onto the back of the black horse.

'We will only be an hour,' Elizabeth promised.

'Don't hurry on my account,' she replied. 'Enjoy yourselves.'

She watched them go and, once out of the yard, they put the horses to the trot and soon vanished down the tree-lined drive. Dora turned back towards the house. She was still feeling the effects of her exertions of the night before and was looking forward to spending a quiet hour sitting in the garden. She wandered around for a while, looking for the ideal spot, and came suddenly on Mrs Warrender, who had set up an easel in front of a weeping willow, under whose branches the grass was studded with crocuses. She would have turned back and looked elsewhere, but she had been seen.

'Good morning, Dora. I hope you slept well.'

'Very well, thank you.'

'Where is Elizabeth?'

'She has gone riding with Edward.'

'That is very remiss of her. You are her guest. Her time should be spent with you.'

'Oh, please don't blame her. I told her I was rather tired and would be glad to sit quietly for a while.' It was a lie, but a harmless one.

Mrs Warrender indicated her canvas. 'Do you paint? If you would care to join me, I can lend you the necessary materials.'

'Thank you, no. I have no talent for it.'

Mrs Warrender raised her aristocratic profile and looked down her nose at Dora. 'You don't paint, you don't play or sing. Do you have any accomplishments, other than dancing?'

Dora returned her scrutiny. 'Accomplishments? No, I suppose not. I do, however, have some skills which I think may have a more practical use.'

Mrs Warrender turned back to her painting with a small shrug. 'Of course, I forgot for the moment that you have your own way to make in the world. The accomplishments expected of a lady, particularly of the wife of a gentleman engaged in one of the professions, would not be of any great use to someone in your position.'

Dora gazed at the back of her head. The implication of what she had said was clear. She must not consider herself as a suitable wife for Edward. Her hostess was under the impression that she had set out to entrap him. She berated herself for having allowed such a suspicion to arise. She had been very foolish and her behaviour had been misconstrued. She was in danger of making herself a laughing stock, or the object of malicious gossip, and she must take steps to correct the false impression.

She said, as coolly as she could manage, 'I mustn't disturb your concentration any further. Excuse me.'

After searching the garden she found a rustic bench in a secluded corner and sat with her head buried in her hands. Had Elizabeth, or Mr Warrender, formed the same impression of her behaviour? Worse still, how had Edward construed it? How could she ever look him in the face again?

The rest of the day, which should have been a day of pleasure, was instead a torment. The picnic, which Mr Warrender had suggested, duly took place. To Dora's relief, there was a shortage of places in the dog cart, the only vehicle suitable for the narrow tracks they were to follow. Mrs Warrender pleaded a headache and stayed at home and Edward offered to come on horseback, leaving Elizabeth and Dora and Mr Warrender to bring the picnic baskets. When they reached their goal, a sandstone tower set in a grassy space at the top of Leith Hill, they found that another party of friends, who had also been at the dance the night before, were already there. The two groups joined forces and there was a general chatter, which allowed Dora to remain quietly in the background. Once or twice, Edward approached her, but she pretended to be absorbed in the view, which was indeed spectacular, encompassing, she was informed, thirteen counties. Alternatively, she began to talk to some other member of the party, so they never had anything approaching a tête-à-tête. In spite of that, it was a relief when the sun began to dip towards the horizon and the remains of the picnic were stowed into the dog cart.

Reaching Lillden, Dora pleaded a headache and retired to bed. Next morning, they had to be off early to catch the train that would take them back to London and there was little time for farewells. She thanked Mr and Mrs Warrender and turned to Edward. He took her hand and kept hold of it, in spite of her efforts to retrieve it.

'We shall see each other in London. I'm determined that we shall be regular attendees at concerts. You can rely on me.'

'I – I am not sure. You know we have to work shifts. It may not be possible.'

'We shall find occasions; depend on it,' he returned, and handed her up into the trap.

As they trotted away Dora looked back and felt a sudden pang of regret. After the grimy streets where she had grown up Lillden seemed like the the Garden of Eden, but, like Eve, she was fated not return to it.

After the excitements and disturbances of the holiday it was hard to settle back into the routine of the hospital, but she forced herself to concentrate on caring for her patients and little by little, as the days passed, the memory began to fade. As her personal distress became less sharp, one aspect of what she had experienced came to the forefront of her mind. She had tried to ignore the contrast between the opulence and extravagance of the Warrenders and the extreme deprivation that she had witnessed on a daily basis in the workhouse and again in the slums of London, but now she found herself increasingly troubled by it. It should not be allowed to continue, but what possible remedy could there be?

She voiced her thoughts to Lily and through her drew Pearl and Phil, who seemed to have developed a close friendship, into the discussion. Their talk returned frequently to the Bill that Mr Gladstone had laid before Parliament, but which now seemed to be mired in a slew of amendments. In the absence of any immediate prospect of a political solution, they looked for something they could do at a personal level and saw that there was one form of practical help which was within their power. When their shifts in the wards allowed it, the four of them began to visit the mean streets of Shoreditch, using the skills they had acquired to treat those who could not afford the attentions of a doctor. They dared not use the bandages and other supplies from the wards, so Phil undertook to buy whatever they needed and, since she seemed to have no shortage of money, they accepted her offer.

Tentatively as first, and then with increasing confidence, Dora began to employ her old herbal remedies again. It was not always easy to find the plants she needed, though the gardens surrounding the hospital provided some of them. It was Phil who had a sudden inspiration.

'The Chelsea Physic Garden!'

'What is that?' Dora asked.

'I don't know much about it, but I know where it is. I think we should go and have a look.'

They found the garden close to the bank of the Thames. Dora would have hesitated to go in but Phil marched confidently through the gates and accosted a gardener working in one of the beds.

'Who is in charge of this place?'

'Mr Moore's the curator. His office is over there,' the man replied.

Phil tapped on the office door and a voice bade them enter. A small man with a ragged beard and a face like well-worn leather looked up from a large tome on his desk.

'Yes?'

'My name is Phyllis Verney. My father is Lord Delamere. This is Miss Dora Latimer. We are both training to be Nightingale nurses.'

The little man rose and came round his desk. 'How do you do? I'm delighted to make your acquaintance. Now, how can I help you?'

'Miss Latimer is an expert on the use of herbal remedies. She is finding it difficult to obtain the herbs she needs in London and we are wondering if you can help.'

Mr Moore turned his attention to Dora. 'An expert in herbal remedies?'

Dora blushed. 'No, my friend is very kind, but I would not call myself an expert. But I do have some knowledge, which I inherited from my mother, and I have proved that many of my remedies are efficacious.'

'This is very interesting!' The man's expression had become quite animated. 'I expect you know that this garden is properly called the Garden of the Society of Apothecaries? It was gifted to them by a benefactor two centuries ago, at a time when herbal remedies were the only medicines available. Sadly, in recent years they have fallen out of favour, which I believe is a great mistake. Please, take a seat. Now, tell me, which herbs have you found most useful?'

For the next half hour he engaged Dora in a detailed discussion of the preparation of various herbal remedies and their effects. At the end of that time, he personally conducted them both on a tour of the garden and allowed Dora to pluck whatever herbs she required. They departed with an invitation to return whenever she needed to replenish her stores.

'You are a genius, Phil,' Dora said, as they waited for the omnibus to take them back to Surrey Gardens. 'I would never have thought of that – and I would never have dared to walk in and make myself known like that.'

'Ah well,' Phil said with a wry grin, 'I have learned from experience that the mention of my father's title does tend to open doors. I disapprove of it in principal, but there are times it seems justified.'

Before long, the Nightingales, as the local people called them, and in particular Dora, were known all round the area called the Old Nicol as angels of mercy, who brought comfort and healing without asking for payment of any kind.

*

Edward kept his word and it was not long before Elizabeth received a note inviting them both to join him for a concert. To Dora's relief, it was on an evening when they were both on duty, so they had to decline. The same thing happened with the next invitation, but inevitably a day came when there was no excuse for refusing. Dora thought of claiming a bad headache when the evening approached, but she was eager to experience a proper orchestral concert and with the passage of time her anxiety about what Edward might think of her had faded. She told herself that, after all, Elizabeth would be with her, and they would be in the constant company of other people. There could be no opportunity for any embarrassing tête-â-têtes.

In the event, Edward behaved as if there had never been anything more between them than the courtesy a man might show to his sister's friend. For Dora, the evening was a revelation of another kind. She had never heard the music of a full orchestra, and the performance of Beethoven's Fifth Symphony raised her to a level of exultation that was almost transcendental.

There was nowhere in the Manor House or in the hospital itself where Dora could prepare her remedies and she knew that any request for such facilities would be met with disapproval. Instead, she made use of Lily's mother's kitchen and Lily's house became the headquarters of their operations in Shoreditch. It was also a meeting place for men who belonged to the Reform League and Dora and her team listened to many animated discussions about how the government could be forced to accept the proposals in Gladstone's Bill.

One evening, Phil brought the conversation to a halt by remarking, 'You all spend so much time trying to get a vote for ordinary working men. Has it ever occurred to you that women should be able to vote as well?'

There was a moment of stunned silence and then a low rumble of laughter. 'Women voting?' Lily's father said. 'What would you vote for? A reduction in the price of knitting wool?'

'A fair wage for men and women, so that children are not left to starve,' Phil replied crisply.

'Aye, well, we'd all vote for that,' he said. 'But that's why you can leave it to us men. We understand the way the world works. Politics is not something for women to get involved with.'

'We understand how the world works well enough,' Phil said. 'We are the ones who go out into those slum streets and see babies dying because their mothers do not have enough milk for them, and children with rickets for lack of fresh food, and old women coughing their hearts out in rooms with holes in the roof where the rain comes in.'

'And then you go back to your comfortable lodgings,' one of the men put in, 'and when you've finished your training you'll go home to your father's acres and marry a rich man and forget all about us.'

'Never!' Phil said vehemently. 'When I am qualified I shall look for a position in a hospital where people like you come to be cared for, when accidents or illness prevent you from working. I shall be entrusted with returning you to health and sending you back to your families. And yet I cannot be trusted to vote for the man who represents me in Parliament?'

'Now, now,' Lily's father said pacifically. 'Let's not get the cart before the horse. First we need to get the vote for the ordinary working man. That's our priority. We can't afford to muddy the waters asking for the impossible.'

And the men drew together and lowered their voices, excluding the women from the discussion.

Not long after that, at the beginning of June, Phil came into the dining room carrying a copy of *The Times* and looking triumphant.

'You remember that argument I had with Mr Baker and the other men about women's suffrage?'

'Very vividly,' Dora agreed.

'Read this!'

She had folded the paper back to one of the inside pages and pointed to a short article. It reported that on the previous day, Mr John Stuart Mill MP had presented to the House a petition requesting that the franchise should be extended to all women who fulfilled the property qualifications which applied to men.

'Signed by one thousand four hundred and ninety nine-women!' Phil said. 'If only I'd known about it I'd have made it one thousand five hundred!'

'Will it have any chance of succeeding?' Dora asked.

'Who knows? But there is a lot of talk about reform at the moment. If Mr Gladstone could be persuaded to include that in his bill ... Imagine! Women like us being able to vote, to influence what happens in our own country. Isn't it about time?'

'Perhaps,' Dora said. 'It would be all very well for you, probably, but it would make no difference to people like Lily or Pearl – or to me, for that matter.'

Phil sat down abruptly. 'I'm sorry. That was thoughtless of me. But it would be a start, wouldn't it? If women were given the vote on the same basis as men at present, and then the franchise was extended to working men as Mr Baker wants, wouldn't it have to include women as well?'

'I don't know,' Dora said. 'You saw how those men reacted to the idea. They are not going to campaign for women to vote.'

'No, that is true,' Phil said with a sigh. 'But at least the possibility is in the air. If Gladstone can get his Bill through, who knows what might follow?'

Her optimism was dashed very quickly. On 28th, June dissension among Liberal MPs over the Reform Bill brought down the government headed by Lord Russell and Mr Gladstone, and the Tory party took power.

Now that the summer had come, it was tempting in their time off to take their ease in the gardens round the manor house, but Dora and her friends continued with their visits to Shoreditch. One evening in July, Lily's father came back from a meeting, just as they were about to gather up their things and head for home, with an expression of excitement on his face.

'It's agreed! There is going to be a big demonstration in support of the Bill.'

'When?' Lily asked.

'On 23rd July. A week next Monday. We're to meet in Holborn, at the league's headquarters, and march to Hyde Park. Our president, Mr Beales, and some of his friends, will take the lead and the members of all the London branches will follow. We expect several thousand supporters.'

'Will the government allow it?' Mrs Baker asked.

'It will not matter whether they do or not. It is going to happen.'

'Can we join in?' Phil asked.

'I don't see why not. The more the merrier.'

'What shift are we on that day?' Lily asked.

There was a moment's silence while they calculated. 'We are on the morning shift,' Dora said. 'We shall not be free till two o'clock.'

'What time is the march due to start?' Phil asked.

'Two thirty. But don't worry. It'll take a while for everyone to get into marching order. If you jump straight into an omnibus you can still be in time.'

'I don't think Mrs Wardroper will approve,' Pearl said doubtfully.

'I'm sure she won't,' Phil agreed, 'which is why we shall not tell her.'

Riding back in the omnibus Phil and Lily chattered enthusiastically about the prospect of the march. Dora said little. She felt as strongly as ever about the injustices in society, but she was unsure whether they might best promote their cause by breaking the law. Also, she had to admit to herself, the possibility that Mrs Wardroper might somehow find out about their participation alarmed her. She could not afford to be dismissed from the school. She thought of her benefactor, Mr Rathbone, and wondered what his attitude would be.

The day before the march, Dora returned from the hospital at two o'clock in the afternoon and was astonished to see Edward standing outside the main door of the manor house.

'What are you doing here?' she asked, forgetting the normal courtesies.

'Waiting for you,' he responded. 'The dragon in there refused to allow me inside.'

'Of course not,' Dora said. 'Gentlemen are not permitted. What did you tell her you wanted?'

'Oh, don't worry. I told her I was Elizabeth's brother and I had a message for her from Father.'

'Elizabeth's not back yet. She had to redo a dressing because Sister Andrews didn't like the way she had done it. What is the message?'

'There isn't one. That was just an excuse, to pacify the dragon. It's you I want to see.'

'Me?'

'Don't look so surprised. I love my sister, but I wouldn't be inviting her out so often if it wasn't the only way I can get to spend some time with you. And even then, we never have a chance to talk on our own. So I thought I would take the afternoon off and call on you.'

'We are not supposed to have gentlemen callers.'

'But who's to know? I covered my tracks.' He looked at her with a kind of appeal. 'Can we take a walk in the gardens?'

'I suppose so,' she agreed uneasily. At least it would take him out of sight of curious eyes in the windows of the house.

He offered her his arm and they strolled along one of the shady walks that ran through the grounds. Surrey Gardens had been designed originally as a pleasure ground and, although it had fallen out of favour, the trees and shrubs with which it had been planted were still cared for and offered a welcome respite from the heat. They had also been designed to lead to small bowers where a couple could be concealed from any casual passer-by. Edward conducted Dora to such a spot and suggested that they might sit for a while. She assented unwillingly. His sudden appearance had reawakened her sense of shame at having given a false impression of her feelings for him when they were at Lillden, and his deliberate manoeuvring to get her on her own alarmed her.

To forestall any embarrassing remarks on his part she said, 'Have you heard that there is to be a big demonstration in Hyde Park tomorrow, in support of the Reform Bill?'

He looked confused. 'No. Why should I have done?'

'Of course, there's no reason for you to know. It's just because one of the students here, a girl called Lily – her father is a member of the Reform League.' She was rambling and began to wish she had not introduced the subject. But it was too late to go back. She plunged on. 'Some of us have been going to the slum near where she lives, to help the people there who cannot afford to see a doctor. That's how I know about the march.'

He looked at her in some surprise. 'I didn't know you were interested in politics.'

'Oh, I'm not really.' She hesitated. It was what he expected to hear, but it was not the truth. 'Well, I suppose I am, in a way. You remember what I said on the evening of your father's party, about how wrong it is that some people should have more to eat than they can manage, while other people are starving? I was thinking of the people who live near Lily. She took me there one day, and it's horrible, Edward. People are living in hovels not fit for animals. The children don't get enough to eat and have no shoes on their feet. It cannot be allowed to go on.'

He was frowning. 'I do not see how this demonstration is going to change that.'

'Not at once, of course. But if the husbands of those poor women, the fathers of those children had a vote, don't you think eventually they would make sure that things changed for the better?'

He shook his head. 'I do not believe that giving that sort of power to the ignorant masses can be a good thing. What do any of them know about how the country should be governed?'

'You might be surprised. I've listened to Lily's father and his friends discussing things. They are not ignorant, or stupid.' A sudden idea struck her. 'You told me that when you qualify you want to defend the weak against the oppression of the powerful.'

'Yes, because I shall have the education and the position to do that. That is not the same as putting power in the hands of men who know nothing more than the politics of the gutter and the ale house.'

'Come with me!' she said urgently. 'Come and meet Mr Baker and the others. You'll see what I mean. Come and join the march.'

'You don't mean to tell me that you intend to take part in this ... this fiasco?'

'Yes!' Suddenly all her doubts had vanished. 'Yes, I do.'

His face had clouded. 'Dora, you must not do this. Heaven knows what will happen. The mob cannot be trusted to behave properly. And I have no doubt that the march will be forbidden anyway.'

'We don't care about that. We shall march anyway.'

'You would break the law?'

'If that is the only way that these poor people can make their voices heard.'

'But why must you involve yourself? You are not one of them.'

She stood up. 'You forget, Edward. I have lived for years among people who were even poorer, even more deprived than they are. I do not come from the sort of background that you had. We may share interests and tastes, but when it comes down to it we really have nothing in common.'

She began to walk away. He came after her and caught her hand. 'Dora, don't say that! Do not be angry with me. I don't care who your family were, or whether you have money or not. Who am I to give myself airs, when my own father grew up in the back streets of the East End? I am only concerned for your welfare. This could be dangerous. You don't know what might happen. You could be trampled underfoot if the crowd panics.'

'Come with me, then,' she challenged him. 'Come with me and protect me.'

He looked into her face for a moment. 'I dare not. There may be arrests. If it were to be known that I had taken part in an unlawful action it would be the end of my career. I could forget being called to the Bar. You must see that.' His eyes appealed to her.

She sighed. 'Yes, I do see. But don't try to stop me going. I owe it to my friends, and to the people I am trying to help.'

He made a small gesture of regret and disappointment. 'This isn't what I came for.'

'I know,' she said.

He reached for her hand again. 'Don't let this little ... disagreement ... come between us, please! You know, you must know, that I – care for you.'

She felt the colour coming into her face. 'Yes. Of course. I hope we shall always be ... friends.'

'Friends? That is not ... not what I hope for.' His eyes searched hers and then he bent his head and kissed her on the lips. Instantly, her body remembered the only other time she had been kissed by a man and the image of Jem rose in her mind's eye. But at the same time, her senses responded as they had done then, sending her blood racing, turning her insides to liquid.

She pulled back, gasping. 'I must go! I must go in. Elizabeth will be looking for me.'

He nodded slowly and let go of her hand. 'Very well. But you understand now? You know how I feel, and I believe you feel it too.'

Without answering, she turned away and set off back towards the house.

She was met by Phil, waving a copy of the newspaper.

'The Home Secretary has declared the march illegal and issued a Police Notice!'

Chapter 12

There was no time to change at the end of their shift next day. Still in their uniforms they ran to the gates of the Gardens and jumped on the first omnibus. Even so, by the time they reached Holborn the crowds were choking the adjoining streets and they had to abandon the omnibus and make their way on foot. Dora would have hesitated to push her way through but Phil was not deterred. Taking Pearl firmly by the arm she led the way forward.

'Excuse me! Can we pass, please? Thank you. Thank you.' Her patrician tones produced an immediate, respectful response, reinforced by sight of their uniforms.

Little by little they worked their way forwards until they were within sight of the League's headquarters in Adelphi Crescent. They were just in time to see a cab containing several gentlemen in top hats set off at a walking pace towards Oxford Circus. A group of men dressed in sober Sunday best followed, some of them wearing sashes or badges denoting their position in the League, and the main body of the marchers fell in behind them. Even so, the crush was so great that it was some time before Dora and her friends were able to make any progress. Eventually, they found themselves marching along in the middle of a cheery, good-tempered crowd.

Men tipped their caps and grinned a welcome to them and she heard 'Good for you, miss!', 'Thanks for your support, ma'am,' and similar phrases. There were women in the march as well as men, though they were in the minority, and Dora noticed that among those wearing rough working-men's garb there was a sprinkling of the better dressed, prosperous traders perhaps or clerks. The whole route was lined with men wearing sashes marking them as stewards, and they were quick to quell any sign of potential trouble, but the vast majority of the people were on their best behaviour and the stewards had little to do. As they got closer to central London she saw that the pavements were lined with spectators, many of whom shouted encouragement as they passed.

Everything seemed to be going well until they neared Marble Arch. Then the pace slowed until they came to a standstill.

'What's happened?' Dora asked, of no one in particular. She was answered by shaken heads and shrugged shoulders, but after a while the crowd began to grow restive and there were a few shouts of 'Let us pass!', 'Move on ahead there!', 'Out of the way!'.

'Let's see if we can find out what's happening,' Phil said, and she employed the same tactics as she had used before to make a way through the press of people.

It was harder this time, but they squirmed and ducked and nudged their way forward until Dora was able to see, between the shoulders of the men in front of her, the reason for the halt. The gates into Hyde Park were locked and barricaded by a line of omnibuses and in front of them stood rank upon rank of policemen. In front of them was a man mounted on a horse. Angry words were being exchanged between him and the leaders of the protest. She could not hear exactly what was being said, but their meaning was clear.

'Who's the man on the horse?' she asked a well-dressed man standing beside her.

'That's the Commissioner, Richard Mayne,' he replied. 'And that is our president, Mr Beale, arguing with him.'

As he spoke there was a sudden movement in the crowd. Some had lost patience and surged forward as if intent on forcing their way through. Immediately, at an order from the officer on the horse, the police advanced and began to lay about them with their truncheons. The protestors fell back, but a hostile roar rose from the crowd.

The stalemate continued for some time and some of the marchers began to filter away along the roads bordering the park, some towards the Bayswater Road and others down Park Lane. After a while they heard shouts from that direction and more people moved off towards the sounds.

'Let's see what's happening down there,' Phil said.

So they allowed themselves to be carried along with the general flow and soon saw what it was that had attracted the attention of the leaders. Someone had noticed that the railings enclosing the park were weak at that point and had begun to sway them backwards and forwards. Now, several burly men were lending their weight and, as Dora and her companions watched, a section of the railings collapsed and with a loud cheer the marchers stormed through the gap and into the park.

'Come on!' Phil said and followed them.

Dora picked up her skirts and picked her way over the collapsed railings and followed the others. Once inside, there was nothing to hold them back and they were swept along over the grassy expanses and round flowerbeds in full bloom until the crowd came to a standstill in an open area around a large oak tree. More men and women appeared from another direction and it was clear that the boundaries of the park had been breached in several places. Soon the whole area round the tree was packed with people. A way was cleared for a group of men in top hats and someone produced some crates to make an improvised platform. The man she now recognised as Mr Beale got up on it and began to address the crowd, though his voice did not carry to where she was standing.

The crowd had quietened to listen but suddenly a new roar of fury arose. An army of police, some on foot, some mounted, had charged into the margins of the crowd and were laying into them indiscriminately. The yells of protest increased in volume and then missiles began to fly. Stones and bricks rained down and Dora saw several policemen collapse to the ground. Beside her, Phil was yelling encouragement.

'Got him!' she shouted triumphantly and pointed to the Commissioner.

It was true. Mayne's hat had been knocked off and blood was streaming down his face. He was rapidly hustled away by some of his comrades.

A new shout arose, different in tone. 'The Guards! The Guards!'

Peering over the heads of those in front of her Dora saw the plumed helmets and shining lances of a detachment of cavalry. Her stomach contracted.

'Now we're for it!' she exclaimed to Lily, who stood close beside her.

'Don't you worry, miss,' said a man nearby. 'The soldiers won't attack the ordinary people. I served with them once and I know them. They're good lads, not like these swine of policemen.'

He was right. The Guardsmen kept their distance and contented themselves with manoeuvring in different formations, without attempting to interfere with the protest. A cheer went up. 'The Guards! The people's Guards!'

The police had withdrawn to the margins of the crowd, but it became clear that there was no possibility of restoring sufficient calm for the speeches to be heard and word was passed along that instead there would be another meeting the following evening in Trafalgar Square.

'I can't see that being allowed to happen,' Phil commented.

It was growing late and the shadows were lengthening on the trampled grass, but the crowd was unwilling to disperse. A new ripple of interest passed over it as a little group of gentlemen drove up in a hansom cab and joined the leaders. One of them mounted the platform and raised his voice and this time Dora heard what was said.

'My friends, Mr Leno and I have just met with Mr Walpole, the Home Secretary, and pointed out to him that if the meeting tomorrow is met with the same violence as today the danger of considerable bloodshed cannot be ruled out. He has, reluctantly, agreed and the meeting will go ahead without interference from the police.'

A cheer went up and then the people began make their way slowly back towards the road. Neither the police nor the Guards were anywhere to be seen.

'Now what?' Lily asked.

'Find an omnibus and get back to the hospital,' Dora said. 'I don't know about you, but my feet are killing me!'

Two days later when they returned to the manor house at the end of their shift, they were greeted with the message that Mrs Wardroper wanted to see them at once in her office. Phil and Dora exchanged looks.

'You don't think ...?'

'Why else would she want to see the four of us?'

'But how ...?'

'Heaven knows.'

A sick chill went through Dora's guts as they climbed the stairs to the office. She'd had her reservations about joining the march and it had only been Edward's presumption in trying to stop her that had finally decided her. What right had he to forbid her? That had been the thought at the back of her mind. Now she remembered why he had said he dared not come with her. It would be the end of his career. Now it looked as though it might be the end of hers.

Mrs Wardroper's face left them in no doubt about the trouble they were in. On her desk was a copy of the *Illustrated London News*, opened at a page headed 'Riotous Assembly in Hyde Park', and showing an engraving depicting members of the crowd. She pushed it across the desk.

'Look at this. Can you deny that this is a picture of the four of you?'

Quite clearly pictured among the figures were four young women in the uniform of the Nightingale School, though the faces were only a blur.

'How do you know it's us?' Lily blurted.

'When the picture was brought to my attention I made some enquiries. It seems the four of you have often absented yourselves when you are not on duty. That is your affair, of course, but it had been noted. No one could recall having seen you here on the afternoon in question, but Mr Greaves, the hall porter, remembered having seen you leaving the hospital in a hurry, still in uniform at the end of your shift, and heading towards the omnibus. Do you deny being there?'

'No,' Dora said. 'We cannot deny it. We were there.'

'What possessed you to associate yourselves with such an undertaking?'

'It was my fault,' Lily said. 'My father was one of the organisers. He told us about the march.'

'But we joined in voluntarily,' Phil said. 'It was not Mr Baker's idea.'

'Why? What possible reason could you have?'

'We have seen the conditions that the poor people live in,' Phil said. 'We believe that the best chance of changing things is giving a vote to ordinary working men.'

'I am amazed that you, of all people, can advocate the rule of the masses,' Mrs Wardroper said. 'I cannot imagine what your father's attitude to that might be. However, that is something that we shall shortly find out. You have brought the school into disrepute and shown yourselves unfit to wear the uniform of Nightingale nurses. You will be dismissed. I shall write today to your parents – or in your case, Latimer, to Mr Rathbone, your patron – informing them of my decision and the reasons for it. You will serve till the end of the week and leave at the end of your final shift.'

Pearl burst into tears. 'Oh, ma'am, please don't send me away! I've got five little brothers and sisters. My ma's relying on me to bring in a decent wage. She'll never forgive me if I don't qualify.'

'You should have thought of that before you allowed your friends to lead you into such a foolish escapade,' Mrs Wardroper returned bleakly.

'I do not see that we have done anything to injure the reputation of the school,' Phil said. 'The cause was just. We were trying to support the disadvantaged. It was our duty as Christians.'

'Do not presume to lecture me on our Christian duty! Your duty, as probationers, is to respect the authority of your elders and to uphold the standards expected of your profession. That does not include taking part in a riot!'

'It was not a riot! It was perfectly peaceful until the police started attacking us.'

'Enough!' Mrs Wardroper rose to her feet. 'You have heard my decision. Now go – and think what opportunities you have so foolishly thrown away.'

Outside the room Pearl was still inconsolable. Phil put her arms round her. 'Don't cry, my dear. I will make sure that you and your family don't suffer. There are ways and means. I'll take care of you, I promise.'

Lily's reaction was anger. 'It's not fair! We did nothing wrong! It's just typical of the way working people are treated. They think we're dirt under their feet. It's all very well for you, Phil. You can go back to your father and your big house. This will not make a difference to your life.'

'That is where you are very wrong,' Phil told her. 'I have no intention of going back. I will admit that I have an advantage, in that I have money of my own so I can support myself. But I will not go back and bury myself in the country and marry some boorish farmer. I will find work of some kind. If I cannot be a nurse, there must be other things I can do.' She looked at Dora. 'What about you? What will you do?'

Dora took a long breath. 'I suppose I will go back to working in the infirmary at the workhouse. But instead of being there as a qualified nurse I shall . . . I shall be no more than any of the other paupers who volunteer to help.'

'A pauper?' Phil said. 'Oh, come now!'

'It is what I am,' Dora said bitterly. 'I have no means of supporting myself. Qualifying as a nurse was my only way to change that.'

She looked round at their shocked faces, then turned away and went to her room.

When it was time for tea to be served she considered remaining there, unable to face her colleagues, but Elizabeth tapped on her door.

'Dora, I've heard what has happened. We all think it's terrible. You were so brave to go on that march. I would never have done it. We really admire you – all of you. Please come down to tea!'

In the dining room Dora joined Phil who was still trying to console Pearl. 'Where's Lily?' she asked.

'She went home, to warn her parents. Better to hear it from her than by letter from Mrs W. she thought.'

'I wonder what her father will think,' Dora mused. 'He can't be angry with her.'

'But I'll wager he's furious with Mrs W.,' Phil responded.

After a sleepless night Dora headed for her shift in the wards with a sense of unreality. There seemed little point in continuing. It seemed, however, that the nursing staff had not been informed of her disgrace and she soon found herself caught up in the business of caring for her patients. It was some comfort, she reflected, that she could still continue with the work she loved, when she went back to the infirmary, and she would bring new skills that she had learned in her months at the school. The question that distressed her more than anything was what Mr Rathbone would think of what had happened. He would regard her as ungrateful, unworthy of the help and the money he had given her. It was a poor return, after all he had done for her.

Returning to the manor house when the shift was over they were surprised to see a small group of men and women in working clothes gathered outside the main door.

'I recognise that woman!' Dora said. 'I treated her baby for croup last week.'

'And that is the man whose leg I dressed when he had that ulcer,' Phil said.

Lily said nothing but ran forward to hug her father, who stood at the front of the group.

As they approached, the front door was opened and Mrs Wardroper appeared. Her expression was severe, and in her black dress and white cap and veil she looked to Dora like the very personification of unrelenting authority.

'I am told that you refuse to disperse until you have spoken to me,' she said. 'What is it you want?'

Mr Baker stepped forward, his cap held respectfully in his hand. 'Beg pardon for disturbing you, ma'am, but we think you are about to commit an act of injustice.'

'Injustice!' Mrs Wardroper's nostrils flared in contempt. 'How dare you accuse me of that. What is this about?'

'It's about these four young women you are about to dismiss.'

'And what is your interest in the matter?'

'One of them is my daughter ...'

'Ah-ha! Now we are coming to the point. Your daughter has behaved in a way incompatible with the standards we expect of our students. There is no more to say on the subject.'

Baker was not to be intimidated. 'We believe there is, ma'am. We think there are what the lawyers call "extenuating circumstances".'

'Oh? And how do you arrive at that conclusion?'

Baker looked around and seeing Dora and Phil and Pearl on the outskirts of the group beckoned them forward to join Lily. 'Over the last couple of months, these four young women have given up their free time to take care of the sick and poor in our neighbourhood. Many of them cannot afford a doctor's fees, and until then if they were sick or wounded they had to make what shift they could to heal themselves, and very often that was not enough. These girls have dressed their wounds and soothed their fevers and poulticed their children's chests. There are men and women here who have good reason to be grateful to them and it seems wrong to us that they should be sent away and prevented from carrying on with their good work.'

His last words were almost drowned by voices from the crowd, calling out instances of how they had been helped or healed.

Mrs Wardroper raised a hand. 'We cannot conduct a discussion like this on the doorstep. What is your name, sir?'

'I'm William Baker, ma'am. Lily's father.'

'Very well. If you will select two or three of your companions to speak for the rest, you had better come up to my office, where we can talk in a civilised manner.'

She turned away and Baker looked round at the others. There was no shortage of volunteers and he quickly picked out two women and a man, who seemed to have gained the most benefit from the care they had been given. The four of them disappeared into the house, leaving Dora and her friends surrounded by the rest.

'I don't know how to thank you!' Dora said. 'To have come here specially to speak up for us! It's so good of you.'

'It's nothing to what you've done for us,' someone said. 'When we heard from Lily what was going to happen, well, we just couldn't sit back and do nothing.'

'Do you think it will work?' Pearl asked timidly.

'I wouldn't rely on it,' Phil responded. 'Mrs W. will not like to back down.'

It was some time before Baker and the others reappeared.

'Well?' Lily asked. 'What did she say?'

'She wants to talk to all four of you. I'm not sure if we have made our case or not, but at least she is thinking it over.'

241

'She's just as likely to haul us over the coals for acting without her authority,' Phil muttered pessimistically, as they mounted the stairs.

Once again, they stood in a line in front of Mrs Wardroper's desk. She regarded each one of them in turn.

'Whose idea was it to go into that slum and offer to care for the sick?'

'It was mine,' Dora confessed. 'I'd seen how terribly bad conditions were and I thought it was the only way I might help.'

'And what made you believe that you had sufficient skill and knowledge to treat these people?

'I knew we couldn't do much, but we do know how to dress wounds, and how important it is to keep things clean,' Phil said.

'From what I have heard, you did more than that. You administered medication of various sorts.'

Dora swallowed. 'That was me, too. I ... I have some knowledge of herbal remedies, which I have used in the infirmary and found efficacious. It seemed to me better that the poor people I was caring for should have them rather than nothing.'

'Have you discussed these "remedies" with any of the doctors?'

'I – I did try, once, ma'am. Dr McIntyre called them medieval superstitions.'

'I am not surprised! Yet you still persisted in administering them.'

'Because I know they work!'

Mrs Wardroper fixed her with a long stare. Then she looked at the others. 'And did you three participate in these ... experiments?'

'We don't have the knowledge Dora has,' Phil said. 'But we did see the results. She is right. Her medicines do work.'

'Hmm.' Mrs Wardroper's eyes scanned them all for a moment. 'I can see that you were motivated by Christian charity, which is commendable. But you exceeded the limits of your knowledge and expertise and could have done more harm than good. I shall reconsider my decision, but do not take too much comfort from that. I may yet decide that your conduct in joining that march outweighs any good intentions you may have had. You can go. I will give you my decision later.'

None of the four had much appetite for their dinner and afterwards Dora wandered out into the garden to be away from the fruitless speculation of her friends. She was sitting gloomily contemplating the fish in an ornamental pond when Lily came running towards her.

'Dora!' she cried breathlessly, 'you're wanted. Mrs Wardroper has sent for you.'

'Just me? Not all of us?'

'No, just you. She's got a gentleman with her.'

Dora climbed the stairs with a greater sense of foreboding than ever. She knew that she had transgressed more profoundly than the others. She had taken it upon herself to treat her patients with remedies that were not approved by the medical profession, and she guessed that the gentleman with Mrs Wardroper was probably some senior doctor from the hospital – or perhaps even a policeman. She was not sure whether what she had done was legal.

With a pounding heart she knocked at the door and was bidden to enter. Mrs Wardroper was in her usual place behind her desk and beside her stood a familiar figure.

'Mr Rathbone!'

'I received Mrs Wardroper's letter this morning and took the first train,' he said.

'Oh sir,' Dora gasped. 'I'm so sorry! You must think me wickedly ungrateful. I never meant to let you down. I'll do anything ... anything I can ... to make it up to you.'

Mr Rathbone came round the desk and took her by the hand. 'My dear Dora, I am not angry with you. I totally approve of your actions. Mrs Wardroper has told me of your charitable efforts to help the poor people in that slum. It is just what I would have expected from you. And I completely endorse the principles behind that march. It is more than time that respectable working men should have a vote. I came down not to reprimand you, but to intercede with Mrs Wardroper to allow you to continue your training. And I am happy to say that she has acceded to my request.'

Dora looked from him to Mrs Wardroper. 'Does that mean all of us, ma'am?'

She returned the look frostily. 'I can hardly excuse you and refuse the same indulgence to the other girls. You may all stay – but on the condition that if you wish to continue your efforts with the poor you must persuade one of the senior nurses to accompany you. I cannot allow unqualified girls to carry out that work unsupervised. Also, you will refrain from taking part in any political activity.'

The relief was so great that for a moment Dora felt as if her legs might buckle under her. She caught a breath. 'Thank you, ma'am. I promise we will abide by all your rules. And I will do my very best to prove that you were right to give me a second chance.' She turned to Mr Rathbone. 'And thank you, sir. I don't know how to find the words to tell you how grateful I am.'

He smiled a trifle wryly. 'As to that, I am not sure that my intercession was the deciding factor. Mrs Wardroper has told me about the deputation that came to see her this morning. I think their words carried more weight than mine could ever have done.' He took up his hat from where he had placed it on the desk. 'Now, if I am to catch my train I should be on my way. Goodbye, Mrs Wardroper, and thank you for listening to me.'

'Not at all, sir. It has been a pleasure to discover that my nurses have such an ardent supporter. I wish you a safe journey.'

Outside the door Dora said, 'Please, sir, if you can spare the time, I should like you to meet my friends. They will wish to thank you too.'

'I shall be delighted,' he replied. 'It seems to me that they must all be remarkable young women.'

In the hall, Phil and Lily and Pearl were waiting anxiously. The look on Dora's face was enough to tell them what they wanted to know.

'It's going to be all right!' Phil exclaimed.

Dora introduced them to her patron, who shook hands with each of them, saying, 'It is a privilege to make the acquaintance of three such dedicated nurses. As you probably know from Dora, I take a great interest in the welfare of those who are treated in our hospitals, particularly those who cannot afford to pay for their care. With nurses like you, I can feel confident that they will always receive the best possible care. And if any of you in the future should need help in furthering your careers or finding suitable positions, you may apply to me for a reference. Now, I must go or I shall miss my train. Good day to you.'

Tea time was very different from dinner as the four friends rejoiced in their reprieve. The rest of their watch shared their delight – except for Julia.

'Personally, I think you were all mad to get involved with those people,' she declared. 'They are the dregs of society and if they can't help themselves they don't deserve charity.'

Dora rounded on her. 'You don't know what it is like to be poor. I've worked with people like that all my life. Yes, some of them have brought it on themselves by drinking or by idleness, but the vast majority are decent people who have just fallen on hard times through no fault of their own. You have never wanted for anything in your life. You don't have a right to judge them!'

'Well said!' exclaimed Phil.

'Don't you take the high tone with me like that!' Julia said. 'You are in the same position, with your land and your titled father.'

'I know. But I can see how fortunate I am and do something to correct the balance.'

'Oh, you! I'm sick of this holier than thou attitude!' Julia said and flounced off.

The mood of euphoria was dampened when they were bidden once again to Mrs Wardroper's office.

'I have been considering the appropriate action to take in your case. You cannot be allowed to escape completely unscathed. So I have come to a decision. Over the month of August it is my intention to allow a few members of each watch to take a few days holiday, on a rotational basis. You will not be accorded that privilege. You will work your shifts without a break until I feel you have adequately made up for your earlier behaviour.'

Chapter 13

'But you will not be able to come to Lillden!' Elizabeth's disappointment was clearly genuine.

'I know,' Dora responded, unsure whether she was sorry or relieved. She had not seen Edward since the day before the march. He had kissed her and she had not resisted. So where did that leave their relationship? She did not know if she wanted to see him again or not, and at the back of her mind was the memory of her last letter to Jem. Was he still waiting for her to return to Liverpool? She had thought she was in love with him, but now that seemed to belong to another life.

'Edward will be furious,' Elizabeth said, as if she had read Dora's mind.

'Furious? Who with? Me?'

'Oh no, I didn't mean that. Furious with Mrs Wardroper for cancelling your holiday.'

'It's my own fault. He tried to persuade me not to go on that march, so if he is angry with anyone, it should be me.'

'He won't be angry – not really. Just disappointed. So am I. We were planning to teach you to ride, remember?'

'Oh, as far as that goes, I don't mind,' Dora said. 'As I said, I shall never have the chance to ride regularly.'

'You never know! Things don't always turn out the way we expect,' Elizabeth said, and there was something in her voice that made Dora wonder if she meant more than she was saying.

All through the long, hot days of August, Dora, Phil, Lily and Pearl worked their shifts in the hospital. The others went away and came back with stories of home comforts, country walks or days by the sea. All, that was, except for Julia, who went and never returned. No explanation was given, but none of them were surprised.

The four also continued their visits to the Old Nicol, though they were less frequent than before. This was not from any lack of interest on their part, but because of Mrs Wardroper's decree that they must always be accompanied by one of the qualified nurses. After a long shift on the wards, it was not surprising that most of them were reluctant to trek out to Shoreditch to do more of the same work. Word had gone round, however, about the deputation that had arrived to support the four students and the consciences of some of them had been sufficiently stirred to prompt them to agree to Phil and Dora's urgent requests.

Once they saw how dire the situation was, they made their own representations to Mrs Wardroper and as a result they were allowed to take medical supplies from the hospital to help in the work. Dora was pleased by that, but the embargo on the use of her herbal remedies was a source of frustration and distress. Her one-time patients begged her for the medicines that had relieved their pain and eased their fevers, but she did not dare to provide them.

One day a new, young doctor appeared on the wards. His name was Dr Frankby and he was tall, with hair and beard that had a chestnut gleam and eyes that sometimes looked brown and sometimes green. His arrival caused quite a flutter among the nursing staff and Dora derived considerable amusement from watching their efforts to impress him. He was recently qualified and obviously determined to show that he knew his job and did not need to refer to anyone else for advice, but on the other hand his attitude was less dogmatic than Dr McIntyre's and he was interested in the latest developments in medical science. When Phil discovered this she was quick to engage him in discussions about new ideas and he was clearly impressed by the fact that she took the trouble to read articles in medical journals.

'You know,' he remarked one day, 'I know a lot of doctors who are less well informed about the science of medicine than you are.'

'So why should women not become doctors?' Phil challenged him.

He shook his head. 'I don't think people are ready to accept the idea of a woman doctor. It is just too extraordinary. But that doesn't mean women cannot make very, very good nurses.'

'Hmmph,' said Phil, and left it at that.

One of the shifts they all dreaded was the surgical ward. It was right next to the operating theatre and the screams of the patients undergoing amputations or other procedures were hard to bear. One day, a young man came back to the ward after having his leg amputated, but no one had heard him scream.

'You are a brave lad,' Dora told him as she held a cup of water to his lips. 'You never made a sound all through it.'

'Didn't hurt,' the boy mumbled.

'It must have done,' she said; but he had closed his eyes and seemed to have drifted off to sleep.

Shortly afterwards, Dr Frankby came to check on his patient and Dora said, 'That boy must be made of stone. He told me it didn't hurt.'

'Of course,' the doctor said with a smile. 'He will not have felt a thing.'

'Do you mean that the leg was so far gone he had lost all feeling in it?'

'Not at all. He was simply unconscious all the time.'

'He fainted?'

'No. I rendered him unconscious with a substance called chloroform. It has been known for some years but it has only recently been used in general surgery.'

Phil, who was nearby, pricked up her ears. 'I read something about it. Didn't the queen use it when Prince Leopold was born?'

'Yes, that is correct. It was originally introduced by a Scottish doctor called Simpson for the purpose of alleviating the pain of childbirth.'

'And does it really render people so deeply unconscious that they do not feel something as painful as an amputation?' Dora asked.

'You have just heard this young man say so.'

'But why don't all surgeons use it? We have heard such heart-rending screams when Dr McIntyre operates.'

Frankby sighed and shook his head. 'It is still controversial in some quarters. There is the religious argument, that after the Fall, God condemned mankind to suffer for the sin committed by Adam and Eve, and to interfere with that is to go against his edict. Then there are those who feel we are interfering with nature or who doubt the safety of the procedure. I have even heard people say that a man, particularly, should be able to withstand pain and this is a proof of his manliness. But there is one more cogent argument. The fear is that once the patient is anaesthetised, the surgeon may be tempted to take longer over the operation, or to attempt more complex forms of surgery than have been possible hitherto.'

'I take it you don't subscribe to any of those arguments,' Phil said.

He smiled. 'I see my duty as being to relieve suffering whenever and wherever it is possible to do so.' He considered a moment. 'Have either of you ever witnessed an operation?'

They both shook their heads and Dora said, 'I couldn't bear to see someone suffering so much.'

'But if there was no suffering involved ...?'

'I should certainly like to watch,' Phil said.

'I am about to operate on the small boy who was brought in yesterday with an inflamed appendix. You can come and watch, provided you obey my instructions to the letter.'

'You are going to operate?' Phil said. 'I did not know it was possible to do that.'

'It is a very new procedure. The first such one was only carried out a few months ago by an American surgeon called Willard Parker. But it has been extensively reported and I saw the same procedure carried out by the surgeon under whom I studied.

'Have you done it before?' Phil asked.

Dora caught her eye and shook her head. The question seemed impertinent. But Frankby said quietly, 'No. But I have no doubt in my mind that that child will die a very painful death if I do not attempt it. Now, do you want to come and watch?'

'Yes!' said Phil, and Dora, after a moment's hesitation, nodded.

At that moment two of the hospital porters walked into the ward carrying a stretcher on which lay a small boy. He was struggling to get up and sobbing frantically.

'No, no! I don't want him to cut me open. Let me go! Let me go!'

Frankby moved quickly to the stretcher. 'What have you been saying to the child?' He laid his hand on the boy's shoulder. 'It's all right, Timmy. No one is going to hurt you. I promise. Just lie still and we'll have you better in no time.'

The child looked up into his eyes and stopped struggling, though he continued to whimper.

'Put him down here for a moment,' Frankby instructed, indicating an empty bed. He turned to Dora and Phil. 'Go into the operating theatre and wash your hands very thoroughly in the basin you will find there. You will notice the water has a strange smell, but don't let that worry you. Then come back to me.'

'We have already washed our hands, before we came onto the ward,' Dora said.

'I know. But I want you to wash them again.'

They did as they were ordered. The water was cloudy and did indeed have a strange, sickly-sweet smell.

When they returned Frankby said, 'Can you lift him between you?'

'Yes, of course,' Dora said.

'Then carry him through to the theatre.' He looked at the two porters. 'You can wait here. I do not want you in the operating theatre.'

The two looked mildly affronted but shrugged and moved off to find a seat. Dora carefully lifted the little boy in her arms. He was so thin and light that she could carry him easily. He was still whimpering and she could feel him shaking with fear.

'Don't worry, little one,' she murmured. 'You heard what the doctor said. No one is going to hurt you.'

Inside the operating theatre Frankby had spread a clean sheet on the table. 'Lay him down here,' he instructed. He picked up a large metal cylinder with a nozzle at one side and a handle on the other. 'This is another new discovery. This contains a solution of carbolic acid. A Scottish surgeon called Lister has discovered that by spraying the room and the patient and all the instruments with this it is possible to vastly reduce the danger of infection. It works like this, see?'

He pumped the handle and a yellow mist, with the same sickly-sweet smell, filled the room.

Frankby turned to Phil. 'Can you hold this? It's heavy, I warn you.'

Phil took the contraption and nodded. 'Yes, I can manage.'

'Right.' The doctor moved over to where the little boy lay. He was clinging to Dora's hand, silent now, his eyes wide with terror. Frankby leant over him. 'I'm going to put something over your mouth and nose, Timmy. It will smell a bit funny, so if you don't like it, just blow the smell away. Now, don't worry. I've promised I shall not hurt you. Do you believe me?'

Timmy swallowed and nodded.

'Good boy.'

He produced a small metal mask with perforations that reminded Dora of a tea strainer, and took a bottle from the table beside him. He poured some liquid onto a piece of lint and laid it over the mask. Then he laid it over the boy's nose and mouth. 'Now, lie still and take deep breaths,' he instructed.

The boy took a breath and then suddenly began to struggle, trying to pull the mask off. 'Hold him still,' Frankby instructed and Dora put her free hand on the child's shoulder and pressed him back onto the table. 'Remember what I said?' Frankby repeated. 'If you don't like the smell, blow it away. Take a big breath in and blow. That's right. And again ...'

Abruptly, the small body under Dora's hand went limp and the terrified eyes closed. Dora looked up in alarm. 'Is he ... is something wrong?'

'Not at all. He is unconscious, that is all. Now, take this,' He handed her the bottle. 'If he shows any sign of coming round, put a few more drops of chloroform on the lint.' He looked at Phil. 'Right, give a good spray with that carbolic.'

Phil obeyed and Dora and Frankby and his patient were enveloped in the yellow fog. The doctor removed a cloth that was covering a tray of instruments, which gleamed dully in the misty atmosphere. He lifted the boy's gown to expose his belly. 'Now, let's see what is going on in here.'

Dora watched him make the first incision. Then she decided it would be better to concentrate on watching Timmy for any sign of movement. A new and even more unpleasant stench filled the air and Frankby murmured, 'Ah yes. This is the scene of the putrefaction.' Dora was aware of him working and muttering to himself, occasionally interspersing his internal monologue with instructions to Phil. 'More spray here, please. Yes, enough ....' But she kept her eyes averted.

After what seemed a long time she realised that he was stitching the wound together. There was a good deal of blood and pus on his hands and on the cloth he had been swabbing the wound with, but he looked satisfied.

'Well, I think we can be hopeful of a cure,' he said. 'At least the child has a chance now. All right, you can remove the mask now, Nurse Latimer.'

Dora did as he said and waited for Timmy's eyes to open. Nothing happened. She looked at Frankby in alarm. He placed his fingers on the boy's throat and nodded. 'The pulse is quite strong. Give him a few minutes.'

At last Timmy took a sudden breath, his eyes opened and he tried to sit up.

'It's all right, dear,' Dora said soothingly, 'You're all right. Don't be afraid.'

He sank back and looked around for the doctor. Frankby was engaged in washing his hands.

'When is he going to do it?' the boy whispered.

'It's all done,' Dora told him. 'You've been asleep and the doctor has finished.'

Timmy raised his head and peered down at the bandages on his stomach. Frankby returned. 'You are a very lucky boy. Not many doctors know how to do what I have done.

Now, you can go back to bed and very soon you will be up and about again.'

He opened the door and called the porters. 'You can take this little lad back, now.'

Timmy was carried away and Frankby said, 'I hope you have both learned something this morning.'

'We certainly have!' Phil said emphatically. 'Thank you so much for letting us watch.'

'You did not just watch. You were a part of the process and a very useful part, too. Now, you must wash your hands again before you leave. The most important lesson I want you to take away is the importance of the use of antiseptics, especially in surgery. Everything must be kept sterile.'

'Does that mean that you believe in Dr Pasteur's theory about germs?' Phil asked.

'It seems to me to be the only real explanation for how infections are passed from one person to another.'

'Ah ha!' Phil said, with an expression of triumph.

A week later Dora was returning from a shift when she once again found Edward waiting outside the manor house.

'Good morning.' She forced her voice to take on a casual tone. 'I hope you had a good holiday.'

'I did, up to a point,' he said, 'but I missed seeing you.' He offered her his arm. 'Can we walk a little?'

She slid her hand into the crook of his arm and felt a sudden flutter in her stomach. They began to stroll through the grounds and after a pause he said, 'We had a ... a disagreement last time we met. But I hope I made it clear in the end that I didn't want to quarrel.'

'Yes.' She could think of nothing else to add.

'Perhaps I overstepped the mark a bit when I tried to persuade you not to go on that march, but I really was only concerned that you might be putting yourself in danger.'

'You were right, in a way,' she conceded. 'But it was not during the march. I was perfectly safe there. It was afterwards.'

'Elizabeth told me all about what happened. I really admire you for going out into that dreadful slum to help those people. Thank heaven they were sufficiently grateful to come and speak on your behalf to Mrs Wardroper.'

'Thank heaven for Mr Rathbone, too,' she said.

Edward nodded. 'He must think a great deal of you, to come rushing down to London like that.'

'It has nothing to do with me, personally,' she said. 'He has made an investment, and if I don't go back to the infirmary as a qualified nurse he has wasted his money.'

He gave a deep sigh. 'I hate the idea of you going back there. I can't bear the thought of not seeing you.'

She glanced sideways at him. 'There are trains that go between London and Liverpool, you know.'

'You mean you might come to visit?'

'I was thinking more that you might come to Liverpool.' She saw from his face that she might have suggested he take a train to the moon.

'It's not enough,' he said, 'whichever way we did it. I am going to miss you so dreadfully.'

She hesitated. 'I shall miss you, too – and all the wonderful concerts and things you have taken me to.'

He stopped suddenly and turned to face her. 'Don't go! Stay here!'

'And do what?' she asked.

For a moment he stared at her in silence, and in that pause a vision flashed across her mind of Lillden, with its wide lawns and shady woodlands, its opulent furnishings and luxurious lifestyle.

'I don't know,' he said. 'There must be some way.'

Dora dragged her mind back to reality. 'No, Edward. There isn't. I have to go back to Liverpool.'

'I can't accept that!' He seized her by the shoulders and tried to pull her into his embrace, but she resisted and freed herself.

'No!' Then more gently, 'I am sorry, but that is the way it has to be. And as it does, I think it is better if we don't see each other again.' He began to protest but she overrode him. 'I know it seems hard and I am very sorry if I have ever given you reason to think that things could be different. But you will forget me quite quickly, once I am far away. And I shall do my best to forget you. Now, I must go. Goodbye, Edward.'

She turned quickly and walked away. At the end of the shady path they had followed she looked back. He was standing where she had left him, staring after her, but his expression was not so much stricken as that of a man trying to solve a particularly knotty problem.

Later, alone in her little room, she went over in her mind what had been said. She was sure that she had done the right thing. The relationship was impossible – had been impossible from the start. It was much better to end it now than to let it drag on. It was common sense, but more than that it was a matter of pride. So she told herself, but something inside her, that knew nothing of pride or common sense, was weeping.

*

The first rumours of an outbreak of cholera reached the hospital towards the end of August. It began in the downtrodden areas of east London, close to the waters of the River Lea and, although everyone expected it to spread, it seemed after a while that it struck only those living in that area. Dora's immediate reaction to the news was one of anxiety for her friends in the Old Nicol, which was in the heart of the affected area. Lily too was worried because although the street where her family lived was comparatively respectable, the slum was very close. As soon as their shifts allowed, they set off for Shoreditch, without bothering to persuade one of the qualified nurses to accompany them. After all, they reasoned, they were not intending to treat anyone.

The Bakers were all well, to Lily's profound relief, but Mrs Baker told them that horrific stories were reaching them from the mean streets nearby. When they proposed to go and see for themselves, she begged them with tears in her eyes to stay away.

'You only have to touch one of them, or breathe the same air!' she pleaded. 'I don't want you going and catching it and then bringing it back here.'

Lily hesitated. 'Mum, I must go and find out if Peggy is all right, and her little one. But if it worries you, we won't come in here afterwards. Then there will be no chance of us carrying the sickness to you.'

'But what about you?' her mother wailed.

'Oh, don't worry about us,' Lily said. 'We know how to keep ourselves safe, don't we, Dora?'

'Oh yes, of course.' Dora knew it was a lie. They had no more idea of how the disease was spread than Mrs Baker, but the assurance was enough to calm her down.

Lily kissed her and hugged her little brothers and they set off into the narrow lanes and alleyways of the Old Nicol. Dora noticed immediately that something had changed. There were no children playing in the streets, no women gossiping, no men working at trades or standing idle. The whole area was disturbingly quiet, but the smell of ordure was stronger than ever. Lily led the way to the crumbling tenement where Peggy lived. The place seemed to be deserted. Lily called up the stairs, but there was no response. She and Dora exchanged looks and then, without the need for words, they began to climb. On the first floor an open door showed the interior of a room, where the only furniture seemed to be a broken down bed. On it lay an old woman, her body twisted at an unnatural angle and her face turned up towards the ceiling. Dora went to her and put a hand on her cheek, but she knew already what she would find.

'She's dead, Lily.'

'Oh, God!' Lily whispered, and went on up the stairs.

At the door of Peggy's room they both paused, afraid of what they would find.

'Peg?' Lily called softly. 'It's me, Lily. Can we come in?'

There was no answer.

Seeing that Lily was hesitating, Dora pushed the door open. They both stepped back, with an involuntary cry of disgust. The room reeked of excrement and vomit. Holding one hand over her mouth and nose, Dora advanced inside. Peggy was on the bed, curled into a foetal position. The sheet was soaked with excrement, which had dribbled down onto the floor. Dora forced herself to cross the room and put her hand on Peggy's neck. She was cold, and there was no sign of a pulse.

Dora straightened up. 'I'm sorry, Lily. She's gone. I think she had been dead for at least a day.'

'Oh, God!' Lily said again, this time it came out as a high-pitched wail. Then she looked wildly round the room. 'What about the little one?'

They found him in his cot, as filthy and as cold and immobile as his mother. Lily went to pick him up but Dora caught her arm.

'Leave him, Lily. There's nothing we can do and there's no point in exposing ourselves to contagion any more than we have done.' She looked round the room. 'Didn't Peggy say she had four children?'

'Oh, God!' This seemed to be the response that came automatically to Lily's lips. 'Where are they, the poor mites?'

'Let's search the rest of the house,' Dora said.

Out on the stairs Lily sank down and buried her face in her hands, sobbing. Dora hesitated a moment, then said, 'You stay there. I'll look.' Steeling herself for the worst, she climbed carefully up the creaking stairway. To her relief, the rooms on the next floor were empty, though there were signs of a hasty departure. The attics above were also deserted. She went back to Lily.

'There's no one up there.'

'So what's happened to the children?'

Dora heaved a sigh. 'Heaven knows. Perhaps they've been taken in by someone. We'll have to knock on a few doors.'

They made their way back to the street. There Dora hesitated, looking around her. 'Perhaps we should see if there is anyone we can help. There must be people still alive in some of these houses.'

Lily shuddered and began to weep again. 'I can't, Dora! I just can't bear to see any more sights like that.'

Dora put her arm round her. 'I know, I know. I feel the same but ...'

The unnatural silence was broken by the sound of wheels on the cobbles and a handcart came into view, pulled by two men. On the back of it were two coffins and hung on the side was a notice: Thos. Graveny and Sons, Undertakers.

Dora gave a gasp of relief and stepped forward.

'Stop, please!'

The men halted and the elder of the two looked them up and down as if torn between surprise and resentment at their presence. 'What do you want? This is no place for young ladies.'

'Where are you taking those coffins? To the cemetery?'

A mirthless grin appeared on the man's face. 'Bit early for that, seeing as they're empty.'

'Empty? Then you have come to collect a body – or two bodies? Where from?'

'Wherever we find them,' he answered. 'We've been charged by the council to collect and bury any that have been left lying. Can't have them spreading infection.'

'Oh, thank goodness!' Dora exclaimed. 'You are just the men we need.' She pulled herself together. 'My name is Dora Latimer and this is my friend Lily Baker. We are students at the Nightingale School of Nursing. We just called in to see whether Lily's friend, Peggy, was in need of help.' She paused, swallowed and forced herself to be professional. 'She's dead and so is her baby boy. And there is an old woman in another room, in that house behind me. The deaths need to be reported, but we don't know where to go to do it. And there are three other children who are missing. We need to find out what has happened to them.'

The man looked at her for a moment, then he said, 'Wait there.'

He disappeared into the house and returned after a brief pause, looking grim.

'You're right. Nothing to be done there.' He considered them for a moment. 'You're a brave couple and no mistake. All right. You can leave them to me. I'll see they're done right by. What were the names again?'

He produced a grubby notebook from his pocket and took a stub of pencil from behind his ear. Dora looked at Lily.

'Do you know Peggy's married name?'

'Stone,' Lily said, then clasped a hand to her mouth in dismay. 'Her husband! He must be told.'

'What's his full name?' the undertaker's man enquired.

'Oh, I don't know. I can't remember. Yes, I can. It's Sidney.'

'Know where he works?'

'No, I'm afraid not.'

Across the street a door opened a crack and a face peered out. Then the door was opened wider and a small woman came out. She was hugging a shawl tightly round her narrow shoulders and her face could have belonged to anyone between the ages of thirty and sixty. She advanced timidly to where Dora and Lily were standing.

'You're Peggy's friend, ain't you? I seen you going in and out. And you and her,' indicating Dora, 'you're the nurses from St Thomas's, ain't you?'

'Yes, that's right.' Lily reached out and caught hold of the woman's arm. 'Peggy's dead and the baby, and we can't find the other children.'

'I got two of them here, with me,' the woman said. 'The girl, Polly, she come home a couple of days ago. Came running over to me in tears 'cos she'd found her ma dead and the little one, and her little brother clinging to his ma's body and howling. I took them in. Well, what's a body to do?'

'Oh, thank you! Thank you!' Lily exclaimed. 'It's so good of you.'

'What about the eldest one, the boy?' Dora asked. 'Didn't he work for a chimney sweep?'

'Fred Biggins,' the woman confirmed. 'I sent my eldest round to tell him what had happened. He's kept the boy with him. He'll take him as an apprentice, so there's no need to worry about him.'

'What about the two with you?' Dora asked.

'I'll keep them, for now anyway – if we're all spared. Pol's a good girl, and she brings in a bit of money, and the little un's no trouble.'

The undertaker's man shifted his feet. 'Look, I've got a job to do. I can't stand around here all day. I'll see to the bodies. The rest's up to you.'

He and his mate lifted one of the coffins off the cart and disappeared into the house. Lily shivered. 'Let's go, Dora. I can't bear it here any longer.'

'Just one more thing,' Dora said. She turned to the little woman. 'Do you know how to get in touch with Peggy's husband?'

'Him?' The woman's lip curled in a sneer. 'He scarpered as soon as the first few went sick. I ain't seen him for days.'

Dora looked at Lily. 'In that case, I don't think we need to stay. The undertaker will inform the necessary authorities and it seems the children are being cared for.' She reached into her reticule and found a florin, which she held out to the woman. 'I know that it isn't easy to feed two extra mouths. This may help a little.'

The woman looked at the coin, pride and gratitude struggling for supremacy in her expression. 'I don't need charity,' she mumbled.

'I know,' Dora said. 'But this is just a way of saying thank you for your kindness. Please take it.'

The woman hesitated a moment and then nodded and reached for the money. 'It'll come in very useful, there's no denying. Thank'ee, miss.'

Dora turned away and put her arm round Lily, who was shaking. 'Come along. Let's get you back to the hospital. We've done all we can here.'

Chapter 14

The first cholera cases arrived at St Thomas's soon after that. There were one or two on the first day, six the next, and very soon the staff were forced to discharge all those who could walk or who could be looked after at home and clear two wards to accommodate the influx. The older nurses had seen cholera before but for some of the young ones it was a new experience, and a very difficult one. The symptoms of the disease were distressing enough. The victims suffered from violent stomach cramps and diarrhoea; they vomited continually and their skins turned a clammy bluish white. They were constantly thirsty and complained of aching limbs. Some of them thrashed around wildly, so intense was the pain, others lay supine without the strength to complain. What was worse was the realisation that no one, even the most experienced doctors, had any idea how to treat the disease. Most of the patients suffered for a day or two and then died. All the nurses could do was try to keep them clean and make sure they had water to drink.

'Now as never before,' Sister Andrews said at the morning briefings, 'it is vital to maintain the strictest hygiene. We do not know how this disease is spread but it is probable that, like so many others, it is caused by the miasma arising from dirt of all sorts. I know it is going to be very hard, but the wards must be kept spotless at all times, and you must wash your hands at every opportunity.'

Normal shifts were abandoned. Nurses and students worked for twelve hours at a time, and sometimes longer.

Dr McIntyre examined each patient and prescribed his usual treatment. They must be bled. Watching, Dora thought that in their weakened state this must be the last thing they needed, but she dare not say so.

Later, when Dr Frankby came on duty, she said, 'Is there really no treatment, other than bleeding?'

'None that have proved effective,' he said sadly. 'When it first appeared in India doctors there tried all sorts of remedies, some of them too brutal even to contemplate, but nothing worked. The trouble is, we don't know what causes it, so it is hard to think of possible cures. But there is hope, perhaps not for these poor souls, but hope that we may be able to prevent further outbreaks.'

'How?' Dora asked.

'There is a school of thought that suggests that the disease is spread through contaminated drinking water. Some years ago, there was an outbreak in Soho and the local physician, a man called John Snow, noticed that all those affected were drawing water from the same pump. The only people not affected were the inmates of the nearby workhouse, which had its own well. He prevailed upon the local council to remove the handle from the pump so it could not be used and the outbreak stopped. If you believe in germ theory, as I increasingly do, it seems quite reasonable to suggest that the water may have contained germs.

Unfortunately, the majority of established medical men still cling to the miasma theory and think it is transmitted through breathing bad air.'

'If it is water, what can be done to prevent it?' Dora asked.

'Much has been done already,' he said, 'with the new sewer system and filtration plants, and now that companies are no longer permitted to draw water from the tidal section of the Thames the quality of water is much better.'

'So, why has this outbreak happened?'

'It is interesting that it seems to be confined to one area. I think the water must be supplied by the East London Water Company. I hope some investigation is being carried out to see if they bear any responsibility.'

'Is there anything people can do to avoid being infected?' Dora asked. 'Lily's family live in Shoreditch and she is almost out of her mind with worry.'

'Well,' Frankby said slowly, 'it may be a long shot, and I would probably be shouted down by doctors with more experience than I have, but I would suggest that for the time being they boil all their drinking water. It certainly won't do any harm, and, if I am right about the cause of the outbreak, it may protect them.'

'I'll tell Lily as soon as I get a chance,' Dora promised.

Unable to visit her family, since they were all confined to the hospital until further notice, Lily immediately wrote home with that advice. Two days later she received a reply, promising that it would be heeded.

Dora discussed Dr Frankby's theories, as she usually did, with Phil.

'I read something in the paper the other day suggesting that water supplied by the East London Water Company might be to blame,' Phil said, 'I don't know if the matter has gone any further.'

Two days later she came to breakfast with a copy of *The Times*. 'There's a letter here from a Mr Greaves, the water company's engineer, flatly denying any responsibility. He says—' she consulted the paper '—"not a drop of unfiltered water has for several years past been supplied by the company for any purpose".'

'So perhaps Dr Frankby is wrong, after all,' Dora said.

'Or perhaps Mr Greaves is lying through his teeth,' Phil retorted.

The controversy went on over several weeks, while the epidemic showed no sign of abating. One day Phil came into the dining room red-faced with fury. She flung down a copy of *The Times* in front of Dora.

'Read that!'

It was a letter from a Mr Beardmore, the engineer to the Lea River Trust, denying that the disease was the result of contaminated water. Instead 'overcrowding, deficiency of drainage, and inferior articles of food are more likely to have promoted cholera than impurity or deficiency of water'. The East End, he went on, was populated by '... dock labourers, sailors, mechanics in the new factories and great numbers of laundresses, all social groups whose poverty, irregular lives and underdeveloped sense of personal hygiene made them especially susceptible to the disease.'

Dora shook her head sadly. 'This is typical. I've seen the same attitude in Liverpool to people in the workhouse infirmary. No one ever blames the fact that they are sick on the dreadful conditions they are forced to live in, or on low wages and unemployment. They prefer to think that they have brought it on themselves by drinking or gambling or sheer idleness. How can you blame people for being dirty when six families have to share two privies and the only water has to be drawn from a communal pump? It is so unjust!'

'It is an injustice that has to be abolished!' Phil was still angry. 'I see more than ever why ordinary men want the vote. Things will not change until people like that have a say in government. If women had a chance to make their voices heard, conditions like the ones you describe would not be tolerated for a day!'

At last the number of new admissions began to decrease and it seemed that the epidemic was over. Lily and Dora made a long-delayed visit to her family and discovered that they had all survived. They were convinced that Dr Frankby's advice about boiling water had saved them, and they had passed it on to other families nearby, none of whom had contracted the disease.

The weeks of struggling to cope with caring for the cholera patients had left Dora no time or energy for the consideration of her last conversation with Edward. When she did have leisure to think of him she realised that he had made no effort to contact her, so she assumed that he had accepted her decision that they should stop seeing each other. Then, one day when the fallen leaves were being rattled along the paths in Surrey Gardens by a gusty autumn wind, she received a letter.

My dear Dora,

I must see you! Ever since our last meeting I have been unable to settle to anything and my studies are suffering – my health also. I cannot let you go back to Liverpool without making a last attempt to persuade you to change your mind. I need to talk to you to try to find some solution which will be acceptable to both of us.

I know it would not be proper for me to ask you to meet me alone, so I am writing to Elizabeth to ask for her help. I happen to know that neither of my parents will be in the house in Mayfair next week, as they have engagements in Surrey. I shall ask Elizabeth to invite you to tea and then to give us a few moments alone to talk.

Please, dear Dora, do not refuse to meet me. If you have any kindness for me, give me this one last chance.

> *Your loving friend,*
> *Edward*

Dora had just come off duty after the night shift and had been on her way to bed. She went up to the dormitory and tapped on the door of Elizabeth's room. Her friend was holding a letter in her hand.

'Dora! Come in. We need to talk.'

'Yes,' Dora agreed. 'I know we do.'

'You have got Edward's letter?'

'Yes.'

'I had no idea that ... that matters between you had got to this point. It seems he is in love with you. Did you know?'

'Yes ... well, he says he cannot bear to part with me.'

'I gather you must have tried to break off with him. What happened?'

'He ... he kissed me. I realise that there can never be any ... any lasting relationship between us, so I told him it would be better if we did not see each other again.'

'When did this happen?'

'He came here, just before the cholera outbreak started. He was waiting for me when I came back from the hospital. It has happened twice, in fact.' She looked at her friend. 'I suppose I should have told you, but I was afraid you would think badly of me.'

'Why?'

'I think ... I think I must have given the wrong impression ... that I was, well, "setting my cap" at him, as the saying goes.'

'That would never have occurred to me.'

'It occurred to your mother, a long time ago, when I came to stay at Lillden.'

'Oh, Mother! She is always scheming to marry Edward off to some titled lady. You should not have taken any notice of her.'

'But she was right,' Dora said. 'I don't mean about what she thought of me. I never dreamed of anything like that. But she was right that ... that any sort of relationship between me and Edward would be quite improper.'

'I don't see why. If Edward loves you, there's no reason why he shouldn't marry you.'

'Of course there is! Just think what everyone would say. He, a young lawyer with a successful career ahead of him, marrying a penniless black girl with no family. It would be a scandal.'

'Perhaps it would. But, Dora, isn't this just the sort of thing we are all fighting against? We all want the right to be independent women, making our own decisions, never mind what "society" thinks of us. The question is, are you in love with Edward?'

Dora sank down on the edge of the bed with a sigh. It had been a long night, and she was tired, too tired to make decisions. 'I don't know. I ... I like him very much. I find him very attractive. But I'm not sure if that counts as being in love.'

Elizabeth sat beside her. 'Perhaps you need more time to get to know him. What do you want me to tell him, when I write back? Will you meet him?'

'I suppose I should. But what do you think he wants to say to me? He talks about finding a solution "acceptable to both of us". What do you think he means?'

Elizabeth met her eyes. 'Well, there's only one thing he can mean, isn't there?'

'Would you mind terribly?'

'Mind? No! If he really loves you, and you love him, I can't think of anyone I should rather have as a sister-in-law.'

Dora looked at her and felt tears come to her eyes. 'That means a lot to me. But don't jump to any conclusions. I'll listen to what he has to say, but I still think the whole idea is impossible.'

'Don't make up your mind yet. Let me see. Next week we shall be on the morning shift. I will tell him that we shall be at the house in Mayfair on Sunday afternoon. Will that be all right?'

Dora got up wearily. 'Yes, yes, I suppose so.'

Elizabeth smiled and squeezed her hand. 'That's settled then.'

Dora lived through the intervening days in a state of confusion that kept her from sleeping and made her less attentive to her work than normal. The more she thought about it, the more convinced she became that the whole idea of marriage between her and Edward was impossible. It was all very well for Elizabeth to talk about being independent and ignoring what society would think, but she knew that it would ruin his career.

Beside that, she had her own commitments to consider. She was honour-bound to return to Liverpool and repay the debt she owed to Mr Rathbone. Yet, through all her practical considerations, the mirage of Lillden's green acres floated in her mind. She thought of days spent in country walks and evenings of music; of time to read and talk; of living in surroundings of beauty; of fine food and beautiful clothes. And she could not help contrasting that picture with her memories of the workhouse infirmary; the unchanging routine, the life confined within grey walls; the poverty and the constant struggle to make limited means stretch as far as possible. She remembered that she had once dreamed of being a respected member of society, a lady no less. And with that thought came the memory of Fenella's cruel voice. '*She may be ladylike, but she can never be a real lady.*' That, she told herself, was the reality of her life and that was what she must make Edward understand.

Sunday came at last. In church, Dora prayed for courage to follow the path set down for her and for the humility to accept it. By the time she and Elizabeth reached the Mayfair house she had achieved a degree of calm, which the sight of Edward's golden hair and bright blue eyes threatened to disrupt. For half an hour they drank tea and made conversation, then Elizabeth excused herself and they were left alone.

Edward spoke first. 'Thank you for agreeing to talk to me.'

'I am sorry that you have been upset by our last meeting, but I am afraid that there is very little I can say to make things easier for you.'

'Don't say that! I have thought long and hard about this. In fact, I have thought of little else for weeks. Please don't make any decisions until you have heard what I am going to propose.'

Dora raised a hand to stop him. 'Edward, before you say anything else, you should know this. I, too, have thought long and hard. And I have come to a conclusion. We both have paths laid down for us in life; you as a successful lawyer, me as a nurse. We must follow where they lead. I will not be responsible for ruining your prospects, so there can be no question of marriage between us.'

He looked as if she had hit him with a blunt object. 'Marriage!' For a moment he seemed unable to speak. Then he said, 'Dora, that is not what I was going to suggest. Of course, I understand that it would be quite unsuitable. That is not what I asked you here to talk about.'

Dora felt a blush rising from her heart up to her throat, but at the same time an icy hand seemed to grip her stomach. With some difficulty she rose to her feet.

'Forgive me. It was a … a misunderstanding. I must leave now.'

She headed for the door but he was there before her.

'No! You must not go until you have heard me out. Please! Please sit down again. If you care for me at all, you will not leave me like this.'

She looked at him. His eyes beseeched her and she no longer had the will to resist. She returned to her chair and sat down.

He sat opposite, leaning towards her. 'Listen. I agree with you. We both have our separate paths to follow, but there is no reason why they should not run side by side. I have a suggestion that would make that possible. Your path, as you say, is to be a nurse. I have talked to Elizabeth and she has told me that most of the lady students, once they have qualified, go on to become superintendents at hospitals which do not yet have the advantage of Nightingale-trained nurses. Their job is to train others and to bring the knowledge and techniques you have gained to benefit patients who would otherwise suffer. Is that not so?'

Dora nodded slowly. She had heard of many previous graduates who had taken up positions of great responsibility in hospitals around the country and even abroad, and she knew that already her fellow students were discussing the prospects of such appointments. 'What has that to do with what you want to suggest?'

'Would it not be better if you could take on such a position, rather than going back to work in that infirmary? Your training would be put to much better use in a position of authority. I am sure there must be many hospitals in London that would welcome you.'

'Ah,' she said. 'Now I begin to see.'

'Think about it! If you took a position like that, we could continue to meet. We could go to concerts and the theatre together, you could spend weekends at Lillden ...'

'And is that what you want? All you want?'

He shook his head and hesitated for a moment. Then he drew breath and she sensed that he was coming to the kernel of his idea. 'By next summer I shall have qualified and I shall not wish to continue living at home. I shall want my own establishment. I am thinking of taking an apartment in Half Moon Street, or somewhere similar. Once I am settled there, there will be nothing to prevent you from visiting me, whenever your duties permit.'

She stared at him. It was like looking at a stranger. 'You are suggesting that I should become your mistress.'

'It is not an unusual arrangement.'

'Is it not? And would you introduce me to your friends?' It had suddenly occurred to her that in all their outings together she had never met any of his London friends.

'Well, where it seemed appropriate ...' His tone, so confident a moment ago, seemed to waver.

'And one day, I presume you will wish to marry.'

'I suppose that will become necessary, at some point.'

'And will you introduce me to your wife?'

'Hardly!'

'No, I thought not. So how will you contrive that we shall not meet?'

'Oh, that will not be a problem. She will live at Lillden. She will understand that I need to maintain a pied-à-terre in London for my work and I shall go down to the country at weekends.'

For a moment longer she gazed at him, marvelling that this was the man she had imagined spending her life with. She got up.

'We have nothing more to say to one another. Goodbye, Edward.'

He jumped to his feet. 'Dora, wait! Can't you see? It's the perfect solution ...'

She was already at the door. In the hall, Elizabeth was waiting, an expectant smile on her face. Her expression changed as she saw Dora. 'What is it? What has happened?'

'Your brother!' Dora stopped and forced herself to speak calmly. 'Your brother's notions of morality are not the same as mine. I am leaving now. I'll see you back at Surrey Gardens.'

There was one ward in the hospital that Dora always tried to avoid working in, but sometimes that was impossible. It was the lying-in ward. The sight of women in the pains of childbirth brought back too vivid a memory of her own suffering, but it was the joy on their faces as they took their newborn babies in their arms for the first time that was hardest to bear. She usually tried to make sure that she was busy with clearing up, taking soiled sheets to be laundered, anything that meant she did not have to be near at that moment. Working in the other wards, or chatting to her friends in off-duty moments, she was able to forget the events that had shaped her life nearly five years earlier. She had taught herself not to think about the child she had abandoned, but the sight of happy mothers cradling their infants reminded her too sharply of what she had missed.

Shortly after her last interview with Edward, she was sent to work in the lying-in ward. A woman had been brought in who had already been in labour for more than a day. She was exhausted and for a while she lay in a state of semi-consciousness and nothing seemed to be happening. Then the pains started up again, more violently than ever. They went on and on, but the baby still did not come. The mid-wife examining her stepped back and said quietly to Dora,

'It's a breech birth. Find Dr McIntyre.'

Dora hurried away in search of him, but she went reluctantly. She had seen him at work before and knew how unsympathetic he could be. She found him and delivered the message, but then went in search of Dr Frankby. He was just leaving the operating theatre when she arrived, panting.

'Nurse Latimer? What can be the matter? You look distraught.'

'There's a woman giving birth in the lying-in ward. It's breech, and she's been in labour for days. The midwife has sent for Dr McIntyre, but I know he will not care how much she suffers.'

'So what do you expect me to do?'

'You told us that the queen uses chloroform when she is in labour. Can you not bring some to the lying-in ward for this poor woman?'

Frankby looked worried. 'I cannot intervene between a senior doctor and his patient.'

'But how can you let someone suffer when she need not?'

He hesitated, then said, 'Very well. I will bring the chloroform apparatus. But if Dr McIntyre decides it is not necessary, I must defer to his judgement.'

When Dora reached the ward with Dr Frankby they could hear the woman's screams from outside. Dr McIntyre had removed his coat and rolled up his sleeve and his arm was up to the elbow in the woman's vagina.

Frankby approached and said deferentially, 'May I be of any assistance, sir?'

McIntyre looked up. 'What are you doing here? Do you think I am incapable of dealing with this on my own?'

'Not at all, sir. But I have brought the chloroform. I thought it might be useful in this case.'

'Chloroform? What nonsense is this? Have you no religion, man? What does it say in the book of Genesis? "In sorrow shalt thou bring forth children". This is the punishment for the sins of Eve.'

His words were punctuated by a long, sobbing cry. The midwife said anxiously, 'The woman's at the end of her strength, doctor.'

'I am doing all I can,' McIntyre replied. 'I am trying to turn the child. If I can bring one arm out . . .'

There was another scream. McIntyre withdrew his arm, which was bloody to the elbow.

'It's of no use. There is only one solution. She must be cut. Bring me my scalpel.'

'You would perform a caesarean section, without the benefit of anaesthesia?' Dr Frankby asked, horrified.

McIntyre looked at him for a moment. Then he shrugged. 'Very well. If it offends your gentle sensibilities, you may administer the chloroform.'

Frankby leaned over the woman. 'What is her name?'

'Cora Sykes,' the midwife said.

'Mrs Sykes, I am going to put something over your nose and mouth. There is no need to be afraid. In a moment you will be asleep and you will feel no more pain. When you wake up, your baby will have been born.'

The woman looked up at him with terror in her eyes. He applied the mask and dripped a little chloroform onto it. There was a brief instant of struggle, then the frightened eyes rolled up and the lids closed.

'Very well,' Frankby said. 'You can proceed now.'

McIntyre picked up the scalpel but Frankby intervened. 'Sir, would it not be best to wash your hands first? There is good evidence that the practice reduces the likelihood of puerperal fever. I have brought a bar of carbolic soap with me. I suggest we both use it.'

McIntyre met his eyes and Dora thought she saw a grudging respect in them. 'Very well, as you wish.'

Frankby turned to her. 'Nurse Latimer, a basin of water if you please.'

Dora had anticipated the need and the water was soon produced. Both doctors washed their hands and arms. Then McIntyre picked up the scalpel again. Dora would like to have kept well away while the operation proceeded. She still found that the sight of a body being cut into made her feel faint, but on this occasion she found herself unable to withdraw. She was riveted to the spot, watching in mingled horror and fascination. When the baby was lifted into the air, bloody and wrinkled, she gave an involuntary sob of relief.

'It's a boy,' McIntyre announced. He passed the child to the midwife, who turned it upside down and administered a sharp slap. For a moment there was no response, and Dora saw anxious looks pass between the midwife and the two doctors. Then the baby began to cry. The midwife wrapped him in a towel and then turned and thrust the bundle into Dora's arms.

'Take him. Get him washed.'

At that instant something within Dora that had been under increasing strain for years snapped. The sensation of holding a new life, the warm reality and weight of the child, awoke instincts she had long suppressed. She clutched him to herself and began to sob helplessly.

'What the ...?' exclaimed McIntyre.

'Pull yourself together girl!' said the midwife. 'Get on with your job.'

Dora's sobs became increasingly uncontrollable. 'For heaven's sake!' the midwife said. 'Give him to me if you can't be sensible.'

She tried to take the baby out of Dora's arms, but she backed away into a corner of the room. 'No! No! You can't have him. I won't give him up. I won't give him away this time!'

'For God's sake, get that girl out of the room,' McIntyre roared. 'I'm trying to close up here.'

Frankby came to her. 'Dora, what is it? Tell us what the matter is.' Dora only shook her head and continued sobbing. 'Come now,' he said gently, 'let me have the child. He needs to go his mother.'

'No, no! You can't have him. He's mine! He's mine!' She cowered on the floor, folding her body protectively around the child.

She heard him say, 'Fetch Sister Andrews – or one of the students who work with her. They may be able to talk sense to her. I have to attend to the patient.'

She was vaguely aware of people moving around, of voices coming and going. Then Phil was kneeling in front of her, speaking gently.

'Dora, you can't keep the baby. He's not yours. He needs his mother; she's awake now. She wants to see her baby.'

Dora looked at her through eyes blurred with tears. 'I gave mine away. I want to keep this one.'

'You can't. You know that. Listen, he's crying. He needs to suckle. You can't feed him. Let me take him to his mother.'

'I can't feed him,' Dora repeated miserably. 'I couldn't feed the last one, either.' She thrust the child into Phil's arms. 'Take him. I'm no good to him.'

After that there was a confused period when several voices spoke over her head. She heard Sister Andrews say, 'Get her away from here. Take her up to my office.' Then she was on her feet, with Phil's strong arm round her waist and Elizabeth holding her arm on the other side, and she was being walked up the stairs to the tiny cubbyhole of an office that had been created for Sister Andrews under the rafters. She was lowered into a chair and a glass was put into her hand.

'Take a sip, just a sip now. It's brandy.'

She had never tasted spirits and the brandy burned her throat, but the sensation brought her back to reality. She looked round the room. Sister Andrews was leaning over her and Phil and Elizabeth were behind her, their faces full of concern.

'There now,' Sister Andrews said. 'You look a little better. Do you want to tell us what all that was about?'

Dora shook her head.

Sister Andrews tone became sharper. 'You are going to have to explain yourself sooner or later. Better get it over with now.'

Dora sank deeper into the chair and hung her head. 'What did I say?'

'You said the child was yours. Then you seemed to imply that you had had a child, and gave him away.'

'It's true,' Dora whispered. 'I had a baby son and I gave him away.'

'Why?' It was Elizabeth who could not repress the question, her voice breathless with horror.

'I couldn't feed him. I didn't want him.'

'Why didn't you want him?' Sister Andrew's asked.

'I shouldn't have had a child. It wasn't my fault. I was forced.'

'Forced? By whom?'

'By my half-brother, Hector Latimer.'

'Oh, how terrible!' Elizabeth whispered.

'Who did you give the child to?'

'I gave him back to his father.'

'He was prepared to bring him up, then?'

'He said it wasn't his. But it was! I took him to his house and gave him to the maid who answered the door.'

'And do you know what happened to it?'

'No. They said ... the Latimers ... that I never left him there. But I did. The maid confirmed it. I don't know what happened to him after that.'

'You took him to the house. Where were you living at the time? Where was the child born?'

'In the workhouse. They turned me out onto the street when they discovered I was pregnant. I had nowhere else to go.'

She heard Phil and Elizabeth making sounds of distress and incomprehension. Sister Andrew straightened up.

'I think that's enough for now. I want you two to take Dora back to the manor house and put her to bed. Give her this. It's laudanum. The dose is marked on the bottle. Be careful not to overdo it, and bring the bottle away with you. Stay with her until she is asleep. Mrs Wardroper will want to talk to her in the morning.'

Chapter 15

'Sit down, Dora. I think you know that Mr Rathbone told
me your unhappy story before I accepted you to train here.'
To Dora's relief Mrs Wardroper's tone was calm and there
was no trace of anger in her expression. 'I took you in on
his recommendation and I have to say that until now – with
the exception of that one unfortunate incident of the march
– you have fully deserved his confidence in you. But yesterday's outburst was, to say the least of it, unfortunate. Can
you explain what caused it?'

Dora lowered her eyes to the carpet. Since waking in
the first light of dawn she had been trying to explain it to
herself. 'Ever since ... ever since I gave my baby away, I
have not wanted to hold another one. The sight, the smell,
repelled me. It reminded me so strongly of the way I felt
towards him. You see, I hated him, because of his father
and because of what he made me suffer.'

'But did you have no maternal feelings towards him?
Every woman I have ever attended has loved her child once
it was put in her arms, even if it was not wanted before.'

'But I did not hold him in my arms. The birth was hard,
terribly hard. That was why I felt so much for that poor

woman yesterday. Afterwards, I was ill for a long time. I did not know where I was or what was happening to me. When I did come to myself, I thought the child must be dead, but he wasn't. He was being nursed by a woman in the workhouse who had recently given birth herself and had enough milk for two. When I went to the nursery she put him in my arms and told me I should feed him myself – but I couldn't.'

'That is not surprising, after a long illness.'

'But I did not want to! The thought of suckling him made me feel sick. I just wanted to be rid of him.' She looked up. 'Am I a very wicked woman?'

'No. You should not think that. After what you had been through you had good reason to feel that way. Perhaps if you had been able to hold him immediately after he was born, things might have been different, but that was obviously impossible. But I am told that you said yesterday that you took him back to his father. That seems to me a very strange thing to do.'

'He was responsible for his birth. I felt he should be responsible for his upbringing.'

'Had he shown any sign of accepting that responsibility?'

'No. He denied being the father. His mother believed him, not me, and turned me out of the house.'

'So what made you think he would care for the child now?'

Dora shook her head miserably. 'I don't know. I have asked myself that question. But at the time it seemed the only thing to do. I thought perhaps when he saw him, and knew that he was his own flesh and blood, even though he denied it, he would have some feeling for him. After all,

what future could I have given him? Growing up in the
workhouse he could never have been more than a servant
or a poor tradesman. I hoped he might have a better chance
with his father.'

'Have you any idea what became of him?'

'No. The family denied that I had ever brought him
there, but the maid who opened the door to me confirmed
my story. I suppose they will have given him to some wet
nurse. Perhaps to a respectable couple who were unable to
have a child of their own?' She raised her eyes with a mute
appeal, then dropped them again. 'My great fear is that he
will have been sent to a baby farm somewhere.'

'I am afraid that may be a possibility,' Mrs Wardroper
agreed. 'But that does not necessarily mean he will have
been ill-treated.' She paused and then her manner became
practical. 'What we have to consider now is how this may
affect your future.'

Dora looked at her and felt tears sting her eyes. 'I will
not be able to qualify now, will I?'

'What makes you say that?'

'I know that Miss Nightingale has very strong views
about the sort of women who are suitable. She has written
that it is necessary to be a good woman in order to be a
good nurse.'

'And what makes you think that you are not a good
woman?'

'I did a terrible thing!'

'Perhaps. But it seems to me that you were far more
sinned against then sinning, and since then I believe you
have more than expiated any sin you did commit by your
devotion to the care of the sick.'

Dora looked at her, with the first glimmer of hope. 'Will Miss Nightingale see it as you do?'

'We shall have to wait and see. As you know, she takes a great interest in all the young women who pass through here. She receives regular reports on your progress and your conduct. She knew already about your background. Without consulting her first I should not have felt justified in taking you on. But she has since received favourable reports about your progress and I have good hopes that she will see that, whatever you may have done in the past, you will make a very good nurse. But I cannot guarantee that. It will be up to her to decide when you have finished your course.'

'Thank you!' Dora breathed the words with heartfelt gratitude. 'I was afraid you would send me away at once. I want so badly to complete the course here.'

'That you can certainly do. But there is one thing that disturbs me somewhat. I gather two of your friends were present when you made your confession to Sister Andrews. I cannot say what their reactions may be. If the news has spread all through the body of students we may have a rather unpleasant atmosphere. I should not want that.'

'No, of course not.' Dora had not given any thought to what Phil and Elizabeth might have told the rest of the group, or how they would feel about her now. 'I hope ...' she murmured, 'I hope they will forgive me.'

'It is not a question of forgiveness,' Mrs Wardroper said with a hint of asperity. 'You have done nothing that requires that from them. I hope, and expect, them to show compassion for what you have suffered. It is a cardinal virtue necessary to any good nurse. But I am aware of the temptation to gossip. I hope your friends have resisted it.' She studied Dora in silence for a moment. 'I think you should go now. I am relieving you of your duties for today. You need to rest. But I shall expect you to be back at work tomorrow. Do you think you will be able to do that?'

'Oh yes! Yes, of course I will.' Dora got to her feet. 'That's all I want, just to be able to work. Thank you, Mrs Wardroper. Thank you for ... for your confidence in me.'

'I am sure it will be amply justified.' For the first time she could recall, Dora saw the austere face relax into a smile. 'Go along now.'

She descended the stairs with a pounding heart. She cared little for the opinion of the vast majority of the other students, though she dreaded their sidelong looks and whispered comments. What really mattered was what her true friends thought of her.

It was mid-morning. Blue Watch would be working the morning shift and Green Watch would be sleeping after coming off night duty. Only her familiar comrades of Red Watch would be free. It was a mild November day and she hoped that some of them might have gone out into the grounds for some fresh air. The rest would almost certainly be in the common room. She opened the door with a hand that shook and looked round the room. There was an atmosphere of peace and relaxation. Some of the women were reading or writing letters, some were sewing or mending uniforms and darning stockings. Most of them looked up as she entered, but what she saw in their eyes was not shock or hostility but sympathy and concern.

'Dora?' Lily said. 'Are you feeling better?'

'Yes,' she responded shakily. 'Yes, I am, thank you.'

Phil called her from her usual place on the window seat. 'Come and join us.'

She was sitting with Elizabeth and they moved up to make room for her between them. Elizabeth took her hand and squeezed it.

'What did Mrs W. have to say?'

Dora hesitated, collecting her thoughts. 'She was ... she was very kind. But she knew everything already.'

'Knew it?' Phil said.

'Mr Rathbone told her. He thought she should know before she took me on.'

Phil fixed her with a direct look. 'Was what you said yesterday all true?'

'Yes, it was. Have you ... told the others?'

'What do you take us for? We just told them you were taken ill.'

'I never meant anyone else to know. I shall not blame you if you do not regard me as a friend from now on. I did not mean to deceive you.'

'Oh really!' Phil snorted. 'Does it look as if we don't regard you as a friend?'

Elizabeth said, 'We just feel so sorry for you, and we admire you for the way you have risen above it all. I think many of us would have been completely broken by what you went through.'

Dora said wryly, 'You understand now why I always said any kind of relationship between me and Edward was impossible.'

'Edward is a fool. I made him tell me what he suggested and I'm furious with him. I still think I would rather have you as a sister-in-law than any of the feeble creatures who are likely to accept him.'

Dora felt the ready tears start to her eyes. 'Thank you.'

'I have no idea what you two are talking about,' Phil said, 'though I can make a guess. What is more important is what happens now? Will you be able to complete the course and qualify?'

'Mrs Wardroper thinks so. At least, I can stay and finish the course. Whether I get my certificate at the end will be up to Miss Nightingale.'

She could see a doubt materialising in the eyes of her two friends, but Phil said stoutly, 'She's no fool. She'll see that refusing you a certificate would be a great loss to the profession.'

Dora sighed. 'I hope you're right.'

The final weeks of the course slid by and, as Christmas approached, the talk in the common room was all of the future. Hopeful graduates went to be interviewed for posts around the country and very few failed to be accepted. By early December Dora's friends had all found positions. Phil was to become matron and nursing superintendent at St George's Hospital and Lily and Pearl would go with her as her assistants. Elizabeth would take up a similar position at the Guildford Infirmary, and Hope, pretty, delicate Hope, was going to work in a missionary hospital in South Africa.

Dora listened to their excited discussions but said little. She did not begrudge them these new beginnings, but at the same time the prospect of returning to the workhouse infirmary in Liverpool was not enticing. She reminded herself that when she started her training that had been her whole intention and the achievement of that end would have felt like a triumph. Now she knew that when she returned Agnes Jones would still be in charge and she would be just one, fairly junior, member of the nursing staff. She had a vivid mental image of the high walls and the gloomy interior of the workhouse and the shortcomings of the infirmary buildings; a stark contrast to the surroundings she had lived and worked in for almost a year. She reminded herself that she would no longer be an inmate, so she would be free to come and go when she was not on duty, and that Liverpool had its concert halls and theatres that could rival those of London, but she would have to attend performances alone. There would be no Elizabeth to keep her company. No Edward, either. That should have been a relief. She was well aware of the fool's paradise he had almost led her into and she could not forgive him, but at the same time she missed his company. She told herself that in compensation for the loss of her student friends she would be reunited with Edith, and that was something to look forward to. They had kept in touch by letter during her absence in London, but while Dora's letters had been full of news about what she had learned or about the joys and frustrations of the work, Edith's had grown briefer with every passing month. 'Nothing much happens here, so I have nothing new to tell you' had become a regular refrain.

A week before the course was due to end Mrs Wardroper called them all together.

'You are almost at the end of your training and all of you have done well. I am happy to tell you that you will all be taken to visit Miss Nightingale and to receive your diplomas from her own hands.' A murmur of delight ran through the room. 'As you know, Miss Nightingale suffers from poor health and has to spend much of her time in bed. That does not, however, prevent her from taking a very keen interest in all of you. She has received regular reports from me about each of you and is interested to meet you all in person. The day agreed for your visit is next Wednesday. A charabanc will collect you from here at two o'clock. I need not emphasise, I am sure, that you must all be in uniform and that it must be impeccable. Thank you. That is all.'

As the students filed out Dora lingered until she was left alone with the matron.

'Well, Nurse Latimer?'

'Me, too?' Dora asked, anxiously. 'Am I to go with the others?'

'Of course. Why ever should you not go?' was the austere reply. Then Mrs Wardroper's expression softened. 'Yes, Dora. You too. You have richly deserved to receive your diploma at Miss Nightingale's hands.'

As they boarded the charabanc at the appointed time there was a hum of suppressed excitement. To meet the great Miss Nightingale in person was something they had all dreamed of, but they knew that their behaviour must be beyond reproach and too much hilarity would be frowned on.

In the drawing room of her home in South Street they found Miss Nightingale reclining on a couch. There was a fire blazing in the grate, but in spite of the cold December afternoon a window was open. It was obvious that she acted upon her own axiom about the importance of fresh air. Beside her was a low table, strewn with papers and bearing an ink-well and a number of pens. They had all been told that in spite of her ill health she still maintained a heavy workload, writing papers and compiling statistics, for which she had a special talent. Closer to hand was a pile of files which, they discovered, contained the reports she had been given about each of them.

One by one, as their names were called, they went forward to kneel beside the couch. Miss Nightingale had a few words for each of them, very rarely needing to consult the files beside her. To Phil she said, 'You are a young woman of considerable intelligence and strong character, both admirable traits. Be careful that it does not cause you to dismiss the opinions of others without giving them careful consideration.' To Elizabeth she said, 'There will be many young men who will be eager to offer you a life of ease and luxury. I hope you will always put duty before your own pleasure.'

When Dora's turn came she found herself the focus of a steady, curious gaze.

'Where did your mother come from?'

'From Jamaica, ma'am.'

'I wondered as much. You remind me of a woman I encountered when I was working in the Crimea.'

Miss Nightingale glanced down at Dora's file. 'You have overcome some distressing experiences, which might have crushed another woman. You have great resilience and your skill has earned you high commendations from the people you have worked under. You will do great things.'

Her diploma clutched in her sweaty hand, Dora withdrew.

There was one last bonus, a finale to the discussions about the origin of the cholera outbreak. The newspapers reported that the East London Water Company had finally admitted that, at times of high demand, water had been drawn from two uncovered reservoirs and mixed in with the general supply. The water had been analysed and no evidence had been found of any 'poison' that might have been responsible, but the fact remained that it was illegal to have uncovered reservoirs within five miles of St Paul's cathedral, so the company had been in breach of the law and was duly fined.

Term came to an end a week before Christmas. On the last morning, Dora was packing her trunk ready to leave. Folded away at the bottom of it was the red silk dress, worn just once at the ball at Lillden. She took it out and rubbed the fabric against her cheek. For one night, wearing it, she had felt like a real lady. Now, she could not see any likelihood that she would wear it again. She considered offering it to Elizabeth, but she knew the offer would be declined. Besides, it would be too big for her. No one else she could think of might have a use for it. With a sigh she folded it away again in the trunk. Maybe one day she could sell it and give the money to charity. She packed her other things, closed the trunk and left it for one of the porters to carry downstairs.

The hall was thronged with women waiting for transport to take them off to railway stations, or for friends or relatives to collect them. There were embraces and tearful farewells. Dora went to join Phil and Elizabeth, who were waiting with Lily and Pearl.

'Will we ever meet again, do you think?' Elizabeth said.

'I don't see why not,' was Phil's characteristically robust response. 'It's not as if we were living in the age of the stage coach. These days, the railways can whisk us from one end of the country to the other in hours. For my own part, I have every intention of coming to visit Liverpool. It is, after all, the second greatest sea port in the country.'

'Then I shall come too,' Elizabeth declared.

'I shall be very happy to see you both,' Dora said. Privately, she wondered what her two friends would make of the gloomy prospect of the workhouse.

'And you must come to London,' Elizabeth said. 'You know Edward is going to move out as soon as he passes his exams. So you could come and stay in the Mayfair house, and we'll go to some concerts. Or you could come down to Lillden. That's only a short ride from Guildford where I shall be.'

'I should like that very much,' Dora assured her.

A line of hackney cabs had drawn up outside and the porters began to carry out the luggage. Dora hugged Lily. 'Give my regards to your mother and father. And tell him that I wish him and the Reform League every success in their efforts to get the vote for working men.'

'I will,' Lily promised. 'We're going to miss you, round the Old Nicol.'

'I shall miss all of you, too,' Dora said.

She embraced Elizabeth and turned to Phil, but found that instead of a hug she was offered a firm, masculine handshake.

'Take care of yourself,' Phil said. 'We'll meet again soon.' And Dora thought she detected the faintest hint of moisture in her eyes.

She made her way down the steps and turned for a last look back at the manor house. The others were at the door, waving. She waved back and stepped into the cab.

'King's Cross Station, please.'

Chapter 16

Descending from another cab outside the gates of the workhouse in the early darkness of a winter evening, Dora gazed up at the high, grey walls of the infirmary. Here and there lamplight flickered in a window, but that did little to dispel the forbidding impression. She heaved her trunk out of the cab, paid the driver and rang the bell. A small window opened in the gate and a face peered out.

'You're too late. We're closed for the night now.'

Dora stepped closer so that the light from inside shone on her face. 'It's me, Billy. Don't you know me?'

He squinted at her for a moment, then his face broke into a toothless smile. 'It's you, Dora! Cor blimey, I didn't recognise you. You've gone up in the world, and no mistake! Hold on a minute, I'll open up.' He opened a wicket gate and came out to pick up Dora's trunk. 'You've come back to us then. Or are you just visiting?'

'No, Billy. I'm here to stay.'

She stepped inside and felt the chill dampness, which even the hottest summer could never quite dispel, envelope her. Billy shouldered her trunk and stumped off up the stairs leading into the main part of the infirmary and Dora followed. He dumped the trunk outside Mrs Carter's office and tapped on the door.

'Yes?' came a familiar voice from inside.

Dora started. 'That's not Mrs Carter.'

'Oh no, miss. She doesn't work in the infirmary any more. Miss Jones is Lady Superintendent now.' He pushed open the door.

'Got a visitor for you, ma'am,' he said, with a grin at Dora.

'What, at this time of night? What does he want?'

'Not a he, ma'am, a she. It's someone you know.'

Dora stepped into the room and Agnes Jones looked up from her desk. It took her a moment to recognise her visitor.

'Dora Latimer? It is you, isn't it?'

'Yes, Nurse Jones. It's me. Were you not expecting me? I wrote to say I was coming back today.'

'Of course! Of course! It had quite slipped my mind for the moment. Well, come in! Come in. Thank you, Billy.'

Dora turned and slipped a coin into the porter's hand. He looked at it in surprise. 'Well, thank *you*, miss,' he said and stumped off down the stairs.

Agnes came round her desk and held out her hand, 'Welcome back! So now you are a qualified nurse. Congratulations.'

'Thank you.'

'To be honest with you, I didn't expect you to come back here. Mr Rathbone seemed to think you might be offered a position as superintendent at some big London hospital. That didn't work out then?'

'I expect it could have done,' Dora said, with a hint of annoyance. 'I never applied. I knew I was expected to come back here.'

'Well, I'm delighted to have you. We've lost several of the nurses who came up from London with me.'

'Oh, how?'

'Two of them got married. One had to go home to care for her widowed father. Two were taken ill. We had the cholera here in September, you know, like you did in London. One of the nurses went down with it and died. So we're a bit short-handed.'

'I'm sorry to hear that.'

'There have been a few replacements, of course, but mostly probationers, not fully qualified. Now, you must be tired. I'll get someone to show you where you will be sleeping. There's a proper nurses' wing now, so we can all have our own rooms. Leave your trunk there. I'll get one of the porters to carry it for you.'

The room Dora was shown into was brighter than she expected. There was a fire in the grate and chintz curtains with a floral pattern at the window, with a matching bedspread. Another porter brought her trunk in and Agnes left her to unpack. She took off her bonnet and her cape and combed her hair and washed her face and hands in the basin on the washstand in the corner. Then she set out for the wards, in search of Edith. She had expected that her old friend would be the first to meet her, but concluded that she must be on duty.

The wards looked all too familiar. Agnes Jones had brought about a transformation when she first arrived, with fresh paint and polished floors and the installation of water closets, but since then little had changed. To Dora's eyes, used to St Thomas's even in its temporary home, the beds were too close together, the bed covers were shabby and there were no flowers, nothing to brighten the aspect.

She found Agnes on her rounds.

'There's no need for you to start straight away, Dora,' she said. 'Tomorrow morning will be soon enough.'

Dora looked at her properly for the first time and was shocked to see how thin she was. There were lines at the corners of her eyes and shadows under them.

'Forgive me for saying it, but you look tired. Are you well?'

'Yes, perfectly. A little fatigued, but that's normal. There is always work to be done. You are the one who should rest, after that long journey.'

'I should like to find Edith, please. Which ward is she working on?'

'Edith?' Agnes Jones's expression became sombre. 'Oh dear, I am afraid I have bad news for you. Edith is not well. In fact, she is extremely sick.'

'How? What is wrong with her?'

'You will recall, I am sure, that she was originally admitted to the infirmary because of a weakness in her lungs.'

'But that was years ago. She was cured.'

'Not completely, I am afraid. I believe she never spoke much about it, but it never quite left her and over the last few months it has steadily worsened.'

'Is it consumption?'

'I am afraid so, yes.'

'And what is the prognosis?'

'I am sorry. You must prepare yourself to lose her within weeks, days even.'

'Oh no!' The words felt as if they would choke her. 'Is there really nothing that can be done?'

'You know yourself that there is no cure. Perhaps if she could have gone to somewhere warmer, Italy perhaps, her life might have been prolonged by a few months, but that is a solution only available to someone with considerable means. For Edith, as for so many others, that is not an option.'

'Can I see her?'

'Of course. I know she has been eagerly awaiting your return. She is at the far end of the women's ward. We have put screens round the bed to give her a little privacy.'

Dora hastened down the length of the familiar ward without looking to right or left. Once she would have paused to check on a patient here or there, or been called over by one of them, but they were all strangers to her now.

Edith was propped on pillows, her face pale but showing the hectic patches of colour on her cheeks that betokened fever. Her eyes were closed but opened at Dora's approach.

'Dora! You're back. I am so glad!' Her voice was weak hardly more than a whisper.

Dora sank down by the bed and took one of her hot hands in her own. 'Oh, my dear! I am so sad to see you like this. I had no idea. Why didn't you write to tell me you were so ill? I would have come back sooner.'

'That's why I did not write,' Edith replied. 'I would not wish to be the cause of you failing to get your diploma. You have got it, haven't you?'

'Yes, I have.'

'I'm so glad for you. And you have come back to work here?'

'Yes, as I promised.'

'But now you are an independent woman, with a job and an income. Not one of us paupers any longer.'

Tears stung Dora's eyes. 'I could never think of you as one of those poor creatures. You should have been properly paid for what you did. It is unjust! You should not have had to spend so many years of your life in this place.'

'I have not been unhappy here,' Edith murmured. 'The work was satisfying, even if it was unpaid. And I particularly treasure the memory of those years when we worked together.'

'I was looking forward to working together again,' Dora said. 'I owe you so much, Edith. You helped me at a time when I thought my life had become unbearable. I believe without your support I might have killed myself.'

'Not you! You are too strong for that but if I was able ...' Her words were cut short by a fit of coughing. Dora supported her until the paroxysm passed and saw, with a sinking heart, that the handkerchief she had pressed to her lips was stained with fresh blood.

'Lie back and rest,' she said softly. 'We can talk again tomorrow. You must not tire yourself.'

Edith nodded, wordlessly, and closed her eyes. Dora sat by her for a while, until she thought she had fallen asleep. As she got up, Edith whispered, 'I am so glad I was able to wait until you came back.'

Dora passed a restless night and before dawn she got up, dressed and made her way to Edith's bedside. She was sleeping so Dora tiptoed away. Wandering back through the ward she saw a shaded lamp burning on a table at the far end and found Agnes sitting there, writing.

'You are up very early, Miss Jones,' she commented.

'You, too.'

'I went to see Edith, but she is sleeping.'

'That's good. By the way, now that we are to be colleagues, I think it is only right for you to call me Agnes – perhaps not in front of the patients, but when we are alone. For the patients, I am now Matron and I think you should be called Sister Latimer. Is that agreeable?'

'Yes, certainly. But Nurse Latimer would be good enough.'

'Well, we must discuss your duties, but not just now. After breakfast perhaps?'

As soon as she had eaten Dora went back to Edith's bedside. She found her awake and restless, the bright spots of fever more pronounced on her cheeks.

'Oh, Dora, do you still make your herbal medicines?' she whispered. 'I should dearly love some of that willow bark preparation. I remember that that was so effective in reducing fever.'

'I have not made anything like that for months now,' Dora told her. 'It was frowned upon at St Thomas's. But if it will bring you comfort, I will find a way to produce some.'

She sought out Agnes Jones and told her of Edith's request.

'I remember your herbal remedies,' Agnes said, 'and I recall that they did seem to be effective in some cases.'

'I'm afraid that was not the attitude I encountered from the doctors at St Thomas's.'

Agnes gave her wry smile. 'I am afraid that most doctors are very suspicious of anything that might make their own methods seem ineffective. But I have no such prejudices. If you wish to take up your old habits, I shall not object.'

'In that case, may I take some time today to find the herbs I need?'

'Yes, you may. We can discuss your formal work later. I shall be glad of anything that will ease Edith's last hours.'

Dora made her way to the little garden where she had grown her herbs. It was neglected and overgrown with weeds but many of the herbs she had planted were weeds themselves, in other contexts, so they had survived. She found yarrow and feverfew, both effective in fever, but the willow was not something that she could have grown in that limited space. When she had been an inmate she was not at liberty to seek out her ingredients and Dr Wentworth had found them for her – until he decided it might be detrimental to his career to be associated with her. Now she was free to come and go, but she was unsure where to look. The recollection prompted her to wonder whether Wentworth was still working at the infirmary. She hoped not.

She knew that willows grew by water, so the obvious place to look was along the banks of the Mersey, but not in the centre of the city, where they were lined by docks. It occurred to her to ask Billy, the porter.

'Why not try the canal?' he suggested. 'You can walk along the tow path easy enough.'

His advice proved fruitful and by midday she returned to the infirmary with a basket of strips of willow bark and a collection of other useful herbs that she had come across on her walk. She headed straight to the kitchen and started work. By evening she was able to offer Edith a dose which she hoped would enable her to rest. Edith swallowed it gratefully, in spite of the bitter flavour.

Dora shook up her pillows and settled her against them. 'Making this reminded me of Dr Wentworth. I haven't seen him about the wards yet.'

Edith gave her an ironic look. 'Oh, Dr Wentworth doesn't work here any longer. Not since he became famous. He has consulting rooms in Rodney Street now and a very exclusive clientele, so I hear.'

'Famous?' Dora queried. 'What for?'

'For getting a paper published by the Royal Society of Medicine.'

'A paper? On what subject?'

Edith paused and a faint, bitter smile twisted her lips. 'On the efficacy of herbal remedies.'

'You mean ...?'

'I mean that all the time he was working with you, he was storing up information that he might be able to use. He took notes, didn't he?'

'Yes. But I thought it was just so he could use some of the remedies himself.'

'Oh, he probably does, on some of his ladies and gentlemen. But that was not his main purpose, obviously. He has made his fortune out of your work.'

For a moment Dora stared at her, then she began to laugh.

'You think it is funny?'

'Well, what is the point of being angry? I should have known when he dropped our connection after he found out about – well, you know – what had happened to me. He was a nasty little opportunist, only interested in his own advancement. And if it means that some of my mother's remedies are being taken seriously – well, so much the better.'

The potion began to have its effect and Edith's eyelids drooped. Dora waited a few moments, then got up and crept away.

Over the next day or two Edith's condition steadily worsened. Dora tried all the remedies she could think of but it was clear that they could only ease her final moments. She was busy in the wards most of the time, but whenever she could she spent time sitting by the bedside of her old friend. One evening, when she had given her another draft of the willow bark infusion, Edith seemed to rally a little.

'Dora, I want to ask you something. I hope it will not bring back painful memories. Do you every think of the child you gave away?'

Dora dropped her gaze. 'Not often. There was – an incident – at St Thomas's, when I was working in the lying-in ward. A woman gave birth after a very difficult labour to a baby boy. It brought it all back so strongly that I – well, I broke down. But mostly try not to think of him.'

'Perhaps that's best,' Edith murmured.

'There's something I wanted to ask you, too. Did Jem ever get my letter?'

'Oh yes. He came as he had promised on that Thursday afternoon and I gave him your letter.'

'What did he say?'

'Nothing. He read it all through, then he thanked me and left.'

'Did he seem – very distressed?'

'He looked like a man who had been given a blow and was stunned by it.'

'Oh dear! Did he ever come back?'

'No. I never set eyes on him from that day forward.'

'I feel bad about treating him like that.'

'I have no doubt he recovered. Men do not pine away like women.' She sighed. 'I'm tired now, dear. I think I might sleep.'

Dora held a cup of water for her to take a sip, settled her on her pillows, and kissed her on the forehead. 'Sleep well, my dear.'

Next morning Agnes came to tell her that Edith had died during the night. 'She passed away in her sleep, quite peacefully. We should be glad that her sufferings are over.'

It was Christmas Eve.

This was the fifth Christmas that Dora had spent in the workhouse, and although some things were different, too much was still the same as ever. In the morning there was the obligatory service in the chapel within the walls, the branches of holly with which it was decorated the only splash of colour most of the residents ever saw. This year, she sat towards the front along with Agnes and the other nurses, in a pew just behind the governor and the visiting dignitaries, but she was still aware of the ranks of whey-faced paupers behind her, men on one side, women on the other, in their drab workhouse clothes. More heart-rending still were the rows of children, bony shoulders and knees sticking out through clothes that were a size too small. If she had not given him away, she reminded herself, her own boy would have been among them.

After the service came the moment they were all looking forward to – the Christmas dinner. It was, she well remembered, the best meal any of them would have that year. There was roast beef, donated by the charitable members of the Vestry, the body charged with running the workhouse, and after the beef, plum pudding. It was almost the only sweet thing the paupers ever tasted and when Dora took her first mouthful the memory of how almost unbearably sweet it had seemed in previous years almost brought tears to her eyes. It made her aware of how different her life had been for the past year.

Once the festivities were over, life returned to its normal routine and Dora lived through the days in a blank numbness of spirit. Without Edith's companionship the infirmary seemed bleak indeed. She got on well with the other nurses, all of whom came from the same kind of backgrounds as the 'lady' probationers she had trained with. They were dedicated and efficient and the younger ones, who had joined the staff while she was away, treated her with respect as an 'old hand' who knew the ropes, but she could never forget that Agnes, and the longer serving nurses, knew that she had once been one of the paupers they were there to care for. It was hard under those circumstances to make friends. Her defence was to concentrate on her work and prove herself as competent as any of them.

Mr Rathbone came to visit early in the New Year.

'I am delighted that you chose to come back to us, Nurse Latimer,' he said. 'I was afraid that you might be tempted to take up a position at a London hospital.'

'I would never have done that,' she told him. 'It would have been a very poor return for your generosity.'

'I am told that you showed yourself to be one of the most able and dedicated students,' he said. 'I knew I was right to invest in your education. I can imagine a day when you may find yourself in charge here.'

'Oh no,' Dora said. 'That is Nurse Jones's place. I would never presume to that position.'

'Well, do not undervalue yourself,' he said. 'I expect great things of you.'

Little by little, as the weeks passed, Dora's gloom lifted and she began to consider how vastly her lot had improved, rather than dwelling on the sameness of her surroundings. She was no longer a pauper. She had a regular salary and though it was not great, since her board and lodging were free, she had enough to pay for various small pleasures. She often bought flowers to brighten her little room or to deck the wards and sometimes she allowed herself to buy a pretty scarf or a new hat. She had no need of fashionable clothes, other than those she had, but she could never resist adding a touch of colour. She could come and go as she pleased when she was off duty, and she began to explore what the city could offer in the way of entertainment. She made tentative enquiries among the other nurses and found two of them who loved music almost as much as she did and together they attended concerts at the Philharmonic Hall and St George's Hall. Sometimes they went to the music hall, though Dora found that a bitter-sweet occupation, reminding her too vividly of the first time Edward had taken her and Elizabeth out.

There was one thing she dreaded whenever she left the confines of the workhouse, and that was an accidental meeting with her stepmother or one of her step-sisters

– or worse still with Hector. She recalled, however, that her erstwhile family had never shown any interest in music, so she was unlikely to encounter them at a concert, and, as she told herself, Liverpool was a big city. The chance of bumping into one of them in the street was very small.

At work, too, there were developments that cheered her. She was put in charge of the children's ward. At first she was reluctant to accept the position. Any involvement with children brought too many unanswered questions about the fate of her own boy. But after a little she began to find great rewards in caring for these small invalids. There were heart-rending days when a child was brought in with no hope of recovery, and all she could do was to make its last days as pain-free as possible. But the infirmary's reputation was growing and it was no longer seen as a place where people came to die, but as a place where they came to be healed. A good many of her young charges came in with diseases for which there was a hope of a cure, with care and good nursing. Many times she was reminded of the dictum passed on from Florence Nightingale herself, that the nurse's job was to create an environment where Nature could perform its healing function. Her greatest joy came when a child was declared well enough to go home and the parents came to collect him or her. Very often, at the moment of farewell, the child's arms would be thrown around her neck with heartfelt thanks for the care she had given.

Another course of satisfaction was the fact that she was no longer barred from using her well-tried herbal remedies. As the infirmary expanded, so had the medical establishment. There was now a medical superintendent with three doctors working under him. Dr Fletcher, the doctor in charge of the children's ward, was a genial, elderly gentleman whose greatest desire was to make life as easy for himself and everyone else as possible. So when he discovered that Dora's soothing syrups quieted fractious children he was happy to give her carte blanche.

As spring approached she began to cultivate her little herb garden again. She remembered with envy the plants she had seen in the Chelsea Physic Garden and wondered if any of them would grow in Liverpool's mild but damp climate. She wrote to Mr Moore and received in return not only advice but several packets of seeds, which she sowed and carefully tended. She also made use of her new freedom to make expeditions into the countryside in search of plants that grew wild in the hedgerows and along the banks of streams. By careful experiment she extended her repertoire of medicines and saw them prove useful in the wards.

In October Phil came on her promised visit. Elizabeth was not with her. She wrote apologising and explained that she was engaged to be married and was too busy with arrangements for the wedding. Phil took a room at the Adelphi, which relieved Dora of her anxiety about accommodating her in the gloomy confines of the infirmary, and Dora asked for and was granted a few days off – the first she had had since returning to Liverpool. Together, they explored the city and Dora took pleasure in showing her friend that it could compete on level terms with London in the magnificence of its new public buildings, all of them the result of the beneficence of public spirited individuals. There was an element of tension, however, when it came to explaining the source of this prosperity. They both knew that it was ultimately founded in the slave trade and she sensed a hesitation on Phil's part when it came to discussing the matter. She decided to tackle the subject head on.

Early one morning, as they set out again, she remarked, 'Of course, when my father brought my mother back here the slave trade had been illegal for years. She was a free woman – though I suppose her parents were probably taken to Jamaica as slaves.'

'You've never spoken about your mother before,' Phil said. 'I thought you were adopted.'

Dora realised that she had opened a subject that might have been better left closed, but it was a relief to speak honestly. 'That was what I told everyone at the training school, but it wasn't exactly correct. I lived with my mother until I was twelve. When she died, my father took me into his own home, to live with his wife and daughters.'

'Your father?'

'Captain Latimer was my father.'

'I see.' Phil absorbed this information in silence for a moment. Then she said, 'It cannot have been easy for you.'

'It was not too bad as long as he lived. Even when he was away at sea, his wife was quite good to me, because she knew he would be angry when he got back if I complained of my treatment. It was when he went down with his ship that things got ... difficult.'

Dora could tell that Phil was putting together what she had just said with her outburst in Sister Andrews's office after her breakdown. After a moment she said, 'You don't need to tell me any more unless you want to. You have just reinforced what I said before – I think it is admirable that you have been able to overcome all those early problems to do what you do now.' She slipped her hand under Dora's elbow. 'Shall we go down to the river? I should like to see the ships coming and going.'

They stood on the dockside and Phil marvelled at the number and variety of the craft out in the Mersey estuary and tied up in the docks.

'Don't you think it's romantic? All those ships, coming from heaven knows where, bringing cargoes of heaven knows what. Oh, look! There's one of the new steam ships. It's the first one I have ever seen. I wonder where she's bound.'

'That'll be the Royal Standard, outward bound for Australia.' The voice took them by surprise and they turned to look at an old man sitting nearby on a bollard, smoking his pipe. 'The White Star Line's latest ship, that is.'

'Australia!' Phil said. 'Just think. I wonder what it would feel like to stand on deck and watch the shores of England vanish in the mist and know that you were bound for the other side of the world.'

'Doubt you'd see much of anything, for the smoke and smuts in your eyes,' the old man said grimly.

'You don't like steam ships?' Phil asked,

'No, I don't. And that's not just because they put an end to my life as a seaman. No place for old sea dogs like me on those new-fangled contraptions. But just look at the difference! See that clipper sailing into the estuary right now and then look at that abomination belching out smoke. Which would you rather sail on?'

'It's true the sailing ship is much more beautiful,' Phil agreed. 'But the steamers get to their destination quicker, don't they?'

'Aye, if speed's all you care about,' the old man grunted.

Memory stabbed at Dora. She said, 'I treated a man once, who had worked as a stoker on one of those ships. His lungs were clogged with soot and he was sent to the infirmary.'

'See what I mean?' the old man said.

'Well, just the same,' Phil mused, 'I can see the attraction of getting on a ship and setting off for somewhere new and strange. I think if I had been born a boy I might have decided to go to sea. Come to that, I suppose there's nothing to stop me going as a passenger.'

'Don't you dare!' Dora said. 'You are needed here.'

Phil looked down at the old man. 'You must have seen some comings and goings here, over the years.'

'Oh, aye. More goings than comings though. Irish mainly, escaping from the famine over there, heading for Australia, some of them, but most of them to America.'

'Poor souls,' Dora murmured.

'No need to go to sea to see the world,' he went on. 'Sit here and the world comes to you. I see history being made, right out there in front of me. I'll lay a wager you ladies don't know that the last act of the American Civil War took place out there.'

'In the Mersey Estuary?' Phil said. 'How is that possible?'

'You may well ask!' The old man was obviously enjoying having found an audience. 'But it's a fact. See, it was like this. There was this ship, the *Shenandoah* – not that she was called that when she was launched up in Scotland. She was the *Sea King* then, but the Confederates bought her and changed her name. She was what they called a commerce raider, meaning her job was to sail the oceans looking for ships belonging to the Yankees, or trading with them, and steal their cargo and then send them to the bottom. She took on some crew from here before she started out and because she got all the supplies she needed from the prizes she took she sailed clear round the world without needing to put in at another port. Trouble was, her captain and crew had no way of knowing that the war was over. When they did find out it was three months later and that meant they'd been acting as pirates for all that time. So what were they to do? Put in at an American port, and like as not be hanged? Or go somewhere else and have the ship impounded and the crew arrested?'

'So what did they do?' Phil asked.

'In the end, they came here. Dropped anchor behind a Royal Navy ship as happened to be visiting, hauled down their flag and surrendered. So that was the final act of the war.'

'What an amazing story!' Phil exclaimed.

'What happened to the men on board?' Dora asked.

The old man chuckled. 'Ah, well. That's the best bit of the story. The authorities here didn't know what to do with them. In the end, word came from London that all the Americans could go free, but any English on board were to be arrested. It was against the law, see, for any of us to fight on either side, because England was supposed to be neutral.'

'That doesn't seem fair,' Dora objected.

'No, and it didn't seem fair to the men on board, either, I should guess. Strange thing is, though quite a few of them had started out from here, turns out that when the roll was called every single man jack of them was American born and bred!'

Phil and Dora laughed delightedly. 'So they all went free?' Phil said.

'Had to, didn't they? There was no way anyone could prove different.'

He knocked out his pipe on the bollard and the two young women took that as a sign that the conversation was over. Dora felt awkward. She thought he might expect some reward for entertaining them, but did not know how to offer it without giving offense. Phil, as always, was more worldly wise.

'It's been a pleasure talking to you. If I was a man, I'd ask you to join me for a glass of ale, but that would not be quite suitable, under the circumstances. Instead, would you do us the honour of drinking our health next time you happen to be in a tavern?'

She reached out and coins changed hands. The old man touched his forelock. 'I'll do that, and with the greatest pleasure, ma'am. Good day to you.'

As they walked away Phil chuckled happily. 'Our very own Ancient Mariner! Now my visit is complete!'

Chapter 17

In what seemed to Dora far less than a year, another Christmas was upon them, and soon they would be wishing each other all the best for 1868. Her mood was a great deal lighter than the previous year and it seemed to her that her colleagues were more cheerful and less solemnly dedicated than a year earlier. She persuaded some of them to accompany her to the carol concert in the Philharmonic Hall, which put them all in the right mood for the festivities. Then Mr Rathbone invited them all to a New Year's Eve party at his home. It was not possible, of course, for everyone to leave the infirmary at once, so they drew lots to decide who should stay, and Dora was one of the lucky ones who was free to go. Only Agnes Jones refused to take part. Her place, she insisted, was in the wards, whatever the season. It was not the first time she had made the same response. Dora had tried on several occasions to persuade her to join them at a concert, or to come walking when the weather was good, but she always refused. Dora was growing concerned that her devotion to what she perceived as her duty was having a detrimental effect on her health.

The celebrations over, the infirmary settled back into its normal routine and, waking one morning, Dora remembered that it was her birthday. Birthdays were not generally celebrated in the workhouse and it took her a moment to calculate how old she was. The answer was twenty-three. It entered her mind that this was how her life would be from now on. It was not a bad prospect, she decided. She loved her work, she got on well with her colleagues and there were enough small pleasures and amusements to compensate for the long hours and the gloomy surroundings. It seemed that she was not destined to marry. The only men she met were either patients, or the male paupers who worked as porters and cleaners, or the doctors, all of whom were married men in middle age. She thought briefly of the dreams she had once entertained. The fantasy, so cruelly dispelled, of marriage to Doctor Wentworth; her equally improbable dreams of marriage to Edward; her almost-engagement to Jem. That was the only one she really regretted. There had been a realism about that. She could imagine that they might have married and settled in a home he had bought for them. By now she would probably have had a child, maybe two. When she reflected that she would probably never know what it was to hold her own child in her arms, to care for him or her, to watch them grow up, that did give her pain. She told herself sternly that she had no right to feel regret. She had a child somewhere. She could have kept him. It was her choice to give him away. Now she had to compensate herself for the loss by caring for other women's children, and she was lucky to have that much comfort.

It was summer when a new volunteer arrived. Her name was Lizzie Findlay and she told Agnes that she had at one time been employed as a nursemaid in the home of a wealthy couple. Because of her experience with children Agnes put her in Dora's charge. Dora soon perceived that she had suffered a shock of some sort. She was very thin, not an unusual state for new inmates of the workhouse, but beyond that it seemed that something had happened to her to destroy her confidence in the providence that shaped her life. Dora knew well how that felt, and set about trying to restore it.

After a little, Lizzie's story began to come out. She had been employed as nursemaid to a little girl who had been adopted by an Irish couple, the husband a wealthy tea importer. She felt that the child was not being well treated, the mother's idea of discipline being extremely harsh, but she, Lizzie, had tried to compensate by showing the child affection and standing between her and authority where possible. In the end the parents had decided to send the little girl away to a boarding school and Lizzie had no longer been needed. Instead, she had been offered a job in the warehouse owned by her employer, where her father also worked. That, she said, had been less enjoyable than her previous position, but at least it was work. Then something had happened. She seemed unwilling to say exactly what, except that someone had come asking questions about the whereabouts of the little girl. Her employer had found out they had spoken to him and both she and her father had been given the sack. The shock had killed her father, whose health was already poor, and the landlord of their little house had turned her out because she could not pay the rent. So Lizzie had found herself destitute, with no other recourse than the workhouse. She had volunteered to work in the infirmary as a way of giving herself some purpose in life 'so that I don't feel completely useless' as she put it. Dora understood that well enough, and gave her responsibility for the care of two children who had recently been admitted to the ward with whooping cough. Her devotion to them soon proved that Dora's confidence had not been misplaced.

One day Dora looked up from attending to one of her charges to see a respectably dressed young man hovering in the doorway. When she asked what he wanted he told her he was looking for Lizzie. Dora called her over, but occupied herself with some work within earshot, in case he had brought bad news of some sort. It was clear that Lizzie recognised him and her attitude was reserved but showed a quiet dignity. The young man began by apologising profusely for being the cause of her present position and Dora deduced that he must be the person whose enquiries about the missing girl had resulted in Lizzie and her father being dismissed. She heard Lizzie ask eagerly if 'Angelina' had been found. The man replied that she had not, but the search was still in progress. Then Lizzie called to her.

'Dora, you've been here for a few years, haven't you? Do you ever remember a little girl with golden hair who was dumped outside the gates one night?'

For a moment Dora was confused. She had not realised that the child in question had originally been left in the workhouse. Then the description sparked a memory.

'Golden hair? Did you say her name was Angelina? There was a child they used to call Angel.'

The young man seemed quite excited by her words. 'Did you know her?' he asked.

Dora explained that she only knew the child from what she had heard. She told him about the fire in the dormitory and the girl whose hands had been burned rescuing a friend. 'All she was worried about was the child she called Angel. She couldn't wait to get out of here and go back to the nursery to make sure she was all right.'

The young man was staring at her. 'The girl, do you happen to remember her name?'

Dora racked her memory. 'Mary, was it? Or Mabel? No, May, that was it? Why do you ask?'

She saw him flush suddenly and he made some remark about possibly having met her, after she left the workhouse.

Dora regarded him shrewdly and thought, that's not the whole story. She's more to you than a casual acquaintance, by the look on your face.

But she said nothing and the young man turned the conversation by remarking that he was surprised at the cleanliness and order in the wards. She told him that it was all due to the efforts of Agnes Jones. At that moment a child called out for her and she hurried away, leaving Lizzie to see him out.

She thought little more of the incident until a day or two later when Lizzie came to find her with a glowing face.

'Mr Breckenridge has found me a job!'

'Who?'

'The young gentleman who was here the other day. His mother happened to know of a couple with three little ones, whose nursemaid had to leave them at short notice to look after a sick relative. They are desperate for help. The husband came here this morning to talk to me, and I've got the job. I start straight away.'

Dora reached out impulsively and gave her a hug. 'I'm so glad for you, my dear. You deserve a bit of luck.'

Lizzie's expression sobered. 'I feel ungrateful, going off like this. You have been so kind to me and there is such a lot to do here. In a way, I feel I should stay.'

'No!' Dora said. 'You have the chance to stand on your own feet. You must take it. I shall miss you, but I wouldn't dream of holding you back.'

Lizzie hugged her in return. 'I'll never forget how good you've been to me.'

'Well, come back when you can and let me know how you are getting on.'

'I will! I promise.'

Over the years she had worked there, Dora had never known a time when there were no patients in the fever ward. She had been in London when the major outbreak of cholera hit Liverpool, but there were many other contagious diseases that were sent to be treated in the infirmary. Typhus, smallpox and yellow fever were endemic and there were usually two or three patients being treated for one of the other. Then, later that summer, there was a major outbreak of typhoid fever. The numbers threatened to overwhelm the infirmary's resources and, as at St Thomas's when the cholera outbreak reached its peak, wards had to be evacuated to make room for the new patients.

Led by Agnes Jones the entire nursing team, including Dora, found themselves working twelve-hour days, or even longer. Sufferers were brought in complaining of severe headaches and pains in their stomachs; some had diarrhoea and all had a high fever. Upon examination, they were found to have a rash of small pink spots on their bodies.

There was little that anyone could do for them, other than sponge their faces with cool water and satisfy their raging thirst, though Dora's fever medicine of willow bark and yarrow seemed to bring some relief. Some of them, the strongest, recovered. Many died.

The cause was a question that nagged at the back of Dora's mind. She had no doubt that the London cholera outbreak had resulted from the water company's use of contaminated water from uncovered reservoirs, though that had never been conclusively proved. Could typhoid be traced to the same root? It was plain that the majority of sufferers came from the over-crowded slum areas of the city, where for generations human waste had accumulated in middens and cess pits far too close to the area where people slept and ate, but in recent years, through the efforts of Dr William Strange, the Medical Officer for Health appointed by the city council, many of these insanitary arrangements had been replaced by modern water closets. There were those who blamed the sickness on the effects of alcohol and the slovenliness of the inhabitants of those areas, just as they had in London the previous year, but middle-class families were affected too, which gave the lie to that hypothesis. Dora put the problem to the back of her mind. Her job was to deal with the effects, not worry about the cause.

As always, no one worked harder than Agnes. More than once Dora, dragging herself back to the wards after a few hours' sleep, found her already bending over one of the beds.

'Agnes,' she asked the third time this occurred, 'have you been to bed at all?'

'Oh, I'm afraid I nodded off in my chair over there for a while,' was the reply.

'What do you mean, "I'm afraid"?' Dora said. 'You need to rest just as much as the rest of us. You cannot keep going indefinitely without sleep.'

'I'll sleep when this is over,' Agnes said. 'Until then, God will give me strength.'

Dora admired her faith and her total dedication to her duty, but she was tempted to repeat the old adage that 'God helps those who help themselves'. But she saw the look on Agnes's drawn face and the light in her eyes and decided to say nothing.

Next day she was shocked to find Agnes in one of the water closets, bent over the bowl, retching.

'Here.' She handed her a cloth to wipe her face. 'Now, come with me. You need to rest.'

But Agnes shook off her hand. 'It's nothing. I ate a boiled egg for breakfast. It must have been off. I shall be all right in a moment.'

'You look flushed. Are you feverish?'

'No, no. I have a slight headache, that's all. It will pass.'

In spite of Dora's pleas to her to lie down for a while, she insisted on going back to work, but an hour later she collapsed in a dead faint. Dora and one of the other nurses carried her to her room and undressed her and Dr Fletcher was summoned. He felt her forehead and then opened the front of her nightgown and Dora suppressed a cry of anguish when she saw the tell-tale rash.

The doctor straightened up. 'We must do all we can for her, but I fear she has exhausted her strength.'

'She will get better!' Dora averred. 'She is too valuable to lose.'

'We can only hope so,' he responded.

For two days Dora spent every moment she could spare from the wards at Agnes's bedside. She had never had a strong religious faith, but in those moments she prayed with a despairing fervour. Agnes's belief had been unshakeable and Dora felt, though she knew it was illogical, that if there was a God surely he would wish to preserve such a faithful servant. It was to no avail. Agnes's condition deteriorated. She tossed and turned on her pillow, in spite of every remedy that Dora could summon from her repertoire, and soon began to lose touch with reality. In her confusion she tried several times to get up and go back to her work, only to relapse onto the bed, muttering incomprehensibly. The other nurses hovered near whenever they could get away, and many of them wept. In the small hours of the third night Agnes sank into a coma from which she never recovered. Going through her papers afterwards Dora was shocked to discover that she was only thirty-five years old.

With a bitter irony, the epidemic seemed after that to have burnt itself out.

The funeral service in the chapel was attended by a number of city dignitaries, led by Mr Rathbone, who was visibly moved. All the nurses who could be spared were there, Dora among them, together with all three medical officers attached to the infirmary. Dora remained dry-eyed all through the service and the subsequent burial, but alone that night she wept bitterly for the loss of a woman who had done so much to shape her life. She had never been close to Agnes; very few people were. It seemed her dedication to her duty had left little room for personal attachments. Nevertheless, the whole infirmary, staff and patients, felt as if a guiding light had been extinguished and they were left groping in the dark.

Some days later Dora was summoned to appear before the chief medical superintendent, Doctor Gee, and members of the Vestry committee that was responsible for the running of the workhouse. She approached it in a mood of mild irritation at being called away from her essential tasks.

Gee opened the proceedings. 'I do not need to make you aware that, after the tragic death of Nurse Jones, the position of Lady Superintendent of the infirmary is now vacant. As a committee we have the task of choosing a successor and we are considering you for the post.'

Dora caught her breath and swallowed. 'Me? But why? Why me?'

'You are not the only candidate,' Gee said. 'There are two other nurses whom we are also considering, and there has been a suggestion that we might ask for someone to be sent up from the school at St Thomas's—' a low grunt from one of the committee made clear that person's disapproval of this last idea '—but there is a general feeling that someone local, someone with roots in the community, might be a better choice.' He consulted his notes. 'We have received a report on your progress during your training from Mrs Wardroper, which is very favourable, and we are, of course, aware of the good work you have done since you returned. But until we have had an opportunity to interview the other candidates we cannot make a final decision. All I wish to know from you at this moment is this: if you were offered the post, would you accept it?'

Dora was finding it hard to breathe. 'I ... don't know ... I suppose ... No one could replace Nurse Jones but ... Yes, if you think I am the right person for the job, I should be very honoured to accept.'

'Good!' Dr Gee rose to his feet. 'Thank you, Nurse Latimer. That will be all for the moment.'

Outside the room Dora stood still and pressed her hand to her heart. It seemed to be trying to jump out of her chest. Nothing had prepared her for this offer and she still found it hard to believe it had been made. After a few moments she remembered that there was work she needed to do in the ward and her feet carried her automatically in that direction. It was not until sometime later, when her shift came to an end, that she was able to think about what had been said.

She remembered her feelings at the end of her course at St Thomas's, when her friends were applying for and gaining places as nurse superintendents at large London hospitals. She had thought then that she was just as capable as they were and the idea of such a prestigious position had seemed very attractive. Two considerations had held her back. The first was her sense of duty to Mr Rathbone and the idea that she had an obligation to return to Liverpool. The second was subtler, one she hardly acknowledged even in her most secret thoughts. The friends who had taken those posts were 'ladies'; women like Phil, whose father was a lord, or Elizabeth whose father was a wealthy businessman. How could she, the illegitimate half-caste daughter of a dead sea captain – an outcast, a fallen woman – aspire to such a position? Again and again Fenella's cruel words echoed in her memory – *'she may be ladylike, but she will never be a real lady.'*

Now these thoughts resurfaced. Did the Vestry Committee know her history? Mrs Carter had known, and Mr Bellow, who was the chief superintendent when she first came to the infirmary. And the governor of the workhouse knew. But Mrs Carter and Mr Bellow had been replaced and it was possible that the Vestry would not think it necessary to consult the governor about this appointment. Mr Rathbone knew, but she felt sure that he would not stand in her way. But did she have the right to accept – assuming she was offered the position – without making the committee aware of her history? The question went round and round in her head but she could not find an answer.

Over the following days, Dora performed her duties automatically. She found herself thinking, 'If I get the job I shall change that ... If I was in charge I would have a word or two to say to that young probationer ... If it was up to me, I would ask for extra funding to provide this or that ...' She also found herself watching her colleagues, trying to decide who were the other two candidates. There were four nurses now who had come from London with Agnes Jones and so were theoretically senior to her, but she knew that one of them was on the verge of getting engaged and one other said frequently that she would like to find a place nearer to her home in Hampshire. Did the Vestry know that? Looking at their faces as they went about their work she tried to deduce if they had been spoken to in the same terms as herself, but no one mentioned it and she felt it would be improper to ask.

Not long afterwards, she was carrying a tray of empty dishes back from the children's ward, which was now in full operation again, when she heard a familiar voice.

'Pardon me, I'm looking for a Miss Dora Latimer. Does she still work here?'

Deep and resonant, self-assured but courteous, the sound seemed to reverberate somewhere inside Dora's own body. She turned to set the tray down on a nearby table but in her confusion she misjudged the distance and the tray and its contents clattered to the floor. She dropped to her knees and began grovelling for the broken pieces.

The voice, above her head now, said, 'You don't have to get down on your knees, you know. It's only me.'

Dora looked up into warm brown eyes. 'Jem! You've come back! What ... what do you want?'

'A few words, that's all – for now.' He knelt beside her and began to collect the pieces she had missed. 'When can we talk?'

She collected her scrambling thoughts with an effort. 'I'm on duty now. My shift finishes at six o'clock. If you wait for me outside the gates ... perhaps we can, I don't know, go for a walk?'

He smiled. 'No need to wait for the last Thursday in the month, then?'

She stood up, with a sudden surge of pride. 'I'm not a pauper any more. I'm a qualified professional nurse. I can come and go as I please.'

He stood too. 'Of course you are. I knew you did the right thing, going to London.'

'You don't ... blame me?'

'Not at all. I was disappointed when I couldn't see you, but I knew it was the right thing for you to do.'

A nurse came along the ward, her shoes tapping briskly on the wooden boards. As she passed she glanced curiously at Dora and Jem. Dora said, 'You had better go now. I can't talk at the moment. I'll see you at six.'

'I'll be there,' he promised.

He was there, waiting outside the gates for her. Looking at him properly for the first time she saw that he was well-dressed and his face had the sheen of health and prosperity.

He extended his hand. 'Thank you for agreeing to see me.'

'No,' she said, taking it. 'I should thank you. I thought you would probably never want to see me again.'

'No chance of that,' he said. 'I would have been here sooner, but I was out of the country.'

'Out of the country? Where?'

'Jamaica.'

'Jamaica! What made you go there?'

'It's quite a long story,' he said. 'We can't talk very well standing here. Can we find somewhere we can sit down?'

People were passing and she was aware of casual glances in her direction.

'Of course,' she said. 'There's a pleasant little public garden behind St George's Hall. We could sit there if you like.'

'Excellent.'

He offered his arm and they began to stroll down Brownlow Hill towards the river. It was late summer, a mild evening with sunlight glancing through slow-moving clouds propelled by a gentle westerly breeze. It was the end of the working day and people were coming out of offices and shops. Bowler-hatted clerks with rolled umbrellas hurried homewards; business men in top hats hailed hansom cabs. On the steps of the Adelphi Hotel a little group of ladies dressed for afternoon tea stood murmuring together as they waited for their carriages. At the bottom of the hill, as they passed the windows of Freeman's Department Store, a gaggle of young women, laughing and giggling, burst out from the alleyway leading to the staff entrance. Rounding the corner they came in view of the impressive frontage of St George's Hall on its raised platform and behind it the law courts. Behind that, as the land sloped away towards the Mersey, was the public garden Dora had mentioned. They found a bench and sat looking over the river to where the sun was beginning to go down behind the Wirral peninsula.

'You look well,' she told him.

'So do you, and more beautiful than ever. It's good to see you in some nice clothes, instead of some kind of uniform.'

She was wearing the heather-mixture tweed skirt she had bought for her weekend at Lillden and a new lilac-coloured blouse edged with cream lace, topped off with a bonnet trimmed with violets and purple ribbon. She felt herself blush, but at the same time there was a glow of pleasure deep inside her.

'So, tell me. What made you go to Jamaica?'

He took a moment to collect his thoughts. 'Well, after I got your letter I didn't know what to do, but I felt that I didn't want to stay here, where I could see the workhouse every time I passed. It reminded me too much that you were not there inside, any longer. So I wanted to get away and I suddenly thought, why not go to Jamaica and see the place my ancestors came from. I thought I should like to find out how things are there, now there's no more slavery. So I found a ship that was heading there and I signed on.'

'Not …' she interrupted him.

'No, no, not as a stoker. I learned my lesson there. No, I got taken on as a steward and it was the luckiest chance I could have had.'

'Oh, how so?'

'One of the passengers was a gentleman called Sir Henry Storks. He was a very affable gent and didn't mind talking to someone like me. He was on his way to head a commission of enquiry into how the island was being governed. I didn't know it then, but Jamaica was in a bad way. The economy relied on sugar, growing it and exporting it, but when slavery ended the planters couldn't find enough labour to keep the plantations going, so things got very difficult. Most of the black ex-slaves had got themselves bits of land in the interior to cultivate and they didn't want to go back to work on the plantations, even as free men. There was a lot of bad feeling between them and the white planters – not surprisingly. I'm not clear exactly what happened, but a black man was arrested for trespassing on an abandoned plantation and at his trial a riot broke out. The trouble spread and it became what the people in charge called the Morant Bay rebellion. Turns out it wasn't really a rebellion, just a bit of local trouble, but the governor, a man called Eyres, decided to crack down. The militia was called out and hundreds of blacks were killed. Most of them had never been anywhere near the rioting, but that didn't stop the killing. Dozens of others were flogged, men and women – even women who were pregnant ...'

'Oh, that's terrible!' Dora exclaimed. 'How could that be allowed to happen?'

'That's just what the government here wanted to know, which is why they sent out Sir Henry to hold an enquiry.'

'I don't see what this has to do with you, personally,' Dora said. 'Why was it lucky for you?'

'I was coming to that. I liked Sir Henry, so I made a point of looking after him, and he seemed to like me, too. Towards the end of the voyage he asked me if I intended to stay with the ship and come back to England and I told him no, that I wanted to stay in Jamaica, if I could find a job. He said then that he would need to set up his own establishment while he was on the island and would need his own staff. I'd mentioned how much I love working with horses. He knew he was going to need a horse to get around the island, and his wife and daughter who were travelling with him like to ride out, so he needed someone to buy suitable mounts for all of them and to look after them. And the upshot was, he offered me a job.'

'Ah, now I see! And you took it, of course.'

'Of course I did.'

'And it worked out well?'

'Better than I could ever have expected. Sir Henry took to me, and gave me quite a lot of responsibility. He used to take me with him when he was investigating matters around the island. In the end, Governor Eyres was dismissed and sent packing with his tail between his legs and Sir Henry took over as interim governor, while the authorities back home looked for a good man to appoint permanently. After a few months, they appointed a chap called Sir John Grant, and when Sir Henry left he recommended me to the new man, who took me on. Not as a groom any more. Officially I was his steward, but in fact he used me as a go-between with the black population. He reckoned being black I'd be trusted more by them, but being new to the island I couldn't be associated with the troubles, so the whites wouldn't have any reason to object.'

'That sounds to me as if you had a pretty responsible job,' Dora said, impressed.

'It turned out that way,' Jem agreed. 'When the government picked Sir John they got the right man for the job. You wouldn't believe the difference he has made in a very short time. There's a big new irrigation scheme and he's building roads and elementary schools and – this will appeal to you – hospitals.'

'And you have been part of it.'

'A small part, yes.'

'But you've given it up and come back. Why?'

'I couldn't settle, not until ...' he broke off. 'I had to find out what had happened to you.'

'Will you go back?'

'That depends.'

'What on?'

'On the answers to two questions.

'What questions?'

He shook his head. 'I'm not ready to ask them yet.'

'So, is this a kind of holiday, or are you looking for work?'

He laughed. 'I can't afford to use up my savings sitting around idle. I shall have to find a job.'

'You won't find anything as ... as important as what you were doing.'

'No, probably not. That won't matter for now.'

Somewhere nearby a clock struck seven. The sun was almost down. Jem stood up and looked at her.

'Would it be against the rules for a single gentleman to ask a single lady to have dinner with him?'

'I don't know. I don't see why not.'

'Then will you do me the honour of having dinner with me?'

She stood up and took his arm. 'With great pleasure.'

Chapter 18

Over the following days Dora met Jem whenever she could get away from the infirmary. They went for walks and sat in tea shops and once, when she had the whole afternoon off, they took the ferry across the Mersey and strolled through the grassy expanse of Birkenhead Park. And they talked, endlessly. She was fascinated by all he had to say about Jamaica and about the improvements being made there, and he was equally interested in her stories of life at the nursing school, and particularly in the work she had done in Old Nicol and the march for voting rights for ordinary men. It did not take long for Dora to recognise that she had found a man whose attitudes and interests chimed with her own; someone with whom she could realistically imagine spending the rest of her life. When describing her time in London she touched briefly on her friendship with Elizabeth and her visit to Lillden, but she never mentioned Edward.

One evening he said, 'Well, I've found myself a job.'

'Oh, where?'

'You'll never guess. Back at the livery stable where I worked before.'

'Oh!' She looked at him, thinking he must feel that this was a definite step backwards from the position he had reached in Jamaica.

'It's not as bad as all that,' he laughed, interpreting her expression. 'I've taken over the management of the place. The owner has gout and can't get about like he used to, so he was glad to find someone he could trust to help out. I'll still be working with horses, so it suits me very well – for the time being at least. He's got a new house out Toxteth way somewhere, so he's renting me the old place attached to the stables.'

The excitement of Jem's return had almost driven out of her head the interview with Dr Gee and the members of the Vestry. That night the recollection came back to her with a shock. If Jem did ask her to marry him, how should she answer? Which did she want, marriage to him, or the post of superintendent? Of course, she might not be offered the position, and if she turned down Jem's proposal she might be left with nothing. But then, maybe she was mistaken about Jem's intentions, although that was hard to believe. She recalled Florence Nightingale's words to Elizabeth. 'I hope you will not choose personal pleasure over duty.' Well, Elizabeth was getting married, so she had made her choice. Agnes Jones had chosen celibacy and duty, so had Miss Nightingale herself. Was that the path she should take? The questions kept her awake most of the night.

Next day he arrived at the workhouse gates in a smart pony trap, and took her to visit his new quarters. There was a strong smell of horses, even inside the house, and to her eyes it needed a good scrub out, but there were two bed-rooms and a new bathroom with the luxury of piped water, and a modern water closet in the yard. When he had shown her round he took her in his arms and kissed her for the first time since his return and she felt the old fire running through her blood.

After a moment he drew back slightly and looked into her eyes. 'I think you know what I came back here to ask you, don't you?'

She caught her breath. 'I ... I think so.'

'Then, what's the answer?'

She hesitated and suddenly he dropped to his knees. 'Very well. You want me to do it properly. Dora Latimer, will you do me the honour of becoming my wife?'

Dora gazed down into his face. Every instinct screamed at her to say 'yes' but she could not reconcile that with the dilemma she had faced last night. She swallowed and passed her tongue over her lips. 'Jem, I want to marry you. I want it more than anything else in the world. But I'm not sure that I can.'

He stood up. 'I don't understand. Why not?'

'Because ... because. It's too difficult to explain! Please, can I have a few days to think about it? There is something I have to decide. I'm sorry. Can you bear to wait a little while longer?'

He studied her face and she could see in his eyes how disappointed he was, but in the end he said, 'Well, I've waited nearly three years. I suppose I can wait another day or two.'

He kissed her once more and then led her out to where the pony waited and drove her back to the workhouse.

After another sleepless night Dora woke to the news that an epidemic of whooping cough had broken out and six new patients had been admitted to her ward. It was clear very quickly that they were just the forerunners of many more and Dora and her team were soon working at full stretch. She scribbled a quick note to Jem, telling him not to call for her until she told him that the pressure had eased and begging him to believe that this was not simply a way for her to delay her decision. Over the next days her mind was too concentrated on looking after her patients for her to think about his proposal. It was saddening work. Whooping cough was a killer and usually only the strongest survived, but with careful nursing the less robust could pull through. When the epidemic began to subside, some three weeks later, she was exhausted, but she knew that children were going home, restored to health, who might have died without her care.

It was at this point that she was summoned once again to a meeting of the Vestry committee, to be held the following morning. She did not know what that might portend but presumably they had made their choice. If they were going to offer her the position as superintendent she could not delay her decision any longer. Waking in the dawn, she suddenly knew what her answer was going to be.

'Nurse Latimer, thank you for attending again,' Dr Gee began. 'I have asked you to come because we, the Vestry and I, have arrived at a decision. It has not been an easy choice between some very strong candidates, and there has been much discussion, but I am able to inform you ...'

'One moment, sir, if I may,' Dora broke in. 'Forgive me for interrupting you, but I think I should tell you, before you go any further, that I wish to withdraw.'

'Withdraw! On what grounds?'

'I plan to get married.'

Looks were exchanged between the committee members. She saw consternation and in some faces anger. There were irritated murmurs and someone said, 'well, really!', and another voice muttered, 'what did I tell you?'

Dr Gee looked infuriated. 'When you were first invited to apply you assured us that you would accept the post if it was offered.'

'I know,' Dora said apologetically. 'I am really sorry to go back on my word. But perhaps you did not intend to offer me the position?'

'Of course we did! Why do you think we sent for you?'

'I can only apologise, sir,' Dora repeated. 'The fact is that my circumstances have changed. I no longer feel able to continue my work here.'

There were more looks exchanged and then Gee said, 'Very well. There is no more to be said. You have placed us in a very difficult position.'

'You said there were several strong candidates,' Dora pointed out. 'I am sure you will find someone who will do a better job than I would have done.'

'That is as may be,' Gee spluttered. 'The fact is we shall have to start the selection process all over again. Oh, very well, very well. You can leave. There is no more to be said.'

Dora closed the door behind her and felt herself trembling, but she was quite sure she had done the right thing. She sat down and wrote a note to Jem, telling him that she was now free to meet him and asking him to call for her the following evening.

As before he picked her up in the trap and on the way back to the stables they talked of anything but what was uppermost in Dora's mind. Once the pony had been handed over to a stable boy and they were in the kitchen, Jem set the blackened kettle on the hob to boil and then seated himself opposite her at the table. Dora felt a flutter of nervous excitement in her stomach. *This was the moment. Now he would ask her.*

Instead he said, 'Do you ever think of that child you gave up?'

She drew back, feeling a sudden chill. 'Yes, of course. Not all the time, but whenever I see mothers with children I wonder what I have missed. And whenever a new boy is admitted to the hospital I find myself thinking, could this be him?'

He nodded. 'If you knew where he was, would you want him back?'

'I don't see how I could, under the circumstances.'

'But if circumstances were different ...?'

'Then yes, of course I should.'

'I think I know where he is.'

'What?'

'I believe I have found him.'

'How?'

He settled himself in his chair and leaned towards her. 'Have patience and I'll explain. My real reason for coming to see if there was a job for me here, at the stables, was not just that I liked the work. It was because of something I discovered the first time I worked here. One Sunday afternoon, a man came to hire a horse. I didn't take to him. He was very high-handed and impatient; thought himself too good for the likes of me. His name was Hector Latimer.'

'Hector! I don't remember him ever going riding.'

'I'm not surprised. It was easy to see he was far from comfortable on horseback. But in spite of that he brought the mare back two hours later in a lather, as if he'd been riding hard.'

'Where had he been, I wonder?'

'Wait a bit. I took a look in the book where the owner listed regular bookings and there he was, last Sunday of the month, going back as far as the book went. So I asked myself, why does a man who doesn't enjoy riding hire a horse once a month for two hours? And the answer, of course, is, to get somewhere he can't go by train or omnibus – somewhere in the country.'

Dora caught a quick breath. 'You're thinking of one of those places you told me about – a baby farm.'

'That's exactly the idea that came to me. I was going to tell you about it, but then I got your letter saying you were going away, so I couldn't see much point in following it any further. But I never forgot, and when I started here again the first thing I did was check the bookings, and there he was, regular as clockwork every month. Hadn't missed one the whole time I was away in Jamaica, as far as I could tell. Last Sunday was the last in September, so I had a horse ready for myself, and I followed him. He set off eastwards on the road towards Woolton. It wasn't hard to keep him in sight without making myself obvious as long as he stuck to the main road, but then he turned off along a country lane in the direction of Allerton, where there was very little traffic, and I realised if I followed him there he might spot me, so I turned back. I hadn't been here long before he arrived back, so I knew he couldn't have gone much further. So, later in the week, as soon as

I could get away, I rode out that way and sure enough I found what I was looking for. A cottage, with a little bit of land, enough for a few hens and geese and a pig or two. There was a woman weeding in the garden and a gaggle of children running around her, all ages from toddlers to youngsters of six or seven. I pulled up and asked if I could water my horse at the trough, and while he was drinking a boy came round from behind the cottage. He was filthy and I guessed he had been cleaning out the pig sty, but underneath the dirt it was obvious he was black – well, our colour, maybe a shade lighter.'

'You think that was ... was my son?' Dora asked breathlessly.

'Doesn't it seem likely? But there's more. I called him over and asked him to hold my horse for a minute, so I could get a better look at him. His eyes are blue.'

'Then that is him!' Dora exclaimed. 'It must be. Oh, Jem! I can't believe you found him.' Then, in a moment of doubt, 'Can we be sure it is him?'

'Listen, I made out I was surprised to find someone of our colour there and asked the woman if she knew anything about his parents. She said no, all she knew was that a fine gentleman came from the city once a month to give her money for his keep. '

'Then that proves it!' Dora's pulse was racing and so many emotions were whirling through her brain that she felt dizzy. She was silent for a moment, forcing herself to think clearly. 'So ... what do we do now?'

'Do you want him back?'

'Yes!'

'You are sure?'

'Of course!' She paused. 'I understand why you are asking. I gave him up and all these years I have made no effort to find out where he was – but I didn't know where to start, Jem. I didn't even know if he was still alive. But now ...'

'Now, you want him?'

'Yes, I do ... but ...'

'I know what you are going to say. How can you look after him, in your present circumstances.'

She dropped her eyes. 'Yes.'

'There is a simple answer. If we were to marry, we could bring him here to live with us. I ... we could adopt him. No one need know the real story.' He leaned across the table and took her hands. 'Well, what do you say?'

Dora bit her lip. 'If I say yes now, you will always wonder if it is because I really love you, or just so that I can find a home for my son.'

His mouth twisted in a wry smile, but she could see the pain lurking behind his eyes. 'There is that, yes.'

'If only you had asked for my decision before you told me about him.'

'Why do you say that?'

'Because if you had asked then, I would have told you that some weeks ago I was summoned to a meeting of the Vestry. They told me they were looking for a new Lady Superintendent and were considering me for the place. They wanted to know if I would accept, if it was offered, and I said I would.' The shadow of pain was deepening in his eyes and she hurried on. 'Yesterday they sent for me again, and said they had chosen me for the position ...'

'And you accepted.' It was a flat statement, in a voice in which all emotion had been suppressed.

'No! That's what I wanted you to understand. I told them I had changed my mind – that I expected to be married.'

She saw his chest heave as he drew a deep breath. 'Then the answer is yes?'

'Yes. And it would have been yes even without this wonderful gift you have given me.'

'Gift?'

'My son!'

He came round the table and dropped on his knees beside her chair, folding her in his arms. 'Oh, my darling! My sweet love! You are the one who has given me a wonderful gift, a gift beyond price. Thank you!'

He kissed her and she clung close to him with a sudden feeling of homecoming, as if some deep part of herself had cherished the memory of his embrace and had been yearning for it ever since.

After a while he drew back and brought his chair round to sit close beside her.

'So, now. What next?'

'I shall have to give notice. I suppose the end of the month will be acceptable.'

'And we shall have to have the banns called, so that means three weeks at least. We could set a date for the beginning of November. Will that suit you?'

'Oh yes! Very well.' She paused for a moment. 'But what about the boy? Did ... had she given him a name?'

'Dan, she called him. Daniel.'

'Daniel. I like that. Will we have to leave him where he is until then?'

'Not necessarily. I could go back and say I like the look of the boy and offer to take him on as an apprentice.'

'He's too young to be apprenticed, surely.'

'I doubt whether she'll care about that.'

'I don't know,' Dora said doubtfully. 'She is getting a regular monthly income from keeping him. She may not want to let him go. Or she may feel she has to ask permission from Hector.'

'Why should he mind? He gets rid of a monthly outgoing.'

'That's true, I suppose. Jem, do you think he has been doing it all these years because he feels something for the boy, in spite of denying he was responsible?'

Jem shrugged. 'I doubt it. He can never have spent more than a few minutes with him. If he was taking a real interest he would have stayed longer. I think it was just a way of making sure that he was out of the way, somewhere he could never embarrass the family.'

'Yes.' Dora heaved a sigh. 'That sounds more like him. But the woman may still not want to part with him.'

'Leave it with me. I'll ride out tomorrow and see what her attitude is. I'll tell her I'm prepared to compensate her for the loss, up to a certain extent.'

Dora squeezed his fingers. 'Dearest Jem! You're so good to me.'

'I'll do whatever has to be done to make sure that our boy is with us.'

'Our boy,' she murmured. 'You said "*our* boy".'

'And he will be our boy. We shall be his father and mother. He will never know any others.'

'You don't think he should be told the truth?'

'No. It would be too hard for a child of that age to understand. Maybe when he's older, but not yet.'

Dora nodded. 'Yes, you're right.'

He drew her into a close embrace. 'We have a new life dawning for all of us, my darling. Roll on November the first!'

He called for her again two days later and as they drove through the city streets towards the stables he said, 'Well, I rode out to Allerton yesterday.'

'What happened?'

'I'll tell you when we get home.'

And in spite of her urging he refused to say any more.

As they drove into the yard one of the stable boys appeared and at his side was a small, dark figure dressed in a shirt and breeches several sizes too big for him.

Dora gave a cry that combined joy and shock and gut-wrenching guilt. 'Is that him?'

'It is. Come.'

The stable boy took the pony's head and Jem handed Dora down from the trap. 'Daniel, come here. This is the lady I told you about. This is your new mother.'

The boy came hesitantly closer and Dora dropped to her knees on the cobbles and held out her arms. 'Come here, Daniel. I am so very, very happy to see you!'

The boy drew back against Jem's legs and looked up at him. 'What's a mother?'

Dora was unable to suppress a sob.

Jem said, 'What did you call Mrs Wicks, the woman who looked after you?'

'Ma.'

'And was she kind to you?'

'Sometimes.'

'Well, this is your new Ma, and she will always be kind to you.'

Dora saw that her emotional appeal was only making Daniel uneasy. She stood up and held out her hand. 'Don't be afraid, Daniel. No one is going to hurt you. Will you say "how do you do?" A small, cold hand was briefly placed in her own. 'That's good! How do you do, Daniel?'

'I'm well enough, thank you.' It was obviously a phrase he had been taught and repeated parrot fashion.

Dora had an inspiration. 'Do you like treacle toffee?' She had brought some, because she knew it was Jem's favourite.

'What's that?'

'It's something to stick your teeth together,' Jem said, laughing.

'What?' The boy's face tightened in alarm.

'Don't listen to him,' Dora said. 'It's something very nice to eat and I've got some here in my bag. Shall we go inside, and I'll show you?'

He followed her to the house, but hung back in the doorway until Jem said, 'Yes, go on in, lad.' He added in a lower tone, 'I get the impression he was not supposed to go into the old woman's house.'

'Where did he sleep, then?' Dora asked.

'In a kind of lean to at the back, along with the chickens and two or three other boys, as far as I could make out.'

'Merciful heavens!'

Dora set her bag on the table and sat down. 'Here you are, Daniel. Try a bit of this.'

She held out the paper bag of toffee and the boy hesitantly reached into it a drew out a sticky lump, but he did not put it into his mouth. It was not until Jem took a piece and chewed it with obvious relish that Daniel ate his. Then an expression of such wonder lit up his face that tears came to Dora's eyes.

'Where did you find those clothes for him, Jem?' she asked.

'Jack's mother gave me some of his cast offs,' Jem said, nodding towards one of the stable boys. 'I couldn't let him stay in the rags he was wearing. I thought you would have a better idea what to buy for him than I would. We can go shopping as soon as you have some free time.'

'Would you like that, Jem?' she asked. 'Shall we buy you some fine clothes?'

His only response was to wriggle his thin shoulders, as if the idea was incomprehensible.

'When did you fetch him?' Dora asked.

'Yesterday. I'll tell you all about it after he's in bed. I've got a lamb stew in the oven for dinner.'

Jem had shown an unexpected talent for cookery, for which Dora was grateful. Although she had spent many hours in the infirmary kitchen preparing her herbal remedies, she had never had to cook a meal for herself and would not have known where to start.

Jem took a dish from the oven and Dora quickly laid three places at the table, watched intensely by Daniel. When they were all seated with a steaming plate in front of them she was amazed to see him clasp his hands together and mumble an incomprehensible incantation.

'Seems he's been taught to say grace before meals,' Jem said. 'Perhaps we should do the same.'

So they too folded their hands and Jem repeated, 'For what we are about to receive, may the Lord make us truly grateful.' It had been spoken before every meal at the workhouse and Dora had often repeated it unwillingly, angry that she was expected to be grateful for such poor sustenance. Now she said it with a full heart. Daniel was already wolfing down his portion, one arm curled defensively around his plate. He did not look up, or pause for breath, until the plate was empty and when Jem ladled out a second helping his eyes widened in amazement.

Once the meal was over it was clear that Daniel could hardly keep his eyes open.

'Better get the lad to bed,' Jem said.

'Where is he sleeping?'

'I put him in the spare room next to mine,' Jem said, 'but he couldn't seem to settle, so he ended up in with me. Maybe he'll be better tonight. I'll take him out to the privy.'

He stooped and picked the boy up in his arms. The drowsy eyes opened wide in surprise but he made no resistance. When they returned Dora followed them upstairs and saw that Jem had made up a small bed.

'Where did that come from?'

'Belonged to one of the owner's children. He left it here because the boy'd outgrown it.'

He pulled back the blankets and laid Daniel down. 'There, you close your eyes and go to sleep. Your ma and I will be close by.'

Dora knelt by the bed and stroked the curly hair. 'Goodnight, Daniel. Sleep well.'

He opened his eyes. 'When are you going to take me back?'

The question struck a chill to her heart. 'Do you want to go back?'

'No. It's nice here.'

'Then you are going to stay here, with us.'

'Always?'

'Yes, always. Go to sleep now.' She kissed his cheek and he sighed and squirmed down among the blankets. Within a minute he was fast asleep.

Downstairs, Dora said, 'I didn't know you were going to bring him back with you. How did you persuade the woman to let him go?'

'It was easier than I expected. I told her I'd taken a liking to the boy and wanted to take him on as an apprentice. I expected her to argue, or at least to ask for payment, but she said I was the answer to her prayer. Apparently, the last time the "fine gentleman" came he told her he was not prepared to go on paying indefinitely and when she asked what was supposed to happen to Daniel he said, "put him to work. Let him earn his keep". She thought he was too young and no one would take him on, so she was faced with having to feed and clothe him without any money coming in. You can't blame the woman, she has got six others to look after and from the look of it whatever she is paid is only just enough to keep them from starving.'

'So she just handed him over to you?'

'I gave her some money, to help out with the rest of them.'

'In other words, she sold him to you. You might have had ... well, terrible things happen. Your idea of taking an apprentice could have been a cover for ... Well, you know what I mean.'

'Yes, I do. Luckily for Daniel my intentions are honourable. But it's Hector you should blame. If he refuses to pay, he must know what might happen.'

Dora shivered. 'How can anyone be so unfeeling? He deserves to suffer for what he did to me, and worse for what might have happened to Daniel. But he will get away with it. The likes of him always do.' She considered for a moment. 'I wonder why he suddenly decided to stop paying.'

'Maybe he's going away, so he won't be around to make his monthly visits?'

'Maybe. There was talk, I remember, of him going away to university, but surely he's too old for that now.'

'Perhaps the family is moving.'

'Perhaps, but I cannot think why they should want to.' She dismissed the question with a shrug. 'Most likely he just wants to hang onto the money for himself and he's decided the risk of someone finding out about Daniel's origin isn't too great any more.' A sudden thought came to her. 'She didn't say he was going to stop paying immediately. Has he reserved a horse for the last Sunday of this month?'

'I'll check.' Jem took a ledger from a shelf and leafed through it. 'Yes, he has.'

'I wonder what he will think when he discovers Daniel has gone.' She sat forward with a sudden jolt. 'Jem, you don't think he could trace you, do you? He knows you from hiring horses here. If the woman tells him it was someone of our colour ...'

'Why should he care? Daniel is off his hands. What does it matter where he's gone?'

'I suppose you're right,' Dora said, but she could not dispel a sense of unease.

He came and took her in his arms. 'If I didn't know you for a very moral lady I'd be tempted to suggest you stayed here tonight. After all, in three weeks we shall be man and wife. Do you think God would be very angry with us for anticipating a bit?'

She rubbed her cheek against his and laughed. 'I don't know if He would be angry, but I'm certain Nurse Peters will be furious if I'm not there to take over when her shift ends.'

He sighed. 'Then you will have to go.'

'We can't leave Daniel here on his own. Suppose he wakes up?'

'I've thought of that. Jack will drive you back. He's a good lad, you'll be safe with him.'

He kissed her and went out to call the stable boy to bring the pony and trap round.

Chapter 19

Over the next weeks Dora's emotions were tossed about like a small boat on a choppy sea. At one moment she was filled with joy at the prospect of marrying Jem and settling down with him and Daniel in the first real family she had ever known. The next, she was riven with guilt at what her son had had to endure through her own actions. She told herself repeatedly that the alternative was to let him be brought up in the workhouse orphanage and tried to persuade herself that he would have had a harder time there, but she was no longer convinced. Daniel himself still seemed uneasy with her and she sensed that it would take a long time before he was able to trust her completely. It was not surprising. For the whole of his six years the only mother figure he had known was Mrs Wicks. They had told him that she and Jem were now his mother and father, but he had no conception of what that meant. Dora knew that one day, when he was older, she would have to tell him the truth and deal with his reaction to discovering that she had abandoned him as a baby. She could only hope that by then the bond between them would be strong enough to take the strain. Just now he was more at ease with Jem, but then he spent all day with him and she could only visit when she was off duty. She could only resolve that once she was able to be with him constantly she would make up to him for the years of separation.

One day they tried to take him shopping for new clothes, but the busy city streets so terrified him that they had to give up. Instead, she took his measurements to Freeman's department store and was able to buy breeches and shirts and underwear and a little jacket that fitted reasonable well. She bought shoes, too, but these he flatly refused to wear, pulling them off at the earliest opportunity on the grounds that they hurt his feet.

It was a comfort that Daniel and Jem got on so well. 'He's a worker, all right,' Jem reported. 'He watched my lads mucking out the stables, then without any prompting from me he went and found himself a shovel and joined in. And he's a bright lad. He knows his letters already – the old woman taught him that much at least. He can write his name and the names of some of the animals. We'll have him reading before long.'

In the infirmary the news of Dora's imminent departure was greeted with consternation. To many of the nurses, and to the paupers who had volunteered to train as probation-ers, she seemed like a permanent fixture, as basic to the running of the place as the walls themselves. A nurse who had joined them from the training school in London a year earlier was appointed as Lady Superintendent, and several of the longer serving nurses told Dora that the position should have been hers. She did not let slip that it had been offered to her first. Sometimes, when she thought about her new life, she felt a shiver of anxiety. Nearly seven years of her life, with the exception of her time in London, had been spent within the walls of the workhouse and even though she had earned her independence and was free to come and go, its routines had shaped her days. She wondered what it would feel like to have to order her own life around the unfamiliar duties of a wife and mother.

As well as her work and her visits to the stables there was the wedding to prepare for. She had tried to shrug off the need for new clothes, but Jem had insisted that she should have a proper trousseau, and since she spent so little of her earnings she had enough money saved up to pay for some new dresses and a couple of nightgowns that were rather more glamorous than the plain cotton ones she usually wore. The wedding itself would take place in the workhouse chapel. They had considered asking for permission to have the ceremony in one of the city churches, but since neither of them was a regular worshipper that was not easy to obtain. Dora was not sorry. It seemed fitting that the rather grim little church where she had sat though so many tedious sermons should for once be a place of rejoicing. All her colleagues were invited, and she wrote to Phil and Elizabeth asking them to come. Jem took the arranging of the wedding breakfast into his own hands and refused to tell her the details.

One day, when they were having tea in the kitchen at the stables, and Daniel was playing with the puppy Jem had bought for him in a corner of the room, Jem said, 'I don't suppose you find time to read the newspapers, do you?'

'No, I don't. Why?'

Jem reached into his pocket and produced a folded newspaper.

'I think I may have solved the mystery of why Hector said he was going to stop paying for the boy.'

He handed her the paper, which was folded to the page devoted to society news, and pointed to a paragraph. 'The engagement is announced of Miss Sophia Callaghan, daughter of Mr and Mrs Josiah Callaghan of New Place, Ince Blundell, to Mr Hector Latimer, partner in the shipping company Latimer and Dawson.'

'Sophia Callaghan!' Dora said. 'Trust Hector to do well for himself! The Callaghans are some of the richest merchants in the city. And you think this is why he told the old woman he wouldn't pay for Daniel's keep anymore?

'Well, how would he explain to his new wife why he has to go off into the country once a month on some mysterious errand? And he couldn't trust anyone else to do it.'

'It would be the finish of his engagement if she ever found out,' Dora agreed.

'I've been thinking about what you said a while back, about the chance of him working out that I'm the man who took Daniel. He'll be coming here next Sunday. I'll have to make sure Daniel is well out of the way, and I've sworn the lads to secrecy – but just the same ...'

A chill of fear ran through Dora's veins. 'If he found out ... I don't know what he'd do.'

'What could he do?'

'I don't know. But if he found out that I am here, that we are going to be married ... he couldn't bear the idea that we might betray his secret. He's a cruel man, Jem, and I'm sure he would stop at nothing to make sure his own marriage goes ahead.'

Jem leaned across the table and took her hands. 'Do you remember I said I had two questions to ask?'

'Yes.

'You know what the first one was. Here's the second. Would you consider coming back to Jamaica with me?'

'Jamaica!'

'Why not? I've told you how things are improving out there. We could have a good life – and you could even use some of your nursing skills. The new hospitals that are being set up must be desperate for qualified staff. You wouldn't have to work full time. They would be grateful for any time you could give them. And we would be somewhere Hector Latimer could never trouble us again.'

'And you? Would you be able to go back to working for Sir John?'

'I've got a better idea than that.'

'What is it?'

'Have you ever eaten a banana?'

'A what?'

'A banana. It's a fruit. A long, yellow thing.'

Dora searched her memory. 'I think I might have seen one when my father was alive. I believe he brought some back with him from one of his voyages. But they had gone bad by the time they arrived here.'

'Yes. I can believe that. It was too long a journey in a sailing ship. But everyone eats them in Jamaica and Sir John has encouraged small farmers to grow them instead of relying on sugar cane.' His eyes were bright with enthusiasm. 'Soon, when steam ships can travel faster, it will be possible to ship them to America. Maybe one day to

England, too. There's a fortune to be made by someone who gets into the market early.'

'And you think you could do that?'

'I know a man who is keen to try it. He offered me a partnership, just before I left. I told him I had to come back to England to "settle my affairs" here but that I would try to get back as soon as I could.' He gripped her hands. 'What do you think? We could afford a better house out there. The sun shines all the time. There are elementary schools for Daniel and you could still nurse – at any rate until we have babies of our own. Will you?'

She gazed into his eyes and seemed to see a bright future there. 'Yes, why not? Yes! It will be an adventure.'

'That's wonderful!' He swept her into his arms. 'Oh, my love! We shall share the adventure – all three of us.'

Dora had just finished changing out of her uniform at the end of her shift a day or two later when there was a tap on her door. She opened it to find Lizzie Findlay outside, but a very different Lizzie from the pale, withdrawn girl who had come to the workhouse a few months earlier. Her face had filled out and there was colour in her cheeks, and her eyes were sparkling.

'Lizzie! How nice to see you! You look well.'

'So do you. I hope you don't mind me coming like this, without letting you know in advance.'

'Not at all.'

'I just had to come and tell you my news. I'm going away.'

'Where to? When?'

'Not till after Christmas, but everything has been happening so fast my head's in a whirl.'

Dora took her arm and drew her into the room. 'Come in and sit down, and tell me all about it. How did this happen?'

'You remember the young gentleman who came looking for me, to apologise for getting me the sack?'

'Yes. Mr Brackenbury, was it?'

'Breckenridge. You remember he mentioned a little girl, the little girl who was left here as a baby and then adopted?

'What was it you called her? Angel?'

'Yes, well, it was really Angelina, but I called her Angel. She was adopted by a Mr and Mrs McBride and I was employed as a nursemaid to look after her.'

'I seem to remember she was missing and Mr Breckenridge was looking for her.'

'That's right. Her real father had come back from Africa and wanted to find her, but her adoptive parents had sent her away to school in Ireland. That's when they told me I wasn't needed any more, but I could have a job in the warehouse instead.'

'So what had happened to the girl?'

'She'd run away from school. So her pa employed Mr Breckenridge, who is a solicitor's clerk, to look for her.'

'And did they find her?'

'Yes. She'd been racketing around doing all sorts of things, living with gypsies, even performing with a music hall company. But her adopted father got her back and he didn't want to let her go. It wasn't because he loved her. He just didn't want anyone to know they had adopted a child from the workhouse. So Mr Breckenridge and Mr Kean – that's her real pa – asked me to go with them to help get her away.' Dora shook her head in puzzlement and Lizzie plunged on. 'Oh, it's all very complicated, and we had a real drama, I can tell you. It ended with Mr McBride being arrested ...'

'Arrested?'

'He was mixed up with some kind of smuggling apparently. So after that Mr Kean took Angel to live with him and he asked me to come and work for him, as her nursemaid.'

'So you have got your old job back?'

'Yes, but it's much nicer than working for the McBrides.'

'Is there a Mrs Kean?'

'No, she died. That's why he needed me. But here's the really funny thing. Do you remember Mr Breckenridge asking after May, the girl who burnt her hands?'

'Yes, now you come to mention it. I thought at the time he had more than a passing interest in her.'

'You were right. They're engaged to be married, only she's gone to live with her father in Australia.'

'I thought she was brought up here because she was an orphan.'

'They thought she was, but her father wasn't dead. He'd been transported for stealing.'

'How awful!'

'But now he's a miner and he struck gold! He's a rich man, so May has gone to live with him and as soon as Mr Breckenridge has passed his law exams he's going out to join her.'

'So how does this affect you?'

'He and Mr Kean are good friends, and Mr Kean hasn't got a job in this country – he's some sort of an engineer – so he's decided to go too, and take Angel and me with him.'

'To Australia? How exciting!'

'Yes, it is, isn't it? I feel so lucky!'

'Well, I'm sure you deserve it, after the hard time you had with your previous employer.'

'Wish me luck?'

'I do, with all my heart. But as it happens—' Dora paused and smiled '—I am going away, too, to Jamaica.'

'Jamaica! Why?'

'I'm getting married, to a man whose family came from there, as my mother did. So you might say we are going home.'

'Oh, that sounds wonderful. I'm so happy for you. But you will be missed here. How will they ever manage without you?'

'Very well, I'm sure,' Dora said with a laugh. She glanced down at the watch Mr Rathbone had given her, which she still wore pinned to her dress. 'Now, I must go, Lizzie. My husband-to-be will be waiting for me.' She put her arms round the girl and kissed her. 'I'm so glad things have worked out so well for you. Goodbye, my dear.'

'Goodbye,' Lizzie said, 'and thank you for all the help you gave me when I was really down. I'll never forget that.'

The wedding was to take place on 3rd November, which was a Tuesday, and Jem had found berths for them on a steam ship bound for Jamaica two days later. They would spend the intervening days at the livery stables. Jem had spoken to the owner and explained that he would have to find someone else to manage the business, but his tenancy would not expire till the end of the month.

The last Sunday in October fell on the 25th, and on the Friday before it, when Dora had finished a morning shift and was mending a shirt while Daniel played with his puppy out in the yard, Jem said, 'I was thinking. Hector has not cancelled his booking for Sunday, so I presume he intends to make one more visit to Allerton, at least. It's vital that he doesn't see either you or Daniel when he comes here. It would be a good idea if you took him out for the afternoon.'

'You're right,' Dora said. 'I wonder where I could take him. He still gets very nervous in crowds.'

'He likes going out in the pony trap. Jack could drive you. Why not take a ride along by the river, so he can see the ships? After all, we have to get him on board one very soon.'

'I have been talking to him about ships and the sea, and we've drawn pictures, but he's never seen a real one. I suppose it might be good for him.'

Dora approached the prospect with some anxiety, but in the event Daniel enjoyed the outing. He had grown in confidence over the last weeks and was beginning to respond to Dora's loving care with little affectionate gestures of his own. She had told him about the journey they were going to have and he was excited by his first sight of the great river and the many ships thronging it.

When they got back, and Daniel had gone with Jack to see the pony rubbed down and fed, Jem said, with a curious grin on his face, 'Well, I think I may have put a stop to Hector's marriage.'

'What!?' Dora stared at him. 'What have you done?'

'I wrote a letter to Mr Callaghan. I told him who I was and that for the past six years Hector has been taking a horse for two hours on the last Sunday of every month and I suggested that before he allows the wedding to go ahead he should ask him where he goes, and why.'

'Did you get any response?'

'I did, more than I bargained for. About half an hour before Hector was due, a rather shady-looking character appeared in the yard and said he was a private detective employed by Mr Callaghan, who had sent him to find out what I meant by my letter. I played dumb, of course. Just said I thought it was odd that a man who didn't enjoy riding should want a horse so regularly. So the detective said the only way to know for sure what he was up to would be to follow him, and he asked me to let him have a horse. He waited for Hector to arrive and then set off after him.

'What happened?'

'Hector came back with a face like thunder. "I shan't be requiring your services any more," he says, in that "nose in the air" tone he takes. "Oh, going away are you?" I ask. "None of your business" he says, and off he goes. Ten minutes later the detective comes back, looking very pleased with himself. "You were right to be suspicious," he says. "Mr Latimer was visiting one of those baby farms, but from what I could make out the child he was looking for had disappeared." Apparently, he was able to conceal himself near enough to hear what was going on and Hector and the old woman were having a real row. "Where is he?" Hector was shouting, "I want to know where he's gone." But the old girl wouldn't tell him and he finally jumped on his horse and rode off in a fury.'

'Thank heaven she didn't tell him about you!' Dora said. 'I wonder why she refused.'

'My guess is, she didn't like Hector from the start. She reckoned Dan would be better off with me, so she decided to keep quiet.'

'So what do you think will happen now?'

'Obviously the detective will report what he saw and heard to Mr Callaghan. Do you imagine he will want his daughter marrying a man who clearly has fathered an illegitimate child? I don't see how Hector could talk his way out of that.'

'I suppose not.' Dora looked at him. He was grinning with delight at the success of his scheme. 'It serves Hector right, of course,' she said slowly, 'but I'm not sure it was a wise thing to do. Hector will find out who put Mr Callaghan on his track, and he will want his revenge, Jem. He was a spoilt, vindictive boy and I don't imagine he's changed.'

Jem came to her and put his arm round her shoulders. 'What can he do to us? We've done nothing wrong, and in another week we shall be out of his reach. Don't worry about it.'

With only a week to go before the wedding Dora had too much to think about to worry. Next Sunday Phil arrived, bringing Lily and Pearl with her, and the following day Elizabeth came with her new husband. He was a doctor in the hospital where Elizabeth worked and it was easy to see that they were very much in love. Elizabeth told her that he would have had no objection to her continuing to nurse part-time, but, she confided with a shy smile, as she was already pregnant that was out of the question. Dora took them to the stables and introduced them to Jem, and to Daniel. They already knew, of course, that Dora had had a child, but it took some time to explain how Jem had found him and brought him to live with them. He was shy with all these strangers, but Dora was proud of how well he behaved. In the evening the five old friends dined together at Phil's expense, while Elizabeth's husband tactfully found he had important papers to read in his hotel room.

The wedding day dawned, a crisp autumn morning of sunshine and showers. The grim little chapel had been transformed with great vases of bronze and gold chrysanthemums and autumn foliage and Dora's dress reflected the same colours. She had resolutely resisted any suggestion that she should wear white. The pews were filled with everyone who could be spared from the infirmary and, at Dora's request, the children of the workhouse were there as well. Two of her nursing colleagues acted as bridesmaids, but it was the man who gave her away who raised a murmur of surprise when they entered.

Once she had given in her notice, Dora had felt it was her duty to tell Mr Rathbone in person. She had expected him to be disappointed, but his reaction had been much more generous.

'You deserve every happiness, my dear. You have worked very hard and given your heart and soul to the infirmary and now you should rightfully reap your reward. And I hear great things are afoot in Jamaica. I once met Mary Seacole, who they called "the angel of the Crimea". She lives there now and I shall write you an introduction to her. I am convinced that a time will come when you will wish to resume your profession and she could be instrumental in finding you a place where you can use your expertise and experience. Now, I have one more request.'

'Anything, sir.'

'Your father is dead, you told me.'

'Yes, many years ago.'

'Who is going to give you away?'

'Oh, I hadn't thought!'

'Then might I have the honour?'

So it was on her benefactor's arm that Dora walked down the aisle to stand by Jem. She would have liked to have Daniel by her, too, but that would have been asking too much of the little boy. He sat with Jack, the stable boy, who had taken him under his wing and treated him like a younger brother.

The vows were exchanged, the register signed, and the priest declared them to be man and wife. Dora's heart was full, as she accepted the congratulations and the heartfelt good wishes of her old friends and colleagues.

Jem had taken over the entire space of a local restaurant and the guests were treated to a lavish spread. Mr Rathbone proposed the health of the bride and groom and Jem replied with a dignity and warmth that made Dora proud. Finally, they went outside to find the pony and trap decked out with ribbons and flowers, with Jack holding the reins and Daniel beside him, ready to drive them back to their temporary home.

When they were at last alone, and Daniel had been put to bed, Jem took her in his arms.

'This was the happiest day of my life, but I know for sure that there are going to be many more.'

She nestled against him. 'Yes, of course there are.'

He kissed her and then said, 'You must be very tired. If you feel that all you want is an uninterrupted sleep, I shall understand.'

She looked up into his gentle eyes. 'No. That's not what I want. I want to know what it feels like to lie in the arms of the man I love.'

So they made their way to bed, and Dora learned that the act of love could be gentle and desire could overcome fear, until all worldly cares and doubts were swept away.

She was dragged from the deepest sleep by Jem suddenly leaping out of bed and rushing to the window.

'Smoke! I smell smoke! Wake up!'

She struggled to her feet. He was leaning out of the window.

'By Christ! The stables are on fire. We must get the horses out. FIRE! FIRE!' he was yelling at the top of his lungs.

Dora scrabbled for a shawl and her shoes. Jem was already heading down the stairs and she stumbled after him. The stables were old buildings of wattle and daub on a wooden frame. One wall was already burning fiercely and the fire was spreading up to the thatched roof. As she and Jem ran across the yard the main door burst open and Jack almost fell out. He was clutching a man's cloak.

'It was him!' he screamed. 'It was him. I caught him at it, but he knocked me down and ran away.'

'Never mind that!' Jem yelled. 'Are you hurt?'

'No.'

'Help me get the horses out.'

Dora followed the two of them into the smoke filled interior. In their stalls the horses were stamping and whinnying in panic. Jem flung open the door of one and grabbed the horse by its head collar. It reared and resisted, and then finally made a rush for the open air, almost knocking Dora over.

'Keep back! Leave this to us!' Jem shouted and she stumbled out again into the yard. Gasping for breath she gazed around her and then she screamed in terror. The roof of the house was thatched like the stable and the wind had blown the flaming straw across the space. The thatch was now well alight.

Dora turned back to the stable door and yelled 'Jem! The house! The roof's on fire!' but he was struggling to pull another of the horses to safety and could not hear her above the roar of the flames and the trampling of hooves. Dora ran back into the house.

'Daniel! Daniel! I'm coming!'

She could feel the heat as she clambered up the stairs and as she reached the top a beam came crashing down in front of her. She could hear Daniel screaming, but the beam barred her way. Ignoring the pain in her hands, she grasped the charred wood and heaved with all her strength. For a moment it seemed the weight was too much, then the beam shifted and she was able to shoulder her way past. Daniel was at the door of his room, his mouth a dark round in his puckered face as he howled in terror. She grabbed him up in her arms and turned to go back the way she had come, but as she did so another beam crashed down across the stairs. Dora turned back into Daniel's room and carried him to the window. The yard was now a churning mass of horses and Jem and Jack were trying to calm them and move them out into the paddock.

'Jem! Jem!' she screamed at the top of her lungs. He seemed not to hear. 'Jem! Help me! Jem!'

He turned and looked up and she saw his face change. He ran to stand below the window.

'I can't get down!' she shouted. 'The stairway is blocked.'

He ran into the house and she heard him banging and swearing. Then he came out again.

'It's no good. I can't shift it.'

Dora could feel the heat scorching her neck and pieces of smouldering straw were floating down from above her. She felt a sudden searing pain and realised her night gown had caught fire. Holding Daniel on one arm she managed to beat out the flames.

'We've got to get out!' she screamed.

Jem looked up at her. The house was not tall and the window was less than twice his height above the ground. 'Drop the boy down to me,' he ordered.

'Drop him?'

'It's the only way. Don't worry. I'll catch him.'

Daniel was clinging round her neck like a monkey and she had difficulty releasing his grip.

'It's all right, Dan! Jem will catch you. Don't be afraid.'

She leaned out as far as she could and let him go. Jem reached out, caught him, staggered and then set him on his feet. Jack had seen what was happening and picked the little boy up and held him.

'Now you!' Jem said.

'I can't! You can't take my weight!'

'Yes, I can. Trust me. I won't let you fall.'

The heat was getting worse and more flaming straw was falling on her. She scrambled onto the windowsill, hesitated for a moment and then pitched herself forward. She felt her body collide with Jem's and his arms go round her, as they both collapsed backwards onto the cobbles. Dimly she was aware of the bell of a fire engine approaching, then blackness swamped her.

Several hours later they sat in the smoke-blackened kitchen, drinking strong tea laced with rum. Daniel was fast asleep on Dora's lap, Jem sat close beside her and Jack was slumped over the table with his head propped on his hands. Opposite him sat an inspector from the local constabulary. 'This was your wedding night, I understand.'

Jem gave a twisted smile. 'I know a wedding night is supposed to be an occasion for burning passion, but I didn't expect things to get quite this hot!'

'Jem!' Dora protested. 'What a thing to say!'

The inspector chuckled briefly and returned to his notebook. 'You say you think you know who was responsible for the fire?'

'I know someone who had reason to want to harm me,' Jem replied, 'but whether he started the fire himself or paid someone else to do it I can't say.'

'Who is this person?' the inspector asked.

'His name is Hector Latimer.' Jem went on to explain as briefly as possible the events of the previous Sunday.

'And this is the child in question?' the inspector asked.

'Yes. We think that perhaps Latimer got wind of the wedding and came to spy on us – or sent someone else. If he saw the boy that would have made him even more furious.'

The inspector turned his attention to Jack. 'And you caught him – whoever he was – in the act?'

Jack suppressed a yawn and nodded. 'I sleep above the stables. Something woke me. I could hear that the horses were restless so I went down to see what was the matter. It was dark, and I suddenly smelt smoke. There were some bales of straw stacked at one side and the smoke was coming from that direction but as I went to look a man jumped out from behind them. I tried to grab him, but he shoved me aside and I tripped. He was wearing a long cloak and I managed to hold on to it, but he got away. I couldn't run after him because I had to get the horses out before the fire took proper hold.'

'Quite right too,' Jem said. 'You did well, lad.'

The inspector was turning the cloak over in his hands. 'This is what they call an opera cloak. It's the sort of thing a gentleman would buy if he was concerned about his appearance and keen to be correctly dressed for any occasion.'

'That sounds like Hector,' Dora said.

'No name in it, of course,' the inspector went on. 'That would be too much to hope for. But there is a tailor's label. Quite an exclusive firm. I don't suppose they sell too many of these. It's likely they will keep a record of who has ordered one. If Hector Latimer is on that list we could have some useful evidence.' He got up. 'We'll keep you informed on how the investigation proceeds.'

'We shall not be here to find out the conclusion,' Jem told him. 'We sail for Jamaica on tomorrow's tide.'

'Indeed? Well, then, I shall need you to come to the station and sign a written record of what you have just told me. The sooner you can do that the better.'

'We'll be there,' Jem promised.

Dora sighed. The burns on her hands and one thigh were stinging and all she could think of was the jars of ointment sitting on the shelf in the infirmary kitchen. As soon as the inspector had left she sent one of the other stable lads, who had come to work as usual, with a note asking the new superintendent to send her one. Once he returned with it, and she was able to anoint her wounds with the soothing balm, she felt able to face the rest of the day. Hot on the boy's heels Phil arrived with Lily and Pearl. They had heard what had happened and came to render whatever assistance was in their power.

It was a day that passed in a blur. There was so much to do. The horses had to be checked for injuries and fed and watered. The owner had to be informed of what had happened. He arrived just as they returned from the police station and told them, to Jem's relief, that he had insured the buildings against fire and he would take charge of the rebuilding himself. On top of everything else, they still had to make ready to leave the next morning. Fortunately, all the possessions they planned to take with them had already been packed away in sea chests ready for the voyage and the solidly built chests, though slightly singed, had withstood the flames. A carrier came to transport them to the docks, ready to be loaded on board.

It was impossible to sleep in the house, so Jem found a room for them in a hotel near the docks. Dora took a tearful farewell of her friends, cast a last look around the house that had been for such a short time her home, and mounted the pony trap. In the hotel, Daniel, who had clung to her hand all day, finally allowed her to put him to bed and she and Jem were alone.

'Well, my darling,' he said. 'We've had a dramatic start to our married life. Let's hope for calmer waters from now on.'

She put her arms round his neck. 'I haven't forgotten that wicked joke about burning passions. Do you think it is too late to stoke the embers a little?'

Next morning, they stood on the deck of the *SS Senora* with Daniel between them and watched the city of Liverpool fade into the mist. Dora lifted her eyes and was just able to make out the bulk of the workhouse dominating the skyline.

'No going back,' she told herself. 'A new life begins here.'

AUTHOR NOTE

It is historical fact that Mr William Rathbone, a wealthy philanthropist living in Liverpool, was so impressed by the care given to his dying wife by a trained nurse that he wanted everyone to have the same chance. In 1852 he instituted the first district nursing service, which brought him into contact with Florence Nightingale. In 1865 he invited Agnes Jones, a Nightingale-trained nurse, to head a team of nurses to improve conditions in the infirmary attached to the Brownlow Hill workhouse. He undertook to pay for the first three years of the experiment, so that local taxes did not have to be raised. Agnes Jones transformed the running of the infirmary, but her devotion to her duties wore her out and she died in 1868 at the age of just thirty-five.

While Florence Nightingale did indeed allow both working class and upper class women to become nurses, I have taken certain artistic liberties regarding Dora's acceptance give her mother's background. While Mary Seacole – a British-Jamaican nurse who, like Dora's mother, acquired her knowledge of herbal medicine in the Caribbean, set up the British Hotel behind the lines during the Crimean

War – it would be some time before nurses from ethnically diverse backgrounds would be readily accepted into the nursing profession in the UK.

The full story of Angel's adoption and subsequent disappearance is featured in my previous novel, *Workhouse Angel*.